SHOOT THE MOON

ALSO BY JOSEPH T. KLEMPNER

Felony Murder

SHOOT THE MOON

Joseph T. Klempner

St. Martin's Press
New York

A THOMAS DUNNE BOOK.
An imprint of St. Martin's Press.

Design by Ellen R. Sasahara

Library of Congress Cataloging-in-Publication Data

Klempner, Joseph T.
    Shoot the moon / Joseph T. Klempner.—1st ed.
        p.   cm.
    "A Thomas Dunne book."
    ISBN 0-312-15424-0
    I. Title.
    PS3561.L3866S48   1997
    813'.54—dc21   97-6273
                                                        CIP

First edition: August 1997

10 9 8 7 6 5 4 3 2 1

To my best friend, my biggest fan, my harshest critic, my wife, and my lover—all of whom just happen to be named Sandy.

ACKNOWLEDGMENTS

So long ago that it now seems part of a former life, I was an agent for what was then known as the Bureau of Narcotics of the United States Treasury Department and is now called the Drug Enforcement Administration. I thank my fellow agents for unwittingly contributing some of the incidents, much of the color, and even several of the characters found in these pages. I thank my agent Bob Diforio; my editor, Ruth Cavin and her assistant, Carrie McGinnis; and my early manuscript readers, among them my three children, Wendy, Ron, and Tracy; and my sister Tillie, who promises to finish it soon.

SHOOT THE MOON

[1]

The flat tire is simply the last straw.

Goodman has known from the moment he woke up that it was definitely going to be *one of those days*.

To begin with, the alarm clock in the motel room hadn't gone off when it was supposed to. He realized later that the reason it hadn't gone off was that he'd somehow managed to set it for 7:15 P.M. instead of 7:15 A.M. How was he supposed to know it could tell the difference? But by then he'd overslept, of course, and it was already after eight.

So he'd quickly jumped into the shower, shivering in the cold water before the hot had a chance to come up, nicked himself twice while shaving, gotten into his car, and raced the twelve miles to the Fort Lauderdale Industrial Arts Building. Even as he'd made the turn out of the motel parking lot onto A1A, the squeal from his front right tire had warned him it needed air. He'd cursed himself for not taking the car the Avis agent had wanted to give him in the first place, or even the several he'd been offered at an upgrade for an additional ten dollars a day.

He'd thought about stopping to fill the tire up, but there simply hadn't been time. The days when you could pull into a gas station and spend fifteen seconds adding air to a tire were long gone. Nowadays, you had to find a station with a *machine* that ate quarters. And Goodman had already been running too late to bother getting change and dealing with that. Besides, it was a rental car. If he ruined the tire, he ruined the tire; it would be someone else's problem.

He'd gotten lost twice trying to find the address, and when he'd finally located it, he'd had to spend another five minutes looking for a parking place. He'd settled for the tail end of a spot already taken by one of those subcompact jobs. Still, the back of his car had protruded a good two feet into the crosswalk. He'd left it anyway, playing the odds and figuring a ticket couldn't run more than ten bucks, anyway. Not like New York, where the going rate was fifty-five.

He'd finally arrived for the interview a good thirty-five minutes late, already out of breath and sweating through his shirt. The thing that really upset him was that he was by habit always absurdly early for everything. And now *this*. They'd made him wait another half hour, just to get even with him, he figured. "They" were Mr. Stone and Mr. Baldwin, or Balder, or something like that. Between the two of them, they hadn't smiled once.

Predictably, the interview itself had been a disaster. No, they hadn't received the resumé he'd mailed them from New York a week earlier. Yes, they were looking for an accountant, but they really wanted a CPA, and the fact that Goodman wasn't certified seemed to disqualify him immediately, even though their ad had made no mention of the requirement. And while they seemed to believe that there was really nothing unusual in his wanting to relocate following the death of his wife, they kept eyeing him with a vague look of suspicion, as though there might be more to that story than he was telling them. Did they think he'd murdered his wife? Was that it?

When, after what seemed like barely a polite amount of time, they'd stood and announced that they'd be in touch, he'd been almost relieved at the dismissal.

Back downstairs, the ticket on his windshield had hardly been a shock: By that time, he'd all but expected it. He'd pocketed it without reading it; it wasn't until later that he'd noticed it would set him back thirty-five dollars.

He'd driven around until he'd found a diner. Again, the squeal of his tire as he pulled in reminded him that he'd need to do something about it. But it could wait. At the time he'd picked up the car, he'd been proud of himself for insisting that he wasn't going to take the dark green Toyota Camry they'd had reserved for him. Dark colors were okay for New York. In Florida, it seemed most of the cars were white—which was smart:

White reflected the heat better, so you didn't have to run the air conditioning as much. Less air conditioning meant better mileage. And with gas getting expensive again, better mileage meant saving a buck or two. So he'd asserted himself to the woman at the counter, and she'd checked the computer until she located a pale pink one, which was the closest she could find. It was being held for somebody, but when she checked, she saw the party hadn't showed up, so she finally agreed to let Goodman have it. He remembers wondering at the time who would've reserved a pale pink car. Maybe a starlet, he figured. Or an Elvis wanna-be.

Now it's turned out that it's not so hot anyway, with the temperature barely reaching seventy. Dark green would have been just fine after all. So all Goodman really ended up getting for his trouble was a bad tire.

At a corner booth, he counts his money. Including the change in his pocket, $108.11. Two fifty-dollar traveler's checks. A Visa card that's flirting dangerously with the limit. A Mobil card issued by his last company—which might or might not be usable for a few more days. All told, enough to get back to New York if he leaves right now. If he decides instead to hang around a few more days, trying some of the "Help Wanted" ads and not landing anything, he'll end up being stuck here without enough cash to make it back home. That could be a problem, particularly because back home is where his daughter, Kelly, is. It had been Goodman's hope to land the job, get started at it, and find a place to stay—all before sending for Kelly. In the meantime, she's been staying with her grandmother, trying to get over the death of her mother. No simple task for a six-year-old, he knows.

Surprisingly, he finds that the eggs are okay and the bacon's actually crisp, and for a moment Goodman dares to think that this might be an omen of some kind, that his luck might finally be changing.

He should know better.

But for all his faults, Michael Goodman has always been a person who sees the glass as half-full, even on those occasions when it would clearly appear to an impartial observer to be almost totally empty. So, lingering over his second cup of coffee at the diner, Goodman now takes no small satisfaction over the fact that the coffee is steaming hot, while at the same time ignoring that it's watery and all but tasteless.

Those who know Michael Goodman tend to overlook his slightly bookish appearance, exaggerated by his steel-rimmed glasses and plastic pocket protector with its assortment of plastic pens and sharpened pencils. His repertoire of nervous tics and quirky mannerisms is easily forgiven. Goodman has no real friends to speak of in the true sense of the word—the closest he could list if called upon to do so would be the three buddies from his navy days with whom he gets together Sunday evenings. But then again, he certainly has no enemies, either. By most accounts, he's considered a pleasant-enough fellow to be around, particularly if there are cards to be played, a ball game to be watched, or some other distraction to help pass the time. If one happened to be both charitable and Jewish, one might be tempted to refer to Michael Goodman as a *mensch*, which pretty much translates into a regular, decent, dependable guy—a *man*; but Goodman's also overheard the word *schlemiel* whispered behind his back more than once, and he knows it, too, occasionally applies: For the consensus seems to be that in the game of life, for better or for worse, Michael Goodman is a permanent resident of the losing column.

Still he lingers over his second cup of coffee—long enough to let it cool, long enough for him to pull out a road map and figure the best way to pick up the interstate, and long enough for him to recover just a bit from the series of setbacks that has plagued his morning and pretty much of his recent life. And while he continues to linger inside the diner, figuring and recovering and doing his best to refill himself with hope, just outside the diner, his front right tire continues to empty itself of air.

And yet, when he emerges from the diner into the sunlight of the parking lot, to discover the tire nearly flat, Goodman characteristically manages to blame himself for not having taken care of the tire earlier. Not consciously, perhaps, but just as surely in terms of his reaction to the sight. Forgetting his cavalier attitude of earlier this same morning—that since it was a rental car, it was someone else's problem—he now permits himself but a single sigh before taking off his sport jacket, tossing it onto the front seat, and proceeding to go about the business of changing the tire.

The truth is, changing a tire is something Goodman kind of likes doing, much like mowing a lawn or emptying a dishwasher. There's an orderliness to it, a rhythm that you can actually get into, if you allow yourself.

A thousand miles away, Russell Bradford wakes up in the South Bronx tenement apartment he shares with his mother, his grandmother—whom everyone calls Nana—his two brothers, and his sister.

It isn't the noise that wakes Russell, though there's plenty of that. It isn't the cold air finding its way through the ancient window frames and up between the warped floorboards. It isn't an alarm clock, either: With no job, and no school to got to since he dropped out, Russell has no need of an alarm to wake him.

No, it's something much more basic, more urgent, than any of those things that wakes Russell Bradford this morning. Russell Bradford is sick. Which means it's time for him to go out.

Because it's one of those cars where they hide the spare tire at the bottom of the trunk, Goodman first has to take his suitcase and garment bag out and place them on the pavement. Then he lifts the partition that separates the trunk and the spare-tire compartment. He's pleased to see that they've given him a full-sized tire, not one of those polyspares you can use for only fifty miles and have to drive slowly on. He notices it's bolted down by a big wing nut. He loosens the wing nut a bit, then gives it a good flick with one finger. It spins pleasingly as it works its way almost to the top of the threaded rod. He gives it another turn and a half, and it comes off.

Goodman leans over the spare, grasps it with both hands, and lifts, and is immediately seized with a sudden stabbing pain in his lower back. He lets go of the tire and tries to straighten up, but the damage is done.

Michael Goodman is no stranger to lower-back pain. He's been throwing his back out for half his life, ever since he was in the navy, in his early twenties. He's been to half a dozen doctors, who've given him half a dozen opinions: a herniated disk, a degenerating sacroiliac, a pinched nerve, an asymmetrical spine, weak stomach muscles, and flat feet. Goodman himself has decided it has something to do with mental stress. He notices that when things are going well, his back leaves him pretty much alone. When he's broke and between jobs and can't pay his bills, it's sure to go out on him. It's been doing that a lot lately.

He takes a couple of deep breaths and tries to straighten up again, hoping he hasn't hurt himself too badly. When he was younger, the pain would often be gone by the next morning; if not, it might last a day or two at most. Now that he's reached forty, each episode seems to last longer than the one before it. Sometimes it's close to a month before he's fully recovered.

Goodman returns to the spare tire, determined not to be defeated by it. He's certain it must still be bolted down, so immovable was it when he first tried to lift it. But he can't find anything else that's holding it down. So he lifts one edge. It's heavy, but it moves a bit.

He continues to lift one side of the tire until he gets it to a vertical position in its well. Then, using both hands, he rolls it toward himself, up and onto the lower lip of the trunk. Then he nudges it a little farther, letting gravity do the rest. He poises his hand to catch it on the first bounce and dribble it to a standstill, the way one might control a basketball. But for the second time, the tire surprises him. It barely bounces at all; instead, it makes a thudding noise and falls over on its side.

He bends down painfully and pushes his hand against the sidewall, expecting it to give: It figures that they'd have given him a flat for a spare. But the sidewall is hard to the touch—if anything, it feels *over*inflated.

He stands the tire up again and begins to roll it around to the right front of the car. But it doesn't even roll properly—it seems somehow out of balance. He stoops down and, bracing himself carefully to avoid further damage to his back, he lifts it. It is absurdly heavy.

It occurs to him to let some air out the tire in order to lighten it. (It won't be until much later that he'll remember that air doesn't weigh anything, except in a vacuum. But right now, in his pain and frustration, the idea somehow makes sense to him.) So he takes a ballpoint pen from his shirt pocket, fits the metal opening in the tip of it over the valve stem of the tire, and pushes it slightly to one side. There is the expected hissing noise, but it lasts only a second or two.

He pushes sideways against the valve stem again. Nothing. He feels the tire again; it's softer, but only slightly. Yet, for some reason, no more air will come out.

Russell Bradford slips into a pair of worn jeans and a faded blue T-shirt. He puts on his Nikes, not bothering with socks, and a denim jacket. From under his pillow, he retrieves a crumpled twenty-dollar bill. It's all the money he has.

"Wheah you gon widdout breakfass?" his grandmother asks him as he walks by her.

"Out," Russell says.

Goodman stares at the spare tire. Slowly, it dawns on him: The tire is defective; it won't hold air. Only they've been too cheap to replace it. Instead, they've filled it with sand or something to make it *look* normal, figuring nobody ever bothers to change a tire on a rental car, they just call the company to come out with another tire.

But Michael Goodman is stubborn. Instead of being like everyone else and calling the toll-free "Help" number for Avis, he goes back to the trunk of the car. There, nestled in with the jack, he finds what's he's looking for: the jack handle, rounded and hollow at one end to remove lug nuts, but flattened like the end of a crowbar at the other.

Back at the spare tire, he uses the crowbar end to try to pry the sidewall away from the wheel. There's some adhesive stuff he has to break through, but he manages; after all, there's no air pressure left in the tire to fight him.

He runs the crowbar end of the jack handle around the wheel, separating the tire from it completely. Then he pushes them apart far enough so that he can look inside. At first, he can't see anything but darkness, so he turns the opening around to face the sunlight. Now, as he peers inside, he can see something blue.

Keeping the opening as wide as he can with the jack handle, he uses his other hand to reach inside. He feels something smooth that he's unable to get a grip on. But by running his hand over its surface, he comes to what feels like a corner, which he's able to grasp in his fingers and pull partway out of the opening.

It turns out to be some sort of a blue plastic wrap. He pinches it, trying to break it to see what's inside. But it's either heavy-duty plastic or several layers thick, and it takes him a minute to make a tear in it. When he finally succeeds, a white powder trickles out.

Russell Bradford walks toward 140th Street. He's in a hurry, but he can't walk too fast because of the cramps in his midsection. In spite of the fact that it's forty degrees out, Russell's dark skin glistens with sweat.

At sixteen, Russell looks as though he could be going to school this morning, or on his way to work, or running some errand for his mother or grandmother. But he's doing none of those things. As he walks, clutching his twenty-dollar bill tightly in his fist inside the pocket of his jeans, Russell Bradford has only one thing on his mind, one goal in all of life.

Russell Bradford is going to cop.

Michael Goodman has never before seen real narcotics. He's tried marijuana twice in his life, even inhaled. It made him cough a lot before putting him to sleep. But Goodman has seen movies, and he's not stupid.

Without knowing precisely what the white powder is that has trickled out of the blue plastic, and without having the slightest idea how much of it there is inside the spare tire, he knows he's stumbled upon something serious.

His first thought is that his discovery could get him arrested. That thought alone makes him uncomfortable, until it's replaced by his second thought. It's the second thought—that this stuff could just as likely get him *killed*—that prompts him to act.

He looks around. Spots a pay phone less than a hundred feet away. Walks directly to it. Lifts the receiver. Hears a dial tone. Punches in 911. It rings twice before he hears a recorded voice.

"We're sorry, all available operators are busy. Please stay on the line. Your call will be answered by the next available operator. If your call is not a true emergency, please hang up now and dial the seven-digit number of the agency you would like to reach."

Goodman stays on the line as instructed. Every thirty seconds or so, the recorded voice comes back to assure him that calls will be answered in the order they have been placed. It reminds him to hang up now if it's not a true emergency. That gets Goodman to thinking: Is his call a true emergency? True emergencies are heart attacks, fires, people in distress. He imagines that his call may prevent such a true emergency call from getting through in time to save someone's life. He wonders if, when they finally answer his call, they'll be angry at him for not having hung up and dialed the seven-digit number of the proper agency. But, not sure what the proper agency even *is*, he stays on the phone.

Five minutes go by like this. Ten. The phone is in the sun. Sweat runs down Goodman's neck and forehead. His shirt sticks to his back. His eyes burn. Standing in one place causes his back to hurt even more than before. He changes positions so that he faces away from the car.

After fifteen minutes, he tells himself he'll wait only another minute before hanging up. He gives it three. He's sure that as soon as he hangs up, that'll be the exact moment they were about to get to his call. He decides to give it one *absolutely* last minute.

He turns back toward the car in time to see two kids—boys no more than twelve or thirteen—doing something at the back of his car. He can't see *what* they're doing; they're partially blocked from his view by the open trunk lid.

"Hey!" he yells.

They straighten up and look in his direction.

"Get away from there!" he tells them.

They hesitate an instant before turning away from him and breaking into a run. Goodman smiles to himself. He feels empowered, pleased that he's succeeded in frightening them away, even though they were only boys.

It's several seconds before he notices that they're each carrying one of his suitcases.

He drops the phone and tries to run after them. But his back seizes up before he can even reach the car. By that time, the boys are a full two blocks away, turning a corner.

He figures they weigh about ninety pounds each. They're wearing sneakers. Goodman's ten pounds overweight and wearing Thom McAn loafers with leather soles. Even with his back in good shape, he knows he wouldn't stand a chance. He gives up.

He's too far from the phone to hear the voice of the emergency operator who finally answers his call.

He bends down painfully, picks up the jack handle, and tosses it into the open trunk. He struggles with the spare tire until he gets it upright, then rolls it up and into the trunk and back into its well. He closes the partition that covers it, slams the lid of the trunk, and gets in behind the wheel.

His suitcase and garment bag contained all of the clothes he had with him. With them gone, he doesn't have so much as another pair of undershorts.

Goodman says "Shit" out loud. It's the strongest curse word he ever allows himself.

He feels absolutely drained, too exhausted to do anything. He decides to head back to the motel, maybe spend another night. He figures both he and his back can use the rest, even if it'll mean another thirty-six dollars for the night's stay. He can try calling the police again from there.

Of course, first there's the little matter of the flat tire.

Goodman gets back out of the car, walks around to the tire, and looks at it. He decides maybe it's not quite so bad after all. He remembers an old line about only the bottom of a tire being flat. He guesses he can drive on it, slowly, until he gets to a service station. He gets back in, starts the engine, and backs carefully out of the diner's parking lot.

He drives cautiously in the right lane. Before he's gone two blocks, he spots an automotive-parts store. He pulls in and buys some pressurized tire inflater labeled Jiffy-Spare. He's never used one before, but he's heard that they generally work about half the time. Knowing his luck, he figures one out of three should be more like it. With tax, the three cans come to $10.39. He pays cash.

Outside, he screws the nozzle onto the valve of the low tire until he hears a hissing noise. He can feel the can grow cold in his hand as it empties. To his astonishment, the thing actually works on the first try: The tire fills with air. Some gummy white stuff shows when he unscrews the can.

He drives back to the motel, feeling pretty good about things. With no usable spare tire, he's succeeded in fixing a flat tire by himself. Not everybody could have done that, he decides.

As soon as he turns into 140th Street, Russell Bradford knows he's going to be okay. He sees right away that several of the regulars are out working. Big Red is there. So is Eddie Boy. And the new kid who's got dust.

Russell walks over to Eddie Boy's steerer first. He's a pimply-faced junkie who always seems spaced-out. They call him "Zombie."

"Hey, Zom," Russell says. "What's happenin'?"

"What's happenin'?" may be a term of greeting to others. But on 140th Street in the South Bronx, it's not just a greeting. To the hundreds, or thousands, of the Russell Bradfords of this world, "What's happenin'?" is a very specific question. Loosely translated, it means pretty much this: "What are you selling? How are you selling it? How good is it? And how much is it going for?"

"Night Train," Zombie tells him. "Dynamite, man. Dimes."

Russell thinks over his options for a minute. He knows he needs to stretch his twenty dollars out and make it count.

Night Train is a brand of heroin. The dealer actually stamps his brand name onto the paper in which he sells his product, not very differently from the way boxes and cans in a supermarket are labeled Heinz or Sara Lee or Birds Eye. After all, the customer has a right to know what he's getting for his money. If he likes it, he's going to want to buy it again tomorrow, and the day after, and the day after that. This is the nineties, after all. This is all about competition and marketing and brand loyalty.

"Dynamite" warrants that the product is top-drawer. In this case, that means potent, able to deliver a real high, and, at the same time, stay with you.

"Dimes" are ten-dollar bags. "Nicks" would be fives, "treys" threes. But the smaller bags tend to be weaker. They've often been whacked once more, and they're there for the truly desperate, who don't have the money to buy the better stuff. Even in the world of the addict—*particularly* in the world of the addict—the haves make out; the have-nots suffer.

"Gimme one," Russell says.

"One time," Zombie calls out, and from nowhere another kid appears, one whom Russell hasn't seen before. Russell hands the kid his crumpled twenty; in return, he's handed two fives and a small square of paper. The kid disappears. Russell turns and walks away. All the while, from twenty feet away, Eddie Boy watches. Not once does he touch the drugs or the money, or say a word.

Next Russell walks over to Big Red. Big Red is big, and, as always, he wears his trademark red baseball cap.

"What's happenin', Red?"

"Blues, yellers."

The colors refer to tiny glass vials containing a few rocks of cracks. They are distinguished only by the color of their plastic caps. The blue caps are going for seven dollars apiece today, the yellows five.

"Any good?" Russell asks.

"Ain' nobody bringin' 'em back," Big Red tells him.

"Gimme two yellows," Russell says.

"See the cashier," Big Red says, nodding toward a skinny woman with cornrows. Russell steps over to her and gives her his two fives.

"On the phone," she tells him without looking at him.

Russell turns and walks to a phone booth ten feet away. The phone is broken; the receiver has long ago been cut from the wire cord and never replaced. But on top of the phone, Russell finds two tiny glass vials with yellow plastic tops. He pockets them and walks off.

Back at the motel, Goodman registers for another night's stay, paying the thirty-six dollars in cash. He's given a different room this time, and right away he finds that there's something wrong with the air conditioner: It works, but it's terribly noisy, like maybe it's suddenly about to taxi across the room and take off. But he's already removed his shoes and socks, and he's happy to have the room, so he doesn't complain. Besides which, the bed in this room is nice and hard, which should be good for his back.

At the Formica-topped desk, he goes through his receipts, an old accountant's habit, and counts his money again. Breakfast has cost him

$7.75; along with the three cans of tire inflater stuff and the extra night in the motel room, he's already spent $54.14 today, leaving him with just $53.97. There's no way he's going to make it back to New York, even with the hundred dollars in traveler's checks.

He runs a hot bath, figuring soaking in it will be good for his back. While the water runs, he uses his telephone credit card to call his answering machine in New York. He has to shut off the air conditioner to hear the tape.

There are six messages in all, and for a moment he figures at least one of them has to be a callback from one of the jobs he sent resumés to last week.

He figures wrong.

Three are from collection agencies regarding overdue bills. One is from his former employer, informing him that his medical coverage has been canceled and his gas credit card stopped. Another is from his mother-in-law, telling him that his daughter—who's been staying with her while Goodman looks for a job and gets back on his feet—has been complaining of headaches lately and that she's worried about her. The final one is from his uncle, who's called to announce that his angina is bothering him. Goodman erases them all.

He's about to call his mother-in-law when he remembers the spare tire. He's got to try the police again before he does anything else. But as he dials 911, he becomes aware of the sound of water running in the bathroom. He decides the call can wait until he takes a bath.

He waits until the tub is full, well over the overflow outlet, before he turns the faucets off. The water is hot, so hot that he can barely stand it, and he has to lower himself into it gradually. But once he's able to stretch out in the full length of the tub, it feels good, and he senses his back beginning to loosen up just a bit.

There's an annoying gurgling noise that comes from the overflow outlet, which is several inches below the water level itself. Goodman places a washcloth against the outlet and holds it there with one foot. The gurgling noise stops, though some of the water continues to escape. With his other foot, he twists the faucet marked H open just enough to create a constant trickle of hot water. This combination keeps the tub full and the temperature hot.

Goodman rests the back of his head against the sloped portion of the tub. He imagines he's in a cocoon, warm and protected from the rest of the world.

He thinks of the spare tire. For the first time, he allows himself to wonder just how much drugs are inside it and what they could possibly be worth. He guesses there could be twenty pounds, maybe twenty-five. He has no way of knowing if it's heroin or cocaine, or what. He has absolutely no frame of reference for calculating its value. But even if it's worth a thousand dollars a pound—which he guesses is a pretty conservative estimate—it comes to at least twenty thousand dollars.

He wishes he were a different person, a person who had the nerve to keep the drugs, and the knowledge to turn them into cash. But he knows he has neither the nerve nor the knowledge.

He lies in the bathtub with his eyes closed, soaking until his fingertips shrivel up like prunes. Then he releases the washcloth from its job of damming up the water and turns off the hot faucet with his foot. He listens to the gurgling noise as the water is sucked into the overflow outlet. After a few minutes, the level has dropped and the temperature has cooled. He flicks the drain toggle open with his toe, and the water level drops more rapidly. He pulls himself to a standing position and steps out of the tub, telling himself that he feels a little better.

Wrapped in a towel, Goodman dials 911 again from the phone beside his bed. This time, a real voice answers on the third ring.

"Operator one-one-seven," a woman says in a professional-sounding voice. "What is the nature of your emergency?"

"I've found some drugs," Goodman says.

"What kind of drugs?" the woman asks him.

"I don't know. Narcotic drugs."

"Stay on the line, sir," the woman tells him. There is a click, as though he's been put on hold. But the woman comes right back on without a pause. "I got a jerk wants to turn in some drugs," he hears her say in a different voice, not so professional-sounding. "What do I tell him?"

Goodman says, "Hello?"

There's another click, and now it sounds as if he *is* put on hold. After about fifteen seconds, the woman comes back, using her professional voice once again.

"Sir," she says. "If you wish to surrender a controlled substance, you must bring it to police headquarters during normal business hours. We cannot be held accountable for the actions of this or any other agency until you physically surrender the substance." It sounds to Goodman as though she's been reading the words from some prepared text.

"What are normal business hours?" he asks.

"Monday through Friday, nine to four-thirty." Goodman suppresses a chuckle. That's Florida for you. In New York, normal business hours are more like six in the morning to nine at night.

"Where's headquarters?" he asks.

But all he hears is a dial tone. She's already disconnected him.

From 140th Street, Russell Bradford works his way back uptown to 145th. There, in front of a laundromat, he finds Robbie McCray waiting for him. Even before Robbie spots Russell, Russell can tell Robbie's hurting, from the way he's shifting his weight from one foot to the other and moving his shoulders back and forth, sorta like he's gotta take a piss. Only Russell knows Robbie doesn't have to take a piss.

"Man, where you been *at?*" Robbie says when he finally sees Russell come up on him.

"Takin' care a bizness is where I been at," Russell says.

Russell follows Robbie into a building. It's a five-story brownstone that once belonged to a wealthy white family, years ago. Then it was subdivided into apartments, which were rented to blacks and Hispanics. Now it's abandoned, the glass gone from the windows and replaced with sheets of plywood. There's a padlock on the front door, but it's busted: Somebody sprayed it with a freezing agent, then hit it a couple of good shots with a hammer. Works every time.

They climb the stairs and open the door that leads to the roof. They step out slowly, not knowing if anyone's there. But they're in luck: It's empty, except for hundreds of empty vials, bent needles, torn papers, empty glassine envelopes, a year's worth of other garbage, and a couple of pigeons, which take flight on seeing them. It smells of urine and shit, and they watch their steps carefully as they thread their way to their corner.

"Whatcha got, man?" Robbie wants to know.

"I got some shit, an' I got some cracks," Russell tells him. "Whatchoo got?"

"Nothin', man." Robbie keeps his eyes pointed down at his sneakers.

"Shit, niggah. Wassamatta witchoo?"

"I'll make it up to you, man."

"Fuck that shit," Russell says. But he doesn't have the heart to send Robbie packing. There've been times when Robbie has had stuff and Russell hasn't. Besides, cracking up is better when you're with someone else than it is when you're all alone.

"You got a stem?" Russell asks Robbie.

Robbie produces a small glass pipe and something that looks like a lighter but is called a torch. Russell takes the pipe. He reaches into his pocket, finds one of the yellow tops, takes it out. He unscrews the top and carefully taps what look like two white Rice Krispies into the bowl of the pipe. He lights the torch and holds the flame under the bowl until the two kernels begin to sizzle and melt.

Russell draws deeply from the stem and holds the smoke in his lungs while he passes the pipe to Robbie. They take turns until the bowl is empty. Then they pour the rest of the contents of the vial into the bowl and repeat the process.

Almost immediately, the rest of the world disappears for Russell. Nothing is left but one corner of the roof. There is no apartment, no family. No being out of school and without a job. None of that exists. Robbie's here, but barely. Mostly, Russell is aware of only himself, right here, right now, and an incredible feeling of rising up above everything else, of floating. . . .

Goodman dials his mother-in-law's number. Her answering machine picks up after the second ring, and he hears her voice, along with what sounds like Frank Sinatra singing in the background.

"You've reached two-one-two–five-five-five–two-oh-two-six. I'm not here to take your call. Leave a message after the tone, and I'll get back to you."

He wonders why people think it's necessary to tell you the number that you yourself have just dialed. He can't think of anything to say, so he hangs up without leaving a message.

He stretches out on the bed, studies the ceiling fan for a while. Looks over at the clock. It's the same kind that tricked him into oversleeping this morning. It's 12:03, barely noon, though it feels like the end of a long day already. He lets his eyes close. Figures he can afford the luxury of a nap for an hour or so and still have plenty of time to find police headquarters before the end of their normal business hours.

Russell Bradford's incredible floating feeling has come and gone. He's finding that the feeling, which used to last for what seemed like hours, now lasts only a few minutes. He hears Robbie asking him if he's got any more cracks.

"No," Russell says. "Just the shit."

Robbie forages about on the roof for a while until he finds what he's looking for. He comes back with a rusted metal spoon, the handle of which is bent back under the bowl. While Robbie takes a needle with a rubber bulb attached to it from the inside of his cap, Russell retrieves the paper stamped NIGHT TRAIN from his pocket. He opens it carefully, until it's completely spread out in the shape of a triangle, from which it gets its street name, "pyramid paper." At the very center of the pyramid is a small pile of white powder.

Russell taps half of the powder into Robbie's spoon. He watches as Robbie, not having any water, spits into the spoon, then proceeds to cook the mixture by holding the torch underneath the spoon while gently stirring with the tip of the needle. After a few seconds, the liquid begins to bubble. Robbie sets the spoon down carefully, rolls up one shirt sleeve, and removes the belt from his jeans. He threads the end of the belt through the buckle, creating a loop around his upper arm. By squeezing the bulb attached to the needle and placing the tip into the liquid in the spoon before slowly releasing the pressure on the bulb, Robbie draws the mixture up out of the spoon and into the bulb. Holding the bulb and needle in one hand, he uses his teeth to pull the end of the belt tightly. Russell, who has not yet begun to shoot drugs himself, watches as the veins in Robbie's arm bulge.

With all the competence of a medical technician, Robbie probes into the vein with the needle. Without a syringe, he doesn't have the luxury of pulling back to see if the glass fills with blood. Instead, he squeezes the bulb tentatively for a second, smiles slightly, releases his teeth from the belt, and squeezes the bulb empty. When he withdraws the needle, a drop of dark blood marks the spot.

Russell dips his index finger into the powder that remains on the pyramid paper and raises the finger to his nose. Holding one nostril shut with his other index finger, he snorts the powder. He repeats the process, changing nostrils, until the pyramid paper is empty.

A rush begins to spread through Russell's body. He feels numb, but at the same time warm and happy and safe. He lets the feeling take him, rides with it. He notices that Robbie, who gets off much quicker by shooting, is already beginning to come down, to nod off. Russell turns away from Robbie, back to his own ride. . . .

*   *   *

Goodman awake. Unsure where he is. Sees a ceiling fan overhead. Aware that all he's wearing is a towel. Remembers the motel room, the bath, the spare tire. Looks at the clock: 4:17. He's slept for four hours, and he's blown any chance he had to get to police headquarters, wherever that might be, by 4:30.

He swings his feet over the edge of the bed and pulls himself to a sitting position. His back reminds him it's there, but it feels a little better.

He dials 911 again. A male operator answers after nine rings.

"Operator twenty-seven," he says. "What's your emergency?"

"I've found some drugs," Goodman tells him.

"What kind of drugs?"

"I'm not sure."

"How much?"

"I don't really know."

There's a pause, then the operator's voice again.

"If you wish to surrender a controlled substance, you must bring it to police headquarters during normal business hours. We cannot be held accountable for the actions of this or any other agency until you physically surrender the substance."

"Thanks," Goodman says, and hangs up.

He dials his mother-in-law's number in New York. She answers on the second ring.

"Hello," he says. "It's me, Michael."

"Hello, Michael."

"I got your message. What's with Kelly and these headaches?"

"Where are you?" she asks.

"I'm in Florida. Fort Lauderdale."

"What are you doing *there?*"

"Seeing about a job."

"Don't think for a moment you're taking my only granddaughter to *Florida.*"

"Don't worry," he says, "I didn't get the job. What about the headaches?"

"I had to take her to the doctor this afternoon. Who else was going to do it?"

"What did the doctor say?" he asks.

"They want to do some tests."

"What kind of tests?"

"Tests. How should *I* know?"

"And?"

"And they need insurance stuff first," she says. "That's why I called you. I need the name of the company you work for, and the policy number."

Goodman bites his lip. "There *is* no company, and there *is* no policy number," he says. "They canceled my coverage when I got fired."

There's silence on the other end.

"Let me speak to her, okay?"

"She's asleep."

"It's four-thirty in the *afternoon.*"

"She was tired. Call back in a couple of hours. I'll wake her up for supper." And she hangs up, leaving him holding the phone.

The thought of supper reminds Goodman that he hasn't eaten since breakfast. Though he doesn't feel particularly hungry, he feels guilty about having spent the entire afternoon sleeping in his room. In the bathroom, he brushes his teeth and combs his thinning hair. He cleans the lenses of his glasses, which tend to accumulate fingerprints. He puts on the same clothes he was wearing earlier; they're all he's got.

The Camry's hot from sitting in the sun, and Goodman turns on the air conditioner. He gives it a few minutes to cool the interior before starting off. He decides he's glad he made them give him the pink car. Then he remembers the spare tire. For the first time, the notion occurs to him that this car was obviously intended for someone else, who right about now must be pretty upset. He moves the gear selector to D and pulls out into traffic.

There's a shopping mall on his right after a quarter of a mile or so, and he pulls in, finds a parking spot. At a JCPenney, he buys a pair of jeans, a couple of short-sleeved shirts, three pairs of undershorts, and a package of socks. He picks out a black nylon duffel bag and gets on line at a checkout register. Then, almost as an afterthought, he goes back and picks out a second duffel bag, identical to the first, but in the largest size they have. He tells himself he'll be buying more things sooner or later, and it only makes sense to have two bags.

His purchases come to $89.55. He tenders his Visa card to the cashier and holds his breath while she swipes it through a machine. But there's apparently no problem with it: He must not have reached his limit yet. He leaves the store, his arms full with his new belongings.

He loads everything into the trunk of the Camry, on top of the lid to the spare-tire compartment. Then he starts the car again and pulls out onto the highway in the same direction he's been traveling.

It's a particularly ugly stretch of road he's on, nothing but gas stations, car washes, fast-food places, and U-Haul rentals. He supposes he should eat something, but he still isn't really hungry. He spies a Taco Bell on the opposite side. He actually likes Taco Bell food, even the meat they use in the tacos, which looks a little like dog food. He makes a U-turn at the next intersection and pulls in.

It's cool inside, and almost empty. He orders two seven-ingredient burritos, no sour cream, and a large Coke.

"Here?" the girl asks him.

"Huh?"

"Here, or to go?"

"Oh. To go."

He drives back to the motel, one hand on the steering wheel, the other steadying the Coke container.

It's five-thirty by the time he carries his purchases into his room and sets them down. He locates the remote control for the TV, turns it on, and sits against the headboard of the bed, eating one of the burritos and sipping his Coke as he flicks back and forth between the news and an all country-and-western MTV-type channel.

He enjoys the burritos, is pleased with himself that he remembered to order them without sour cream, which he dislikes. The Coke is a bit watery from the melted ice, but otherwise not bad.

He tries to imagine the person for whom the drugs in the spare tire were intended, and how upset he must have been when he discovered that the car he was supposed to have been given had already been rented to somebody else. Then he remembers that he's given the name of this motel as his local address. For all he knows, the guy may by now have the information and be heading this way. He takes a tiny measure of comfort in knowing that what the guy wants is the car—or, more precisely, what's inside the spare tire—and not Goodman himself. Nonetheless, he gets up and checks to make sure his door is locked. And to be extra safe, he puts the security chain on. It's one of those lightweight brass ones, attached to the wooden molding with a couple of half-inch screws. They go for about $2.98.

The Weather Channel doesn't seem to want to tell him tomorrow's forecast. He's learned that, in southern Florida, that's a sure sign it's going to rain. It seems the chamber of commerce forbids anyone from giving out weather reports that don't call for clear skies and temperatures in the low eighties. He flicks back to the MTV channel, but some cowboy is singing about his faithful Cadillac. He turns the set off.

He dials his mother-in-law's number again. His daughter answers in a small voice.

"Hello, angel. It's Daddy."

"Hi, Daddy."

"How are you?"

"Fine."

"Grandma said you had a headache."

"A little one."

"How do you feel now?"

"Fine. The doctor said Larus can come with me when I go to have pictures made of my head."

"That's good, angel." Larus is Kelly's stuffed animal, her security blanket. It's almost as big as she is, a sort of a cross between a teddy bear and an elephant. No one can remember where it came from or what it's really supposed to be.

"Daddy, when are you coming home?"

"Soon, angel, soon."

"Grandma doesn't know any good stories."

"As soon as I get back, I promise I'll tell you a real good story."

"A long one?" she asks.

"A long one," he agrees.

"With *chapters?*"

"With chapters."

"All right."

"Well, you feel better," he tells her. "And remember Daddy loves you."

"I love you, too, Daddy."

"Let me talk to Grandma, okay?"

"Okay."

After a few seconds, he hears his mother-in-law's voice. "Did you call the insurance company?" she asks him.

"There *is* no insurance," he tells her again.

"Do I have to call a lawyer?"

He ignores that. "What do they think this could be?" he asks her. "The kid's only six years old."

"Six-year-olds can't get sick?"

"Take her for the tests," Goodman says. "I'll find the money."

"You *better* find the money."

He understands it's important for her to get the last word in. "Good-bye," he says.

"Good-bye."

"You got anythin' else?" Robbie asks Russell.

"No, man, thas it."

They had both nodded off, sitting in their corner of the rooftop overlooking 145th Street. Russell awoke first; it took Robbie another twenty minutes. Now, with nothing to keep them there, they stand up, stretch, and head for the stairs. At street level, Russell turns one way, Robbie the other.

"Later, man," Robbie says.

"Later."

As he heads back home, Russell reaches into his pocket and closes his fist around the second yellow cap, the one he's held back from Robbie. The one to get him through the afternoon.

Goodman decides to let the matter of the spare tire take care of itself. He figures he'll just leave the car right where it is tonight, parked just outside his room. Whoever's looking for it will show up sometime during the night. Either they'll break into the trunk and grab the spare or they'll simply steal the whole car. In the morning, Goodman will find out which it was, then notify Avis one way or the other. Then, if they'll let him use his Visa card again, he'll rent another car and hit the road for New York. End of problem.

He turns the TV back on, hunts for a movie, and settles on a National Geographic special about a lone wolf migrating north, trying to find his way home. The wolf is hurt, and Goodman senses that it's not going to make it, so eventually he flicks channels: He doesn't want to see the wolf die.

He settles on a baseball game and watches for a full twenty minutes before realizing that it's the World Series, the Yankees against the Atlanta Braves. He has no real interest in who wins or loses, and he knows almost none of the players' names. But he somehow manages to get absorbed in the rhythm of the thing: three strikes per batter, three outs per side. It's not like football or basketball or hockey, where everyone's in a big rush against the clock. In baseball, you get your three strikes, you get your three outs, you get your nine innings; you can take as long as you need to do it.

After each half inning, there are commercials for cars and beer. Goodman particularly likes one that shows three frogs who learn to say "Budweiser." He eats his second burrito; it's cold, but he enjoys it anyway.

Sometime around ten, he falls asleep.

Raul Cuervas pushes his foot down harder on the gas pedal, watches the needle on the speedometer climb to eighty, eighty-three, eighty-five. He looks at the digital clock on the dashboard: 10:49. He knows the Avis counter at the airport shuts down at eleven. He knows he's still fifteen miles away. He knows he's not going to make it.

He knows he's seriously fucked up.

He was supposed to pick up the car yesterday afternoon. But the night before, he'd gone drinking with Papo and Julio, matching shots of tequila at Fast Eddie's. After half a dozen shots, Raul had been feeling no pain. There was this little *chiquita* kept looking his way, giving him the eye. Finally, he'd gone over to her. They'd talked a while, ended up at a room somewhere.

He swerves to avoid a slow-moving car, fishtails for a moment as he passes it, leaning on his horn. Fuckin' old *maricóns*, he thinks, they oughta get 'em all off the road, give 'em a big mall to drive around in, like bumper cars.

He tries to remember fucking the *chiquita*, but he can't. He can remember her tits, though. Stickin' out real good, with these hard little nipples. . . .

He notices he's having trouble keeping his speed up, with even more cars in his way as he gets closer to the airport. He's doing no better than seventy-five, and it's already 10:54. Cock*suck*er!

He recalls waking up alone this afternoon in some strange motel room, his head throbbing, his wallet gone, not even knowing if he'd got laid or not. And the worst of it was that with his wallet gone, so was the license and credit card Mister Fuentes had given him to pick up the car with. Without which, he didn't even know the fucking name of the guy he was supposed to be.

He comes up fast on a pickup truck with no taillights, seeing it at the last minute, swerving around it with his tires squealing. Another one for the fuckin' mall. He's down to sixty-five, sixty. Still five miles away, and already it's 10:58.

It had taken him all evening to get ahold of Johnnie Delgado and get a duplicate license and credit card. Now he's gonna get shut down at the counter and have to wait till tomorrow to pick up the car. *If* the car's still there, that is. Mister Fuentes is gonna wanta fuckin' tear Raul a new asshole when he hears about this. If he hasn't heard already.

Goodman wakes at around eleven, sees the game is over, that it has been replaced by some postgame analysis show. They're interviewing some player in his underwear.

He flicks the TV off, turns off the light, and rolls over. He's amazed he was able to fall asleep, what with his back and the air conditioner being so loud. But within five minutes, he's asleep again.

It's five after eleven by the time Raul Cuervas pulls into the Fort Lauderdale Airport, almost quarter after by the time he enters the terminal and finds the Avis counter. It's empty and dark. On the counter is a sign,

CLOSED

WILL REOPEN 7:00 A.M.

WE TRY HARDER.

He'd like to take the sign and throw it through the fucking plate-glass window behind the counter, but he notices it's chained to the counter. Figures somebody musta done that once already.

Raul's afraid to go home. Johnnie Delgado or Mister Fuentes might be trying to reach him, and he doesn't want to talk to them till he's got the car. But there's no fucking way he's gonna sit in the fucking *air*port for eight hours. He decides to take a ride to Fast Eddie's, see if he can't find his little *chiquita,* break her fucking little neck for her.

Russell Bradford can't sleep. He lies sweating on the sofa in the living room. The room itself is cold, but Russell knows his sweats have nothing to do with the weather. Russell is getting sick again, which means it's time to go out once more.

Though it's dark, Russell has no real idea what time it is. He guesses it's around midnight, but it doesn't really matter: Where he's going, somebody'll be working. It's like that out there.

He pulls the same T-shirt back over his head, slips into the same pair of Nikes. Pulls on a "hoodie"—a sweatshirt with a hood—and his denim jacket. Silently, he moves about the apartment until he finds what he's looking for: his grandmother's purse. She's taken to hiding it on the top shelf of the closet by the front door. But Russell suspects she's not really hiding it at all. Suspects she notices each time there's money missing from it. Has even heard her arguing with his mother, saying she'd rather the boy take a few dollars from her than be out stealing. Russell is "the boy."

From the light coming in the window, Russell can see Nana's got three tens and some singles. He takes one of the tens, goes to replace the purse, thinks a minute. Takes another ten. Tiptoes out of the apartment, closing the door quietly behind him.

2

Goodman gradually becomes aware of daylight slanting through the slats of the venetian blinds. His first thought is about his daughter, Kelly. He tells himself that her headaches may be nothing more than a child's way of asking for attention following her mother's death. It's been awhile now, but he's read somewhere that kids can have delayed reactions to these things. And because they find it hard to talk about their feelings, they start having nightmares, wetting the bed, developing stomach cramps and headaches. Makes a lot of sense, when you think about it. He's pretty sure that's all this is. He says a little prayer that he's right.

He says little prayers like this from time to time, asking for things to happen or not happen, or giving thanks for things that have somehow managed to work out okay. He says them to nobody in particular. He hasn't been inside a synagogue since he was married fifteen years ago, and doesn't consider himself a religious man. But he continues to say his little prayers and thanksgivings anyway. And they seem to work for the most part, as long as he's careful not to ask for too much, and remembers to give thanks when something works out.

His second waking thought is about the car. He can't remember hearing any noises outside the door during the night. But that doesn't mean much: He knows he was tired and that he probably slept pretty soundly. And with the air-conditioning running, he figures he could have missed a *plane* taking off from the parking lot, let alone a car.

His bet is that the car itself is gone. That certainly would be the easiest thing for the people to have done, to take the whole car, rather than to start messing around with breaking into the trunk and taking the chance of stealing the tire—something that would also be a lot harder to explain if they got caught at it.

He gets up slowly, testing his back. It's sore, but not as bad as it was yesterday. The night's sleep on the hard bed has done him some good. He walks to the window, separates two of the venetian blind slats with his fingers, and looks out.

He sees the Camry, just as he left it.

As he showers, Goodman convinces himself that they must've stolen the tire out of the trunk after all. Figures whoever came looking for it must have come alone, and since the guy already had a car, he had no real choice—hard to drive two cars at once, after all. Goodman remembers years ago, trying to figure out just how you could manage to do that best— get two cars from point A to point B all by yourself. Would you drive one car a little ways, then walk back for the second one, pull it up to the first one? Maybe even leapfrog ahead a bit? Or were you better off driving the first car all the way to where you were heading, then walking back for the second one? He never could figure out which would work best.

He lathers his body for what he realizes is a very long time. Suppose, just suppose, the tire's still in the trunk. What then?

He rinses the soap off his body. What then, he tells himself, is that he drives to police headquarters, lets his problem become their problem. No other choice, plain and simple.

He steps out of the shower, dries off, wraps a towel around his waist. He sits on the edge of the bed and dials the information operator. He succeeds in getting the nonemergency number for the Fort Lauderdale Municipal Police Department, and dials it.

"You have reached the main switchboard of the Fort Lauderdale Police Department. Our telephone hours are nine A.M. to four-thirty P.M., Monday through Friday. If your call is an emergency, dial nine-one-one."

He looks at the clock: 6:51. More than two hours to kill. He shaves, taking as much time as he can. He dresses slowly, removing each tag and pulling each pin from his new JCPenney clothes. When he's done, he stands in front of the mirror in stiffly creased dark blue jeans and a short-sleeved white dress shirt. He feels like a redneck.

Outside, he looks around before opening the trunk of the Camry, but there's no one in sight. He unlocks the trunk, lifts the lid over the spare, finds it still nestled in its well. Closes it up.

He decides to leave the car there while he takes a walk to find some breakfast. He wonders if he's giving them one last chance to come and make off with the car. No, he decides: It's just a nice time of day to be out, before the sun heats things up too much.

Raul Cuervas is back at the Avis counter in the airport by 6:30. His skin is a bit paler than usual, his hair a bit more mussed. His mustache even seems to droop a little more. Raul has had less than two hours' sleep during the night.

From the Avis counter, he'd gone back to Fast Eddie's, but he hadn't found the *chiquita* who'd ripped him off the night before. Instead, he'd spent three hours drinking Cuervo Gold and making frequent trips to the men's room. Not to relieve himself, but to snort the better part of a gram of cocaine to stay awake.

From Fast Eddie's, he'd gone to the Miramar Lounge, where he'd hung out to closing time. And from there to Rico's, an after-hours spot in Miami. There, they'd let him lie down for a couple of hours in one of the upstairs rooms that on busy nights are reserved for the *putas* and their johns, twenty dollars for thirty minutes, or until you come, whichever happens first. By 5:45, he was back on the road, determined to be the first customer on line at the Avis counter.

The rental agents show up around a quarter to seven, but they spend the next ten minutes setting things up and giggling like schoolchildren. It's five of seven when he finally gets one of them to talk to him.

"My name is Velez," he says, "Antonio Velez." To prove his point, he displays the driver's license Johnnie Delgado has supplied him with, the second one. "I was supposed to pick up a car the day before yesterday. I got delayed."

"Let me see," the woman says. She has reddish hair and big tits. She takes the license, reads from it as she punches his name into her computer.

"I'm sorry, Mr. Velez," she says after a minute. "We had to cancel your reservation. You were more than twelve hours late."

"I had a problem," he explains.

"You should have phoned our eight hundred number," she says.

"Would you like me to see if we can find you another car?"

"Yes. No, I mean. I want the same car."

"No problem. I can give you the same car. A Toyota Camry, right?"

"It's gotta be *ezzackly* the same," he says. "It's gotta be the pink one."

"Excuse me?"

"The car," he says. "I need a pink one. I promised my little girl we'd rent a pink car." He's pleased with himself for his quick thinking. "See, it's her birthday," he adds.

The redhead plays with her computer some more. "I've got a pink Lincoln Town Car," she says.

"Gotta be a pink Toyota Camry," he says.

More playing with the computer. "I only show one of those," she says. "And it's already rented."

Cuervas feels a knot in his stomach. "Who'd you rent it to?" he asks. "That was supposed to be *my* car."

"I'm sorry," she smiles. "We're not allowed to give out that information."

"When's it due back?" he asks.

She smiles again.

"C'mon," he pleads. "It's my little girl's *birth*day. I *prom*ised."

She punches some more keys on the computer, then looks around to make sure nobody's listening. Like this is top-secret information, national security stuff.

"Noon."

"Noon today?"

She nods.

"I gotta have it," he says, feeling the knot in his stomach loosen up a bit.

"I can reserve it," she says. "I'll need a major credit card."

He's already handing her the card Johnnie Delgado gave him.

"Lissen," he says while she punches numbers. "I'm gonna wait for it, okay? Case the guy brings it back early. You don't see me, you page me, okay?" He extends his hand over the counter, showing just the corner of a fifty-dollar bill. She sees it, looks around again. Then she covers his hand with some papers while she takes the fifty from him.

"Don't give my car away again," he tells her.

"Don't worry," she says with a smile.

As soon as he gets his license and credit card back, Cuervas walks away from the counter. Too dangerous to wait there, he knows.

He steps outside and wanders around for a while until he finds the sign he's looking for.

AVIS

RETURN RENTAL

CARS HERE

Goodman dawdles over breakfast at an imitation Dunkin' Donuts place called The Duke of Donuts. Several times he looks at his watch, imagining that even as he's eating his pancakes, thieves are breaking into the Camry back at the motel. It's 7:50 by the time he finishes his second cup of coffee and pays his check—$6.50, with the tip.

He walks back slowly, pretending to enjoy the sights, hoping that by the time he gets to the motel, the car—and his problem—will be gone.

Finds it parked, exactly as before.

Inside his room, he packs his few new possessions into the two JCPenney duffel bags. His plan is to get to police headquarters as soon as they open up, tell them his story, let them take the spare tire and give him a receipt for it, drive to the airport to drop off the car, and rent another one if he can, one-way to New York.

He checks the rate schedule posted on the inside of the motel door, notes that checkout time is 11:00 a.m. Decides to hang on to the room key for a while, just in case he needs to stop back in the room later, like maybe to use the bathroom. He doesn't mind using a public restroom for urinating, but when it comes to sitting down, he likes his privacy. And he figures even if he doesn't come back, he can always drop the key in any mailbox, just like the writing on the green plastic tag tells him.

Even though he's unsure of the way and drives extra slowly, Goodman arrives at police headquarters a full twenty-five minutes before nine. Finds a parking lot, but it's reserved for municipal vehicles. A block and a half away, there's another one, for visitors. He guesses he qualifies as a visitor. Pulls in at the sign marked ENTRANCE, finds a spot, shuts off the motor, and waits.

At the airport, Raul Cuervas waits, too. He's positioned himself right outside the Avis drop-off area. He wants to be there when the clown who took his pink Toyota Camry brings it back. He wants to see the car at the earliest possible opportunity, make sure there's nothing wrong with it.

Maybe follow it through the drop-off process, slip a coupla bucks to the guy's supposed to check it out, see that he's good and quick about it.

He also wants to get a look at the driver. Just in case it turns out there's a problem.

As he begins his wait, he lights a cigarette. He'll go through a pack and a half before the morning's over.

In his South Bronx apartment, Russell Bradford finally falls asleep. He's been out most of the night, copping and smoking, copping and sniffing, hanging out on corners, on rooftops, in alleyways. It was already getting light when he sneaked back into the apartment. He thought he heard somebody saying something in one of the bedrooms. Probably his grandmother, Nana. She never seems to sleep. But she didn't come out to the living room.

Spaced-out from the dope but still jumpy from the crack, Russell had lain on the couch for what seemed like a couple of hours. Then, just as he began to hear people waking up and moving about, he finally crashed. . . .

In the days that follow, Michael Goodman will try to reconstruct just what it was that went through his mind as he sat behind the wheel of the pink Camry in the visitors' parking lot, waiting for the beginning of normal business hours to begin at the Fort Lauderdale Police Department headquarters. He will remember thinking about how hopelessly in debt he was, and how little money he had to his name. He will remember worrying about his daughter, shuddering to think what headaches could mean in a six-year-old, not daring to imagine how expensive the tests would be and how he would possibly figure out a way to pay for them.

He will recall that there had been no one thing in particular that he could put his finger on. It had just seemed at the time, as he had added things up, that everything seemed to be in the debit column and nothing in the asset column, with no prospects anywhere on the horizon. And he had suddenly felt terribly tired; and the old, seductive fantasy of falling asleep and never waking up again had entered his thoughts as he sat there. And the only thing that had finally brought him out of that was the realization that while that might be fine for *him*, it wasn't going to do much for Kelly.

And he will remember that it was somewhere right about then that it had come to him: that he *did* have an asset after all; that there was indeed a prospect on the horizon. Not floating vaguely way out there somewhere, but sitting right under him, not five feet behind his butt!

He will recall looking at the clock on the dashboard, seeing that it was still ten minutes before nine, becoming acutely aware of the annoyance he felt at having had to call the police repeatedly, listen to their stupid recordings, drive to *them* (when by rights they should have dropped everything and come rushing over to *him*), and then wait on their bankers' hours. He will remember sitting there behind the wheel of the Camry, feeling his annoyance begin to steam and simmer, until it reached the full boil of anger. Anger at the mechanical voices of the operators he'd had to listen to. Anger at the bureaucracy that forced him to respond to its stupid rules and adjust to its rigid schedule. Anger at the officials he'd be sure to encounter as soon as he walked inside and tried to explain his discovery of the contents of the spare tire.

He will remember imagining being told to wait interminably, being shuttled from one department to another, being required to repeat his story over and over again, being compelled to sign affidavits, being told he couldn't leave the state while they investigated the situation, maybe even being accused of knowing more than he was letting on.

And the next thing he will remember is having moved his right hand slowly but deliberately toward the key that still sat nestled in the ignition. Giving that key a ninety-degree turn to the right. Hearing the engine catch. Moving the gear-selector lever gently from P, past R, past N, until it reached and settled into D. Feeling the car begin to move him forward. Allowing it to take him back to the entrance sign of the parking lot—which from the inside of the lot read THIS WAY OUT—over the cut in the curb, out onto the street beyond, and back in the direction from which he had come.

Raul Cuervas looks at his watch for the hundredth time in the past two hours and sees he's finally made it to nine o'clock. He's been told the pink Camry isn't due back until noon, but he knows he doesn't dare assume that the renter won't bring it back early. He's fucked up once already, he knows, and he can't afford to do it again. In the business he's in, there doesn't tend to be a lot of second chances.

*   *   *

Goodman drives directly back to the motel. Almost involuntarily, he pats the outside of his left pants pocket, feels the room key attached to its plastic tag. One of the things he'll think about in the next several days is whether he'd really held on to that key for no better reason than just to be able to use the bathroom in privacy. He will wonder if even then he was beginning to set some plan in motion, some plan for which that key might come in handy.

He turns into the parking lot, sees that the spot in front of his room is still vacant. Instead of pulling directly into it, he swings the Toyota around, then backs into the spot so that the trunk of the car ends up closest to the door of his room.

He gets out, walks around to the trunk, opens it up. He removes the two duffel bags and, unlocking the door to the room, carries them inside. As he does so, he looks around, satisfies himself that no one is watching him.

Returning to the trunk, he raises the lid that covers the spare. Bracing his back carefully, he frees the tire from its well, rights it, and rolls it up and out of the trunk and into the room. He returns to the car and retrieves the jack handle before closing the lid and slamming the trunk.

Back in his room, he closes the door and fastens the chain, which suddenly strikes him as foolishly flimsy, but will have to do. He studies the tire; it looks brand-new, as though it's never been driven on. He decides it's clean enough to lift onto the bed.

With the jack handle, he separates the tire from the rim, pulling it almost completely free. He sees now that the tire is packed to its capacity with blue plastic packages, each pressed tightly against the ones to either side of it. He removes the first one carefully, with some difficulty; the remainder will come free more easily.

Each package is roughly the size of a brick, and, Goodman figures, each was originally shaped much like one. Wedged into the tire, however, the packages have conformed to the interior of the tire, and as a result, they are rounded on one side. As he handles them, he tries to judge their weight. He uses sugar as a reference: They're somewhat heavier than a one-pound box, but considerably lighter than a five-pound bag. He ends up guessing they go about two pounds each, maybe a little more.

As he continues to remove them from the tire, he lines them up in a neat row on the bed. When he's finished, he counts an even twenty bags. If he's right about what they're worth, he's looking at forty thousand dollars.

Forty thousand dollars.

He refits the tire around the rim. He empties his two duffel bags of their few items. In the smaller bag, he finds the two remaining unused cans of Jiffy-Spare. He shakes the first one, then threads it onto the valve of the tire until it hisses. He feels the tire begin to harden in his hands. The second can completes the job. A small amount of white adhesive remains on the valve; he wipes it off with a towel from the bathroom.

He lifts the tire from the bed. It's fully inflated and, for the first time, weighs what a tire ought to. He lowers it to the floor, notices that it bounces now, the way a tire's supposed to. He feels immensely pleased with himself.

He removes the pillowcases from three of the four pillows in the room and divides the packages among them. Then he tightly knots closed the opening of each pillowcase. Two of them he places in the larger duffel bag, the third in the smaller one. He covers them with his JCPenney possessions.

He takes what's left of his money out, peels off a ten-dollar bill, and leaves it on the desk. Wonders for a moment what pillowcases cost, can't remember ever having bought one. Adds a five.

He tosses the room key onto the desk and lifts the two duffel bags onto the floor. They're heavy but manageable. He steps out into the parking lot and looks around, sees nobody. He opens the trunk of the Camry and raises the lid to the spare-tire well. He rolls the tire from the room to the car and stows it in its well. He bolts it down tightly with the wing nut, and replaces the jack handle. Closes the lid over it. Retrieves the two duffel bags from the room, carries them to the trunk, and places them in it. Slams the trunk closed.

As he pulls out of the parking lot, Michael Goodman tries to think of the most reckless thing he's ever done in his life up to this moment. The best that he can come up with is the day he and Herbie Schwartz stole two six-packs of Pepsi from the A&P on Eighty-sixth Street. He'd saved his six bottles without opening them for a month, so sure he'd been that the Pepsi Police were going to come to his home in the middle of the night to arrest him and demand their return. He'd been ten at the time, maybe eleven, but he can still remember his fear as though it had all happened yesterday.

Now, thirty years later, Goodman drives toward the Fort Lauderdale Airport with two duffel bags containing twenty packages of white powder. He's not sure precisely what the white powder is, but he's certain it's worth more than all the Pepsis in all the A&Ps he's ever been in. He's equally certain that if the police catch him, it won't be a matter of returning a six-pack of Pepsis; he'll spend the rest of his life in prison. He turns on the radio and tries not to think about that. The local weatherman tells him it's going to be clear skies, with temperatures in the lower eighties.

3

Raul Cuervas is so busy opening a new pack of Marlboros that he doesn't notice the pink Toyota Camry until it's almost alongside him. He follows it on foot, which is easy, since the car return area is crowded. He sees a uniformed attendant signal the driver to pull into a spot. Cuervas walks closer, but not too close. He wants to get a look at the driver, but he'd rather not be noticed. So he walks behind a minivan and melts into the family that's just climbed out of it.

When Cuervas sees the driver step from the Camry, he can't help smiling. The guy is short, maybe five six. He's not fat, but *soft*-looking. Got this curly Jew hair with a little bald spot just starting to show. He's maybe forty. Looks like he never did a real day's work in his life. A pencil pusher. But the thing that really gets Cuervas is the way the guy's dressed. Got on this girlie shirt and a pair of jeans that look like they just came off a rack, real dark and still perfectly creased. Best of all, they're turned up about four inches at the cuffs. This guy is a *bufón*, Cuervas says to himself, a real clown.

Goodman unloads the two duffel bags from the trunk. He tries to act casual about it, telling himself to treat them as though they contain nothing but personal belongings. An Avis attendant wearing a WE TRY HARDER button checks him out, then directs him to a shuttle bus that will take him to the terminal. He pays no attention to a family returning a minivan nearby.

He boards the bus. When the driver goes to help him with his duffel bags, Goodman politely declines the offer. He rides the bus with the bags on his lap. He realizes he's only drawing attention to himself, tells himself he's going to have to try loosen up a little bit.

"Hey, that's my baby," Cuervas tells the Avis attendant who's about to get into the pink Camry. When the attendant, a large black man, looks at him quizzically, Cuervas explains. "I got her next, special for my daughter's birthday. She likes pink."

"That's nice," the man says, as if he couldn't care less.

"I 'preciate it if you could turn her around real fass for me," Cuervas says, and to show just how much he would appreciate it, he extends a fifty-dollar bill in the man's direction. The man takes it, never taking his eyes off Cuervas's.

"*Real* fass," Cuervas repeats. "An' let 'em know at the counter as soon as it's ready. I'm in a *big* hurry."

"No problem," the man says.

At the main terminal, Goodman finds the Avis counter and gets on line. When he makes it to the front of the line, he asks the rate for a one-way rental to New York City. After punching up some numbers on the computer, the attendant, a young man with blond hair, gives him the news.

"For a midsize car, I can give you a rate of forty-six dollars a day, unlimited mileage—"

Goodman is pleasantly surprised, and is in the process of multiplying forty-six by two, then three, when he hears the bad news.

"And there's a one-way drop-off charge of two hundred and fifty dollars."

Goodman knows his credit card can't take a hit like that. "Thanks," he says. "Let me think about it a bit." He turns, lifts his bags, and walks away from the counter.

*   *   *

Goodman is gone less than a minute when a Hispanic man with a droopy mustache ignores the line and walks directly to the Avis attendant with the red hair and the big breasts.

Cuervas pays no attention to the complaints muttered by the people waiting on line. "My pink Camry," he tells the woman. "She's back."

"Oh, Mr.—"

"Velez. Antonio Velez."

"Mr. Velez," she repeats. She checks her computer. The people on line mutter some more, but she ignores them, too. "I'm sorry," she says, "they're still servicing it."

"I don't need it serviced," Cuervas tells her. "I need it *now.*"

"Let me see what I can do," she says, and picks up the phone.

Goodman stops at the Delta counter, asks about a one-way ticket to New York.

"I can put you on our flight five-sixty-two to Kennedy," he's told. "It leaves at twelve-oh-one."

Goodman has a theory about the number 562. He's convinced it comes up more often than any other three-digit number. Were he a gambler, he'd play the number. But he doesn't even know how you go about betting on a number. Nonetheless, he figures flight 562 is a good omen.

"How much would that be?" he asks. He's down to $47.47, plus a hundred dollars in traveler's checks.

"That would come to two hundred and twenty-nine dollars."

"Okay," he says, and fishes out his Visa card. Again he holds his breath, but it seems that Delta isn't checking credit cards too closely this day. A machine spits out his ticket and boarding pass.

"How many bags will you be checking?"

Goodman freezes for a moment. Do they search bags? Run them through an X-ray machine?

"I don't know yet," he says. "I'm going to buy a few things before I check them in. Is that okay?"

"Sure."

After a few minutes on the phone, the redhead tells Raul Cuervas that his car is ready. She gives him a big smile, like maybe she expects another fifty. But Cuervas is finished with her.

He takes the stupid little red bus to the pickup area and spots his Camry. He opens the trunk and lifts the lid covering the spare tire. It's there, good as new, nicely bolted down. He gives it a push with his thumb; it feels nice and hard. He closes the lid, slams the trunk.

He gets in behind the wheel, starts the engine, and pulls out of the spot. He knows a little turnoff about ten minutes away, where he can make sure that everything's the way it's supposed to be.

Goodman looks at his watch, sees he's got an hour to kill before his flight. He decides he's going to have to take a chance and check his luggage, at least the larger duffel bag. They'd only take it away from him at the gate: It's much too big to carry on.

While he knows they don't make you open checked-in luggage on a domestic flight, he has no idea what they do to the bags before putting them on the plane. But he figures he has no choice.

He buys a newspaper, wanders into a souvenir shop. They've got all this Miami Dolphin and Florida Marlin stuff, picture frames covered with shells, and plastic dolphins and killer whales that can spout water. He buys Kelly a dolphin. Then, as an afterthought, he buys his mother-in-law a bottle of toilet water called Florida Breeze. He figures a little peace offering can't hurt.

His purchases come to $19.85, leaving him $27.62.

He finds a quiet corner to unzip the big duffel bag. He rearranges the contents until they look like nothing but clothes and dirty laundry. He puts the dolphin and the toilet water on top, then zips the bag closed again. He finds a piece of string in a trash can and uses it to tie the zipper pull closed. Then he goes back to the Delta counter and checks the big duffel bag with them.

Cuervas pulls the Camry off the highway and into a little turnoff between the north and south lanes. It's a heavily wooded portion of the divider, where he can back his car between the trees in such a way as to make it invisible to passing traffic. He knows the spot because a friend of his who used to be with the Highway Patrol pointed it out to him. The cops use to use it to "coop"—to catch some sleep on the job—or even to conduct a quick out-of-court settlement of a speeding infraction committed by some pretty young thing who's afraid of losing her license.

He opens the trunk and lifts the lid, revealing the spare tire. He unscrews the dust cap from the valve. Using the blade of a silver pocketknife, he presses against the valve stem to let air out of the tire. He knows there's supposed to be twenty kilos inside, so he figures there can't be much air, maybe only five or ten seconds' worth.

To his surprise, air keeps hissing out. Fifteen seconds, twenty, thirty. As the tire empties, Cuervas fills with panic. By the time the hissing noise stops, the sidewall of the tire is soft enough to push away from the rim.

Though he could easily pry the tire from its rim by hand to inspect the inside, Cuervas instead stabs at the rubber with the blade of his knife, cutting into it and ripping it.

"Fuckin' gringo!" he shouts. "Fuckin' gringo *maricón!*" He continues to slash away at the empty tire until the knife blade closes across his fingers, drawing blood. He slams the lid and the trunk, gets back into the car, pulls out onto the highway in a violent spray of cinders and dirt, and heads back to the airport.

He covers the seven miles in just over six minutes, weaving in and out in the midday traffic. He remembers making the same drive, more or less, last night, only to arrive at the Avis counter after closing time. This time, it's not the Avis counter he's racing to; it's the guy in the rolled-up jeans who's stolen the twenty kilos from the spare tire.

Cuervas has no idea how the guy knew the stuff would be there. He figures *some*body has to have tipped him off; he just doesn't know who or why yet. The thought that the guy might have stumbled onto the drugs by pure accident never once occurs to him. In Raul Cuervas's business, there is no such thing as coincidence; there *are* no pure accidents.

He pulls the Camry right up to the terminal and leaves it there. They can tow it back to fuckin' *Japan,* for all he cares. He strides into the terminal, starts with the United ticketing area, then heads to American. . . .

Goodman hears the first announcement for his flight at twenty minutes to twelve. From the fact that there are passengers waiting to get on as standbys, he figures he was lucky to get a ticket when he did.

He listens for the announcement that they're boarding his row before getting on line. When he was married and traveling with Shirley, she always said it didn't matter, and insisted that they line up as soon as the very first announcement was made, the one for travelers with small children, or those requiring special assistance. But, without his wife's bravery, Goodman's afraid they might catch him boarding before his row's been called, so he waits his turn.

Finally, at quarter of twelve, they announce that everyone can board, and Goodman takes his place at the rear of the line, the smaller of his two duffel bags tucked under his arm like a football.

It's ten minutes to twelve by the time Cuervas works his way to the Delta gates, just in time to see Mr. Rolled-Up Jeans handing his boarding pass to a ticket taker at gate 22 and disappearing from view. Immediately, Cuervas runs to the counter, pushes past several people waiting for standby seats, and gets the attention of a man behind the counter.

"I gotta get on that flight!" he shouts.

"Sorry, sir," the man tells him. "That flight's actually *over*sold."

"You're actually an asshole!" is all Cuervas can think to say. People turn to stare at him. After a moment, he walks off, but not before taking a look at the sign above the door through which the guy disappeared.

GATE 22

FLIGHT 562

NEW YORK–JFK

[4]

Michael Goodman sits looking out the window of the plane, watching the Florida coastline recede beneath him into the distance, and wondering exactly what it is he's doing.

He has lived on this planet for a shade over forty years, and his entire life has been conventional to the point of absolute boredom. Or so it seems to him. For as long as he can remember, he has gotten up in the morning, showered, shaved, and gone to school or to work. He has a wife and a daughter. *Had* a wife. He has a studio apartment he rents, debts he owes, and cards made out of plastic that somehow manage to get him to the next crisis.

Up until this moment, Goodman's only link to the world of illicit drugs has been the two marijuana cigarettes he puffed unsatisfactorily years ago. He knows nobody who traffics in narcotics, and can't even come up with anyone who he knows for sure even *uses* narcotics, though he has his suspicions about the McPherson's teenage son, the one who wears the earring.

Yet now he suddenly finds himself sitting in a plane, resting his feet on top of a duffel bag containing thousands of dollars' worth of narcotics, while stapled to his ticket is a claim check for another duffel bag containing twice as much. He has absolutely no clue as to what he can do with the white powder inside those duffel bags in order to convert it somehow into money. And yet he knows that that's precisely what he's going to try to do.

* * *

Unable to get onto the same plane as Mr. Softee, Raul Cuervas toys with the idea of getting a ticket on the next available flight, but there are no nonstops to JFK for another hour, which means he'll miss the guy at the other end. He heads to a bank of pay phones, feeling as if he's about to enter a confessional booth. Only difference is, he knows Mister Fuentes isn't going to be satisfied with telling him to say five Hail Marys and five Our Fathers.

It takes him twelve minutes and three phone calls before he finally gets to speak with Johnnie Delgado and explain things. Then he holds on for Mister Fuentes. But when next he hears a voice, it's still that of Johnnie Delgado.

"*El viejo* is so pissed off, he won't talk to you," Delgado tells him.

"Tell him I'm real sorry," Cuervas says. "Tell him I make it up to him, however I can."

"He wants to know if you got a good look at the guy," Delgado says.

"Yeah, yeah," Cuervas assures him. "I could spot this guy in the fuckin' Orange Bowl, man."

There's a pause. Cuervas can hear Delgado relaying his answer to Mister Fuentes in the background.

"Okay," Delgado says. "He says for you to come to the hotel. Right away."

It will be another fifteen minutes, while he's driving back to Miami, before it dawns on Raul Cuervas that his ability to recognize the man may turn out to be the only thing that's going to keep him alive. At least until they get the stuff back, that is.

In his business, that's called reassurance.

Goodman drinks a Bloody Mary, emptying only half of the vodka in the tiny Smirnoff bottle they give him. He figures half will calm him down a bit, without depriving him of his ability to function. But then he uses a little more of the vodka to mix with what's left in the can of Bloody Mary mix. Never much of a drinker, he feels a definite buzz even before draining the last of the mixture.

The person to his right, a young man with a ponytail, listens to music through headphones. The music is so loud that even Goodman can hear it. It sounds like rock 'n' roll, though Goodman actually isn't too sure what

rock 'n' roll really is. The music and the ponytail cause Goodman to wonder if the young man knows anything about narcotics. But he figures it
would be a mistake to bring up the subject with a total stranger.

They bring him lunch, a turkey and cheese sandwich on a hero-type
roll. Goodman knows that most people hate airplane food, and he understands it's fashionable to complain about it. But the truth is, he secretly
likes the meals you get on planes. He spreads mustard onto the sandwich
from a little plastic packet, shakes on just the right amount of salt and pep-
per from individual containers, and eats slowly. Even the fig bar that's supposed to be dessert is moist and good.

Tommy McAuliffe is working steady days at Kennedy all week. McAuliffe is a member of the New York Port Authority Police. He's been given
a computer-generated printout of a dozen incoming flights he and his partner are to meet that afternoon. "Meeting" a flight means checking the bags
as they come off the baggage trains, right before they're put on the con-
veyer belts that take them into the claim areas.

The seventh flight McAuliffe and his partner are to meet is due in at
Gate D-17 at 3:37 P.M. It is Delta 562 from Fort Lauderdale. As always,
McAuliffe and his partner will be looking for drugs. Almost all of the flights
on their list are from South Florida. Statistical studies have consistently
demonstrated that, along with Houston and New Orleans, those are the
ones it pays to meet.

Because all of the flights are domestic, McAuliffe knows that only an
external examination of the bags is permitted under law. Except in the
case of customs agents dealing with international flights, the Fourth
Amendment of the United States Constitution prohibits opening bags in
the absence of a search warrant or probable cause to believe that they contain controlled substances.

Under different circumstances, the prohibition might constitute an in-
surmountable obstacle to McAuliffe, given the fact that luggage tends to
be opaque rather than transparent, and the further fact that controlled
substances have a way of not showing up as much of anything on the X-
ray machines.

This is where McAuliffe's partner comes in handy. He has an uncanny
ability that makes him ideally suited for his work. He is a four-year vet-
eran of the K-9 division, a ninety-five-pound German shepherd named
Rommel, trained to lie down whenever his nostrils detect an airborne con-

centration greater than three parts per hundred thousand of heroin, co-caine, marijuana, or methamphetamine.

Goodman is one of those travelers who follows the suggestion to keep his seat belt fastened throughout the flight. (He even pays close attention to the demonstration on how to inflate the life jacket he's assured is under his seat, and studies the laminated card that locates the emergency exit nearest him.) So he's ready to descend long before the first announcement comes over the intercom.

He dries his palms on his pant legs. He tends to perspire at normal times, and this is no normal time. He's worried about his daughter and her headaches, and how he's going to pay for the tests she needs. He's worried about the landing: Planes make him nervous, especially right before they touch down. He worries they may go into a skid, may blow a tire. The brakes may fail. The pilot may overshoot the runway. A little plane may be crossing in front of them as they roar down the tarmac. The possibilities are endless.

He's worried about how to get home from the airport. He doesn't think he's got enough cash for a cab, which could run thirty dollars into Manhattan. He's heard about the "train to the plane," but he doesn't really know what it is. Certainly there's no subway stop at Kennedy. But if there's a "train to the plane," doesn't that mean there's got to be a "train *from* the plane," too?

Most of all, he's worried about his bags.

The one he's carrying is okay. It's the one he checked that he thinks about now. Did they search it? Run it through an X-ray machine? Suppose it's been stolen or lost? Does he dare put in a claim for it? Is he going to be able to manage it on the train from the plane? Can his back take the weight?

About the only thing he *doesn't* worry about is the one thing he *should:* Rommel. And, in particular, Rommel's nose. But he has no way of knowing about that.

He tightens his seat belt and prepares for impact.

Bobby Manley is "catching" this afternoon for Delta Baggage Crew 2. This means that his partner, Teddy Siskowitz, will lift each bag as it comes off the unloading ramp of the plane and, in the same motion, toss it to Bobby.

Usually, the toss isn't really a toss at all: The bag is in Bobby's hands even before Teddy lets go of it. But occasionally, mostly with smaller items, the toss is really a toss, especially with Teddy, who's got muscles in places where some people don't even have places, and who likes to show off a lot.

It's Crew 2, Teddy Siskowitz and Bobby Manley, that is assigned the first run to Delta 562 at Gate D-17. Teddy drives a little tractor that pulls five baggage cars snakelike to the belly of the plane. Bobby walks to meet him. Regulations prohibit anyone but the driver from riding on the tractor or the cars, ever since Walter Mayberry slipped between two of the cars he was straddling and broke his leg.

The walk is a long one, and it's made worse by Bobby's hangover. He woke up this morning with a major-league headache, vowing never again to mix rum and vodka, no matter how cool it may seem at the time.

It is this same hangover that has kept Bobby's sense of balance slightly off all day, as well as his sense of timing. Usually, he and Teddy get a nice rhythm going: As Teddy brings each bag up, Bobby's reaching for it. But today they've been just a hair off at times. It's cost Bobby a number of close calls and two outright errors, which Teddy has been quick to broadcast to an invisible crowd on his imaginary public-address system.

It just so happens that Bobby makes one more error this afternoon, as they're unloading Delta 562.

Not only is his timing off again but the weight of the bag surprises him. True, Teddy isn't supposed to call out "Heavy!" unless the bag is heavy for its *size*. But for some reason, Bobby just doesn't expect the weight of this one, and it slips right through his hands, hitting the tarmac with a thud.

"And the big *E* lights up once again!" Teddy announces for anyone within earshot.

Since it has landed upside down, Bobby has to stoop to roll the bag over before picking it up. But even if he wasn't tired and hungover, Bobby Manley's nose is simply too insensitive to pick up the faint odor of Florida Breeze that has just been released by the breaking of a small glass bottle at the top of the black duffel bag.

But that same odor proves to be the undoing of a far more sensitive nose than Bobby's. While not noticeable enough to arouse the suspicion of Tommy McAuliffe five minutes later, the odor is just strong enough to mask the scent of anything else in the bag, and Rommel obediently stands his ground as it passes him. He will, in fact, suddenly lie down twenty-seven bags later, alerted by the smell of a five-dollar bag of marijuana inside a backpack belonging to the young man who had sat alongside of Michael Goodman during the flight from Fort Lauderdale.

Goodman thanks the flight attendants as he steps from the plane and begins the long walk to the baggage-claim area. Some of the passengers are met by families and loved ones. Little children run forward for hugs and presents, causing Goodman to remember his own daughter and worry about her headaches.

Although he feels a momentary pang of jealousy toward those lucky enough to have people waiting there to meet them, in a sense he need not: For the truth is that Michael Goodman has a waiting party, too. As Goodman walks, clutching the smaller of his duffel bags tightly against his side, two men fall in behind him at a distance. Their names are Antonio Rodriguez and Sixto Quinones, but on the street they are known as "Hot Rod" and "Six." They work for one Pedro Aguilar, who in turn answers to a Mister Fuentes from Miami. They tend to kill people. But not today. Today, they have come to the airport with instructions to meet Delta Flight 562, spot a little middle-aged gringo who'll be wearing turned-up jeans and carrying a black bag, and follow him to find out where he goes.

By 3:45 that afternoon, as they walk through the terminal, they've already completed half of their assignment. Michael Goodman, of course, is totally oblivious of their presence.

He reaches the baggage-claim area, where for the first time he glances around to see if there's anyone who looks like he might be a police officer. But Goodman realizes he has no idea what a police officer would look like out of uniform. Would he be a big man, of Irish or Italian extraction? Might he be wearing mirrored aviator-type sunglasses? Would he look like Clint Eastwood, or maybe Sylvester Stallone?

All he sees are people like himself, intent on retrieving their luggage, paying him no attention whatsoever. He decides things are as safe as they're going to get.

There is a ringing noise, and the carousel belt begins to move. Bags appear: brightly colored suitcases, duffels of all shapes and sizes, and cartons wrapped with rope and tape. It isn't long before Goodman spots his own large black duffel bag. He lets it go around once, not so much out of caution, but because he's simply unable to get close enough to the conveyor belt to grab it the first time. The second time by, he pulls it free, noticing as he does so that there's a wet stain near the zipper. There's also an odor coming from it, a perfume smell he can't quite place.

The train from the plane turns out to be a thing of the past. These days, the poor man's trip to the city starts out with a bus ride. Goodman boards, lugging his two duffels, envious of the business travelers who have only their attaché cases to carry, and, in particular, of the two Spanish men across the aisle, who are empty-handed. One of them is nice enough to help Goodman lift his larger duffel onto the overhead rack, grunting under its weight.

The bus brings them to a place called Howard Beach, which is actually a subway stop and not a beach at all, as far as Goodman can see. He boards the A train, finds a seat. He remembers hearing of Howard Beach. It was where John Gotti lived when he ran the Mafia. He looks around the train for Italian types with pencil-thin mustaches, but sees only blacks, Puerto Ricans, and airport commuters like himself.

The train seems to take forever as it winds its way past Ozone Park, Rockaway Boulevard, East New York, and Bedford-Stuyvesant, and then on to Flatbush and downtown Brooklyn, before plunging under the East River and into subterranean Manhattan. Goodman clutches both his duffels in his lap, one on top of the other, the smaller reaching almost to his chin.

At the Broadway/Nassau Street stop, he changes for the Lexington Avenue line, struggling down the connecting corridor under the weight of his bags. He rides the express to Eighty-sixth, where he exits, leaving himself a six-block walk home. He could change once again and take the local to Ninety-sixth, but the four-block walk back would be uphill and more than his back can take.

It's after five by the time he lets himself into his walk-up studio apartment on Ninety-second Street between Lexington and Third. He leaves his bags on the floor, bolts the door, and collapses onto his sofa. He is sweaty, exhausted, and in pain. But he's home.

"We took him home, boss," the one called Hot Rod says into the pay phone on the corner.

"Good," comes the reply. "Was he carrying a lot of stuff with him?"

"Yeah, a shitload. Want us to go in an' get it? We could get in an' do this guy easy."

There is a pause, then Hot Rod hears, "No, don't do nothin'."

It isn't simple caution that has prompted the answer, and it certainly isn't morality. It comes down to a lack of trust, trust being an exceedingly rare commodity in the world of Antonio Rodriguez and Sixto Quinones. Pedro Aguilar, the man on the other end of the phone, has no doubt that Rodriguez and Quinones could break into the apartment in a minute, get the stuff, and do the guy without blinking. The problem is that there's too much product involved to trust them to bring it in. They could skim it, whack it, or even go south with the whole load. No, better to wait, see what Mister Fuentes wants to do about it.

It is only this lack of trust that now keeps Michael Goodman alive upstairs, sprawled out on his sofa, snoring lightly.

Goodman awakes to darkness, and it takes him a moment or two to figure out that he's back in his own apartment in New York.

He peels his clothes off as he heads to the shower, tripping and stumbling over the larger of two duffel bags he now remembers about.

He lets the shower send its needles of water over his body for what seems like a long time. Maybe he should forget about those duffel bags, he thinks, dump the narcotics into some garbage can before they get him into trouble. No amount of money could possibly be worth risking ending up in jail. Not even forty thousand.

He towels off, puts his glasses back on, and stares at his reflection in the mirror of the medicine cabinet. His skin is pale; you'd never know he just got back from Florida. His hair never looks thinner than when it's wet. He's taken to fluffing it dry not because curly hair has finally become stylish, but because he looks less bald that way. Somebody once asked him for his autograph before mumbling, "You're not Billy Crystal, are you?" and walking away.

He dials his mother-in-law's number. She answers "Hello" in her scratchy voice.

"Hi," he says. "It's me. Michael."

"Where are you?"

"I'm home," he says. "I'm back."

"Good. Maybe *you* can take her for the test tomorrow. I'm exhausted."

"Sure," he says. "How's she doing?"

"So-so." This is pretty good, Goodman knows. In mother-in-law, *so-so* means good to excellent, while *terrible* could suggest anything from a mild cold to a bad hangnail. *Dying* is where you first begin to get worried.

"What kind of test?" he asks.

"I don't know, an MRS, or something like that."

"What time should I pick her up?"

"I gotta leave at eight-thirty."

"Okay," he says. "I'll be there. Can I talk to her for a minute now?"

"Hold on."

After a half minute, he hears his daughter's little voice. "Hi, Daddy."

"Hi, angel. How you doing?"

"I'm scared."

"Don't be scared."

"They're going to put me in a big ma*chine.*"

"I'll be with you, angel," he tells her. "I'll take care of you."

"Promise?"

"Promise."

"Are you remembering about the story, Daddy?"

"Absolutely," he assures her.

It's only later that it dawns on him that the only reason his mother-in-law's so anxious for him to take Kelly for the test is that that way he'll end up being the one who has to pay for it. His eyes travel to the duffel bags lying on the floor.

He decides that even if he's going to throw the stuff out, he's not ready to do it quite yet. So he may as well put it away. And since he's no doubt looking at big jail time if he gets caught with it, putting it away is transformed to hiding it. But where do you hide three pillowcases full of narcotics in a studio apartment?

He looks around. An amateur, he thinks amateur thoughts: inside the clothes hamper, underneath the sofa, up in the back of his closet, in the oven. He knows just enough to know that those are probably the very first places anyone would look. And yet he can't come up with anything better.

As a temporary measure, he removes the pillowcase from the smaller duffel and adds it to the two in the larger duffel, which he takes down to the basement of the building. There, each tenant has been given a small storage locker in exchange for a $7.50 monthly increase in rent. The lockers are cages that you can see into. All Goodman keeps in his are a couple of cartons of books and old tax records. To safeguard them, he went out and bought a cheap combination lock, which he keeps set at 0-0-0 so he won't forget the numbers. He once figured out that if he lives to be seventy-five, the locker will have cost him about three thousand dollars. Now he figures he might as well start getting something for his money.

Back upstairs, he fixes himself an American cheese sandwich, with mustard on one slice of bread and mayonnaise on the other. He pops open a can of Pepsi, sits down on his sofa, and clicks on the TV. The first channel he hits, they're showing *Rocky,* the original one, where this down-and-out bum of a club fighter gets given a shot at the heavyweight title, a zillion-to-one underdog. It's one of Goodman's all-time favorites, and he's caught it right at the beginning. He kicks off his shoes and settles back.

Life could be a lot worse, he thinks.

5

Goodman is up by six. He showers, shaves, and dresses, downs a cup of instant coffee with nondairy creamer and a strawberry Pop-Tart. He's at his mother-in-law's apartment a few minutes after eight.

"You're early," she tells him.

Kelly comes into the room, still in pajamas. She drags Larus with one hand, rubs her eyes with the other. To Goodman, who hasn't seen her for a week, she looks tiny and frail.

"Hi, angel," he says softly. He feels his back twinge when he squats down to be her size, but he deals with it.

"Hi, Daddy," she says, folding herself into his arms.

It turns out the MRS test is really an MRI. Goodman is allowed to stand off to the corner of the room as they slide his daughter into a tremendous machine that reminds him of a photograph he once saw of something called an iron lung, which they used to put polio victims in. She cries the entire time, not (it seems to Goodman) because she's afraid of the machine, but because they won't let Larus into it with her.

Afterward, they tell him the film the MRI machine has made of Kelly's head will be delivered to her doctor. They're pleasant enough, but they won't tell him how it looks, and that worries him.

At the cashier's station (and Goodman realizes he must have missed that point at which doctors' offices started having cashier stations), Kelly dries her tears against Goodman's shirt while Goodman signs a form promising to pay the eleven hundred dollars himself if it turns out his insurance doesn't cover it. He figures that ought to buy him about three weeks.

From there, he takes his daughter for lunch at McDonald's, where he eats his own Big Mac and finishes most of her Happy Meal. He wonders how long she can survive on french fries and Coke. She looks so pale and thin to him.

He presents her with the plastic dolphin he bought her at the Fort Lauderdale Airport. She seems to like it, but asks him if he can carry it for her. She explains to him that she has to carry Larus, and Larus is very big.

They go to Carl Schurz Park and watch the boats that go up and down the East River. They find a bench to sit on, and Kelly curls up in his arms.

"I'm ready for the story," she announces.

"Are you certain you're not too tired?" The truth is, he's never been a very good storyteller, and he has no particular idea for one in mind.

"I'm certain," she assures him.

So he does his best.

The Little Princess

Once upon a time, in a far-off kingdom, there lived a little princess —

"Was she a ballerina?"

"Of course she was a ballerina."

The Ballerina Princess

Once upon a time, in a far-off kingdom, there lived a Ballerina Princess. The name of the kingdom was Yew Nork. It was a kingdom much like the city where we live, except that instead of having tall buildings all around, it had hundreds and hundreds of tall castles. And instead of being surrounded by rivers, it was surrounded by a wide moat. And one other thing: It was a magical kingdom. It was magical because it was a place where things could come true if you wished for them hard enough, and if you tried hard enough to make them come true.

Now the Ballerina Princess was six years old. She had been born to

a beautiful mother and a loving father. But there came a time when her
mother had to go away, and of course that made the Ballerina Princess
very, very sad.

"Did her mother go to heaven?"

Her mother went to heaven, yes. And that meant that her grandmother had to look after the Ballerina Princess for a while, because her
father was so busy with work. But she also had someone else to help look
after her. And that was the brave and loyal Prince Larus. So, in a way,
the Ballerina Princess was luckier than most little girls, because instead
of having just two people to protect her, she had three. And that's an
awful lot, especially when one of them is the brave and loyal Prince
Larus.

Even with his eyes closed, he can tell from her rhythmic breathing that
his ballerina princess has fallen asleep in his arms. As he looks down at
her little face, her tiny mouth slightly open, Goodman aches with worry.
The worst part about flying down to Florida was leaving his daughter behind, even for a couple of days. The thought that he might lose her, that
she could actually *die*, is simply too much to imagine.

"Please let my angel be okay," he says softly. He has always believed,
for some reason, that if you give thanks or say prayers out loud, even in
just a whisper, it counts more than if you just think the words to yourself.

"Please," he repeats.

That evening, Goodman drops Kelly back at his mother-in-law's. She cries
when he leaves, and he promises her that it won't be long before she can
come and live with him. His own eyes water as he walks home to his own
apartment.

For some reason Goodman's key won't fit into the lock of his door, and
he's forced to ring the Tony the Super's bell on the first floor. Together
they trudge up the four flights, where Tony finds he can't get the master
key to work, either. He bends down to inspect the lock.

"Aha!" he announces as he extracts a broken piece of toothpick from
the lock. "Here's the problem."

But it turns out the toothpick is only a symptom of the problem. As soon as Tony opens the door, Goodman sees that the place has been trashed.

"They put the toothpick in the lock to jam it, in case you get home while they're still inside," Tony explains. "You go to get help, that gives them time to split."

It takes Goodman two hours to clean up the mess. Every drawer has been dumped onto the floor, every item of clothing thrown from the closet. The cushions of his sofa have been cut open, the sofa itself tipped forward onto his wooden coffee table, which has buckled under the weight.

It is only later, almost as an afterthought that comes to him while he lies exhausted on his ruined sofa, that it occurs to Goodman that absolutely nothing is missing as a consequence of the break-in.

The thought sends a chill through him. Until this very moment, he has not once considered the possibility that this was anything other than a routine burglary. He's read or heard that when burglars can't find anything worth stealing—which would certainly have been the case with whoever broke into his apartment—they often get annoyed and vandalize the place.

But they haven't even taken his TV set, or the coins he'd left on top of his coffee table. Everything—right down to his postage stamps—can be accounted for. Thrown around, ripped up, or whatever—but accounted for nonetheless.

So sometime after midnight, Goodman finds a flashlight, tiptoes down to the basement, and checks his storage locker. To his relief, he sees the duffel bag still safely inside. As an extra security measure, he decides to reset the combination lock, figuring maybe 0-0-0 is a bit too obvious. He's afraid that if he picks some random number, he won't be able to remember it. He thinks of his birth date, then remembers reading once that crooks think like that, too. So he chooses his magic number, setting the lock at 5-6-2. He's so pleased with himself for being clever that he neglects to move the cylinder off the new numbers before heading back upstairs.

[6]

Goodman spends Sunday afternoons with three buddies of his from his days in the navy. They call themselves "the Walking Wounded." Not because they were actually wounded during any war: There *was* no war going on during their stint, which was back in the mid-seventies. The name is more a reflection of their own shared awareness that the four of them are misfits of one sort or another.

Goodman himself is probably the least remarkable of the group. True, he has an erratic employment history and is out of work altogether at the moment. He certainly has his share of peculiar habits, of strange likes and dislikes, of obsessive little mannerisms. But compared with the other three, he's positively *normal.*

Krulewich is a diabetic who refuses to take his insulin because he suspects his doctors at the VA hospital are trying to poison him. As a result, he's lost one leg and several toes of the other foot and is nearly blind. He needs surgery to remove cataracts that have formed over his eyes, but he continues to put it off, because every time he checks into the hospital, he seems to come home with fewer parts. As a result, he squints out at the world through lenses so thick that the weight of them seems to lower his head and thrust it forward permanently at an odd (and seemingly belligerent) angle.

The Whale is pretty much that. In his navy days, he was five nine and

180 pounds. He's still five nine (give or take an inch), but has ballooned to the point where he's closing in on the three-hundred-pound mark. He drives a cab for a living, but is constantly getting his hack license suspended for refusing to get out and help passengers load or unload their luggage at the trunk. "I don't *refuse,*" he's explained to the Taxi and Limousine Commission over and over. "It's just that by the time I get out from behind the wheel, they *think* I'm not gonna do it."

And then there's Lehigh. His true name is Lehigh Valley, given him when he was found abandoned in a boxcar on the Lehigh Valley Railroad, somewhere between Altoona and Pottsville. A black boy raised by white foster parents in the coal towns of western Pennsylvania, Lehigh talks of repaying "Mommy and Daddy" by buying them a retirement home to replace their twelve-foot trailer. He works as a dishwasher at a cafeteria on Avenue C and lives above it in a single room. They pay him $4.56 an hour. So far, he's saved up a little over two hundred dollars.

Goodman's aware that he himself is a cut above the rest of the Walking Wounded—not only in terms of his superior mental health but educationally, professionally, and socially, as well. Yet it's precisely this awareness that keeps him from dropping out of the group. He's afraid the others might regard it as a snub and end up feeling hurt. So he stays, as much for their sake as his.

They meet at Krulewich's this Sunday afternoon. They usually meet at Krulewich's, not because his place is any grander than those of the others (it isn't), but because of the simple reason that it's hardest for Krulewich to get around.

The Series is on. It's either game three or game four—Goodman's not sure. It's the top of the fifth, with the Braves leading five to nothing. The Whale wants to bet on the outcome, or the final score, or who'll win the Series, or who'll be named MVP. But nobody'll bet with him. The Whale is a recovering gambler, and he'll bet you on tomorrow's weather if you give him a chance.

They watch the game to the end. The Braves win five to three. "I coulda won fifty bucks!" the Whale moans. They send out for pizza. There's talk of playing cards, but they can't agree on a game. They've given up playing poker—it's too hard for the Whale to keep it a friendly game.

"You guys know how to play hearts?" Lehigh asks.

No one seems to know.

"I could teach you, easy," Lehigh offers.

But Krulewich's eyes are bothering him, and Goodman's not really up for it, either. For the last hour, about all he's been able to think about is Kelly's MRI.

They decide to put off hearts till next Sunday. Around eight, they break up.

[7]

Russell Bradford is awakened by the sound of a woman's screaming. He's been dreaming, and in his dream he was standing out in the rain in nothing but his undershorts, and it takes him a minute to figure out where he is and who's doing the screaming.

"Nana! Nana!" he hears, and finally remembers that Nana is his grandmother, and the screaming voice belongs to his mother.

"Russell!" she calls. "Get in here and help me!"

He forces himself up from the sofa and follows his mother's voice into Nana's room. What he sees is his mother crouched over the body of his grandmother, who lies on her side on the floor. Russell's first impression is that Nana is dead, and he stands stupidly in the doorway, not knowing what to do.

"Don't juss *stand* there, boy!" his mother shouts. "Help me!"

Russell takes two steps into the room, and can now see that his grandmother isn't dead after all. She's twitching, her whole body shaking in these spastic little movements. Her eyes are wide open, but where the pupils should be, Russell can see only the whites of her eyes. A string of spittle runs from the corner of her mouth down to the threadbare rug beside her bed.

"Don't die, Nana," Russell says in a voice barely above a whisper. The remainder of his thought he keeps to himself: If you die, where am I going to find money to cop?

* * *

While Russell Bradford worries about money, so does Michael Goodman. He sits in his apartment this Monday morning, drinking a cup of weak coffee and reading through the "Help Wanted" ads in the classified section of *The New York Times*. There are always ads for accountants, but most are for CPAs or college graduates willing to start as trainees with big firms. No one ever seems to want an over-forty bookkeeper without so much as a junior college degree.

He circles four ads and, beginning at two minutes after nine, starts calling the numbers listed. The first job is already filled. The second place would prefer someone with more education; the third one is looking for someone just a bit younger. The fourth one, the Bronx Tire Exchange, is more promising.

"You know it's only two afternoons a week?" a young woman asks him, cracking her gum as she speaks.

"That's okay."

"What are your salary demands?"

"Whatever the job pays," Goodman says. He knows this isn't the time for pride.

"Can you come in to talk to Manny tomorrow?"

"Sure. What time?"

"Anytime," she says. "He's here by seven."

"How about today?" Goodman asks. "I could come in right now if you like."

"No, today's no good. He's having a boil lanced today."

"He must have a trap in there," says Pedro Aguilar to Antonio Rodriguez and Sixto Quinones as the three of them huddle over Cuban coffee at Victor's Restaurant. A trap is a specially constructed hiding place, often discoverable only by the pressing of a button or some other remote device. "There's no other way. You saw him go in with it, and he never came out with it."

"No way, man," says Hot Rod. "We turned that place upside down. There was a trap, we woulda found it."

"Yeah," says Six. "It's not like you can hide twenty keys in a fuckin' coffee can, boss."

"Didja find out who this guy *is?*" Aguilar asks.

"I went through his shit, like you said to," Hot Rod says. "Best as I can tell, he's some kinda bookie or banker, or something like that. Got all these ledgers with columns of numbers in them. Couldn't figure out what they all mean, though."

"That's it!" Aguilar announces. "He's their moneyman—he washes the money for them. What else would a banker do?"

"Thass it."

"Yeah."

"But who are *they?*" Aguilar asks. "Who does he work *for?*"

None of them has an answer for that question.

"You guys stay on him," Aguilar says. "See who he meets. Sooner or later, he's gotta take you to his people."

Around eleven, Goodman's phone rings. He answers quickly, nervously, as he always does. Unlike life itself, which he embraces with unjustifiable optimism, the phone is something Goodman rather fears, and he is constantly afraid that it's ringing with news of some disaster.

It's only his mother-in-law.

"The insurance is no good," she tells him.

"I know. I told you it was no good, remember?"

"They called to tell me. They won't send the test results to the doctor until you make other arrangements."

"Other arrangements?"

"Cash or certified check."

"I'll take care of it," he assures her. He figures it must have been someone from the cashier's station who called. "How's Kelly doing?" he asks.

"It's hard to tell. She tells me it doesn't hurt, but every once in a while I'll see her wince when she doesn't think I'm looking. I think she's afraid that I worry too much about her, so she pretends she's better to protect me."

His mother-in-law can be a pain in the rear sometimes, but she reads people like Goodman reads balance sheets.

Russell Bradford's grandmother is taken by ambulance to Jacoby Hospital. Russell's mother rides in the ambulance; Russell meets them at the emergency room. By the time they arrive, the EMS team has stabilized Nana, and she's no longer in seizure. But it's soon determined that she's suffered a cerebrovascular accident—a stroke, they explain—whether as a result of the seizure or the cause of it, they're not sure. She's admitted to ward 7-D. She cannot speak, and the entire right side of her body seems to be frozen and beyond her power to control. She's listed as being in guarded condition.

Russell leaves his mother at the hospital and goes home. There, he goes to the front closet, reaches up, and finds Nana's purse. He searches through it, finds ten dollars.

"Shit," he mutters.

He takes it and goes back out to cop.

Goodman goes back to the office where they did Kelly's MRI. The receptionist directs him to the cashier's station. There, they tell him that since he has no valid and current medical coverage, they will release the test results only upon receipt of cash or a certified check, just as his mother-in-law has reported.

"I'll get the money," he promises. "In the meantime, can you just tell me how the tests *look?*"

"I'm sorry," he's told by a stern-faced woman in white.

"This is my *daughter,*" he tells her. "She's *six,* for God's sake."

"State law prohibits us from releasing any films, information, or opinions to anyone but the referring physician." He's reminded of the Fort Lauderdale Police Department's policy regarding narcotics you want to turn in to them.

Walking home, he thinks of the black duffel bag in his storage locker. He doesn't notice the two Hispanic men who fall in behind him.

Russell Bradford spends his grandmother's ten dollars on two yellow caps of crack that he buys from Big Red. But when he tries to get a couple of dime bags of heroin on credit from Eddie Boy, he's turned down.

"How 'bout you give me somethin' on consignment, man?" he asks. "I'll sell 'em down on the Concourse for you, and you can gimme a cut of the take?"

"Sorry," says Eddie Boy. "Things are tight right now. I can't be doin' no favors for nobody."

Russell knows he should save the crack for later, when he'll be needing it more. But his lack of money causes him to feel apprehensive and depressed, and he detours on the way home to an abandoned basement apartment where he keeps a stem and a torch. He smokes the contents of one vial but still doesn't feel quite right. Ends up smoking the second one, as well. The feeling he finally gets is good enough to take the edge off and allow him to stop worrying for a while. But it will last him less than an hour.

That evening, as he sits in front of his TV set waiting for his frozen macaroni and cheese dinner to cook, Goodman sees a news item on Channel 4. The reception is bad, because Goodman can't afford cable and his set is an old eleven-inch model with a coat hanger for an antenna, but he watches intently as the commentator describes the seizure of a large amount of cocaine from a warehouse in Queens. A high-ranking police department spokesman is interviewed; he announces that the seizure definitely represents a major blow to organized crime.

"Perhaps," says the commentator, "this is an indication that in the war against drugs, the tide of battle is at last beginning to turn our way."

Across the Harlem River and three miles to the north, Russell Bradford spends a very difficult night. His mother returned from the hospital around 8:30 with the news that Nana's expected to live but may need to be hospitalized for a month or more. When Russell asked his mother for money, she snapped at him that she had none and that if anything, she should be asking *him* for money, he being a grown boy and all.

He went out around ten, made the rounds, checking every dealer he knows, hoping that someone would give him something on credit, trust him with something to sell on consignment. But Russell already owes too many dealers too much money, and no one will give him anything unless it's "C and C"—cash and carry.

Back home shortly after midnight, Russell's already sick from the beginnings of heroin withdrawal and irritable from his craving for crack. Unable to sleep, he alternately watches TV, sits by the kitchen window overlooking the fire escape, and paces the floor. Finally, he rolls himself into a ball and lies on his side on the living room rug, not unlike the way he's seen his grandmother lie following her seizure. He readies himself for the chills and the sweats and the waves of nausea that he can feel even before their arrival.

All Russell knows is that he's got to cop tomorrow. No matter what it takes.

In his Ninety-second Street walk-up, Michael Goodman lies awake, too. He worries about his job interview tomorrow, worries about his daughter, worries how he's going to get the money to get the test results released.

It's nearly four o'clock by the time either of them falls asleep, these two very different men from very different worlds, whose lives are being drawn closer and closer toward collision.

Despite his lack of a good night's sleep, Goodman is up early by habit. He showers and shaves. He realizes he has no idea what one should wear to an interview at a place called the Bronx Tire Exchange. He knows that a blue suit would be much too dressy, but he's afraid of showing up *too* casual. He settles for a sport jacket, a yellow shirt, and a pair of tan slacks. He studies himself in the mirror, decides to put on a tie. Figures he can always take it off and stuff it in his pocket.

The Bronx Tire Exchange is located at 155th Street and Jerome Avenue. Goodman gets out his Yellow Pages and finds the subway map, sees that the number 4 train stops at 149th and again at 161st Street. Either way, he'll have to walk six blocks.

He takes a last look in the mirror, straightening his tie but forgetting to button the two little buttons on the collar of his shirt. To make sure he doesn't have bad breath, he makes a last stop in the bathroom, where he squeezes a gob of toothpaste onto his finger, then rubs it on his tongue. He looks at his watch: 7:05.

He steps outside, feels the October chill. He walks to Eighty-sixth Street, gets the number 4, and heads uptown. The train is surprisingly empty. Evidently, everyone else seems to be headed downtown this time of day.

* * *

At just about the time that the number 4 train that carries Michael Good-man rises from deep underneath the street and climbs the elevated tracks that cut through the South Bronx on their way north to Woodlawn Ceme-tery, Russell Bradford wakes up. Perhaps it's even the sound of Goodman's train that rouses him.

Russell turns over on the sofa, searching for a cool spot on his pillow. He keeps his eyes closed, trying to put off the day as long as he possibly can. But it proves to be a losing battle.

Raul Cuervas is also up uncharacteristically early this morning. Barhop-ping last night, Raul heard from three different people that Mister Fuentes was looking for him.

Under normal circumstances, this would be good news for Raul. It would mean that Mister Fuentes has a job for him to do. It would mean he was back in action. Most of all, it would mean money.

But Raul is not so sure that these are normal circumstances. For one thing, he knows that Mister Fuentes was very displeased about Raul's being late picking up the car, and enraged that twenty keys disappeared as a result. Although Mister Fuentes seemed to believe Raul's story about being drugged and ripped off by the *chiquita*, you could tell he didn't think it was much of an excuse.

Raul had been able to provide a detailed description of the guy who returned the car, and that was good. Mister Fuentes had gotten Johnnie Delgado to call some people in New York, and they'd succeeded in spot-ting the guy as he got off the plane. At the time, Raul had thought that was good, too. Now he's not so sure: If they're sitting on the guy up there, then it figures they don't need Raul anymore to point him out. And that could be very bad.

Raul knows this can be a cruel business, in which people tend to have exceedingly short memories. Do the right thing fifty times, they take you for granted. Fuck up once, and right away it's, What has Sheraton done for me *lately?*

So Raul wakes up early this morning. He knows he's got a decision to make: Does he go see Mister Fuentes and face the music, however bad it is, or does he split for a while, disappear until they recover the twenty keys, everybody's happy again, and they all forget about his little fuckup?

By 7:30, he's still sitting up in bed, but already he's smoked eight cig-arettes. Smoking helps him at times like this, when he's got to think hard.

*   *   *

Goodman notices that he's the only one in the subway car who isn't black or Hispanic. He knows that wasn't the case when he got on, though he vaguely remembers a lot of white people getting off at Ninety-sixth. He also notices—not for the first time—that people who ride the subways tend to be short, like he is. He wonders if anyone's ever done a study on the subject. And if he's right, if there *is* a correlation between shortness and subway riding, what's the cause-and-effect relationship? Does being underground stunt your growth, as it seems to in the case of a mole or a groundhog? Maybe being deprived of sunlight? You never see a giraffe underground, do you?

He feels better when the train suddenly emerges from the darkness in the Bronx. He stays on past 149th Street, having decided to get off at Yankee Stadium. He can't remember the last time he was there. His father used to take him to ball games when he was a kid, but that seems impossibly long ago, as if it was in a different lifetime altogether. In this life, for as long as he can remember, all Michael Goodman has done is work. And now, out of a job for three weeks, here he is, trying to find work again.

Russell Bradford finally gives up his battle to fall back asleep. He dresses without showering and doesn't bother with breakfast: Despite the fact that he's had nothing to eat in twenty-four hours, food is the last thing on Russell's mind.

He knows he's already taken the money from his grandmother's purse, but force of habit compels him to check it anyway. Finding it empty, he silently curses, then feels bad because he knows Nana's always been good to him, up to now.

Before leaving the apartment, he tiptoes into the room where his two younger brothers are sleeping. On the floor, in a pile of comic books and video-game accesories, he finds a black plastic water pistol, designed to look like an Uzi or a Mac-10. He picks it up and stuffs it into the waistband of his jeans, covering the handle with his T-shirt.

The walk from Yankee Stadium to 155th Street takes Goodman only five minutes, and he spots the sign for the Bronx Tire Exchange. He's expected it to be an office building of some sort—not fancy, but at least an office building. After all, they've advertised for an accountant. So he's somewhat surprised to see that instead it's really nothing but a big garage that spills out onto the sidewalk. In addition to the sign giving the name of the establishment, there are numerous other signs, some attached to the brick front of the building, some wired to the metal bars that cover the windows, a few even standing on the sidewalk or in the street itself.

TIRES NEW & USED

RECAPS

FLATS FIXED WHILE "U" WAIT

BEST PRICES IN THE CITY

TIPS ACCEPTED

Although it's barely 7:30 in the morning, it seems like rush hour at the place. Three cars are jacked up out in front, another four or five inside. Most of them are taxis—not the yellow cabs you see in Manhattan, but the "car service" ones, the gypsy cabs that service the outer boroughs, where the yellow drivers are afraid to go. The employees working on the cars are all black or Hispanic, and most of them seem to be little more than high school age. They wear grimy jumpsuits that look like they've never been washed. They work quickly, using what look like electric drills attached to air hoses to remove and replace the lug nuts on the wheels.

Goodman wanders inside, where the noise from the compressors and drill things is even louder. He asks one of the employees where he can find Manny.

"Jes look for a doughnut, man. He be sittin' on it." When Goodman looks puzzled, the man points toward a door. A handwritten sign has been taped to it long ago.

OFICE

YOU KEEP OUT!

Goodman knocks, gets no answer. Knocks again, more loudly.

"Yeah?" comes a gruff voice.

"I'm here about the job," Goodman tells the door.

"Wha?"

"The job," Goodman repeats. "The accounting position."

Nothing happens for a half a minute. Then Goodman hears locks being slid open, and the door swings out, hitting him squarely in the shoulder.

"Careful!" says the man who's responsible for the door swinging. "I'm Manny."

Manny is half human, half black bear. Goodman has never seen a human being with so much hair on his body. His arms, his neck, his chest, his shoulders—he wears a sleeveless undershirt, as though he's proud to display his pelt—are covered with thick black hair. The back of his hands are hairy. He has hair sprouting from his ears, from his nostrils. The top of his head is bald, but it's fringed with more of the same black hair, which seems to grow like some weed straight out of a science fiction movie.

"C'mon in," Manny says.

Goodman enters and waits while Manny resecures three dead-bolt locks.

"Have a seat."

The room is loaded with clutter, but Goodman sees only one chair, and that's occupied by what looks like a tiny white inner tube. He moves toward it.

"Not there! That's my doughnut." Manny ambles over to it. "Know what a sebaceous cyst is?"

"No," Goodman says, not sure he wants to, either. He remembers being told yesterday that Manny was having a boil lanced. That's good enough for him.

"Sa fuckin' pain in the ass, is what it is!"

Manny lowers himself gingerly onto his doughnut. He points to the other side of the desk, where there is indeed a second chair. This one contains a stack of tire catalogs, magazines, and loose papers. The stack is probably no more than two feet high.

"Put that shit on the floor," Manny tells him.

Goodman complies, locating a bare spot only with some difficulty.

"Whadjousay your name is?"

"Goodman. Michael Goodman." Though he's sure it's the first time he's said it.

"Right. Goodman. You come in two aftanoons a week, Monday and Thursday, one to five. You can use my office right here, plentya privacy. Twenty-five bucks an hour, cash. Okay?"

"Okay."

"Come in Thursday. That way, Marlene'll show you what to do. That's her lass day. Stupid broad got herself knocked up. Tell you the truth, I'm supprised she could figger out how to do it. Okay?"

"Okay what?"

"Okay Thursday?"

"Okay."

Michael Goodman has a job.

Raul Cuervas has a problem. He smokes twelve more cigarettes while he tries to think of places to go where Mister Fuentes and his people won't be able to find him. But with no friends or family, and no money to speak of, he realizes that Mister Fuentes and his people are Cuervas's only people, too: He has no one else to turn to, no place to hide.

So he showers and shaves and dresses, and prepares to take his chances with *el viejo*. He will acknowledge that he made a mistake. He will humble himself and ask forgiveness. Surely his record is such that he'll be given another chance.

Instead of heading down to 140th Street, where he's known, Russell Bradford walks north towards 150th. He's never done anything quite like this before. Sure, he's done a little boosting from cars from time to time. He's shoplifted. He's even sold a little crack when somebody's given him some on consignment.

But his situation is different now. A couple packages of frozen meat or a Blaupunkt tape deck aren't going to do it this time. What he needs is cash, and he needs it fast.

Almost involuntarily, his hand moves to his midsection, where he feels the outline of the gun beneath his clothing. He no longer regards it as a toy. He thinks of it as real. It's going to help him get paid, get what he's entitled to for all he's had to put up with.

He reaches 150th Street, continues walking uptown. He imagines he's a panther out looking for prey. Nobody ever blames the panther, after all, do they? He's just out there doing what comes naturally, doing what he's got to do to survive. Why should we think of people as any different?

Rather than retracing his steps back up to 161st Street, Goodman decides to walk down to the 149th Street station. As he walks, he replays in his head the interview—if you could call it an interview—with Manny. Four hours at twenty-five an hour is a hundred dollars; double it and it comes out to two hundred a week, cash. Cash is good: It means no withholding, no taxes. But it also means no benefits: no health insurance, no workmen's comp. And while it'll pay the rent and put some food in his refrigerator, it sure isn't the answer to Kelly's MRI bill or the rest of Goodman's mounting debts. But they say beggars can't be choosers, and Goodman was coming pretty close to being a beggar. So he's grateful to have the job, and for the moment it takes his mind off everything else. Which is a mistake, because, as he nears 150th Street, he forgets to pay attention to his surroundings.

Halfway between 151st and 152nd, Russell Bradford spots an elderly black woman pushing one of those fold-up grocery carts. The cart's empty, so he figures she's headed to the supermarket. That means she's got money on her.

Russell sizes her up. She's got a purse slung over one shoulder. He could grab it before she'd even know what's happening.

But something makes Russell hesitate. The woman reminds him a little bit of Nana, and that causes him to hesitate—not so much because of the resemblance, but because he remembers that Nana generally uses food stamps to shop with. He doesn't want to risk everything for a handful of fucking *food* stamps. He lets her pass by him.

Closer to 152nd, there's a wino going through someone's trash. Russell figures the guy probably doesn't have a dime on him; he walks by him.

Then he sees the white dude. This guy is made to order. He's short; he's got narrow shoulders, glasses. He's wearing a sport jacket and a *tie*, like this is fucking Wall Street or something. Dude doesn't look like he ever gets his hands dirty. And on top of everything, he looks like he isn't even paying attention to what's going on.

Russell does a quick check across the street, then up and down the block: nobody but the old lady and the wino. There are some kids up ahead, but they're all the way up at 153rd, playing some game on the sidewalk. Couldn't be better.

He waits till the guy's almost alongside of him before he says something to him.

"Hey, man, you got the time?"

The dude stops, startled by Russell's voice. Almost involuntarily, he raises his left hand to look at his watch.

"Five after eight," he says.

"Nice watch, man," Russell tells him. The truth is, Russell can't tell a Rolex from a Timex. The dude doesn't say anything.

"Think you could help me out with a little change?" Russell asks him.

This seems to make the guy uncomfortable. He starts looking around. But, of course, there's no one there.

"I'm afraid I don't have any change," he says, and then adds, "sorry."

"Any folding money?"

"Sorry," he says again.

"Me, too," Russell says. And to show how sorry he is, he reaches to his waistband and lifts the bottom of his T-shirt just enough to reveal the handle of his gun.

Goodman's first thought upon seeing the gun is that he's about to lose control of both his bowels and his bladder at the same time. So intense is his concentration in attempting to keep this from happening that he's unable to react to the situation in any other way: Not only does he say nothing; he can't even begin to *think* about speaking.

"Putchya hands down," the kid says.

"What?"

"Your hands. Put 'em down."

Goodman looks, and sure enough, he's raised both hands slightly, the way a stagecoach passenger might once have signaled surrender to the bad guys in an old Western. He tries to lower them, but they won't go all the way down.

"Give it up," he hears the kid telling him. "Your money, your wallet, your watch. Whateva you got." As he speaks, the kid glances around nervously, up and down the block.

For Goodman, everything seems to be happening in slow motion. Gradually, he regains control of his sphincter muscle and mastery of his urinary function. He wants to speak, wants to assure the kid he's ready to give up everything. But still he can't get his voice to cooperate.

The black kid doesn't seem to know what to do with Goodman's paralysis. He starts looking up and down the block and across the street. Goodman follows the kid's glances, trying to see what he's looking at. When he sees nothing, he suddenly thinks, This kid is as scared as I am. It is that realization that manages to break the spell for Michael Goodman and liberate him from his paralysis. Intellectually, he knows he should be afraid for his life; but in spite of himself, he begins to feel like he's in a movie scene, that all this is happening to some different person and that he's just an observer, watching it all from someplace else.

"You heard me, man!" he hears the kid say. But while the kid tries to make it sound menacing, to Goodman it comes out plaintive, as though he's now being *begged* for his money.

Goodman the accountant does some quick calculation. He figures he has maybe twelve dollars on him, give or take a token. He knows he should give it up—he's always reading about people getting killed over pocket change. But no sooner does he think that than his mind starts wandering to the gun. Something about it didn't look real. And why isn't the kid pointing it at him? He's reminded of one of those drawings in a magazine or comic book, where there are all sorts of mistakes you're supposed to find: What's wrong with this picture?

So he lies. "I've only got two dollars," he says. "The watch cost me four bucks on Canal Street." That much is the truth.

Goodman waits for the kid's reaction. He expects disbelief and anger. He's prepared to be hit, to be searched, to be commanded to turn his pockets inside out. But none of these things happens.

Instead, the kid says, "Fuck," as if he's just scratched the coating off an instant lottery game and lost. He doesn't seem angry at all, or even particularly surprised. Mostly, he seems *tired* all of a sudden.

So Goodman says, "Sorry."

The kid seems to shrug his shoulders ever so slightly.

"Is that real?" Goodman asks, gesturing toward the kid's waistband, where the gun is again covered by the T-shirt.

"Uh-uh," the kid shakes his head from side to side.

"Looks like a water gun."

The kid doesn't say anything. He just stands there, looking like he's liable to start crying at any moment. For the first time, Goodman notices how thin he is. He wonders when the last time was the kid had something to eat.

"You hungry?" he asks the kid.

"No."

"Sick?"

"Sorta."

"Anything I can do to help you?"

The kid smiles and does something that comes out like half laugh, half snort. "What I need, man, you don't got."

And slowly, finally, it dawns on Goodman: This kid is a junkie.

Suddenly, there is a single *blip* of a siren, and both Goodman and the kid turn their heads toward the street. A police car pulls up to the curb next to where they're standing. The words 40 PCT are stenciled on the side. Two uniformed officers step out. One is a white male, the other a black woman. They approach, each resting a hand on a holstered gun. It is the white male who speaks.

"Everything all right here?"

It is clear to Goodman that the question has been directed to him. And it's just as clear that he can have the kid arrested with as little as a shake of his head, silence, or even sufficient hesitation. But he hears himself speaking.

"Yes, sir" is what he says. "Everything's fine."

The officer is apparently less than convinced. Gently, he manages to place his body between Goodman's and the kid's; just as gently, he steers Goodman away from the kid, until Goodman realizes that the four of them are now standing in pairs: the white officer with Goodman, the black officer with the kid.

"What's going on here?" the officer asks him.

"I was just asking him directions to the subway."

"A little bit out of your neighborhood?"

Goodman notices how young the officer is, wonders if he can really be twenty-one.

"I work up here," he tells him.

"Where?"

"The Bronx Tire Exchange."

"Who's your boss?"

"Manny."

"Tell him Brian says hello, okay?"

"Okay."

"And be careful around here."

"I will be," Goodman says. "Thanks for stopping."

"No problem."

Goodman watches as the officers get back into their car and pull away from the curb. He hears the kid say something, but it's said so quietly, it takes him some time to realize it was "Thank you."

"No problem," says Goodman, who liked the sound of the phrase when the officer said it to him a moment ago. He turns toward the kid and extends his hand. "My name's Michael."

The kid takes his hand and they shake. "Russell," he says. For Russell, it's the first white hand he's ever shaken.

"Can I tell you somepin?" Russell asks.

"Sure."

"Don't be walking around up here. Getcha inna trouble."

"Thanks. Can I tell you something?"

Russell nods.

"Don't be robbing people. You're no good at it." He reaches into his pocket, fishes out a ten-dollar bill, and offers it to Russell, who stares at it for a moment before accepting it with a sheepish smile.

"Would you do me a favor, Russell?"

"I guess I owe you one."

"Meet me tomorrow?"

"Whafor?"

"I got something I want you to check out for me."

"You gonna bring the cops?" Russell asks.

Goodman smiles. "You know I'm not," he says.

"Yeah." Russell nods. "I guess you had your chance."

"Twelve noon," Goodman tells him.

"Here?"

"Shit, no," says Goodman, who almost never swears. He's in no hurry to come back to this particular spot. Yet he's not ready to invite his new acquaintance to *his* neighborhood, either. He decides on neutral territory. "Ninety-sixth and Lexington," he says.

"Bet," Russell says.

"What?"

"Never mind. I be there."

Raul Cuervas's meeting with Mister Fuentes takes place at the Hotel Fontainbleu in Miami Beach, where Mister Fuentes has a permanent suite of rooms on the top floor. Johnnie Delgado is there, along with Papo and Julio, who also work for Mister Fuentes. There's another man there, too, a scary-looking guy with a full black beard, whom Cuervas has never seen before. Nobody bothers with introductions.

"Hello, Raul."

"Hello, Mister Fuentes," Cuervas says. "I feel very bad I've caused you this problem."

"Me?" Mister Fuentes smiles. "I don't believe I have a problem."

The words send a chill through Cuervas, and he doesn't respond. He tries to think of different meanings Mister Fuentes's statement might have, but he came up with only one.

"Raul," Mister Fuentes says, "I want you to go with Papo and Julio and Gatillo here. They got a job to do, and they need your help. They'll fill you in on the details on the way there."

"Mister Fuentes, I'm real sorry—"

But Mister Fuentes stops him by raising a hand. The meeting is over.

Walking from the room, following Papo and Julio, and aware of the bearded one following *him*, Cuervas takes no comfort from the fact that, translated into English, the word *gatillo* happens to mean "trigger."

That evening, Michael Goodman sneaks down to the basement again. He notices that the combination lock on his storage bin is still set to the digits of his lucky number, 5-6-2, and therefore not really locked. He resolves to be more careful in the future.

By the light of his flashlight, he unzips the duffel bag, unties one of the pillowcases, and makes a little cut in one of the blue plastic bags. He squeezes a small amount of white powder into a sandwich bag. Then he tapes up the cut and replaces everything. This time, he makes sure the lock is locked.

Back upstairs, he goes into the bathroom, which has the brightest light in the apartment, and looks at the powder in the sandwich bag. It's the best look at it he's had so far. In the clear plastic bag, he can see it has a slightly grayish color to it.

"Now," he says to the powder, "we're going to find out what you are."

Back in his apartment, Russell Bradford tries to sleep the rest of the day away. He wasted no time spending the ten dollars the guy gave him on two nickle bags of heroin, but they wore off pretty fast. Still, with only what they call on the street a "sniffin' habit," he hasn't gotten that sick yet.

As far as meeting the guy tomorrow, he's not sure. Could be some kinda setup, even if the guy didn't snitch him out to the cops when he had the chance to.

He'll wait till tomorrow, see how he feels.

* * *

Michael Goodman feels tired as he lies on his sofa bed, but he also feels hopeful. He's got a job of sorts, he's survived a mugging attempt, and he's made a start at the business of figuring out some way to become an alchemist who can turn white powder into green money.

The sandwich bag lies underneath his pillow.

Shortly after midnight, two officers from the Miami Police Department make a grim discovery. Investigating a car parked underneath an overpass on I-95, they find a body slumped over the wheel. The car will turn out to be stolen. The body is that of a male Hispanic, thirty to thirty-five years old.

It isn't the small-caliber bullet hole in the back of the man's head that the officers find remarkable. They've seen plenty of homicides during their years in what's become known as the nation's murder capital. It isn't even the ligature marks around the man's neck. It's what they find later, at the morgue, when they see that the man's penis has been neatly sliced off and stuffed into his anus.

The older cop, who's seen just about everything in his day, is able to decipher the message for the benefit of his partner and the morgue attendant: "Just somebody's cute way of telling the world that this guy fucked himself."

Raul Cuervas has become the first victim of the twenty kilos. He will not be its last.

9

Goodman lies on his back on his sofa bed, hands underneath his head, and waits for morning to come. He can't see the sky from his apartment— his only window faces a brick wall across a narrow alley—but he watches as his ceiling gradually changes from black to charcoal to gray, signaling the arrival of another day.

What keeps him awake this morning is not just his daughter's headaches and his own mountain of debts. What keeps him awake is what he knows he's about to do before this day is over.

He thinks back to the moment he drove the rental car out of the visitors' parking lot of the Fort Lauderdale Police Department headquarters. In one respect, all he'd really done at that moment was to reject having to do things according to their convenience: He'd simply gotten fed up with their bureaucratic nonsense.

But as soon as he tells himself that, Goodman knows he's denying the obvious. He drove off because, on some level, he'd wanted to keep his options open at least. Because he didn't know what he wanted to do about the narcotics, he'd held on to them until he could decide. And, since he was about to return the car in any event, holding on to them had necessitated moving them from the tire to the duffel bags. Next, since he was returning to New York, he'd had no choice but to bring them with him. And, once home, it had made sense that he put them somewhere where they'd be safe—and it turned out to have been a good thing he'd done that.

Each of those actions he can group under the heading of keeping his options open. All he'd really done was to retain the *possibility*—however remote—that at some point he might actually decide to try to do something with the stuff.

But now it's different. Now he's about to push off from shore. Now he's about to *do that something*. And he finds that while the thought terrifies him, it also excites him just a little bit. What he finds difficult—what he finds all but *impossible*—is to focus on the immorality of what he's about to do. Now he forces himself to do just that.

He knows it's wrong; that's easy enough. But he also knows it's wrong to let his daughter go untreated for something horrible that might kill her. He makes himself mouth the words he hasn't dared mention to his mother-in-law, hasn't allowed to let form in his own vocabulary until this moment. He says them out loud now as he lies staring at the gradually lightening ceiling.

"Brain tumor," he says.

And if narcotics are the scourge of the city, if they kill people and enslave children and cause crime, are they any worse than his only child dying of a brain tumor because her father stood by hopelessly and did nothing to save her?

He doesn't know the answer to that question. But he knows that if he lets his daughter die, his own life is over, too. And he knows that no matter how criminal, no matter how wrong, he will go and meet the kid named Russell today. He will choose his daughter's life over the hundreds or thousands of lives that may be jeopardized or lost in the bargain. That will be his sin; that will be his crime; he'll answer for that.

Lenny Siegel is at his office before eight this morning. In fact, except for a few of the secretaries, he's the first one there. What brings him in early is a pile of reports on his desk. This being the first week of October already, the September monthly reports of everyone in his group have been turned in. As leader of Group Two, it's now Lenny's job to review those reports, evaluate each person's performance, total up the statistics, and compile a report of his own summarizing the activity and performance of the group during the preceeding month.

The problem is that Lenny already knows that the reports are going to be high on bullshit and low on results. The truth is, it's been a slow month for the whole office. But this will mark the third month *in a row* that's been slow for Group Two, and Lenny knows the district director isn't going to want to hear it again. As he thumbs through the first of the reports, Lenny keeps remembering the director's words at the last supervisors' meeting: "What we need is *production,* fellas," he'd explained. "Think of us like you'd think of any other company. Without production, we're out of business." At the time, no one in the room had quarreled with the point. Lenny himself had wanted to say, "But we're not just *any other company,*" but he'd thought better of it and had kept his mouth shut. You know what they say: The boss may not always be right, but he's always the boss.

So as he goes through report after report now, Lenny knows it's time to convey the director's message to his group. It bothers him a little bit, because the truth is, they aren't all part of some Fortune 500 company. For one thing, they're dealing with human beings. For another, all you've got to do to understand the difference between them and some manufacturing company is to take a look at what kind of *production* you're talking about. Some companies produce automobiles; some produce refrigerators; some produce barbecue sauce. Here, we're in the business of producing seizures and arrests. That's how *we* measure success.

"Seizures and arrests," Lenny says out loud, pleased at the double entendre he's discovered. He could be a cardiac surgeon talking. And wasn't his mother always telling him he could have been a doctor?

He can almost hear her voice. "Look at you. You could've been a doctor, a lawyer, a *CPA!* But no, you had to become a *cop!*"

"I'm not a cop, Mom," he'd explain for the umpteenth time. "I'm an agent."

"Agent schmagent. What kind of a Jewish boy gives up all that education and becomes a secret agent?"

"Not a *secret* agent, Mom. Just an agent."

"Better you should keep it secret."

But after twenty-one years, it *is* no secret: Lenny Siegel is an agent—in fact, now a group leader—in the New York Office of the Drug Enforcement Administration, otherwise known as the DEA. And this morning, as he thumbs his way through the last of the monthly reports of the twelve field agents who work under his supervision, he knows that, like it or not, he's going to have to do something to get some more production out of them: more seizures, more arrests.

He wonders what the average cardiac surgeon with twenty-one years' experience makes in a year. Two hundred thousand? Three? Half a million? There's gotta be a few out there pulling in 2 or 3 million.

Lenny Siegel, as a grade 13, step 6, with twenty-one years in (make that twenty-three, counting his two years in the military), makes $58,156—before taxes.

Mom was right once again, after all. So what else is new?

Michael Goodman is up early, too, this morning. He showers and shaves, breakfasts on a bowl of Special K. He eats it dry, without milk—partly because he likes it crunchy better than soggy, partly because milk is expensive. He stirs some powdered grapefruit Tang into a glass of tap water and drinks it down. He's tried orange Tang and doesn't care for it, but the grapefruit is almost like the real thing. And, as everybody knows, New York City tap water is the best in the world. He once read that it keeps beating all these fancy bottled waters in taste tests where they blindfold the participants. And on top of that, it's *free.* Just one of the many reasons I love this city, thinks this man who, not twenty-four hours ago, found himself the victim of a broad-daylight mugging attempt.

But Goodman knows that it's that very mugging attempt that may turn out to be his lucky break, the entrée he so desperately needs to the underworld of drugs. At the same time, he knows he can't count too heavily on his new friend Russell. All he knows about him for sure is that he's young, he's black, he tries to mug people, and he's very bad at it. Chances are he won't even show up for their meeting. But since Goodman's got the day to kill—it's Wednesday, and he doesn't start at the Bronx Tire Exchange until tomorrow—he'll go and see. And he'll take his little sandwich bag with him.

Lenny Siegel assembles his field agents for a group meeting shortly after ten o'clock.

"These reports suck," he tells them, waving the stack of them dismissively. "We're running a law-enforcement agency here, not a creative writing class. The DD is tired of excuses. He wants *numbers,* as in numbers of arrests made and amounts of drugs seized."

His eye catches a hand raised in the back of the room. It's on the end of an arm connected to the body of Jimmy ("No Neck") Zelb. Before he became a DEA agent, No Neck was a small-team all-American football player who went on to become a cop in Toledo. He's one of Siegel's best men.

"Yeah?" Siegel asks.

"Maybe it's a good thing the numbers are down," Zelb says. "I mean, can't we say it's 'cause we been doing our job so well?" There's a murmur of approval around the room, a nodding of heads.

"You can say it, but the old man isn't saying it," Siegel says. "He goes to Washington in November to defend our budget. All they want to hear down there are *numbers*. Not theories, not sociology—*numbers*. Is that so hard for you guys to understand?"

"Things are tight out there," says Frank Farrelli. Another murmur, more nodding heads.

"You'll see how tight they are when they take our overtime budget away," Siegel says. "Or when they make us turn our cars in at the end of the day. See how you like riding to work on the subway." That seems to hit a nerve. The murmuring subsides; the heads stop nodding.

The meeting breaks up shortly after. By eleven, Siegel's left alone in his office, staring at a blank form in front of him entitled "Group Two Monthly Activity Report."

He lights a cigarette. It's his fifth one of the morning.

Russell Bradford is awakened by his mother's voice, helped considerably by the fact that it's aimed directly into his left ear.

"Get up off that sofa, boy!" she shouts. When he's slow to react, she adds, "Don't you be sleeping another day away!"

Russell rubs his eyes. His back is sore where it's been pressed against the hard part of the sofa.

"What day is it?" he asks.

"It's Wednesday," she says as she moves about the living room, straightening up. "I'm goin' to visit Nana at the hospital. You can come with me, or you can get your butt up and go lookin' for a job. But you are *not* goin' to lay around the house all day."

Russell has a vague recollection that there's something he's supposed to do today, but he can't remember what.

"What time is it?" he asks.

"Almost noon."

Noon. Noon today is when he's supposed to meet the white guy. He sits up.

"*Ezzackly* what time is it?" he asks his mother.

She stops what she's doing and looks at her watch.

"Eleven-twenty," she tells him.

Russell raises his body from the sofa, stretches the muscles in his back.

"So?" she asks. "You comin' with me, or you goin' lookin' for a job?"

"I can't go with you," Russell says. "I got a interview at twelve o'clock."

"What kind of interview?"

"With a white guy," Russell tells her. "About a job."

"Where?"

"Ninety-sixth and Lexington."

"What's at Ninety-sixth and Lexington?"

Russell thinks. "A store," he says. He figures he can't go wrong there.

"Well, break a leg."

Russell figures she means he should get going. He heads for the shower.

Even though it's only a four-block walk to Ninety-sixth Street, Goodman arrives fifteen minutes early. He views Ninety-sixth as a sort of line of demarcation between the white world to the south and the black and Hispanic world to the north. As a gesture of accommodation, he crosses the street and waits on the uptown side. There, he melds into a small group of people waiting for the crosstown bus. He tries to remember what Russell looks like, wonders if he'll recognize him, or if he's going to be guilty of being one of those white people to whom all blacks look alike.

Every so often, he reaches his right hand into his rear pants pocket and feels the sandwich bag.

Fifteen minutes go by. Twenty, twenty-five. Four westbound buses come and go. Goodman wishes he'd asked Russell for his phone number. Then he realizes Russell might not *have* a phone, so he's glad he didn't ask. He decides he'll give it until one o'clock.

Goodman once worked for an accounting firm that had a black kid who ran the mailroom. He was a nice kid and everybody liked him. Thing was, he was supposed to be in each morning at nine, but he never made it before ten or ten-fifteen. When Goodman commented on it to one of the other accountants, the response he got was that the kid was on CPT.

"CPT?" Goodman had asked.

"Yeah. Colored people time."

Now he wonders if Russell maybe runs on colored people time. Or black time. Or Afro-American time. Whatever. He's wondering what the next politically correct phrase will be, when he feels a tap on his shoulder.

Russell offers no reason for being late, and Goodman asks for none. It is enough that he's come. "Hello, Russell," he says.

"Hello."

Goodman looks around. The corner is a crowded one, but then it's pretty crowded both ways along Ninety-sixth, and up and down Lexington, as well.

"I got something I want to show you," he tells Russell, "but . . ." He lets his voice trail off. Russell doesn't say anything. Goodman wishes he'd take some initiative, help out a little here. But he knows Russell has no clue about what he has in mind.

"Got a few minutes to take a walk?" Goodman asks him.

Russell looks at Goodman warily, as though maybe he suspects that a sexual proposition of some sort is coming next.

"Don't worry," Goodman assures him. "I'm not like that."

Russell only looks more confused, but he says, "I ain't worried."

Goodman leads the way as Russell falls in half a step behind him. They zigzag south and east until they reach the upper tip of Carl Schurz Park. They walk in silence, these two strangers to small talk.

Once in the park, they continue to the wrought-iron fence at the edge of the East River. There are a few people in sight but no one really close by them. Goodman moves up to the railing and stands there as though he's looking out over the water. Russell takes a similar stance at his side. Goodman reaches into his back pocket and retrieves the sandwich bag. He holds it in his palm so that Russell can see it.

"Please don't be offended," he says, "but I figured you might possibly know more about this than I do."

Russell stares at the baggie. For a minute, Goodman fears that he *has* offended him, has been wrong to leap to the conclusion that just because he's black, he must be a drug user. Then he reminds himself that there *was* the little matter of the mugging attempt.

Russell continues to study the baggie. "What is it?" he asks.

"I was hoping you could tell me."

Russell looks around furtively before reaching for the baggie. He gives it a shake, holds it up to the light, and squints at it. He opens it and looks inside. Then he moistens the tip of his little finger, dips it into the powder, and withdraws it. A surprising amount of the powder clings to his fingertip. This he first smells, then touches to the tip of his tongue. He gives it a few seconds, appears to swallow the powder.

He dips his fingertip into the baggie a second time, extracting even more of the powder. He hands the baggie back to Goodman in order to free it to hold one nostril closed while he moves his fingertip directly beneath the other nostril. There is a sudden single sniffing sound, and the powder is gone.

For a moment, Russell just stands there as though waiting for some reaction, and the thought occurs to Goodman that the forty pounds he's lugged all the way from Florida is going to turn out to be talcum powder, or baking soda. Then he sees Russell reach out with both hands and grasp the rail in front of him. At the same time, he hears a low noise that sounds like "Ooooooooh." It takes him a second to realize it's coming from Russell.

A full minute goes by before either of them moves or makes another sound. Then Russell turns to face Goodman, who can see that the pupils of Russell's eyes have contracted to something approaching pinpoints.

"Wowwwww," Russell says.

Between *ooooooooh* and *wowwwww,* it's pretty clear to Goodman that we're not talking talcum powder or baking soda here. "What is it?" he asks.

"It's *dynamite,* man. That's what it is." He seems to be speaking in slow motion, or like when the batteries of a tape deck are real low.

"No," Goodman says. "What is it *really?*"

"It's heroin." (Only Russell pronounces *heroin* in a way that Goodman's never heard before—*her'oyne,* is how he says it.) "An' it's fuckin' outa sight."

It takes a moment for the news to sink in. Not that the stuff is potent—Goodman figured as much, seeing as it had been packaged in bulk containers, and also knowing that it comes from southern Florida, which he figures must be a place where it comes into the country. No, the news he tries to digest now is that it's heroin. For some reason, he's assumed up to this moment that it was cocaine. That seemed easier to live with somehow.

"You're sure it's heroin?" he asks Russell. "It's not cocaine?"

Russell smiles. "Yeah, man," he says. "Lemme show you." He opens his hand, and Goodman hands the baggie back to him.

"First thing is," begins Russell the teacher, "it's heavy. Coke is feathery stuff, real light and fluffylike. Sneeze on it an' it's gone. Heroin (again he pronounces it her'oyne) is more like a powder. See how this packs down real nice?" And he demonstrates by shaking the bag back and forth gently. Though to Goodman, it still could be grayish talcum powder he's looking at.

"Any idea what it's worth?" Goodman asks him.

"This right here?"

Goodman hesitates. He's reluctant to tell Russell how much he has.

"I'd say you maybe got a half an ounce here," Russell says. "I'd also bet my butt it's *pure.*" He says the word *pure* almost reverently. "On the street, this little bit here be goin' for over five hundred dollars."

Goodman is aware that his own mouth has opened but that no sound is forthcoming.

"Course, we *really* wanna make money," Russell continues, "we whack it up."

Goodman notices the "we," realizes that they've suddenly become partners. He finds his voice. "Whack it up?"

"Step on it. Cut it. This shit should take a six, maybe even a seven."

This is all new to Goodman, who can only ask, dumbly, "What does that mean?"

"Means we get aholda some milk sugar. Mix this up with it. One parta this stuff with like six partsa sugar. Then we bag it up."

"Bag it up?"

"Yeah. Put a little bit into lotsa little bags, the kind you then buy on the street for like five bucks each. This here half ounce, you could take right now—before even steppin' on it—and make three bundles outa it."

"What's a bundle?" Goodman needs to know.

"Twenny-five nickle bags, five-dollar bags," Russell explains. "Course you don't wanna do that."

"Don't want to do what?"

"Bag it up pure."

"Why not?"

"First thing is, you'd be givin' up the chance to make *real* money, six or seven times as much. But on topa that, you'd be killin' people."

"Killing people?" All of this is too fast for Goodman.

"Yeah, man." Russell slows it down, as though he realizes he's dealing with someone who has no clue. "You put pure shit inta nickle bags, guys that're useta sniffin' or shootin' street stuff, they getta holda one a your bags and don' know the diffrince, they gonna do the whole bag unsuspectin' like. Next thing you know, you gonna have people OD'in' all over the place."

"OD'ing?"

"OD'in', as in overdosin'," Russell says. "As in *dead?*" he adds, as though maybe Goodman can understand *that.*

Goodman stares out over the water. It's gray and flat, but from his navy days he can sense that there are treacherous currents at play here.

If the terminology is all new to him, the numbers come easily to Michael Goodman's accountant's brain. If the half ounce would make three bundles of twenty-five of these "nickle" bags each, that's seventy-five bags. An ounce would make twice as much, 150 bags. With sixteen ounces to a pound, that means each pound would make 2,400 bags. If each of the blue plastic bags from the spare tire weighs two pounds, it means you could make close to five thousand bags. Multiply that by twenty—since there are 20 blue bags—and you've got 100,000 bags. At $5 a bag, that's $500,000.

But that's without cutting it. Dilute the pure powder first so that you end up with six times as much—as Russell says you've got to do—and you're talking about three million dollars.

A tugboat pulls a string of barges downriver. The barges are piled high with garbage, and seagulls follow it, making occasional dives at the load. Goodman watches in silence, as does Russell, who's apparently talked out, unaccustomed to the role of teacher.

Michael Goodman has no need of three million dollars. All he wants is enough money to pay for his daughter's tests, so they'll release the results to her doctor. Nor does he want to go into the business of diluting drugs and putting it into little bags for poor souls like Russell to sniff or inject into their bodies. He wants no part of that.

"Suppose," he breaks the silence, "suppose I just wanted to sell what I've got, as it is."

"Pure?"

"Yes."

Russell seems to think a minute. It strikes Goodman that, in a way, this is all as new to Russell as it is to him.

"How much you got?" Russell asks tentatively.

"A lot."

"More than a few of those?" Russell glances at Goodman's pocket, to where the baggie has returned.

"Yes."

"As much as a *pound?*" As though he's almost afraid to say the word.

"As much as a pound," Goodman confirms.

"A *key?*"

Goodman's stumped again. "What's a key?"

"A *kilo,* man." There is a touch of reverence in his voice. "That's how it usually comes inta the country."

"How big is a kilo?"

"Two point two pounds," Russell explains with a touch of pride. Goodman has the feeling he may have tapped into the only math lesson Russell ever paid attention to in school. But he also realizes he's going to have to revise his own calculations slightly upward: That's what the blue plastic bags must be, kilos. He's going to have to add 10 percent to everything.

"Okay," he says to Russell. "Let's say I have a kilo."

Russell whistles softly. Goodman notices that his pupils have returned to more or less normal size.

"An' you're lookin' to sell it?"

"Let's say I am."

"Kilo a pure, right here in New York." Russell seems to be figuring out the numbers for a minute. "You could prob'ly get fifty thou for it, just like it is. Course you'd have to know how to unload it."

Goodman says nothing. He figures the partnership pitch is about to surface again.

Russell doesn't disappoint him. "You gonna need some help here, man." It isn't a question. They both seem to know it's a fact.

"What kind of help?" Goodman asks.

"Help findin' a buyer, a customer."

"You could do that?"

"Shit, yeah."

Goodman looks at Russell's pupils again. He wouldn't be too surprised to see them change into dollar signs.

"I'm gonna need a sample," says Russell, his eyes traveling once again toward Goodman's pocket.

Goodman reaches for the baggie. He hesitates a moment, realizing that, just like arranging the meeting with Russell, giving him a "sample" will constitute an affirmative step forward in this business. But he hands the baggie over.

"Gimme a day or two to get this checked out," Russell says, placing the baggie down the front of his pants.

Goodman nods. "How about we meet back here Friday, twelve o'clock noon?"

"That's cool," Russell says. He looks around. "We should leave here separate. Some cop is gonna see the two of us together, me black an' you Caucasian, an' decide he wants to search us."

That seems to make sense to Goodman. "Okay," he agrees. "Go ahead."

He watches Russell walk away, notices a little bounce to Russell's walk that wasn't there before. Then the accountant in Goodman goes to work again. Sixteen ounces to a pound means there're thirty-two ounces in two pounds. Add 10 percent and it means there're about thirty-five ounces to a kilo. If a kilo's really worth fifty thousand dollars, then the half ounce he's just handed Russell is worth a little over seven hundred dollars.

He hopes he hasn't seen the last of Russell Bradford.

{ 10 }

Even though Goodman doesn't have to report for work at the Bronx Tire Exchange until one o'clock in the afternoon, he's up early Thursday morning, sharpening pencils, gathering pens and ledgers and pads of paper, changing the little battery in his pocket calculator. He's decided not to bring his solar-powered one; he figures there's probably not enough light in Manny's office to operate it.

He arranges and rearranges his supplies, not knowing if he's packing too much or too little. Manny never did get around to telling him just what it is he wants Goodman to do, so Goodman figures it'll be the books—payroll, taxes, checks, whatever needs doing.

He lays out some clothes to choose from him. He decides against a jacket and tie—Manny is definitely an informal kind of guy. But no jacket means no large pockets. So he retrieves an attaché case—he's accumulated four of them over the years—from his closet. He picks a Samsonite one a client gave him a few years back. It's the nicest one of the four. It's vinyl, but it could pass for real leather, and it's lightweight. He once saw it advertised in an Innovation Luggage catalog for $29.95.

While he breakfasts on an apple Pop-Tart and a glass of grapefruit Tang, he wonders what Russell Bradford is doing.

* * *

What Russell Bradford is doing is sleeping. Russell didn't go home after leaving Goodman in Carl Schurz Park yesterday afternoon. He went and found Robbie McCray, and together they went to the rooftop of the building on 145th Street. There, Russell showed Robbie the half ounce of heroin he'd gotten from Goodman. They'd sniffed some of it, but Russell wouldn't let Robbie cook any of it up to shoot; he was afraid that Robbie'd OD if he mainlined it. And after sniffing it, Robbie'd had to agree—the stuff was pure dynamite.

They'd come back downstairs, found Big Red, and traded a small amount of the heroin for a half a dozen vials of crack. Then they'd gone back up to the roof, where they'd spent the rest of the afternoon and most of the evening, alternately sniffing the heroin to get wasted and smoking the crack to keep from nodding off. It had been dark by the time Russell got home, and in the condition he was in, he'd had a hard time convincing his mother he'd been out interviewing for a job. Too strung out to eat, he'd lain down on the sofa and was soon in a deep sleep, dreaming of huge mountains of white powder.

Around ten, Russell is awakened by a noise that he finally realizes is someone banging on the front door. He has no idea how long the banging's been going on, but he figures long enough to mean that he's the only one home. He pulls himself up from the sofa and makes his way to the door. His head aches and his entire body feels sore.

"Who is it?" he calls.

The banging stops.

"Robbie."

Russell unlocks the door and staggers back to the sofa. Robbie comes in, closing the door behind him.

" 'Sup, man?" Russell asks him.

"Shit," Robbie says. "I thought you was dead or somethin'."

"I ain't dead."

"I seen Big Red lass night," Robbie says. "He wantsa see us."

"What about?"

"I dunno. But he says it's real important like."

Big Red is something of a legend in the South Bronx. In addition to being the man to see if you're looking to buy crack on 140th Street, Big Red has a reputation as someone who's *endured*. The story is that back in the seventies he was one of Nicky Barnes's lieutenants, that he killed a cop in a shoot-out in the early eighties, for which he got sentenced to twenty-five to life, but that the case was reversed when a later investigation revealed that the bullet removed from the cop's head had been fired from his own partner's gun. The DA then tried to get Big Red to turn state's evidence against the cop's partner, but Big Red refused. Because of that, the word is that Big Red now has what they call a "license"—meaning the cops pretty much look the other way when they see him. He may get picked up now and then for something minor, like driving his Bentley without proof of insurance or something like that. But he always seems to get out the same night.

Russell zips up his jeans and slips into his Nikes. If Big Red wants to see him, that's good enough for him.

Around the same time as Russell Bradford slips into his Nikes, Ray Abbruzzo slips into the meeting room on the second floor of a gray stone building on Alexander Avenue at 138th Street. Abbruzzo slips in because he's late, exactly twelve minutes late by his own watch. But the truth is, he hasn't missed anything. The briefing that's under way is virtually identical to dozens of others Abbruzzo's attended over the past eight months, and his role in what's being planned is the same as it always is. Abbruzzo will act as a member of the backup team on what's known as a "buy and bust" operation.

Ray Abbruzzo is a detective, and the gray stone building is the 40th Precinct station house—or, to Ray Abbruzzo and every other cop in the Bronx, the Four-O.

A buy-and-bust operation is the principal tool used by the New York Police Department in combating street-level narcotics trafficking. First, a geographical area is targeted, usually a block known to be filled with small-time dealers. Occasionally, civilian complaints will determine the location.

An undercover officer, often black or Hispanic, will be provided with money in small denominations. The money is "prerecorded," meaning that it's been photocopied with the serial numbers showing. The undercover will drive an unmarked car to a spot near the targeted area, park, and proceed on foot to the designated block. There, he'll walk the sidewalk, asking anyone he sees, "Who's working?" In street parlance, that translates to "Who's selling drugs?" Sometimes he'll be followed by a second undercover, whose role is simply to observe. He's called a "ghost."

Because street selling has become such a competitive business, it's not long before the undercover is told exactly who's "working," what he's selling, and how much it's going for. A deal is struck on the spot, and the person whom the undercover has encountered (the "steerer") takes the undercover ("steers" him) to someone else to complete the transaction. That someone else (the "moneyman") takes the undercover's money and gives him change if necessary. He may give him the drugs right then and there (in which case he is not only the moneyman but the "hand-to-hand man," as well) or send him to yet a different hand-to-hand man. Or he may direct him to a phone booth, a car bumper, or a vacant lot where the drugs are hidden. There may be one more member of the selling group, a "lookout," who scans the block for signs of the police.

Once he has the drugs, the undercover leaves the area, heads back to his car, and radios the backup team. He tells them where he's made the buy, and gives them a brief description of the cast of characters involved—the steerer, the moneyman, the hand-to-hand man, and the lookout. He'll refer to a suspect by his most identifying feature: J. D. Sideburns, J. D. Boots, or J. D. Tattoo. J.D. stands for John Doe, a suspect whose true identity is not yet known.

Within minutes, the backup team swoops into the block, grabbing as many of the group as they can find. Once they've done this, they radio the undercover and tell him to drive by the spot where they're holding the suspects. This the undercover does (in what's come to be called a "drive-by ID"), following which he uses the radio once more to inform the backup team whether they've picked up the right individuals.

The suspects are arrested and searched for money and drugs—"cash and stash." Money seized from them is checked for serial-number matches against the photocopies of the money with which the undercover started out; drugs are compared with the drugs bought by the undercover. Either will provide powerful corroborative evidence at trial.

Because he's neither black nor Hispanic, Ray Abbruzzo is invariably relegated to being a member of the backup team, which is okay with him. The team works on a rotating basis, meaning they take turns "taking the collars." In other words, they alternate being the officially designated arresting officer.

Today, by virtue of the fact that he arrived late to the meeting, Ray Abbruzzo will be "batting cleanup." That means he'll have to wait until the fourth and final buy the undercover makes to be the arresting officer.

Whoever gets grabbed for participating in that buy will become his prisoners.

Russell Bradford and Robbie McCray spot Big Red as soon as they turn
the corner from Walton Avenue into 140th Street. Robbie's for walking
right up to Big Red, but Russell knows better and holds him back: You
don't just walk up on a man like Big Red. Better to hang back a half a
block away and wait.

It doesn't take long for Big Red to spot them. He signals one of his men
to take his place, then heads their way.

Big Red stops directly in front of Russell and greets him with a broad
smile. Russell is tall, just under six feet, but Big Red towers over him and
outweighs him by a hundred pounds.

" 'Sup, Russell?" Big Red says. He says nothing to Robbie, acts as if he's
not even there.

"Not much, Red."

"How's your grandmama?"

"Okay, I guess." Russell wonders how Big Red's heard about her, but
he doesn't ask.

"Take a walk with me?" It's spoken like a question, but Russell knows
it really isn't. He falls in step with Big Red as they head east. When Robbie begins to follow, Big Red finally seems to notice him. He stops and addresses him for the first time.

"You wanna work?" he asks him.

"Sure," Robbie says.

Big Red seems to think for a minute, tugging at the brim of his red baseball cap. "Go see Tito on Thirty-eighth Street. Tell him I said to put you
to work."

Robbie looks surprised, as though he's disappointed he's not going to
be part of whatever business Big Red wants to talk over with Russell. But
he's not about to pass up a chance to work for Big Red. So he hesitates
only a moment before nodding and heading off toward Thirty-eighth
Street, which is, of course, really 138th Street.

Big Red resumes walking, Russell alongside him. They cover a full
block before Big Red says anything.

"Your friend back there be messin' around with needles, huh?"

Russell shrugs. "I dunno," he says.

"You know. You jus don't wanna say."

It seems Big Red knows just about everything there is to know.

"You know what I want to talk with you about?" he asks Russell.

Russell has a pretty good idea, but he shakes his head as though he doesn't.

"You don't talk much, do you? That's good."

They keep walking, past storefronts and boarded-up brownstones. Five or six Puerto Ricans standing in front of a bodega make way for them to pass, something Russell knows wouldn't happen if it was just him who was walking by.

Big Red waits till they're alone before he gets to the point. "That shit you traded yesterday," is what he says.

"Yeah?"

"Your buddy says there's a lot more where that came from."

"My buddy's got a big mouth."

"That he does," laughs Big Red, "that he does. But he seemed to know what he was talkin' about."

Russell doesn't say anything. He's trying to figure out if this is good or bad, Big Red getting involved in this. He knows it's good in one respect, because Big Red has all sorts of money, can surely buy the whole kilo himself if he wants to. But it could be bad, too, because as soon as Big Red gets involved, it'll become his show, and Russell will get squeezed out.

"How much are we talkin' about here, Russell?"

"I dunno. Maybe a lot."

"What's a lot?"

Again, Russell says nothing. He doesn't want to tell Big Red, but then again, he doesn't want to lie to him, either.

"Unnastand, Russell, I don't want to take this *away* from you," Big Red says, as though he's read Russell's thoughts. "I want to work *with* you. See, you got the contact, right? But that's only half of it. The other half of it is the money. And you *don't* got the money."

Here, Big Red abruptly stops walking and faces Russell. No more than a foot separates them. Russell feels forced to answer.

"Right," he says.

"Me," Big Red says softly, *"I got the money."*

Russell wants to think it over, but he suddenly feels so crowded by the bigger man that he finds thinking all but impossible.

"How would this work?" he manages to ask.

"Like magic," Big Red smiles.

"Partners?"

"Absolutely. You get what's called a 'finder's fee.' All you gotta do is cut me into the source. I do the rest. My money, my people, my risk. Whatever I make on it, you get ten percent."

Russell's not sure. He's not too good at percentages. He thinks Big Red may be taking advantage of him. But he's not sure what choice he has.

"What kinda weight we talking about here?" Big Red asks him. The smile is gone; this is all business now.

"I think the guy's got a key."

"Same quality as yesterday?"

"I think so."

"We're talkin' big money here, Russell. We pay him maybe thirty grand, turn it into a *hundred* and thirty! You're looking at *ten thousand dollars,* partner. For makin' one little introduction. You gonna beat that for an hour's work?"

"I guess not," Russell admits. But he says it looking down at his feet.

"Hey, man, I want you to feel *good* about this," Big Red says. "Tell you what, make it fifteen percent. That's *fifteen grand.* Sound better?"

Russell looks up. It's his turn to smile. Truth is, he was ready to do the deal for the 10 percent. But by the simple trick of looking unsure, he's managed to outbargain Big Red, and he feels good about that.

Were he older and smarter, of course, Russell Bradford would realize that it was all too easy, that a man like Big Red doesn't just throw away five thousand dollars in order to make somebody else feel better. But Russell is young and not too smart, and he misses this nuance completely.

Big Red extends his hand. Russell reaches out with his own, and they meet in a three-stage inner-city handshake that seals the deal as surely as any notary's stamp ever could.

It's only later, walking home, that Russell has a chance to realize that maybe he hasn't bargained too well after all, that when it comes down to it, even 15 percent isn't really much of a partnership. Aren't partnerships supposed to be fifty-fifty?

But then again, fifteen thousand dollars is an awful lot of money.

Before leaving for work, Michael Goodman phones his mother-in-law. As much as he wants to find out how Kelly's doing, he's put off the call because he knows it will expose him to attack on money issues. But for once, she surprises him.

"I'm really worried about her," she tells him instead. "When I ask her, she tells me her head doesn't hurt her. But then, when she doesn't think I'm looking, I'll catch her with this grimace on her face, like she's really in pain."

The thought of his daughter grimacing in pain is almost too much for Goodman to bear.

"Are you working yet?" she asks him.

"Yes, I am," he tells her. "It's only part-time. But I've got something in the fire that could be big."

"I hope so," is all she says.

"Can I talk to her?"

"Hold on."

A minute goes by; then he hears his daughter's voice. It sounds frail to him.

"Hi, Daddy."

"Hi, angel. How you doing?"

"I'm fine," she says.

He doesn't want to ask her about the headaches, afraid the very question might bring one on.

"When are you coming to get me?" she asks. "I don't like staying with Grandma."

"Soon," he says, "as soon as I can. And I'll see you very soon. Maybe tomorrow, okay?"

"Okay. Daddy?"

"Yes, angel?"

"Larus has a headache."

"Oh?"

"Yup. And it hurts him very, very much."

He feels a lump in his throat, and doesn't dare speak. Is this what kids do, pass their maladies on to their stuffed animals? He hurriedly tells her again that he'll try to see her tomorrow, then gets off the phone just before the tears come. He prays to his God that he might have his daughter's pain, tenfold, if only she could be spared it.

Then he gets ready to leave for his new job.

Ray Abbruzzo rides in an unmarked Plymouth with three other members of the backup team to 136th Street and Gerard Avenue. There, they wait for the first radio transmission from the undercover officer. Ray checks his watch. After seven years on the Job, he unconsciously reads it in military time, the way one who's become fluent in a second language begins to think in it. It's 1222 hours, 12:22 P.M. in civilian time.

There's a short burst of static on the receiver, followed by the voice of a black male. "Okay, I'm about to leave my vehicle and head into a Hundred and thirty-fifth. Do you read me?"

Ray grabs the microphone. "Four by four," he says into it.

"Ten-four," the voice comes back.

"Ten-four," Ray echoes.

The day's buy-and-bust operation has begun.

Goodman takes the subway to 161st Street. He's determined to stay away from the area where he first ran into Russell. He walks the half a dozen blocks to 155th Street rapidly this time, paying careful attention to his surroundings. He arrives ten minutes early, and by one o'clock, he's already at the desk Manny's semi-cleared for him.

It turns out that his predecessor, the pregnant and gum-cracking Marlene, has called in sick on what was supposed to be her final day and Goodman's orientation. So Goodman begins to review the ledgers and checkbooks and tax forms that Marlene's kept in some fashion previously unknown in the history of bookkeeping.

But, he reminds himself, it is a job.

Robbie McCray spots Tito in the middle of the block on 138th Street.

"Red said to see you," he tells him.

"See me about what?" Tito is missing most of his front teeth. He's one of the scariest-looking guys Robbie's ever seen.

" 'Bout workin'."

Tito looks him over. "You worked before?"

"Sure," Robbie lies.

Tito looks like he doesn't believe him. But then he says, "Okay, you be on lookout. You cross over an' stan' right there." He points to the opposite corner. "You see *any*one looks like he could be the Man, you holler 'Five-O!' You hear?"

Robbie nods. After all these years, the only legacy left by an otherwise-forgotten TV series shot on an island paradise half a world away is the phrase used when the police come into the block.

Tito's not finished explaining. "I don' care if they in uniform or plain-clothes, inna car or on foot," he says. "You jus holler good an' loud."

Robbie nods again.

"So get goin'."

Robbie crosses the street. He finds a hydrant to lean against, so it'll look like he's just hanging out. He looks to his left, then to his right. He sees nobody who looks like the Man. This is going to be one muthafuckin' boring job, he tells himself.

But just as it is for Michael Goodman, this is Robbie McCray's first day at work in quite awhile, and after a few minutes, he, too, settles in.

Russell Bradford was on his way home to sniff some more of the heroin in the baggie, but now he changes his mind. He knows if he's going to be a successful businessman, it's important he keep a clear head. Besides which, he's seen the contempt that Big Red holds Robbie in for being an addict.

And Russell, even though he's not the brightest person on the planet, knows this much about himself: If he goes home now, he'll be the only one there. His mother'll be at work, the other kids off at school. He decides to go to the hospital and visit his grandmother. That'll keep him out of trouble for a while, and at the same time, it'll be nice for Nana, who he guesses doesn't get much company. On top of that, Big Red knew about her, and it's possible he also knows that Russell hasn't been to visit her yet.

By 1510, Detective Ray Abbruzzo and the other members of the backup team have completed three waves of arrests, and have a total of seven suspects in the back of an unmarked van off the corner of 134th Street. Three down means one to go, and that means it's finally Ray's turn at bat. Whoever they grab on this one will become his collars.

As before, they wait in the unmarked Plymouth. Ray holds the microphone in one hand. The undercover has already radioed that he was heading into a block—this time it's 138th Street—to try to make one last buy.

They don't have to wait long.

"Chico here," comes the voice.

"Go," Ray says.

"Just bought a couple vials in the middle of the block, downtown side. Two black males: J. D. Gap is an ugly-looking dude with no front teeth, green shirt; J. D. Stud is a light-skinned guy, jeans and a T-shirt, gold stud in his nose."

"Ten-four," Ray says. The driver of the car guns the engine, and they head for 138th Street. Ignoring a red light at the corner, they make the three-block trip in less than a minute, their tires squealing as they pull into 138th. Ray's out of the car even before it comes to a full stop. He grabs a black man wearing a green jacket. Behind him, one of the other officers handcuffs a short, lighter-skinned man with a gold stud in the side of his nose.

"I'm clean, man," insists the one in the green shirt. "You got nothin' on me. This is po-leece harassment!" Each time he opens his mouth to complain, he reveals that he's missing several of his front teeth.

"Wanna make it a triple, Ray?" The voice is that of Ray's partner, Daniel Riley. He's got a skinny black kid by the shoulder. "Soon as we pulled into the block, he starts yellin', pointin' at us. Gotta be a lookout."

Ray looks at the kid. He can't be sixteen. He's wearing a faded orange jacket with SYRACUSE on it in black letters. Had the undercover noticed him and included him in the buy transmission, no doubt he would have named him J. D. Syracuse.

"Hook him up," says Ray Abbruzzo.

As soon as he walks into the hospital room, Russell Bradford is struck by how old his grandmother looks. She's in a ward that has twelve beds; only two of them are empty. She's attached to all sorts of tubes and wires and things, but she recognizes Russell right away.

"Hello, Russell," she says. Only when she says it, she says it out of the corner of her mouth, like the other side of it doesn't work anymore.

"Hello, Nana."

"Don't worry," she says. "I feel better than I look."

"You look fine," he says. The truth is, she looks half-dead to Russell. But she lets him get away with what they both know is a lie.

"What have you been up to?" she asks.

"Nothin' much. Tryin' to find a job."

"Any prospects?"

He thinks of Big Red and his finder's fee. "Yeah," he says. "I got one good prospec' I'm workin' on."

"Good," she smiles. "I just know you're going to surprise us one of these days, make us real proud."

"I'm gonna do my best."

Nana closes her eyes, and for a moment Russell thinks she may have died. But then she opens them.

"Don't worry," she says. "I jes get tired." It seems everyone can read Russell's thoughts these days.

"That's okay," Russell says. "I gotta go, anyway." He bends over to give her a kiss. It's hard to find a place for his lips, there are so many tubes and wires.

"I love you, Nana," he says.

"I love you, too, baby."

He will not see her again.

Manny tells Goodman to knock off around a quarter to five.

"So how'd Marlene leave the books?" he asks.

Goodman wants to be both honest and diplomatic. For all he knows, Manny could be Marlene's father, or the father of the child Marlene's expecting, or even both. He settles for, "Let's just say she had her own interesting style of doing things."

"Yeah." Manny laughs heartily. "That's Marlene awright—*intresting.*" Which doesn't exactly settle the issue for Goodman, but he leaves it alone.

Manny takes a huge wad of money from his back pocket and starts peeling off twenties, licking his thumb between each extraction. He hands five of them to Goodman.

"See you Monday," he says.

"See you Monday," says Goodman.

Back at the Four-O, Ray Abbruzzo takes part in the postbuy meeting. This is the gathering at which the undercovers and backup team members coordinate their accounts, so that when they go to fill out reports and make notes in their memo books, all of their times, locations, and descriptions will be consistent. Each buy gets rounded off to the nearest five minutes (such as 1310 hours); each arrest happens precisely five minutes later (1315); and each drive-by identification by the undercover five minutes after that (1320). Each hand-to-hand transaction is done with the right hand, and all money and drugs are recovered from the right pocket. As little as possible is left to memory.

After the postbuy, Abbruzzo begins processing his prisoners. This consists of getting pedigree information from each of them in turn: full name, address, date of birth, employment (if any), and a host of other similar questions.

Because he's a detective, rather than a police officer, Ray takes a few minutes after each interview to pitch a deal to each prisoner: if any of them want to cooperate with him by giving him information on other dealers, he'll make a recommendation to the DA that they be ROR'd—released on their own recognizance—when they get to court, rather than having the judge set a high bail that's likely to keep them in jail.

J. D. Gap, the guy in the green shirt who's missing his front teeth, tells Ray to go fuck himself. J. D. Stud, he of the gold nose stud, would love to help out, but he explains that he's innocent and therefore doesn't know anybody who sells drugs.

But when it comes to the third prisoner, the young kid with the Syracuse jacket, it's a slightly different story. He's already told Abbruzzo it's his first arrest, and it's the detective's experience that "cherries" are often likely to turn: It seems the fear of jail is at its very worst the first time you're looking at it. Once you've done a little time and survived, the second time's not so scary. Beyond that, the kid seems to have a nasty habit, and already he's showing telltale signs of hurting—he's beginning to sweat, and he's starting to double over like he's got stomach cramps. Not that he's actually in withdrawal yet—he's only two hours off the street—but you can tell that the mere *thought* of it is getting to him.

"You're lookin' at state time here, kid," Ray tells him. "Mandatory one to three." It's not exactly true, but it'll do for now.

"How much I gotta do for you?" the kid asks.

"Coupla things," Ray tells him. "Or one good thing."

"How good's it gotta be?"

"Real good. Gotta be weight."

The kid seems to think for a minute. Then he says, "I might know a guy who's got some pure shit."

"Pure, as in *pure?*"

"Pure, as in *dynamite.*" The kid smiles. It's the first time Ray's seen him smile.

"Now you're talking." Ray can't remember the kid's name, has to look at the arrest report in front of him. "Now you're talking, Robbie."

*   *   *

Goodman's trip home from the Bronx is uneventful: no muggings on the way to the subway, no encounters with the Russells of the world. He stops at the supermarket that's on the corner of Ninety-sixth and picks up a few things. He'd been almost out of food, and the hundred dollars in his pocket represents the first money he's made in almost four weeks.

Goodman's not yet fully used to the idea of shopping for himself. He has to make a conscious effort to refrain from buying Tampax for Shirley or Mallomars for Kelly. He picks out things like packaged macaroni and cheese, tuna fish—he settles for light rather than the more expensive white—generic toilet paper, and some more Pop-Tarts. It fills two bags and comes to $14.97. Still, he feels he's spending too much on himself.

Fumbling for his keys at the door to his building, he feels something brush up against his legs. When he looks down, he sees a cat—or more accurately, a kitten. It's black, though on closer inspection he decides it might actually be gray and just very dirty. It looks up at him and makes a mewing sound.

He tries to push it away without kicking it, but it seems intent on attaching its side to his ankle. He gives up and turns his attention back to his keys. He locates the right one, inserts it in the lock, and manages to push the door open with his shoulder. But as he wedges his body inside, the kitten darts between his feet and slips through the opening, just before the door closes.

"You can't come in," he tells it, feeling foolish to hear himself talking to an animal. The only pets he ever had growing up were canaries, fish, and a one-eyed turtle named Max. Then Shirley had turned out to be allergic to fur, so Kelly's only pet has been the inanimate Larus.

The kitten gives him another *mewww* and continues to rub up against him. When he opens the door to let it out, it moves behind him instead, keeping Goodman's body between it and the door. He gives up and lets the door close again.

"Okay," he tells it, "you can come in. But just for a minute, that's all." Not realizing, of course, that the first part of that message is something universally understood by kittens, while the second part is totally incomprehensible.

In obvious appreciation, the creature remains virtually attached to Goodman's ankles as they climb the four flights to his apartment, and is inside the instant he opens the door.

*   *   *

Russell Bradford gets home around the same time. His brothers and his sister are already there, and his mother's due soon.

Right away, Russell forgets all the good intentions he had earlier in the day. He retrieves the baggie from where he's hidden it underneath the sofa, then heads to the bathroom. He figures a sniff or two won't hurt him. In fact, he's heard that it's best to cut down a little at a time.

It's almost midnight by the time Robbie McCray gets home. Good to his word, Ray Abbruzzo "cut him loose," spared Robbie from being officially arrested and having to go through the system. This isn't something that Abbruzzo had the legal power to do: The law says that once a person is arrested, only the district attorney can "unarrest" him, by filing a form with the court, stating his intention to decline prosecution.

But Abbruzzo simply took things into his own hands, taking the cuffs off Robbie, quietly letting him out the side door of the station house, and deleting his name from the paperwork. Other than the members of the backup team, no one will ever know about Ray's decision, much less complain about it.

Of course, before any of that could happen, Robbie had to spend a little time with Ray, telling him what he knew about a friend of his who's been walking around with a bag of pure heroin. Not that there was much to tell, really. No big deal or anything.

{ 11 }

Goodman is awakened Friday morning by tiny, sharp teeth biting his toes through the blanket, and he's reminded that he relented last night and couldn't quite bring himself to put a certain kitten out. But he'd remembered reading somewhere that you were okay until you fed them, and he'd ignored its cries and refused to share his macaroni and cheese. A night's lodging was one thing, but that didn't mean that dinner was included.

This morning, however, the kitten's cries are more persistent. Well rested but hungrier than ever, it manages to coax a bite of Pop-Tart out of him, first licking the sticky filling and then gobbling down the crust.

"You're eating a *Pop-Tart!*" Goodman exclaims, impressed by his guest's appetite. He opens a second one and downs half of it himself before breaking the remainder into little pieces. He watches in amazement as the kitten inhales them like a vacuum cleaner.

"Pop-Tart," he marvels again, and his new friend looks up, apparently recognizing the name its host has unwittingly conferred upon it.

Before the hour is up, Goodman will make another trip to the supermarket and return with his arms full of cat food, milk, a plastic tray, and five pounds of Kitty Litter, $22.56 poorer.

Robbie McCray is up early, too. He knows there's something he needs to do today, something important, but he can't quite remember what. He thinks back to yesterday: the meeting with Big Red, going to work in Tito's crew, getting arrested, being let go—and then it comes to him: He's got to go warn Russell.

But Robbie's tired; he didn't get home till late. And he knows that as soon as he gets up, he's gonna have to go out and try to cop.

So in order to put that off as long as he can, he turns over and goes back to sleep.

Goodman gets an inspiration. He calls the lawyer who helped him out when his wife died. He's a little embarrassed about doing this, because he still owes the guy money, but he figures he's got nothing to lose but a lecture.

The secretary tells him Mr. Dubin's on the other line, would he like to leave his name and number? No, Goodman says, he'll hold on.

He listens to music while he waits. The theme song from *The Godfather* comes and goes. The one from *Elvira Madigan* is halfway through when he hears Dubin's voice. He likes that song, and is a little disappointed to have it interrupted.

"Hello, Michael, how are you? What can I do for you?"

"Hello, Mr. Dubin," Goodman says. "First, you can accept my apology for not having finished paying your fee yet. I just got a new job, and I'm working on it."

"Good."

"I need to ask you a favor."

"Ask away."

"My little girl's sick. She had some tests, an MRI?"

"Yes?"

"Well, it turns out my medical insurance got a little screwed up, what with the job change and everything. The place that did the test won't release the results to the doctor. And the thing is, Kelly's been having these headaches, and I'm scared to death she's got—" And right here, Goodman's voice cracks, and he has to stop in midsentence.

"Why don't you give me the number of the MRI place?" Dubin says in a voice so self-assured that to Michael Goodman, it sounds like the charge of the calvary.

*   *   *

Within twenty minutes, Dubin has called back.

"They're sending the films over to your doctor later this morning," he says.

Goodman is incredulous. "How'd you do that?"

"I reminded them that this could be a life-threatening situation and that if they withheld test results, they could very well end up being liable in a wrongful-death action."

"Thanks, Mr. Dubin," Goodman says.

"You're welcome. Just be sure you pay their bill, okay? I promised them you'd take care of it by the end of next week."

"No problem."

He hangs up the phone. But when he goes to rise from the sofa, he discovers his knees are suddenly weak, and he has to sink back down. It's not the promise to pay the bill to which his lawyer has committed him without his permission; that doesn't bother him. No, it's Dubin's earlier words that echo in his ears: "life-threatening situation," "wrongful-death action." Goodman sits there stunned, unable to move. Finally, Pop-Tart comes over and jumps up into his lap.

Russell Bradford gets up around ten o'clock. Today's the day he's supposed to meet with the white guy again, tell him he's got a buyer for the kilo.

Russell showers, humming softly to himself. The way he figures, a couple days from now, he should be fifteen thousand dollars richer. Of course, for Russell, being fifteen thousand dollars richer will mean he'll have exactly fifteen thousand dollars. Which, when you think about it, is a lot less than Big Red will have, even less than the white guy. Which hardly seems right, seeing as Russell is really the important guy in this deal. After all, without Russell, Big Red and the white guy don't even know each other; without Russell, they could never pull this deal off.

He gets dressed and watches a little TV, keeping one eye on the clock until it's time to head out for the meeting. Just before he leaves, he pulls out the baggie and takes a couple of quick sniffs, just to brace himself up. No harm in that, certainly.

Goodman leaves his apartment at 11:30. He knows that'll get him to the park too early, but he can't help himself, so strong is his compulsion to be punctual.

As soon as he gets outside, he sees it's overcast, something he couldn't tell from his apartment. He thinks about going back for an umbrella but decides against it. He remembers how his father used to refuse to go back inside once he'd left a place—it was supposed to be bad luck. He smiles at recalling how that little superstition had caused his father to show up at Goodman's wedding without his false teeth, so that Goodman himself had been forced to make an emergency trip across town to retrieve them. He misses his father, misses both his parents. He wonders if his decision now not to go back for his umbrella is some sort of homage to them.

He purposely walks slowly, figuring that Russell will show up late again. He stops to look in the windows of little shops, even though there's not much of interest on the way: a shoemaker, a bagel place, a little grocery store. At one point, he becomes vaguely aware of two men across the street, whose pace doesn't seem to be much faster than his. It just goes to show you the things you begin to notice when you slow down a little in life, he tells himself. And thinks nothing more of it.

At the water's edge, Goodman looks out over the river, to the factories and red brick buildings of Queens. The water is different from how it looked last time. Today it's choppy, with occasional whitecaps. The breeze is backing in from the east, a sure sign that rain's on the way. It feels good against his face, even if it makes his eyes begin to tear.

A uniformed policeman walks by just behind him. Goodman half-turns and their eyes meet, and they exchange nods and small smiles. Goodman can't help wondering what the cop's reaction would be if he knew Goodman was here waiting to meet a black kid from the Bronx about a major heroin deal. He smiles; the thought is truly mind-boggling.

His thoughts go to Kelly again, and how—no matter how criminal, no matter how immoral what he's about to do may be—he's doing it in order to save her life. But he knows there's more to it than that. The way he's begun to look at it is that, at one of life's darkest moments, just when his situation seemed totally hopeless—when he'd seemed trapped on an endless merry-go-round to nowhere—here he's suddenly been given a once-in-a-lifetime chance to reach for the brass ring. Only in this particular case, the ring happens to be pure gold, turns out to be worth a couple million dollars. How can he *not* reach for it?

He tries to shut his mind off by watching the river. There's a strong current today, moving from left to right, down toward the Battery and out into the Atlantic. He watches a log, a timber of some sort, being swept along by it. He imagines himself in the water, trying to swim across to the other side. You'd have to try to do it at an angle, he decides, aiming for landfall far to the south, past Roosevelt Island, past Long Island City, all the way down to Brooklyn.

Goodman the accountant reduces it to numbers: It's maybe a half a mile to the other side, he estimates. It would be a matter of trying to cross that half a mile before being carried past the tip of Brooklyn and out into the open ocean. He's at Ninetieth Street; at twenty blocks per mile, it's four and half miles until you run out of numbers around Houston Street, another mile or so after that. Figure six miles. You'd have to make one foot east for every dozen you'd be swept south. Doesn't sound too hard. Until you figure in fatigue and cold, that is. It's October; the water's got to be sixty degrees, maybe even colder. You'd need a drysuit; even in a wetsuit, you'd cramp up before you could make it. And then there're the waves; all it would take would be one good mouthful, and down you'd go.

The truth is that Goodman—despite his three years in the navy—has always been a weak swimmer, has a difficult time making it across a good-sized pool and back without resting halfway to tread water. Yet he now manages to push that reality aside, and he stands there, continuing to imagine himself fighting the current, defying all the odds, desperately trying to make it to the other side as the current speeds him downriver.

"Hey, man."

He wheels around, to see Russell standing next to him. He's so embarrassed at being caught off guard that he's afraid Russell's aware of what he's been thinking. He even wonders if he's been talking out loud to himself.

But if Russell's aware of Goodman's reverie, he shows no sign of it, to Goodman's relief.

"Hello, Russell," he says.

"Hello."

Neither of them says anything else. Russell takes his place alongside Goodman at the rail, and they watch the river together. It's as though neither of them wants to be the first to bring up the subject that's brought them both back here.

A full five minutes goes by, and Goodman has the thought that the two of them will just stand here, looking out over the water and watching the whitecaps until it's time to leave, and that with that, his notion of selling the drugs will pass forever.

But Russell breaks the silence. "I talked to a guy," he says simply.

"Oh?" And with that one syllable, that one syllable with a barely raised inflection at the end of it, Goodman picks it up again.

"Yeah," Russell says. "He's real innerested."

"Who is he?"

Russell seems to ponder this one a moment. "He's a guy with serious money is who he be," he says. *"Serious* money."

"Fifty thousand?" Goodman's voice cracks over the first part of *thousand.*

"Naw," Russell says. "I was off about the numbers. Turns out a key's only worth about twenny, twenny-five."

Goodman absorbs this news. He knew fifty was probably too good to be true. But he doesn't need to be greedy: Twenty thousand should be more than enough to pay for the MRI, Kelly's other medical bills, the balance of Dubin's fee—

"I'm pretty sure he'll go twenny-five," Russell says.

—his Visa bill—

"Course, if I can getcha twenny-five, you'd hafta give me the five as my cut. Okay?"

"Okay what?" Goodman realizes he hasn't been paying attention.

"Lissen up, man, pay attention," Russell says. "This here is *biz*ness."

"Sorry."

"The guy'll give us twenny-five for the kilo. I get five—that's what's called a finder's fee. You clear twenny. Deal?"

Goodman's brain shuts down. It's not the numbers that throw him—numbers are his language; numbers are his life. But whatever it is, his mind goes totally numb. Finally, from somewhere far, far away, he hears a voice say, "Deal." Vaguely, he recognizes the voice as his own.

There's some more conversation, but, walking home, Goodman is able to recall none of it, other than an agreement to meet Russell back in the park at seven o'clock tomorrow evening. Nor is he the least bit aware of the two men who, from across the street and a half a block behind him, follow him home.

Russell goes straight back to the Bronx. He finds Big Red, as always, on 140th Street. Red notices him and signals him to stay put. Russell chills for five minutes, ten, watching the junkies and crackheads filtering into the block. Buying drugs tends to be an afternoon and nighttime thing; mornings are for sleeping. Here on 140th Street, one of the biggest marketplaces in all of the South Bronx, it's already one o'clock in the afternoon, but the day's action is just beginning to pick up.

When Russell next looks back in Big Red's direction, he doesn't see him. In his place is Black Jimmy, so called because his skin is as dark as skin can get. Russell knows him to be one of Red's crew.

The beep of a car's horn startles Russell, and he looks up, to see Big Red's Bentley pulled up to the curb, Big Red behind the wheel. The car's deep maroon paint is highly polished, and its chrome sparkles. Russell has seen it many times in the neighborhood; everyone knows whose car it is.

Big Red waves Russell over and motions him to get in. Russell circles the car to the passenger's side. He opens the door, slides in, and closes it behind him. It sounds like the door of a huge vault shutting.

It's warm inside, like being in some rich person's living room. Russell is surrounded by the smell of new leather. His body molds into a seat so soft and deep that he imagines he's a ball nestled in the pocket of a fine baseball glove. Everywhere around him is tan leather and grainy wood. Darkly tinted glass obscures the outside world in three directions. Boys II Men sing softly to him from what must be a dozen hidden speakers. The thought comes to him that this is what heaven must be like.

The car moves away from the curb and glides silently west.

" 'Sup, Russell?"

" 'Sup, Red."

"You meet the dude?"

"Yup."

"We got us a deal?" Big Red asks him.

"We got us a deal," Russell says.

Back in his apartment, Goodman dials his mother-in-law's number.

"I've got some good news," he tells her. "I took care of the problem with Kelly's MRI. They're sending the results over to Dr. Saltz."

"I've got some bad news," she says. "They already did, and his office called to say he wants you to bring Kelly in tomorrow. He sounds like he wants her to see a specialist."

Goodman feels his insides shrivel up and knot. He's unable to speak.

"Are you there?"

"Yes," he manages to say. "I'm here."

He waits for her to say something, but she, too, is silent.

"What kind of specialist?" he finally asks.

"I don't know," she says. "I didn't ask."

For once, he can hardly blame her.

Big Red drops Russell off on the corner of 144th Street, and Russell all but floats the rest of the way home. In his mind, he's already spending his money: fifteen thou from Big Red and another five from the white guy. *Twenty thousand dollars!* He imagines himself investing the money in other deals, watching his bankroll grow into a hundred thousand, two hundred—

A car door swings open just in front of him, causing him to break his stride and jump sideways out of the way. A white guy climbs out, a big white guy who's got the Man written all over him.

"Hello, Russell," he says.

Russell stops in his tracks, his mouth wide open. A second door of the car swings open, and before Russell can say a word, he finds himself sitting in the backseat, staring at the backs of the heads of two detectives. There's a squeal of rubber, and they lurch forward into traffic.

Nobody says anything for about ten blocks. By then, they're heading north on the Grand Concourse. The car is nothing like Big Red's Bentley. It's a beat-up Chevy. The plastic seats are torn and lumpy, and there's all sorts of shit on the floor—newspapers, empty coffee containers, crushed soda cans. It smells like moldy bread. Every once in awhile, the two-way radio comes on. It's full of static, and Russell has a hard time understanding the voices he hears.

He spots Yankee Stadium down the hill to the left as they pass 161st Street.

"What's this all about?" he finally asks.

"You know fuckin' well what it's about," says the driver without turning around. He's the bigger of the two, the one who was first out of the car. He's got black hair and a big nose, looks Italian to Russell. Every couple of blocks, he eyeballs Russell in the rearview mirror. The other guy is thinner and looks younger. He's got reddish hair, sort of a crew cut. Probably Irish, Russell guesses.

At the very top of the Grand Concourse, they turn left and go under the elevated tracks at Jerome Avenue before coming to the beginning of Van Cortland Park. At the far side of the park, the Italian one pulls the car over and kills the engine. He turns halfway in his seat to face Russell.

"Hello, Russell," he says again.

Russell says, "Hello."

"I'm Detective Abbruzzo; this here is Detective Riley."

"Pleased to meet you," Russell says.

"Do yourself a favor, kid," says Italian. "Don't be a wiseass, okay?"

"Okay.

"Am I under arrest?" Russell asks. "Or am I free to go?" He once saw on a *Law and Order* episode that you're supposed to ask that when you think you're being falsely detained by the police.

"Whaddayou, a fuckin' *lawyer?*" It's the first thing Irish has said. Russell decides it's one of those rectangular questions, the kind you're not really supposed to answer.

"Russell, my friend," says Italian, "the word on the street is, you been walkin' around with some mighty fine pure shit."

"You must be crazy, man," Russell says, and as soon as the words are out of his mouth, he feels the back of Italian's hand smack him on the side of his head. So fast is the blow delivered that Russell doesn't even have a chance to get a hand up.

"Didn't I tell you not to be a wiseass?" Italian reminds him.

Russell doesn't say anything. His ear stings and feels hot, but he doesn't want to rub it, doesn't want to give these pigs the satisfaction. Instead, he tries to focus on figuring out who's dropped a dime on him.

"Thing is," Italian says, "it's not you we want. Oh, we'll lock your ass up if we gotta. But that's not really what we want."

"Whatta you gonna lock me up *for?*" Russell knows something about his rights, after all.

It's Irish who answers him. "Conspiracy, criminal facilitation, criminal solicitation. How's that for starters?"

"What's that mean?"

"What that means is about ten thousand dollars' bail," Italian tells him. "Mama got that kinda change?"

"No," Russell says.

"Didn't think so." Italian again. "But like I said, it's not you we want."

Russell tries to think. He knows they're bluffing. He's been through the system two or three times—a couple of farebeats and a misdemeanor possession—and he knows that even a Legal Aid'll be able to beat this one, a drug case with no drugs. Problem is, he can't afford to take a chance on getting busted: In the time it'll take him to get out, he'll blow the deal with Big Red and the white guy.

"What do you want?" he asks.

"That's easy," Italian says. "We want the guy you got it from. You give us him, we're finished with you."

"What does that mean—*I give you him?*"

Irish explains it to him. "You tell us his name, that's all. His name and where he lives."

Russell tries to remember the guy's name, he really does. But he's never been good at names—he has this habit of not listening when he's introduced to somebody, so he finds it's not so much that he forgets names; he never gets them in the first place. As to where the guy lives, he's got no clue.

So he says, "I don't know his name, or where he lives."

"Whaddaya call him?" Irish asks.

"Me? I call him 'the white guy.' "

"That narrows it down pretty good," says Italian.

"You got a phone number?" Irish asks.

"Nope."

"How do you get ahold of him?"

"We meet."

"Where?"

"By the river, around Ninetieth Street."

"Which river? The Hudson?"

"No, the other one." Russell can't remember what it's called.

"When's your next meeting?"

"Tomorrow," Russell says. "Tomorrow night at seven."

Irish and Italian seem to think this over for a minute. They don't say anything, but they look at each other as if they're having a conversation without words. Then Italian turns back to Russell.

"You make that meet, Russell. You get your ass there, if you know what's good for you. Do I make myself clear?"

"Yessir."

"And Russell—" He waits for a response.

"Yes?"

"Don't fuck with us. Or you'll find out what it's like to get fucked with."

"Yes, sir," Russell says again.

"Go home now," Italian tells him. "Or wherever you're going."

Which means Russell gets no ride back downtown. He has to get out right there and watch them drive off in the Chevy. Has to walk back to

Jerome, find the train station, hop the turnstile, and ride home.

Fuckin' cops. Think they own the fuckin' world, he thinks.

Jimmy Zelb and Frank Farrelli sit in Peppy's Bar on West Fifty-third Street Friday evening. It's been a long day, and another unproductive one.

"We gotta make a case next week if it kills us," Zelb says.

Farrelli finishes draining a bottle of Corona before nodding in agreement. "Yeah," he says. "Bugsy's counting on us." "Bugsy" is their nickname for their group leader, Lenny Siegel.

"Monday morning," Zelb says, "we start making the rounds, paying visits to all our CIs." CIs are confidential informers. "Put a little pressure on some of those lazy fucks."

"I like that," Farrelli agrees, trying to shake out the little piece of lime from his Corona bottle. "Let's start with Vinnie Ippolito. He hasn't given us squat for months now."

"How 'bout Alfonso Gomez? He's usually good for something."

"If he isn't too strung out," Farrelli says, working his middle finger into the bottle.

"Whaddayou, a gynecologist or something?"

"I'm just trying to get this lime here—"

"Who else we got?" Zelb asks.

"We got Addison, we got Eddie Maple, we got DeSalvo, we got—"

"What a crew of losers."

"No shit," Farrelli agrees, giving up on the lime. "Oh, yeah," he remembers, "we got Dwayne Reddington."

"Yeah," Zelb says, drinking down the last of his J & B. "Why not? It's about time we put some heat on Big Red."

Late that night, Michael Goodman sits in front of his television set, searching desperately for distraction. He spoke to his daughter earlier in the evening, and, even though she denied it, he could sense that she was in pain even as they talked. His mother-in-law got on the phone afterward and told Goodman he's supposed to take Kelly to the doctor at eleven o'clock tomorrow morning.

He changes the channel again, settling for a old black-and-white movie with Gregory Peck. He has no idea what it is, or if he's seen it before.

What kind of specialist could they possibly want Kelly to see? What do they think's the matter with her? All that keeps coming back to him is brain tumor, brain tumor, brain tumor.

Again, almost instinctively, Pop-Tart jumps lightly onto his lap, circles twice before finding a place to curl up, and settles in there. Goodman strokes its back absently until it begins to purr. He marvels at how such a tiny thing can have such a loud motor.

{ 12 }

By Saturday morning, a light freezing rain has begun to fall, and before leaving his apartment, Goodman pulls on an old orange jacket from his navy days and a rain hat Shirley once gave him. Still, he walks the twenty blocks to his mother-in-law's building, not only to save a token but because walking in the rain is one of his secret pleasures.

As he walks, he wonders if it isn't time for his luck to change, for something truly good to happen. Perhaps this'll be the day he finally gets some good news, the day that someone will tell him his daughter's going to be just fine after all.

But no one will tell him anything of the sort this day. As they sit in the doctor's office an hour and a half later, Kelly sitting in his lap and sucking her thumb, it isn't good news that Michael Goodman hears.

"The MRI films show what looks like a small shadow in her brain. And frankly, it shouldn't be there," Dr. Saltz tells him. He holds up a large film for Goodman to look at. It contains many images of what appears to be a brain. "It could be nothing much," the doctor continues. "It could prove to be nothing more than what we call an artifact, a product of the imaging itself. But I'm concerned enough to want her to see a specialist."

Goodman wants to ask him what else it could be, but he doesn't. He doesn't want Kelly to hear the answer, doesn't even want to hear it himself.

Dr. Saltz makes a phone call. He swivels around on his chair so that his back is to them while he talks. When he swivels back, he announces that he's made them an appointment for this afternoon. He pulls open his top desk drawer and fishes around until he finds a business card, which he hands to Goodman.

"He can see you at two o'clock," Dr. Saltz says.

It's only outside, outside in the rain, that Goodman is finally able to look at the card.

SEYMOUR GENDEL, M.D.
Board-Certified Neurologist

1195 Park Avenue
New York, NY 10028
(212) 555-1616

Hours by Appointment

The only word he sees is *neurologist.* Now he knows he's right: The shadow in his daughter's brain is a tumor, a tumor that will kill her, slowly but surely. He feels his entire world crumbling into ruins, crashing down upon him, smothering him. He carries Kelly tightly in his arms, shielding her frail body with his jacket, grateful for the raindrops mixing freely with his own warm tears.

Russell Bradford is awakened Saturday by the sounds of his brothers fighting over which cartoons to watch on TV, *Power Rangers* or *Superheroes.* He tries to cover his ears with his pillow, but it's a losing battle.

In the bathroom, he recalls yesterday's ride with the detectives, remembers telling them he's supposed to meet the white guy tonight. He thinks about calling the meeting off or changing it to a different time, but then he realizes he's got no way to do that: He doesn't know the guy's name, or where he lives, or his phone number. And if Russell doesn't show up as planned, he'll have no way of ever getting ahold of the guy again to set up another meeting. So he's either got to go to the meeting tonight or give up the twenty thousand dollars. And there's no way he's going to do *that.* No fucking way.

He'll just have to be careful, is all.

He gets dressed. It's time to go find Big Red, tell him to get his money ready. Russell figures the best thing is to do this deal quickly, before these cops get a chance to fuck it up.

Dr. Gendel turns out to be a small man without much hair, but with a pleasant manner. He's able to coax Kelly out of Goodman's lap and onto a chair, where he examines her, talking to her constantly, telling her what he's about to do before he does it. Kelly is good about it, and she laughs when he tickles the bottoms of her feet.

He spends a lot of time checking her reflexes, hitting her knees with a little rubber hammer and poking her toes with safety pins. He straps a device around his forehead that looks like a little satellite dish with a hole at the center. He snaps on a light that's part of it, then spends the next few minutes examining her eyes, particularly the right one. Then he asks Kelly questions about her headaches, about school, about her appetite.

"Do you ever see a spot in your eye?" he asks her.

"Sometimes," she says.

"Both eyes, or just one eye?"

"Just one."

"Which one?"

She points to her right eye.

"What color is the spot?" he asks.

"Brown."

He gives her a pat on the head for being so good, then tells her she can put her shoes and socks back on.

He takes the MRI film that Goodman's brought him from Dr. Saltz and clips it up against a thing that's a box with a light in it. Again, Goodman sees the image of his daughter's brain, repeated over and over again. He watches Dr. Gendel study whatever it is he's looking for.

Finally, Dr. Gendel turns the light off and unclips the film. He speaks to someone on his intercom phone. Goodman tries to hear what's being said, but he can't make it out. It seems to have become suddenly hot in the room; Goodman has to dry the palms of his hands on his trouser legs. He's aware of a high-pitched ringing noise in his ears, wonders how long he's been hearing it.

A nurse comes into the room holding a yellow lollipop. She offers it to Kelly, who looks at her father for approval before accepting it.

"Why don't you come with me so your daddy can talk with the doctor?" she asks Kelly. It takes some prodding from Goodman, but eventually Kelly lets the nurse take her by the hand.

Dr. Gendel waits until the door closes and they're alone. "I'm afraid there may be something going on here," he says. "In addition to the shadow we see in the films, your daughter has a spot in her right eye. That could be indicative of pressure somewhere in the brain. One possibility is a growth of some sort. But because the MRI was done without contrast, it's difficult to tell."

"Contrast?"

"Yes. Contrast is when they inject a dye into the spinal fluid. It makes things stand out better in the film. Frankly, it would have been better if they'd done that."

"This growth," Goodman forces himself to say. "You're talking about a tumor."

"That's one possibility," Dr. Gendel acknowledges. "But by no means a certainty."

"What do we do?"

"Well, we could start with another MRI."

"With contrast?"

"With contrast. But even that might not tell us what we want to know. I'd like to do a lumbar puncture first, see what that shows us." He says it matter-of-factly, like a car mechanic might say, "I'd like to check the antifreeze first."

"What's a lumbar puncture?" Goodman asks, fighting a tremor in his voice.

"You've probably heard it referred to as a spinal tap," the doctor says. "We insert a needle at the base of the spine, draw off some fluid, and analyze the cells. It's a good diagnostic tool for letting us know what's going on. In addition, it'll help relieve some of the pressure in Kelly's brain that we may be seeing here."

"It sounds very painful."

"We use a local anesthetic, so it's not as bad as it sounds. Afterward, she may have a headache for a day, but it sounds like that won't be anything new."

The ringing noise in Goodman's ears is louder than ever. "Is she going to be okay?" he asks. "She's only six." His voice breaks on the word *six*.

"If it's up to me, she will be," Dr. Gendel says, giving him a smile that Goodman knows is meant to be warm and reassuring.

On the bus ride home, they find a seat way in the back, in a corner, and Kelly makes him continue the story.

The Ballerina Princess
(Continued)

Now it came to pass that the Ballerina Princess got sick. What happened was, her head began hurting her. Now, since she was a very brave Ballerina Princess, she sometimes pretended it didn't hurt. But her grandma could tell, because she was old enough to be able to tell that kind of stuff. And her daddy could tell, too, because he was the Keeper of the Numbers, and he was generally able to figure things out. And the brave and loyal Prince Larus could tell, because he knew absolutely everything.

So after awhile, the Ballerina Princess realized she might as well say when her head hurt her, since her three best friends knew anyway. And that made things just a tiny bit better for her, because then she didn't have to worry so much anymore about being brave all the time. Instead, she could spend her time concentrating on being the happiest and most beautiful princess in all the land.

Back at home that afternoon, Goodman sits in front of his TV set and watches as the ground crew covers the infield of some stadium with a tarpaulin for the third time in two innings.

His daughter may be dying of a brain tumor. Sometime next week, they're going to stick a needle in her spine to try to find out. Dr. Gendel's fee for the procedure will be five hundred dollars. That's on top of the $250 for his office visit this afternoon. The hospital charges an additional $850, which has to be paid in advance. The unpaid MRI bill is $1,100, and he still owes Dr. Saltz $195. That's close to three thousand in medical bills alone, and that's only if there are no further tests or treatments. Which, of course, there are bound to be.

He remembers he has another meeting scheduled with Russell for seven o'clock. If only Kelly can be okay, he promises himself, I'll throw the drugs away. I'll find some other way to raise the money.

But the truth is, he has no other way. He isn't covered by Medicaid. It could take weeks or months to apply, and Dr. Gendel has made it pretty clear that Kelly doesn't *have* weeks. Even then, Goodman might not qualify for assistance. And even if he did, it would mean taking Kelly to some city hospital and putting her in the hands of some intern or resident he knows nothing about.

As these thoughts go through his mind, Michael Goodman knows he's not going to throw the drugs away. He knows he's going to have to go and meet Russell tonight.

Watching the rain Saturday afternoon, Jimmy Zelb knows that if he hangs around the house, sooner or later his wife is going to get on him about cleaning up the basement. So he calls his partner and asks him if he wants to work.

"Isn't it Saturday?" Frank Farrelli asks him.

"Yeah, yeah, it's Saturday," Zelb says. "But if I don't get outa the house, it's also gonna be divorce day."

"So pick me up," Farrelli tells him.

An hour later, they're heading south on the Major Deegan Expressway, windshield wipers slapping softly.

"Let's go see Vinnie first," Farrelli suggests.

"He's allaway downtown," Zelb says. "How 'bout we stop off and see Big Red first?"

"Good idea," Farrelli agrees.

They exit the Deegan at 138th Street and circle back up to 140th. As expected, they spot Big Red as soon as they pull into the block.

"Fucker doesn't even take rain dates off," Farrelli says.

"Guess wet money's as good as dry," Zelb observes. He's reminded of his days before the DEA, when he was a vice cop in Toledo. Back then, "wet money" was what they snatched when they'd arrested prostitutes and done body-cavity searches. He smiles at his unintended pun.

Zelb pulls the car to the curb alongside Big Red. Farrelli jumps out and grabs him, spins him around, and forces him down onto the hood of the car, where he handcuffs him behind his back before throwing him bodily into the backseat of the car. They drive off.

As soon as they're out of the area, Farrelli unlocks the handcuffs and removes them.

"Good thing I recognized you, man," Big Red says to Farrelli, whom he towers over, even sitting alongside him. "I mighta squashed you othawise."

"Thanks for sparing me," Farrelli says.

Zelb continues driving. "What's going on?" he asks.

"Nothin', man," Big Red says.

"Not the answer we wanna hear," Zelb tells him.

"What can I tell you?" Big Red complains.

Zelb hits the brakes. Both Big Red and Farrelli slide forward against the back of the front seat. Zelb grabs Big Red by the throat.

"You better tell me *something*, mister," he tells him. "I got a boss who wants cases. You're gonna get off your fat butt and give us something, or your license is *history*."

Big Red pulls loose. "Easy, No Neck, easy," he says. "Matterafact, I'm workin' on somethin' for you right now. Should know in a week or so."

"Fuck a week or so!" Zelb roars. "We're coming back to see you *Monday*. And if you don't have something by then, my partner's not gonna take the cuffs off you. Got that?"

"I'll see what I can do."

"Don't see," Zelb says. "Just *do*."

It's still raining lightly as Goodman makes his way to the park for his seven o'clock meeting with Russell. He's halfway there when the thought suddenly occurs to him that maybe he's supposed to be bringing the drugs with him, so the deal can be done on the spot.

He toys with the idea of going back and getting them, but then he remembers his father's superstition. Besides, he decides, if Russell shows up with his buyer, Goodman can always go get the drugs and be back in fifteen minutes.

Once more, he stands by the river, waiting for Russell. This time, there's no uniformed police officer patrolling the area. The rain seems to have kept just about everyone away. The only people in sight are an old black woman looking for cans in the trash containers and two white guys fishing a block or so to the south. He shudders at the thought of eating anything caught in these waters. And the guys don't look that desperate, either: One's a big bruiser with a baseball cap; the other's thinner, hatless, with short red hair.

The breeze is still coming off the river, occasionally blowing a fine mist against Goodman's face. The forecast is for heavier rain tonight, so he hopes Russell isn't too late. He likes walking in the rain, but standing around in it getting soaked suddenly doesn't seem like much fun.

He watches a Circle Line sight-seeing boat move downriver. It looks almost empty; whatever tourists are on board must be inside. Then he notices a couple on deck, a man and a woman huddled under a yellow poncho. They wave in his direction as the boat passes. Goodman looks behind him to see whom they might be waving at, but there's no one there, so he turns back to them and returns their wave. He squints into the mist, trying to make out their faces, trying to tell if they're lovers or friends, but in the darkness he's unable to make out their features. He settles for lovers, oblivious to the weather, and he envies their shared intimacy.

It's almost 7:30 by the time Russell arrives. "Sorry, man. Trains are all messed up," he explains.

"No problem," Goodman says, even though by this time he's thoroughly drenched and beginning to shiver. "What's the story?"

"The story is this," Russell says, looking around with a nervousness Goodman hasn't noticed until now. But the old lady has moved on to other trash cans, and the two fishermen are the only people in sight. "The deal goes down tonight."

"Tonight?" Goodman asks. "It's supposed to rain even harder."

"Ezzackly," Russell smiles. "Rainy Sataday night, my man says there won't be a narc on the street."

"What time?"

"Midnight." Russell smiles again. "My man says that's when the cops change shifts. They all be in the station house, doin' their roll call an' shit."

It does seem to make sense to Goodman, who actually hasn't given much thought to the police, other than the one uniformed cop who passed by last time. "Where do we meet?" he asks.

"Right back here," Russell says. "You have the kilo, my man'll have the twenny-five. It's what we call cash and carry."

"You'll be here?" Goodman asks. Now that the deal is fast becoming a reality, he feels suddenly anxious.

"I dunno," Russell says, looking around again. "It's up to my man. But if I'm not, you'll spot him. Great big guy. He'll walk up to you, tell you I sent him."

"What's his name?"

"Better you don't know his name, he don't know yours." Better for botha you."

All this seems to be happening too fast for Goodman. "You sure this is going to work?" he asks.

"Hey, man," Russell smiles. "This is what I *do*. You just be sure you remember my five thousand, okay?"

"Okay," Goodman nods. "How do I find you to give you that?"

"We meet back here tomorrow, one in the aftanoon, okay?"

"Okay." Goodman feels as if all he's been doing is saying okay, like he's strapped in on some amusement park ride that's started moving, and now it's too late to get off.

"They're moving," Daniel Riley tells Ray Abbruzzo, and they both begin to reel in their lines.

Goodman and Russell split up at York Avenue, Russell angling northwest to the subway, Goodman continuing home. He walks with his hat pulled down hard and the collar of his jacket turned up to protect him against the wind and rain at his back. He is totally oblivious to the dark-haired man and the redheaded man who follow him.

He makes one stop, at the corner of Second Avenue, for a newspaper, a package of instant soup, a loaf of bread, and a can of cat food. It's almost dark by the time he enters his building.

"Home sweet home," Abbruzzo says to Riley as they watch the door close behind the man who's met with Russell.

"Now show us which apartment," says Riley.

They stand in the rain across the street, fishing rods in their hands. A minute goes by, two minutes, three.

"Maybe this guy's a fuckin' *mole*," Abbruzzo says. "Lives in the fuckin' *dark.*"

But finally a light goes on in the corner window of the top floor. A moment later, they can make out the silhouette of the man they've just followed, as he removes his jacket and shakes the rain off it.

"Bingo," says Ray Abbruzzo.

"Let's get outa here," says Daniel Riley.

Cold and wet and tired, they do just that. But to their credit, they avoid the temptation to head for their homes this rainy evening; instead, they drive downtown to 80 Centre Street. Their aim is simple: to get a search

warrant for the left-front apartment on the fifth floor of the building of
the guy they've already nicknamed J. D. Mole.

But in their haste and their fatigue, in their cold and wet condition,
they never pause to wonder just why it was that it took the guy a full six
minutes to climb four flights of stairs.

It doesn't take Michael Goodman six minutes to climb four flights of stairs,
of course; it takes him only one. The first five minutes he spends in the
basement, opening his storage locker, unzipping his black duffel bag, removing one of the blue plastic packages, and then replacing everything
as it was before.

Russell Bradford is cold and wet, too, but he isn't about to go home. From
Ninety-sixth Street, Russell heads directly for the Bronx, for 140th Street.
Russell smells money, twenty thousand dollars of it.

When he gets into the block, he doesn't see Big Red in his usual spot,
but he does see Tito. Tito tells him Red's been expecting him, is waiting
for him in the McDonald's on Walton Avenue. Russell walks the three
blocks. It's dark, and the streetlights are reflected on the wet pavement.

He enters the McDonald's and looks around for Big Red. He spots him
at a table in the back. To Russell's surprise, Red's not alone; he's sitting
with a guy Russell's never seen before.

Big Red sees Russell and motions him over, points to an empty chair
at the table. Russell sits down, eyes the half-eaten burgers and fries. He's
hungry, but he knows better than to say so.

Big Red is the first to speak. "Sup, Russell?" he says.

"Sup, Red?"

"This here's Hammer," says Big Red. Russell and Hammer nod to each
other. Hammer seems to be almost as big as Big Red, though it's hard to
tell, since they're sitting down. He's not too dark, has a beard and mustache. There's an ugly scar on his neck.

"How we doin'?" Big Red asks Russell.

"We doin' good," Russell tells him proudly. "The thing is set up for midnight, jus like you said."

"By the river?"

"By the river."

"Solid," Big Red says. "Tell me what this dude looks like."

"He's Caucasian," Russell says. "Short, kinda weak-lookin'. Got this hair looks like Brillo."

"How old?"

"I dunno." Russell's not too good at ages. "Hard to tell with Caucasians. Thirty-five, maybe?"

Hammer speaks for the first time. "Does he pack?" he asks Russell.

"Pack?" Russell smiles. "This guy wooden know which end of a piece a bullet comes outa."

"How do you know he ain't the Man?" Hammer again.

"You see this guy," Russell tells him, "you gonna laugh you ever axsed that question."

"You betta be right, or you gonna be one sorry nigga."

"You see for yourself."

Hammer leans forward and gets into Russell's face. "I ain't about seein' for myself," he says. "That's your job, and you fuckin' well betta know what you talkin' about."

"Chill," says Big Red in a soothing voice, causing Hammer to sit back. "Russell's done good. It's all gonna go down nice an' easy." He streches out "nice an' easy."

"You want me there for the introduction?" Russell asks.

"No," Big Red says, "we'll take it from here. We'll hook up with you tomorrow."

Russell knows he's dismissed. He gets up and leaves, heads home. But this time tomorrow, he tells him himself, I'll be one rich man.

Still, he could have used a burger, a couple of *fries,* at least.

Ray Abbruzzo and Daniel Riley sit in a large room with Assistant District Attorney Maggie Kennedy and begin drawing up the papers for a search warrant. Abbruzzo does most of the talking. Kennedy takes notes while she listens.

"We got this anonymous call from a citizen," he tells her, "that this guy's been dealing pure heroin out of his apartment. Gives us the exact location. So we begin a surveillance of him. Sure enough, pretty soon we seen him meet with three or four customers."

"Were you able to observe any sales?" she asks.

"Yeah, yeah," Abbruzzo says. "Coupla sales."

"Did you arrest any of the buyers?"

"Uh, no."

"Why not?"

"We didn't wanna blow the thing," Abbruzzo explains. "This guy's very cautious."

"*Very* cautious," Riley echoes.

"We think he may be Italian," Abbruzzo tells her. "Like *connected* Italian, you know what I mean?"

"What makes you believe that he keeps the heroin in his apartment?" she asks.

"The anonymous caller told us."

"That was a while ago," she notes. "Anything else?"

"Yeah," Abbruzzo says. "We see him leave his place with packages, meet his customers, and do the transactions. He always comes back empty-handed. Gotta be the apartment."

"Gotta be," Riley agrees.

"Do you know his name?" Kennedy asks.

"Like I said, the guy's very secretive," Abbruzzo tells her. "But we've got his *street* name." Here he looks around, as though he's fearful someone might overhear him. Then he leans forward and, lowering his voice to a whisper, confides in her. "They call him 'the Mole.' "

"The *Mole?*"

"Shhhhhh," Abbruzzo cautions her. "This is *big.*"

"The guy rarely sees daylight," Riley explains.

Kennedy sits back and looks over her notes. "Well," she says finally, "it's a little on the thin side. But I guess we've got enough probable cause to take a shot at it."

By ten o'clock, Goodman's pacing about his apartment. But because his apartment is so tiny, pacing involves a lot of turns and a fair amount of skill, and more than once he manages to bump a shin on his coffee table or clip an elbow navigating the bathroom door.

He knows this is his very last chance to back out of the deal. And he also knows how absurdly simple it would be to do just that. All he has to do is not show up. With no other way of finding Russell, that'll be the end of it; his career as a drug dealer will be over before it's ever begun.

But by now, he knows he *is* going to show up. He doesn't know if it's just for Kelly, either. He has a vague awareness that he's also doing this to fulfill some peculiar need of *his.*

The thought catches him somewhat by surprise. Saving his daughter is one thing. Even yielding to a golden opportunity is forgivable. But what is this part of him that suddenly has his heart pumping in anticipation of an act that, by all rights, should fill him with nothing but dread and self-loathing? Is this Michael Goodman's great adventure, that life-altering experience that always seems to happen to the other guy? Is this his walk on the wild side?

He pictures himself in a movie scene, the hero (yes, the hero—not once does he stop to consider the possibility that he's really the villain) about to go out and face his defining moment of truth.

He goes into his bathroom, faces the mirror of the medicine cabinet. A short, slightly balding, wiry-haired, bespectacled middle-aged accountant stares back at him. His heart slows down a bit, the spell broken.

For now, at least.

At three minutes past eleven, Detective Raymond Abbruzzo stands in part AR-3 of Manhattan Criminal Court, more commonly referred to as Night Court, and raises his right hand.

"Detective," says Acting Supreme Court Justice Carol Berkman, "do you swear to the truth of the contents of this affidavit?"

Abbruzzo looks the judge straight in the eye. "Yes, I do," he says.

She signs the warrant, complete with a "no-knock" provision authorizing the officers to enter the premises without first announcing their purpose and authority.

Outside the courtroom, the warrant in his hand, Abbruzzo turns to his partner. "Now, or first thing Monday?"

Riley seems to think carefully for a moment. Then he says, "I'm not sure, but I think I got a dentist appointment Monday morning. My gums—"

"Okay, okay," Abbruzzo says. "Let's go for it. We can call for some backup on the way uptown."

Riley checks his watch, realizes they've been on overtime for three hours already. "Good news for the old paycheck," he says.

"Bad news for the Mole," says Abbruzzo.

The rain has turned back to sleet and is falling more heavily as Goodman makes his way back to the river for what will be the last of these strange trips he's been making for what seems like weeks. Still without an umbrella, he leans into the weather, his hands balled into fists inside the pockets of his jacket. As he walks, he can feel the package, stuffed down into the front of his undershorts like he'd seen Russell do it, safe there from the rain.

He knows he's early, but doesn't bother checking the time. To do so would require him to extract his hand and expose his watch to the elements. Never mind, he thinks. He'll wait however long he must; for twenty thousand dollars, he can afford to get wet.

There's no one in sight as he reaches the river's edge. Russell—or Russell's "man"—was right: No police officers are going to be strolling by at midnight on Saturday in the pouring rain. At the same time, however, Goodman's struck by how dark and cold it is, and by how very alone he feels.

What light there is comes from streetlamps behind him, and the movements of branches in the wind cause shadows to dance darkly and wildly. He grasps the icy railing in front of him, imagines he's the captain of a boat, sailing through a stormy sea on a moonless night. He peers out across the waves and studies the lights on the far shore. Somehow, he has to navigate this crossing, has to bring his troubled craft safely into port. He blinks the rainwater out of his eyes, tries to get a fix on the brightest light he sees, the beacon he'll aim for.

"Good evening." The voice startles him, and he whirls around to see a very large black man standing there. "You gonna catch cold standin' out in the rain like this."

"I'll be okay," Goodman says, aware of his own heartbeat. He notices a second man standing behind the first, a bit to one side. He's also black, though lighter-skinned. He's almost as tall as the first one, but not as broad. Neither of them is Russell; in addition to being bigger, they look much older, more sure of themselves.

"I told Russell we gonna try to help you out," says the first man. He's clearly the one in charge, no doubt Russell's "man."

"Right," Goodman says.

"You alone?"

Goodman nods.

"No *po*-leece hidin' in the bushes?"

"No," Goodman says.

"You got the thing?"

Goodman knows better than to say yes. Instead, he asks, "You got the money?"

Russell's man smiles in a friendly way and reaches into his pocket. He comes out with a wad of money that reminds Goodman of Manny's wad at the Bronx Tire Exchange. Only this one is twice as fat. And while Manny's wad was made up of twenties and smaller bills, this one seems to be all hundreds, if the outer bills are any indication.

"Is it all there?" Goodman asks, feeling surprisingly in control of things.

The man smiles again. "All twenny-five large ones," he says, offering it to Goodman. "Count it if you like."

Goodman decides this would be an unprofessional sign of distrust on his part. "That's okay," he says. He reaches down into his pants and retrieves the package. He extends it toward the man, along with his other empty hand, palm up. A simultaneous exchange, he figures—cash and carry, just like Russell said.

Only something goes wrong. The next thing Goodman knows, he's sitting on the walkway, both hands empty. He's aware of a throbbing ache on the left side of his head. Then he's lying on his back, the rain falling onto his face. Someone's pulling at his feet. He fights to catch his breath, is unable to speak. His first thought is that he's being dragged by his ankles, to be thrown into the river or dumped into the bushes. He feels his shoes come loose, then realizes his *pants* are being pulled off, as well.

"Lissen good, my man," comes a voice directly over him. Goodman squints to see, but, looking up into the sleet, he can only make out the silhouette of a large body straddling his own.

"Here's the story, Mr. Drug Dealer. You gonna lie right here for one hour. One hour from now, we gonna come back an' check on you, make sure you still here. We takin' your pants for *in*surance," he's told. "You come afta us, won't be like this again. Won't be about *clothes* nex time."

Big Red and Hammer sit in the Bentley on 125th Street, the heat turned up high. Big Red examines the package in his lap.

"Lookin' good," he says. He fishes the wad of money from his pocket and counts off ten one-hundred-dollar bills, which he folds and hands to Hammer. The remainder of the bills are mostly singles, with a few fives and tens mixed in.

"Thanks for the help," he tells Hammer.

"Anytime," Hammer says, letting himself out of the Bentley.

"Later, man," says Big Red.

"Later."

Big Red picks up a soggy pair of pants and shoes from the floor of the car. The shoes are cheap loafers with a Thom McAn label; he pushes a button that rolls down his window, then throws the shoes out onto the street. He's about to do the same with the pants when he feels a lump in the back pocket. He reaches in and removes a wallet made of imitation leather. He unfolds it and checks the contents: two twenties and three singles, which he pockets; a Social Security card; a telephone calling card, which he ignores; a photograph of a little girl; and a driver's license with a new address inked in.

Big Red smiles. He reaches for his car phone and punches in some numbers. He waits until a male voice says hello.

"Wake up, No Neck," he says. "It's me."

"Shit. What time is it?" the voice asks him.

"Never you mind what time it is," Big Red tells him. "Just write down this name an' address."

"Wait a sec," the voice says. "Okay, go ahead."

Big Red reads the name and new address from the driver's license.

"What's the story?" the voice asks him.

"Guy deals kilos," Big Red says. "Kilos of pure shit. But you better move quick on this one. I hear he's had a bad experience and may be goin' outa bizness real soon. And No Neck?"

"Yeah?"

"You do some good on this one, don't you be forgettin' who your friends are." Then he clicks off. He throws the pants out the window and is about to do the same with the wallet. But at the last moment, he decides against that. Instead, he takes it and, reaching under the front passenger seat, places it in a compartment he's had specially hollowed out among the springs.

Goodman lies helpless on his back in the cold, wet darkness, waiting for the two black men to deliver whatever threat or punch or kick or other humiliation is next. But nothing happens. He lets a few minutes go by before he pulls himself up into a sitting position. The whole left side of his face, from his hairline to his chin, is numb. His pants and shoes are nowhere to be found. His undershorts are twisted halfway between his knees and his ankles. He rises to a crouch, straightening them and pulling them into place, so that at least he's covered there.

He looks around, hoping that they've thrown his missing clothing somewhere nearby, but his vision is blurred, either from the rain or from some blow to his head that the numbness tells him he must have sustained. He feels as if his left ear is bleeding, but at least he can hear out of it.

He gropes around for a minute before giving up hope of finding his pants and shoes. His socks make a squishing sound with every step he takes, and his feet quickly become numb from the cold. His undershorts are soaked through and stick to his skin. He strips off his jacket and ties it around his waist, Boy Scout–style, so that it covers his butt. He begins the long walk home, freezing, wet, tired, and totally humiliated. He's sorry he ever pried open the spare tire of the Camry, sorry he ever met Russell. He promises himself that first thing tomorrow morning he'll take the rest of the packages from his storage locker and dump them into the river he's just come from.

But it turns out that tomorrow morning will have to wait: This night is not yet over for Michael Goodman. As soon as he enters his block, drenched and shivering, but grateful to have made it home without further incident, he sees half a dozen cars double-parked not far from the stoop. One of them is a blue-and-white NYPD car; several of the others have long radio antennas and red lights mounted atop their dashboards. Goodman wonders which building they've responded to, and what the problem is.

He recalls how once, as a child, he was lying in his bed waiting for sleep to come. From far away, he heard the wail of a siren and the telltale horn of a fire truck. He listened as the sounds grew louder and louder, until they came right by his house. He waited for them to speed by on their way to some fire, but instead they slowed and stopped right there, right downstairs. By then, he could smell smoke and hear voices out on the street. He remembers his father coming into the room, telling him to stay in bed, assuring him that everything was all right. But as he lay there, covers pulled up tightly to his chin, the faint odor of smoke reaching his nostrils, he absolutely knew that at any second flames would burst through his door and swallow him up.

Now he has the sensation that he's somehow reliving the experience, only this time it's in reverse. As he draws closer and closer, he begins to realize it's his own building that the police have been drawn to. And as he looks up, using his hand to shield the falling rain from his eyes, he can see that the lights are on in his apartment, lights he knows he turned off on his way out.

A sickening feeling spreads through him. He's considering walking on, pretending he's just passing by, when he hears a man's voice.

"You live in there, pal?"

He looks around but sees nobody. Then he hears a car door open, sees a man approaching him.

"I asked if you live there," the man says.

"Yes," Goodman says, too cold and too exhausted to lie.

"Which apartment?" the man asks. He holds a folded newspaper across his face as protection from the rain, and Goodman can't see his eyes.

Goodman points to his window. "That one," he says.

The man waves his newspaper at Goodman's legs. "Wanna tell me why you're walking around dressed like a half-wit?" he asks.

Goodman can only shrug.

The man pulls what looks like a walkie-talkie out of his back pocket and holds it up to his mouth. "Ray?" he says into it.

He's answered by a staticky "Yeah."

"Looks like Mr. Mole has come back to his burrow. Want me to bring him up?"

Another "Yeah."

Before they even reach the fifth floor, Goodman sees his door has been broken open. Police officers—some in uniform, others in street clothes—are milling about the hallway. Inside, he counts eight of them before losing track. They've set up floodlights, running electric cords across his living room floor. His belongings have been trashed: It's like the burglary, only far worse. The officer who's walked him upstairs takes him over to the one he calls Ray.

"Whadda we got here?" Ray asks.

Goodman squints into the floodlights, speechless.

"Gotta be an EDP," the first officer says. An EDP is an emotionally disturbed person, the NYPD's terminology for a head case. "He just kinda wandered up. I don't think the fucker even noticed it was raining."

"Great," Ray says, shaking his head back and forth slowly. It's clear he's tired.

"Anything here?" the first one asks, looking around the room.

"Nothing but a kitten from hell that ambushed me from the top of the refrigerator." He displays the side of his neck, which bears two rows of tiny teeth marks and dried blood where the skin's been broken. He turns to Goodman. "You live here?"

Goodman nods absently.

"What's your name?"

"Michael. Michael Goodman."

The one named Ray nods, as if he already knew that and was just testing.

"Got your keys on you?"

Goodman looks at him. Can this mean they've already discovered the duffel bag with the rest of the kilos?

"Hell-*o*," Ray says, waving a hand in front of Goodman's face to get his attention. "Your keys?"

It dawns on Goodman that it's keys—not kilos—he's being asked about. After considerable effort, he manages to find the pocket of his jacket. He fishes out his keys and displays them.

"That's it?" Ray asks. "Three keys, is all you got?"

"I guess so," Goodman says.

"Whatta they go to?"

Goodman fingers each key in turn. "This is the downstairs door. This is—was—my door. And this is my mailbox downstairs."

"No car?"

"No."

"No office keys? No safe-deposit box?"

"No."

Ray takes the keys, tosses them to one of the uniformed officers. "Check his mailbox downstairs," he says. "Then we're outa here. Fuckin' lunatic."

Goodman says a silent prayer of thanks to whoever invented the combination lock.

Ray looks down at Goodman's skinny legs and wet socks, then up at the stupid grin on his face. "Fuckin' psycho," he mutters. Then, to the other officers, he shouts, "That's a wrap, fellas! Let's go home."

Goodman watches as they turn off the floodlights and break down the tripods that held them. Within five minutes, they're gone. He inspects the lock on his door, finds it's broken and the security chain snapped. He knows he should make a trip to the all-night grocery store and buy a lock of some sort, but he's simply too exhausted. He walks to his couch and sits down. From nowhere, his attack cat appears in his lap and looks up at him. One of its eyes is swollen shut, and there's dried blood around its nose. Goodman strokes the kitten's back.

"Good Pop-Tart, good Pop-Tart, good Pop-Tart," he says over and over again.

By Sunday, the rain and sleet have stopped, and a warming sun has begun to dry things out.

Goodman spends most of the morning cleaning up his apartment and helping Tony the Super repair his broken door. The new locks cost him $35.76. He tips Tony ten dollars, and can tell from the look on Tony's face that he'd hoped for more. But Goodman's down to his last few dollars, which he needs: Today's the day he gets to spend with his daughter.

He picks Kelly up shortly before noon, early as usual. She seems to be in good spirits and, according to his mother-in-law, hasn't complained about her head since Friday night. Still, as soon as they get outside, he notices that she winces, as though the sudden sunlight seems to bother her.

They walk to the park. Not Carl Schurz Park—Goodman has vowed never to set foot in it again—but Central Park. They visit a little playground that has always been one of Kelly's favorites, but she doesn't want to go on the swings. He doesn't ask her why, but he finds himself watching her constantly for signs of pain. At one point, he thinks he sees her cocking her head back and forth, as though something's interfering with her view. He wonders if it could be the spot Dr. Gendel saw in her eye. But again, he doesn't want to say anything.

They walk onto the Sheep Meadow, but the grass is wet and the dirt muddy from all the rain, and Goodman carries his daughter so she won't ruin her shoes. She puts her head against his neck, and as he feels the

softness of her hair, he asks nothing more than to be able to carry his little girl always, to be able to protect her from spots in her eye and tumors
in her brain for as long as his arms can hold her.

They sit in the sun on the rocks and watch children running and nan-
nies pushing carriages and dogs chasing balls and Frisbees. They talk about
Kelly's school, but she's missed so many days lately that she doesn't have
much to tell him. He asks her if she wants lunch, but she says she'd like
a pretzel from the pretzel man instead. He spends $2.50 buying them two
pretzels, ends up finishing all of his and half of hers when she says she's
full. Then she looks up at him expectantly, as if to say he's put it off long
enough.

The Ballerina Princess
(Continued)

Now, because of her headaches, it became necessary for the Ballerina
Princess to visit some doctors and have some tests. And I must tell you,
these tests were no fun! Some of the doctors would put the Ballerina
Princess into a big machine that could take magical pictures of her head;
and other doctors would hit her little knees with rubber hammers and
stick her little toes with safety pins; and still other doctors would shine
magic flashlights into her little eyes.

But all the time, the Ballerina Princess was very good. Even when
she got tired of all the tests—even when some of the things they did to
her seemed scary and downright mean—she kept being good, because
she knew the doctors were only trying to help her, trying to figure out
a way to make the headaches go away.

And her grandma kept taking good care of her, even if she didn't
know any good stories, and the brave and loyal Prince Larus never left
her side. And her daddy, who loved her more than anything in the kingdom—more than all the castles and the banners and the unicorns and
the winged horses—her daddy promised her that he would work as
hard as he could at his magic numbers, so that he, too, could do his part
in making the headaches go away forever.

By two o'clock, Kelly can barely stay awake and, though the day
seems warm to Goodman, her fingers and the tip of her nose are cold to
the touch. He picks her up once again, and they head for her grandmother's.

* * *

Later that afternoon, Goodman meets up with his navy buddies at Krulewich's apartment. There's no baseball game on—the World Series has apparently ended, unbeknownst to Goodman—and the Giants aren't playing till tomorrow night, on *Monday Night Football.* So Lehigh Valley makes good on his promise to teach them how to play hearts.

They sit around Krulewich's card table, a pretty close relative of Goodman's. Lehigh deals the cards. Krulewich holds his up to his thick glasses. The Whale gets as close to the table as his girth will permit. Goodman, whose facility with numbers makes him a pretty good cardplayer (he and Shirley used to play bridge with her parents), listens as Lehigh explains the rules.

"Everybody gets thirteen cards," he begins. "Whoever gets the two of clubs lays it down. It goes around the table. You got a club, you gotta follow suit. You don't, you can play anything you want. Each heart is worth a point. Only"—and here Lehigh shakes a finger of warning at them—"points are *bad.* There're twenty-six points altogether—thirteen hearts, plus the queen of spades, which is worth another thirteen points."

"All by herself?" Goodman asks.

"All by herself," Krulewich says. "So the winner is the one who gets stuck with the least points."

"So all you gotta do is dump your hearts every chance you get," the Whale decides. "Pretty fuckin' borin', if you ask me."

"Well," Lehigh says, "it would be, except for one thing."

"What's that?" Goodman asks.

"Shooting the moon."

"Hey!" the Whale protests. "I ain't flashin' my butt for a buncha guys!"

"You don't hafta flash your butt to shoot the moon," Lehigh explains. "You gotta get all the points."

"All twenty-six?" someone asks.

"All twenty-six." Lehigh nods. "Do that, everybody else gets stuck with fifty points."

"Suppose you don't make it?" Goodman asks. "Suppose you come close but you only end up with, say, twenty-three or twenty-four?"

"Tough luck," Lehigh says. "You don't get 'em all, they count *against* you. Which is why you better be damn sure you can make it before you try to shoot the moon."

They try a few hands. At first, there's a lot of grumbling. Krulewich has trouble seeing the cards that have been played, and they have to call out each card to him. The Whale wants to bet on the final score. Goodman, who's able to keep track of every card that's been played, is soon winning. After four hands, he's comfortably ahead.

KRULEWICH	36
WHALE	29
GOODMAN	15
LEHIGH	24

They decide to play one more hand before calling out for burgers.

Goodman picks up his cards and studies them. Only three hearts—the two, the four, and the nine. No queen of spades, and no spade higher than the queen. He knows he's home free—all he has to do is to discard his hearts every opportunity he gets.

As play begins, it's clear that everyone else has the same game plan. Krulewich and the Whale dump their hearts, too, but Goodman's so far ahead of them on points that he knows they can't catch him. As for Lehigh, he runs into a streak of bad luck, and is soon groaning as he gets stuck with hearts he's unable to underplay.

"Tough luck, sucker!" laughs the Whale, playing his last heart, the jack, on Lehigh's king.

It's not until the final few tricks that they realize what's been going on. By then, it's too late to stop Lehigh from winning all thirteen hearts and the queen of spades. Final score:

KRULEWICH	86
WHALE	79
GOODMAN	65
LEHIGH	24

That night, secure behind his repaired door and new locks, as Michael Goodman prays for his daughter to be all right, he remembers he was supposed to meet Russell back in Carl Schurz Park earlier in the day. He feels guilty for a moment for not having showed up. Then he tells himself that, for all he knows, Russell was in on the plan to steal the drugs from him. He realizes how stupid he's been to trust someone who only days ago was trying to mug him. He guesses he's lucky to be alive still. He vows to throw away the rest of the drugs first chance he gets. He'll do it tomorrow.

{ 19 }

By Monday morning, Pop-Tart's eye is less swollen and he (and Goodman's finally gotten around to checking, and has confirmed that the kitten he's thought of until now as an *it* is definitely a *he*) can open his eye slightly. Goodman tries dabbing a bit of old antibiotic cream into the eye, but Pop-Tart will have none of that.

As for his own wounds, Goodman sees in his mirror that the left side of his face is slightly larger than the right, but you really have to look to be able to notice. The numbness is gone, replaced by a dull ache, and there's no more dried blood, though he wonders if he's hearing out of his left ear as well as before.

The loss of his pants, shoes, and wallet is another nuisance Goodman has to deal with. The pants were old anyway: He'd worn them because he didn't want to expose a newer pair to the rain. But the shoes were new ones, and he'll have to replace them at some point. As for his wallet, he'll miss the money that was in it, but with no car, he has little need of his driver's license. He'd left his credit card case at home, since the cards had become totally worthless anyway. He remembers being thankful walking back from Carl Schurz Park that his keys had been in his jacket pocket rather than in his pants, and he laughs now at remembering how he hadn't needed them to get back inside after all.

By 12:15, he says good-bye to Pop-Tart, locks up his new lock, and heads to work, grateful for the opportunity to earn another hundred dollars.

First thing Monday morning, even before getting out of bed, Jimmy Zelb remembers Big Red's phone call. Wasting no time, he hits the memory button on his phone that dials his partner's number.

After a single ring, he hears "Farrelli is speaking." He knows Frank copied that line from some movie or something he'd seen, but Jimmy forgets the details.

"Hey, Frankie."

"What's up, Jimmy?"

"Ready to work?"

"Now?"

"I'll let you wake up first, if you insist."

"I guess so," is about as enthusiastic as Farrelli's willing to get.

"I got a call from the Red Man," Zelb tells him. "I think he's got something good for us, but it may take some doing. How 'bout I come by and pick you up in thirty?"

"Make it forty-five?" Farrelli pleads.

"Forty," Zelb says. "And I think we might want to use Cruz on this one, too, so watch what you say."

"No problem," Farrelli says. Cruz is relatively new to the DEA, having come over from the state police less than a year ago, and has only been in Group Two about six weeks. They both know that when you're working with a new agent, you try to do things pretty much by the book. You can't be too careful: You can never be too sure who you're dealing with until you've worked with them a lot and know they're someone you can really trust. Every once in a while, Inspection will sneak one of their people into a field group just to see who's on the take.

Manny isn't in today—perhaps his boil is acting up again—but he's left an envelope for Goodman. Inside is a list of things he'd like Goodman to do this afternoon, like balancing the checkbook, figuring out the right amount of withholding tax for a couple of employees, and trying to find out a way to get a tax deduction or something for giving away worthless tires that can't be recapped anymore. Also in the envelope are forms for

Goodman to complete so that he'll be able to sign checks when Manny's not around. And five twenty-dollar bills.

With the office all to himself, Goodman gets absorbed in his work. The truth is, he's a natural with numbers, and he likes dealing with them. The way some people get joy from completing a difficult crossword puzzle or figuring out the ending of a mystery story—that's how Goodman feels when the numbers in the credit column add up the same as those in the debit column, to the penny. He balances the checkbook (no easy feat, because the legendary Marlene had done her best to translate everything into hieroglyphics), prepares the forms for the withholding, and—with a few phone calls—locates a rubber salvage company that will actually pay by the pound to pick up surplus tires.

With nothing else to do and a half hour to kill, Goodman phones his mother-in-law. Kelly seems okay, she says. And Mount Sinai Hospital called to say that Goodman and Kelly have an appointment for the spinal tap Friday morning.

For the fourth time in two days, Russell Bradford goes to 140th Street in search of Big Red. On each of the previous three trips, Russell has encountered either Tito (who's back out on the street on bail) or someone else who works for Red. Each time, they've told him Red wasn't around and they had no idea when he'd be back.

Russell knows this could be good: It could mean that Big Red is busy cutting and bagging up the product, or even moving it somewhere else. But at the same time, he can't shake the feeling that Red is purposely avoiding him in order to put off having to pay him his fifteen thousand.

Now, as Russell comes into the block, he spots Big Red in his usual spot, and his doubts are put aside. It takes Red a moment to notice Russell, but as soon as he does, he waves him over.

"Yo, Russell, where you been?"

"I been around," Russell says. "Didn' nobody tell you I was lookin' for you?"

"No, man."

"How'd it go?" Russell asks.

"Good," Big Red tells hims. "It went real good."

"And—"

"And you want what's rightfully yours."

Russell smiles sheepishly.

"And so you shall have it," Big Red says. "Ten o'clock tonight, you be at a Hunner and Twenny-ninth Street, over by the Hudson River."

Russell frowns.

"You want big bills or small ones?" Big Red asks him.

Russell shrugs his shoulders. He hasn't thought about that.

"Better off with small ones," Big Red tells him. "Twennies an' tens. Harder to hide, but easier to spend."

"Okay," Russell agrees. "Small ones." The conversation reassures him; he can almost feel the money.

"Good. Bring a bag with you, okay? A strong plastic bag. Best to have two, so you can make a *double* bag, okay?"

"Okay," Russell says. This sounds good.

It's not too long after Russell leaves the block that Big Red calls Tito and asks him to come over, take his place. As soon as that happens, Big Red goes and gets into his Bentley and drives down into Manhattan. He heads south on Lenox Avenue, then enters the Central Park Drive at 110th Street. There, he begins running red lights, slowly but deliberately. He makes it to Seventy-second Street before he hears a siren and sees red lights coming up behind him.

The officers who pull him over seem excited to have nabbed a black man in a car worth $100,000. To their surprise, the man, whose license identifies him as Dwayne Reddington, actually consents to their request to search the car; to their disappointment, they find no contraband. But they do find, through a computer check, that Mr. Reddington's license has been suspended because of two outstanding unpaid moving violations.

For the red lights, they issue him three tickets. For the suspended license, they can either arrest him or issue him a DAT, a desk-appearance ticket, directing an offender who has suitable identification on him to appear in court on a future date. Given the choice, they elect to arrest him and impound his Bentley.

The rain begins again that evening, and Goodman, who's had his fill of it over the weekend, sits in front of his TV set, watching a basketball game. Pop-Tart whines from the kitchen—which is nothing more than one end of the room, comprising a stove, a sink, and a narrow refrigerator—as a reminder that they're out of cat food. But the game is a good one, the

Knicks and Pacers tied eighty-one–all at the end of the third quarter, and he figures by the time it's over, the rain may have stopped.

Russell Bradford shows up at West 129th Street at ten o'clock sharp, the first time in his life he's been on time for anything. He sees right away that Big Red has picked a good spot. He can see cars down by 125th Street, but up here, just four blocks away, it's completely deserted. He pulls up the hood of his sweatshirt and waits for Big Red to show up with his money. In his back pocket is a double plastic bag from the A&P.

After about ten minutes, a car pulls up, but it's an old Mazda, not Big Red's Bentley. A man gets out, and right away, Russell sees it's Hammer, Big Red's friend from the other night. And he's carrying a bag that looks heavy with cash. He walks over to Russell before speaking.

"Sup, Russell?"

"Sup, Hammer?"

"Red sends his regards," Hammer says. "Said to tell you he got tied up, couldn't make it. But he asked me to give you this." And as Russell watches, Hammer reaches into the bag.

His guard lowered by dreams of wealth, it suddenly dawns on Russell that there's no money in the bag. His eyes dart first to the left, then to the right. He sees Hammer smile, sees his hand begin to come back out of the bag. Too late, Russell takes a step backward, then another. He spins around and bolts into the darkness. He gets ten feet, twenty, but suddenly there's something loose under his feet, and he's stumbling, slipping to one knee. He hears Hammer's footsteps coming up fast behind him. He pulls himself up, tries to run again. There's a brilliant flash of light and a deafening explosion, the last sight he sees and the last sound he hears before Russell Bradford becomes the second victim of the twenty kilos.

Reggie Miller scores fourteen points in the final quarter, and the Pacers beat the Knicks, 104 to 99. Pop-Tart seems to sense that the game is over and that, with it, so is Goodman's right to further procrastination. He rubs up against Goodman's legs and—when that doesn't do the trick—begins taking small bites at his ankles. Goodman gets the message. Before he leaves, though, he grabs his umbrella: enough of this walking-in-the-rain stuff.

At the store, he selects three cans of cat food, forsaking the generic type he usually buys, in favor of one called Cadillac. He's decided his new friend deserves something special. He picks out a tuna, a chicken with vegetables, and something called hearty beef stew. He also buys a container of evaporated milk, and a frozen pizza for himself. His purchases come to $12.33.

Back at his building, he unlocks the downstairs door and is about to go inside when he thinks he hears a whimper.

"Please," he says, "no more cats." The sound of his own voice causes him to wonder if maybe he isn't becoming an emotionally disturbed person after all.

But then there's a second whimper, louder than the first, and almost human. It seems to have come from the area underneath the steps, where Tony the Super keeps the garbage cans on nights there won't be a pickup. Goodman peers through the darkness but can't see anything. In spite of himself, he's unable to bring himself to ignore the sound, to turn his back on whatever it is and go inside the building. He is drawn to where it has come from, as surely as iron is drawn to a magnet.

"Hello?" he says softly, prepared for anything from police to panther. "Anybody there?" And he is answered by a sound, this time a muffled sob, decidedly human.

He sets down his bag of groceries and collapses his umbrella. He pokes his way through the garbage cans, shifting them to one side or the other. As his eyes grow more accustomed to the darkness, he finally makes out the form of a person, huddled in a sitting position up against the brick wall, knees drawn up tightly against chest, hands clasped around shins. In the dark, he can't make out if it's a man or woman, an adult or a child.

"Are you okay?" he asks.

"I don't know," comes the answer, in what Goodman judges to be the voice of a young woman.

"Do you need help?" is all he can think to ask.

She ignores his question and says instead, "Please don't hurt me."

"I'm not going to hurt you," he assures her. "Do you need an ambulance?"

"No," she begs him. "Please don't call—"

"Okay, okay," he says. He can now see that she's young—maybe in her twenties, he guesses. Her hair is wet and matted, and her face looks puffy and is streaked with dirt. "Is there anything I can do?" he asks.

There's no answer, only the same low whimpering sound that first drew his attention to her.

"Look," he tells her, "you can't stay in there. You'll freeze to death."

Nothing.

He tries to think of some way to coax her out. "If you don't come out"—What, he wonders, by the count of three?—"I'll have to call the police."

"No," she sobs again.

"Then come out," he commands.

It takes awhile, but finally she lowers her hands to her sides and uses them to push herself into a kneeling position, then a squat. He offers her a hand, but she rejects it, electing instead to crawl out by herself.

Once she's out in the open, she tries to stand, but he has to steady her, so wobbly is she on her feet. He suspects she's his own height, but it's hard to tell: She remains doubled over slightly, as though it hurts her to straighten up.

"How long have you been in there?" he asks.

"I don't know," she says. "Awhile."

"What happened?"

"Oh, nothing much," she says. "I got raped, beaten up, and left for dead."

For a moment, he thinks she's kidding, but then he realizes she isn't. "We've *got* to call the police," he says.

"No," she says. "I only came out 'cause you said you wouldn't."

Which isn't exactly how Goodman remembers it, but he lets it go. She does have a point.

"A hospital?" he suggests.

But she shakes her head. It seems pretty clear to him that she's not a big fan of municipal institutions. "Would you like to come upstairs and wash up?" He fully expects her to reject this offer, too, but she says nothing. Taking this for ambivalence, he places one hand on her elbow. "Come on," he says, "let's get you out of the rain. You've had enough to deal with already; you don't need to get pneumonia on top of everything else."

She makes a sound that comes out as half laugh, half sob. But when he applies gentle pressure to her elbow, she comes along.

It's obvious that she's in a lot of pain, and they have to take the stairs slowly. Goodman unlocks the door to his apartment, turns the light on, and leads her in. He's glad he straightened the place out, even if his visitor's in no condition to notice.

Immediately, Pop-Tart runs over and checks out the new arrival, who sags against the wall, resuming the position in which Goodman first saw her.

"This is Pop-Tart," Goodman says, wishing he'd given the kitten a more traditional name. "My name is Michael."

"I'm Carmen," she says.

In the light, he can see that there are dark circles around her eyes. Her face is bruised and flecked with dried blood, which Pop-Tart now begins to lick.

"Hey you!" Goodman scolds him. "Leave her alone." He lifts the cat and shoos him away before turning back to Carmen. "What can I get you?"

"I think I need a bathroom," she says. "I think I'm going to be sick."

This time, she lets him help her up. He leads her to the bathroom and closes the door behind her. He shakes the rain off himself and sits on the edge of his sofa.

He hears nothing from the bathroom, and the thought occurs to him that maybe he shouldn't leave her alone in there: After what she's been through, she might be suicidal. But then again, he figures, how much damage can she do to herself with one of his disposable razors?

After a moment, he hears gagging sounds coming from the bathroom, followed by flushing noises. They provide strange reassurance that she's all right, in a manner of speaking. When the sounds subside, he knocks on the door gently and asks, "You okay in there?"

He gets a "Yup" in response.

"Would you like to take a bath or a shower?"

After a minute, she opens the door. She looks very pale, and her eyes are red. "A bath would be great," she says, trying to force a smile.

He gets her a couple of clean towels and his only bathrobe, then starts the water running for her.

"Thank you, Michael," she says. "You're very sweet." She goes into the bathroom and closes the door behind her, leaving Goodman and his kitten in the living room.

"Well, Pop-Tart," he says, "I guess it's you and me on the floor tonight."

He will be only half-right, of course. Hours later, as Goodman struggles to find a comfortable position on the shag rug, wedged between the back of the sofa bed and the radiator, Pop-Tart and Carmen will be curled up together on the bed itself, deep in sleep.

The rain that has fallen most of Monday night has tapered off to fine mist by the first light of Tuesday morning. Police Officers Charlie Walsh and Eddie Johnson have been on RMP duty since midnight—actually since 2335 Monday night, since that's when the graveyard shift unofficially begins. Being on RMP duty means taking turns behind the wheel of a radio motor patrol unit, a blue and white police car, cruising the particular sector to which they've been assigned within the precinct and responding to whatever jobs the dispatcher puts out over the air.

Because it's been a rainy Monday night, the tour has been a quiet one. Monday nights are usually slow to begin with, what with the homeboys catching up on sleep and recuperating from the weekend. And rain always helps keep the perps indoors, where the potential for confrontation and mayhem is somewhat reduced.

But quiet nights tend to be long nights, and Walsh and Johnson have already been through a total of eight containers of coffee, four slices of pizza, two doughnuts, and a pack and a half of cigarettes. Now, armed with a couple of buttered rolls and two pint-sized containers of Tropicana orange juice, they pull underneath the elevated West Side Highway on 125th Street. Johnson kills the headlights.

"Hang a right," says Walsh, who's in the recorder's seat. "Don't wanna let anyone see us here and call IAD or something. Mayor might have to convene another commission."

"Right," says Johnson. "God forbid we should eat breakfast." He makes the turn and continues slowly north. To their left, the factories and apartment buildings of New Jersey are still shadows across the river; the only light is to the east, here all but blocked by the highway overhead.

"Pull over there," Walsh points, "by the end."

Johnson complies. Just as he brings the car up to the retaining wall, there's a sudden movement off to the right, followed by the bark of a dog.

"Get lost, Fido," Johnson calls, mostly out of relief.

"I once dated this woman, had a dog named Fido," Walsh says. "Only she spelled it P-H-A-E-D-E-A-U-X. Said she'd read it somewhere, thought it was cute."

"Whadid the dog think?"

"How the fuck should I know? Stupid dog prob'ly couldn't spell."

There's another bark, and this time they can make out the shapes of not one but two dogs, tugging at something heavy by the wall.

Walsh and Johnson look at each other, one of those partner-to-partner looks that needs no words. Walsh takes the paper bag holding the rolls and juice and places it on the dashboard. Each man touches his weapon and reaches for his flashlight. With one noise, each opens his door and steps out of the car.

As soon as the flashlights are trained on them, the dogs turn from whatever it is they've been pulling at.

"Shoo!" Walsh shouts, and they back off. It takes a kicking motion from Johnson to chase them.

Slowly, the officers approach. Each holds his flashlight in his left hand, his right hand resting on his still-holstered weapon. But even before they get any closer, they both know full well they won't be needing their weapons. The early-morning light is enough to show them the object that the dogs were fighting over.

What they have found, of course, is the body of Russell Bradford.

Goodman gives up sleep around six in the morning. He pulls himself to a standing position. His ribs hurt and his hipbones ache from where they've been pressed into the cold, hard floor during the night. He figures he slept for two hours, all told.

He looks over at the sofa bed and sees Carmen, face upturned, arms splayed to either side. A night's sleep seems to have helped her as much as the loss of one has harmed Goodman. Her face still looks bruised in places, but the dark circles around her eyes are less pronounced. Her hair, dirty and matted when he'd first brought her in from the rain, now looks clean and soft. It is a jet black, set off by the whiteness of Goodman's only set of sheets. Tucked against the curve of her waist is the opportunistic Pop-Tart, his eyes as tightly closed as hers.

Goodman heads for the bathroom to shower, wondering how, in less than a week's time, he's gone from a single occupant to the head of a household of three.

At the office of the Chief Medical Examiner at 520 First Avenue, the body of the young black male is fingerprinted prior to autopsy. The prints are analyzed for salient characteristics and reduced to an eleven-digit code, a combination of numbers and letters. That code is faxed to the New York State Department of Criminal Justice in Albany. Within an hour, a return fax has identified the individual from a prior arrest for farebeating.

> BRADFORD, Russell Dwayne
> NYSID#　　31577890F
> DOB　　　1-12-80
> POB　　　Bronx, NY
> Height　　72 in.
> Weight　　165 lbs
> Eyes　　　Brn

The autopsy is performed by Dr. Karen Swiddy. It is somewhere between the five hundredth and one thousandth she's done: She lost track long ago.

Some bodies stubbornly resist giving up the cause of death; a few succeed in refusing altogether, leaving the circumstances forever shrouded in mystery. Russell Bradford is not such a case. The two bullet holes in his upper back leave no doubt as to his last moments. By inserting a probe in the more superior of the holes, Dr. Swiddy is able to track the path of the bullet directly through skin and muscle and into the left chamber of the heart, where she recovers a deformed piece of lead. She initials it "S-1." She places it on a scale and records its weight as 2.7 grams, just under a tenth of an ounce, but enough to end the short life of one human being.

*　*　*

His roommates finally having awakened, Goodman stands at his stove, preparing as complete a breakfast as his modest supplies will permit: oatmeal prepared in a combination of evaporated milk and water, toast with jam—he has no toaster, but by paying close attention, he uses the broiler of his oven to brown bread perfectly—and grapefruit Tang, poured over ice cubes. For Pop-Tart, hearty beef stew combined with some of the oatmeal mixture.

It is only when she sits across from him over his card table that Goodman sees how very pretty Carmen is. The swelling on her face is gone; gone, too, is the dried blood. The bruises that remain look fairly superficial.

"You look much better," he tells her.

"Thank you." She smiles in such a way that her whole face seems part of the process—not just her mouth but also her eyes, her chin, even the line of her jaw.

"You were lucky—" he starts to say, then realizes that's stupid of him and so halts in midsentence.

"No," she agrees, "I *was* lucky. It could have been much worse. And at least I've learned my lesson."

"What lesson is that?" he asks between sips of grapefruit Tang.

"That me and my old man are history."

"This was your *father* did this to you?"

Carmen laughs, her mouth full of oatmeal. Goodman suddenly realizes that maybe oatmeal and grapefruit aren't such a good combination. The acid from the grapefruit could curdle the milk in the oatmeal. But he knows better than to change the subject during a tale of rape and incest.

"Old man means boyfriend," she explains.

Goodman wonders when they changed the meaning of the term, but says nothing.

"Bad enough," she says. "Stayed with him nearly six months. Smart, huh?"

"We sometimes make mistakes," he says.

"Well, when I make them, I *really* make them!"

"What do you do now?" he asks.

"I go it alone, that's for sure."

"Where?"

"I don't know," she says. "I'll have to find a place."

The thought of her leaving as suddenly as she's arrived catches Goodman off guard. He says, "You're welcome to stay here until you—"

She smiles her smile again. "You don't have room for me," she says, waving her arm in a circular motion that takes in the single area that is living room, dining room, library, bedroom, and kitchen.

"Don't be silly," he says. "I've got a bad back, so I sleep on the floor a lot."

"Liar, liar, pants on fire," she sings.

"Nose as long as a telephone wire," he completes the verse. It's not for nothing he has a six-year-old.

Carmen shakes her head. "I can't do that," she says.

"Why not?"

"I don't even *know* you."

"You know I'm not going to beat you up," he says.

Annise Bradford arrives at the corner of First Avenue and Thirtieth Street shortly after one o'clock in the afternoon. She's cold and pale, and shaking slightly. Even before the phone call, she knew something was wrong. She knew it when Russell didn't come home last night, and then again when he still hadn't shown up by midmorning. A neighbor told her how to call Central Booking, explaining that's how she finds out when her husband's been picked up. But Central Booking had no record of a Russell Bradford having been arrested.

She'd called in sick to work and sat by the phone, waiting for it to ring. When finally it did, just before noon, it had taken her five rings to reach for it and lift it to her ear.

"Hello," she had said.

"Mrs. Bradford?"

"Yes."

"This is Detective Morgan," a voice had said, and in that instant she'd prayed that he was going to tell her that her son had been arrested—for anything, even murder. But he hadn't told her that. Instead, he'd said that her son had been involved in an altercation, and asked if she could meet him at the corner of First Avenue and Thirtieth Street in an hour.

This isn't Annise Bradford's first visit to the corner of First Avenue and Thirtieth Street. Nine years ago, she made this same trip. They'd led her into a room lined with square drawers. It had been cold, so cold that she couldn't stop shivering. As she'd stood there, a man wearing a white lab coat had pulled open one of the drawers. On it had been the body of her husband, William. His skin looked like somebody had dusted him with powder. One side of his head was crushed in, and there was a yellow tag tied to one of his big toes.

"Mrs. Bradford?"

She turns and sees a black man in a business suit. He's large enough to be a professional football player, but his shoulders sag just a bit and his face is deeply lined from too many days like this.

"I'm Stanley Morgan," he says softly, and if she'd had any hope whatsoever that her son was still alive—had simply been arrested for some unspeakable crime—that hope ends now.

She follows him inside, through the doors of the office of the Chief Medical Examiner. They stop at the reception desk, where he signs the logbook for both of them.

Sensitivity training has come and stamped its mark upon the bureaucracy, and the gentleman who meets them today wears a tan suit and a striped tie. Instead of being taken into a cold room full of drawers, they are led to a pleasant office, where she is given a seat at a gray metal desk. There the gentleman in the tan suit places a photograph in front of her. It is, of course, a photograph of her firstborn child, Russell. His eyes are closed, and he appears to be sleeping. As she studies his face, large drops of water begin to cover and gradually obscure his features, creating the impression that he's slowly sinking away from her, down toward the bottom of some deep pool.

It takes Annise Bradford a moment to realize that the drops are her own tears.

"If I'm going to stay here, even for just a few days, it's only fair that I help out with the rent when I get some money," Carmen tells Goodman Tuesday afternoon.

"Don't worry about it," he says. "I've got to pay the rent whether you stay or not." He doesn't bother telling her that he's already two weeks late paying it.

"Then let me help with the food, or something."

"You help any way you like," he says. "Just don't worry about it."

"No," she says. "I insist."

And though she seems earnest enough, he also notices that she's in no hurry to venture outside. He guesses she's still traumatized from the experience with her "old man," and he decides not to say anything about it, to give her a little time. But by five o'clock, when Goodman announces he's going to take a walk to buy a couple of things for dinner, Carmen is still wearing his bathrobe—though he's offered to lend her some of his clothes—and makes no move to join him.

At the store, he buys a box of spaghetti, a jar of sauce, some greens for a salad, and a crusty bread. $6.69. He walks past a liquor store on the way home, stops a full block later, doubles back, and picks out a bottle of Chianti, $5.43.

He remembers a game he and his brother Alan used to play when they were boys. It was called rock-paper-scissors. On the count of three, both players would extend their right hands in the shape of certain designated objects: a fist was a rock, a flattened palm a piece of paper, two spread fingers a pair of scissors. There were predetermined rules proclaiming which object would win in head-to-head combat: Rock crushes scissors; paper covers rock; scissors cut paper. The winner of each encounter got to give the loser a "noogie"—a punch in the forearm with the middle knuckle of the fist extended to cause surprising pain.

Now Goodman feels like he's just been in a game of rock-paper-scissors, only this time, the objects displayed turned out to be not rock or paper or scissors, but thrift and recklessness. And, lo and behold, recklessness has completely demolished thrift. He shifts his groceries and the bottle of wine to his left arm and punches the air in front of him crisply with his right fist, delivering a perfect noogie.

Back at the apartment, Carmen takes the groceries from Goodman and orders him to go sit down and watch TV. He does as he's told, and is soon absorbed in the evening news. Only vaguely does he occasionally become aware of scraping noises, pots and pans clanging, and aromas drifting toward him from the far end of the room.

When she announces that dinner is ready, he finds she's created a minor masterpiece: pasta *con tono*, she calls it—spaghetti covered with a rich mixture combining the sauce Goodman bought with chunks of fresh tomato and onion and flaked tuna. There is a green salad drizzled with oil and vinegar. She's warmed the bread and wrapped it in a red bandanna he uses as a pot holder. The Chianti's found its way into two wineglasses he didn't even know he owned, and a red-and-white-striped bath towel of his has been transformed into a tablecloth.

"My God" is all he can think to say, but what it lacks in articulateness, it apparently conveys in spontaneity, and Carmen laughs brightly. Good-man takes his seat at what used to be his card table. He has never been across an ocean, but he instantly imagines that this is what it must be like to dine at a trattoria in Rome or a café in Paris. Lifting his glass, he tries to think of a toast worthy of the occasion, but no words come to him.

"To my rescuer," Carmen says finally.

"To the Ballerina Princess," says Michael Goodman softly.

At 8:15 Tuesday evening, docket number 96N047335 is called for ar-raignment in part AR-4 of the Manhattan Criminal Court. "Reddington!" calls the bridgeman, so called because he stands behind the table—or "bridge"—that separates the lawyers and the defendant from the judge.

A large black man rises from a bench adjacent to the pen area and am-bles over to the bridge, where he takes his place beside his lawyer.

"Docket ending three-three-five," intones the bridgeman, "*People* v. *Dwayne Reddington*. Defendant is charged with violating Section Five-eleven of the Vehicle and Traffic Laws. Your appearance, counselor."

"Morton Wieselheimer, Four-oh-one Broadway, New York, for the defendant," says the lawyer.

"Counselor, do you waive the reading of the defendant's rights but not the rights themselves?"

"Yes." He's never been able to figure out what that means.

"Notices, People?"

"The People serve statement notice," says an earnest-looking assistant district attorney, who then reads from the write-up in front of him. "At the time and place of arrest, the defendant said to the arresting officer, 'You got me.' No further notices."

"Are you requesting bail?" asks the judge, a onetime radical lawyer named William Mogulescu.

"Yes," says the ADA. "The defendant has a lengthy record, including three felony convictions. He's used different names in the past, as well as different dates of birth and Social Security numbers. We're asking for bail in the amount of seventy-five hundred dollars."

"Judge—" Wieselheimer protests, but the judge silences him with an open palm held up in his direction.

"Let me get this straight," Mogulescu booms. "You're asking for seventy-five hundred dollars in a *misdemeanor suspended license case?*"

"Uh, yes, Your Honor. The defendant has seventeen prior arrests—"

"Yes, yes," Mogulescu interrupts. "You told us about his record. Any history of bench warrants?"

The ADA studies a computer printout for a while before saying, "It doesn't appear so."

"Who owns the car, this Bentley Mr. Reddington was driving?"

"It appears the defendant owns it."

"Where's the car now?" the judge asks.

"It was impounded, Your Honor. We're checking it for evidence."

"Oh, I see. You think maybe you'll find a written confession in the glove compartment, or a copy of the VTL in the trunk?" Without waiting for the ADA to respond or for Wieselheimer to say anything, he rules on the request for bail. "The matter is adjourned to November eleventh. The defendant is released on his own recognizance. Next case."

Dwayne Reddington smiles, turns around, and walks out of the courtroom. He will get his Bentley back within twenty-four hours. He'll pay his outstanding summonses and, when he returns to court next month, no doubt he'll be permitted to plead guilty to a minor traffic infraction and pay a fifty-dollar fine. Wieselheimer will get three hundred dollars for an evening's work. But none of that matters, of course. What matters is that Big Red now has an ironclad, airtight alibi for the homicide of Russell Bradford.

The meal turns out to taste every bit as good as it looks, and the three glasses of Chianti he's drunk provide Goodman with a pleasant buzz. Carmen insists on doing the dishes. "I don't have any money to help out," she explains. "It's the least I can do."

Afterward, they sit on the sofa, finishing the last of the wine. Pop-Tart joins them, settling between them and pretending to sleep.

"So tell me about yourself, Michael," Carmen says.

"There's not much to tell. I'm an accountant, though I'm only working part-time right now. I have a daughter who's six years old. She's staying with her grandmother for the moment."

"What about your wife?"

"She's dead, a car accident."

"You're widowed," Carmen says. "How sad. I'm so sorry."

"That's okay."

"And your daughter—what's her name?"

"Kelly," he says, and the sudden crack in his voice causes her to raise an eyebrow. "She's sick," he tells her, the wine overcoming his reticence. "Or at least they seem to think she is."

"Is it serious?" Carmen looks truly pained.

"They're talking about a possible brain tumor. They want to do more tests."

"I'm sorry," she says. "I didn't know."

"Of course not. How could you?"

"Is she the Ballerina Princess?"

"Yes," he smiles. "She's the Ballerina Princess."

They sit in silence for a while, but for Goodman it's not one of those embarrassing silences he's suffered through so many times in his life. It's an okay silence, a pause during which there's simply no need for anything to be said. He wonders about this person who's so suddenly come into his life, but seems to be able to make him feel so good. He wants to do as she did, turn to her and say, "So tell me about yourself, Carmen." But he's afraid he might somehow break the spell. He decides she'll tell him her story when she's ready to.

He sleeps on the floor again that night, but not before Carmen spreads out layers of towels for him to cushion his body. The resulting bed is warmer and softer than last night's, though still not quite good enough for Pop-Tart, who again elects to curl up with Carmen on the sofa bed. He throws Goodman a look somewhere between contempt and pity before settling in for the night.

Fifteen hundred miles to the south, Gustavo Fuentes settles in for the night, too, on a king-sized mattress in his suite on the top floor of the Hotel Fontainbleu in Miami Beach. But sleep does not come easily to Mister Fuentes (as he prefers to be called, and therefore is). Mister Fuentes has a problem. He doesn't yet know the *name* of his problem, but he knows this much: His problem is a smallish man who lives in a particular apartment in a particular building on the East Side of Manhattan, in New York City. It seems the man has something that belongs to Mister Fuentes, something worth *mucho dinero*. That, of course, is not how things should be.

Mister Fuentes suffers from an extremely low threshold of pain. He doesn't like having hangnails, shaving cuts, or blisters. He *especially* doesn't like having headaches. As a result, he decides he's going to be forced to take whatever steps are necessary to see that this one goes away.

Michael Goodman is up early Wednesday morning, a slight headache the price for his three glasses of wine. He showers, shaves, and sneaks out of the apartment while Carmen and Pop-Tart sleep. He returns with the paper and a box of sugared doughnuts.

Carmen is awake, and they breakfast on doughnuts and tea. Goodman tells her he's going to spend the day with his daughter. This time, she asks him if she can borrow some of his clothes, and he readily agrees. He takes it as a good sign that she wants to get dressed, perhaps even go out.

While she showers, he reads the *Times*. There's a small article about a woman from Connecticut who claims to have been raped in Central Park while she slept, a report of a bicycle rider injured by a hit-and-run motorist in the East Village, and a piece describing the alleged beating of a carriage horse by its owner on Fifty-ninth Street as horrified pedestrians looked on.

There is no article about Russell Bradford, no mention of his being gunned down and left for dead on West 129th Street, in the shadow of the West Side Highway, shortly before his seventeenth birthday. Perhaps the omission has something to do with the fact that, unlike the woman and the pedestrian and even the horse, Russell Bradford was not white.

Or perhaps not.

Carmen emerges from the shower wearing the clothes Goodman's put out for her: the new jeans he bought in Florida and a white button-down shirt. Her feet swim in a pair of his sneakers. Although she's the same height as he is, her body is that of a teenager, and his clothes make her look like a child who's raided some grown-up's closet. The bruises on her face have faded almost to the point of being invisible, and her hair has taken on a luster that a day and a half ago would have seemed unimaginable. She is nothing less than stunning.

Goodman says nothing, but he knows full well that the look in his eyes has betrayed his silence. He turns to the phone and calls his mother-in-law, who answers on the first ring.

"Hello," he says. "It's me, Michael."

"Yes, hello, Michael."

"How's Kelly?"

"She seems okay. She's asking for you. This is too much for me, Michael," she tells him. "I'm too old to start being a mother all over again."

The three of them—Goodman, his daughter, and his mother-in-law—had gone together to a counseling agency shortly after Shirley's death. It had been the counselor's suggestion that Kelly move in with her grandmother for a while, just until Goodman could find a new job and get back on his feet financially. At the time, Goodman had suspected that the real motivation behind the suggestion had been the counselor's concern for Goodman's mother-in-law, her perception that she needed Kelly even more than Goodman did at that particular moment. Like her daughter, Shirley had been an only child, and her death had been truly devastating to her mother, who herself had been widowed several years earlier. Allowing Kelly to stay with her grandmother after her mother's death had therefore seemed like a kindness to both child and grandmother, so Goodman had gone along with the suggestion. Now, however, it seems as though it's time for him to reclaim his daughter.

"Let me speak with her," he says.

After a minute, he hears his daughter's soft "Hi, Daddy."

"Hi, angel. You up for some fun?"

"What kind of fun?"

"Oh, I don't know. We'll think of something. I'll pick you up in a little while, okay?"

"Okay. Daddy?"

"Yes?" he says, fearful he's about to hear about her headaches.

"Can Larus come?"

"Absolutely."

Carmen announces she's going out as well, that she's going to visit a girlfriend, see if she can get some "real" clothes.

"You're rejecting my wardrobe?" he asks in mock pain.

"I reject nothing about you," she says, and kisses him on the tip of his nose.

He gives her the second set of keys that came with the new lock to his door. They find Tony the Super, who comes up with a spare key to the downstairs door, but only after giving Carmen a thorough up-and-down and Goodman a knowing wink.

At Lexington Avenue, Goodman and Carmen go their separate ways, he to the west, she downtown. As soon as she's out of sight, he takes his index finger and touches the tip of his nose. It seems to tingle.

The sun feels good, and Goodman coaxes Kelly into going to Central Park, Larus in tow. But after awhile, though she complains of no headaches, he notices her squinting as though the light is too much for her. He blames himself for not thinking of a cap or a pair of sunglasses.

"How would you like to go to the museum?" he asks her.

"Can we have lunch there?"

"You bet."

The museum is *their* museum, the American Museum of Natural History, the one they always go to. They know it almost by heart, from the dinosaurs to the great whale to North America Mammals exhibit. They have their favorites: the pearl-diver exhibit, Peter Stuyvesant coming ashore to meet the Indians, the geological crystals, and anything where you can push a button and make things happen.

Today, they head for Ocean Life and Biology of Fishes, where it's dark and cool. They make their rounds, following the same route they always do. They check on the killer whales, the sharks, the pearl divers in their underwater caves, and watch a tiny movie showing the angler fish cast for its prey for the hundredth time.

Lunch means the cafeteria, where they dine on grilled cheese sandwiches and iced tea at a long wooden table. Kelly cuts her sandwich into tiny squares, which from time to time Goodman has to remind her to eat.

"I'm ready," she tells him between bites.

"Ready for what?"

"Another chapter of the story."

"Ah," he says, though in truth he's at that very moment been working on the next segment and knew precisely what she was ready for the moment she spoke. "The Ballerina Princess. Where was she when last we left her?"

"She was being good even though they kept giving her these tests. Is she finished with the tests?"

The Ballerina Princess
(Continued)

The Ballerina Princess had indeed been very good about the tests. She'd kicked obediently when they'd hit her knee with the rubber hammer, she'd laughed when they'd tickled the bottom of her foot, and she'd said "Ouch!" when they'd stuck her toes with the safety pins, just as she was supposed to do. And the whole time, she never complained once. So it certainly seemed only fair that there should be no more tests.

But, alas! Even in the magical kingdom of Yew Nork, things weren't always fair. And it was decided that the Ballerina Princess needed another test after all.

"Was it the kind of test that hurt her?" Kelly asks him.

"I'm afraid so," he has to tell her. "At least it was the kind that hurts a little bit."

But the Ballerina Princess was very brave, remember. And on the day of the test, she wasn't alone. On one side of her, she had her father, the Keeper of the Numbers. And on the other side, she had the brave and loyal Prince Larus.

"Did she cry?"

She cried a little bit, which was all right, because sometimes crying a bit could actually make the Ballerina Princess feel better. But the test was an important one, because it would help the doctors figure out what the matter was and how to make her all better.

"Can I go back home with you, Daddy?" she suddenly asks him. "Would you like that?"

"If Grandma won't mind."

"We can call Grandma," he says. "I'm sure she won't mind."

"Can I sleep at your house?"

"Of course you can."

On this Wednesday, Annise Bradford uses her lunch hour to travel a hundred and fifteen blocks each way by subway to spend twenty minutes in her mother's room at Jacoby Hospital.

"Hello, Nana," she says, using the name everyone's called her mother by since before she can remember.

"Hello, Ni." She sounds it like *knee*. She still speaks out of the corner of her mouth. One side of her body continues to be virtually paralyzed. The doctors have admitted that they'd hoped for noticeable improvement by this time.

"How you feeling, Nana?"

Her mother totally ignores the question, asks instead, "What's the matter?"

"Nothing," Annise Bradford says, before the tears burst from her.

Nana gives her a minute. "It's Russell," she says then, "isn't it?"

"It's Russell," Annise Bradford sobs. And she falls to her knees beside the bed and lowers her head onto the mattress, her shoulders heaving uncontrollably. Her mother reaches out with the only arm she can move and cradles her child's head in the crook of her elbow, rocking it gently to the rhythm of some ancient, wordless song.

Nana will die in her sleep less than forty-eight hours from this moment. The doctors will attribute her death to complications arising from the stroke. Her death certificate will identify heart failure as the official cause of death.

But in a sense, at least, it can rightly be said that the twenty kilos will have claimed their third victim.

Late Wednesday afternoon, Ray Abbruzzo and Daniel Riley are about to enter an abandoned brownstone on 144th Street in the South Bronx. They intend to use an empty apartment on the top floor as an OP, an observation post. An observation-post operation is a variation on the theme of the buy-and-bust operation. Instead of depending upon an undercover officer to buy drugs before calling in the backup team to make arrests, officers man the observation post, scanning the street below—sometimes with binoculars, sometimes with the naked eye—for drug sales. As they spot a transaction, they radio a description of the buyer to the backup team. As soon as the departing buyer rounds the corner, he's scooped up. After two or three such transactions, the sellers themselves are arrested, and their stash—if the observing officers have been able to pinpoint its location—is seized. The buyers are charged with misdemeanor possession counts and are often permitted to "plead down" in court to disorderly conduct. The sellers are charged with felonies—"observation sales" rather than "direct sales"—but every bit as serious as had they been caught selling to an undercover officer.

Abbruzzo spots a lanky black kid who looks familiar, which is not altogether unusual.

"Hey," he says to Riley, "isn't that Larry Lookout?"

Riley looks. "Yeah," he says, "Syracuse." Even though today the kid's wearing a different jacket.

"Yo!" Abbruzzo calls out, just loud enough for the kid to look over. As soon as he has the kid's attention, he motions him to follow them into the building.

"Hey, kid," Abbruzzo says as soon as they're off the street. "Howya doing?"

"Okay."

"What's your name again? Bobby?"

"Robbie."

"Right, Robbie McCray."

"I didn't do nothin'," Robbie tells them. "I'm clean."

Abbruzzo laughs. "Sure you are," he says. "We got no beef with you, Robbie. It's your friend Russell we're looking for."

"Yeah, we think maybe he jerked us off about that white guy," says Riley. To illustrate the phrase "jerked off," he makes an up-and-down movement with his fist in the area above his crotch.

"That place was clean as a whistle," Abbruzzo says. "Guy turns out to be a fucking *accountant.*"

Robbie eyes both detectives in turn, as though they're jerking *him* off, before saying, "Dint you hear?"

"Hear?" Riley echoes.

"Russell got popped," Robbie says. "Caught hisself a coupla caps downtown." Manhattan is downtown to anyone who lives in the Bronx, even though there are parts of Manhattan that are farther north than parts of the Bronx.

"When?"

"Monday night." This means any time from dark to nine o'clock Tuesday morning.

"Where?"

"Wayova on the Wesside, by the riva. Roun twenny-fif." Which, of course, is 125th Street.

"No shit," says Abbruzzo.

Later, upstairs in the OP, Abbruzzo has a thought. Wiping the coffee from his chin, he shares his thought with Riley. "The way I figure it, maybe it was there after all," he says.

"It?"

"The Mole's stash," Abbruzzo says. "Or maybe not. Maybe he keeps it somewhere else. Either way, someone seems to have got petty pissed off at Russell for putting us onto him."

"Or," Riley says, "somebody wasted Russell for something completely different. Like maybe he dissed the wrong guy. Or owed some fucker twenty cents and was late payin' it back."

"Maybe," Abbruzzo says. "Remind me to check with somebody in the Twenty-sixth. Find out who caught the homicide, see what the word is on the street." He sips his coffee, dribbles some more down his chin, ignores it. "In the meantime, maybe we oughta take a second look at our friend the Mole." The coffee drips from the tip of his chin onto the front of his shirt.

Halfway home, Goodman realizes that he hasn't told his daughter about either Carmen or Pop-Tart. He figures she's had enough surprises lately.

"Hey, angel," he calls out, since she's perched atop his shoulders, holding onto his head for balance. "I've got a couple of guests staying with me. They're both looking forward to meeting you."

"What kind of guests?"

He immediately opts for cowardice. "Well, one's very short, and he's got whiskers—"

"Whiskers?" She laughs.

"Whiskers."

"How many legs does he have?"

"Let me see," Goodman says, pretending to search his memory. "One . . . two . . . three . . . *four!*"

"Does he by any chance go 'meow'?"

"I think he may when he's a little older. Right now, he's only up to 'mew.' "

"You have a *kitten*, Daddy?"

"How come you're so smart, angel?"

" 'Cause you gave me giant hints."

He shifts Larus from one hand to the other.

"Who's the other guest?" she asks excitedly. "Does he go 'bowwow'?"

"No, and he's a she."

That stops her, but only for a moment. "What does *she* say?"

"Oh, she says things like 'Hello' and 'How are you?' and 'Nice to meet you.' "

"She must be a parrot," Kelly announces.

When they reach his building, Goodman unlocks the downstairs door and, to announce their arrival, buzzes upstairs on the intercom. By the time they make it to the fifth floor—Kelly having dismounted and leading the way, Goodman and Larus struggling to keep up—Carmen is waiting at the door.

"This is Carmen," Goodman begins the introductions, "and this—"

"And this must be the Ballerina Princess," beams Carmen, who's somehow managed to lower herself to her knees and become Kelly's height.

"And this is Larus," Kelly announces, rescuing her mascot before her father can drop him to the floor.

"Pleased to meet you, Larus."

A loud mewing sound, followed by the sudden appearance of black fur on the top of the sofa back, informs them that they've slighted someone.

"And this is Pop-Tart," Goodman says, completing the protocol. He watches as Kelly goes immediately to the kitten, questioning his name no more than she's questioned Carmen's. Pop-Tart responds by allowing his head to be scratched and back to be stroked, but he keeps a wary eye on Larus, with whose species he's apparently unfamiliar.

Goodman looks around as he catches his breath. He's already noticed

Carmen's outfit. Tight-fitting black jeans and a matching T-shirt have replaced his own baggy loaner clothes of the morning, and she's had her hair cut or done or something, making her look younger and even prettier than before. Now he takes in the rest of his apartment. His sofa's been turned at a slight angle; his broken coffee table has retreated to the corner, leaving more room to get around. Last night's empty Chianti bottle has found its way atop the radiator and sprouted a bunch of daisies; and somehow the place looks cleaner and brighter than it did before.

Out of the corner of his eye, he notices Carmen looking at him. "Very nice," he smiles. Her return smile suggests a touch of pride, and perhaps even a trace of relief at his approval. He catches himself wondering if her "couple of days" might not have a renewal clause buried in the fine print, and the thought fills him with an undeniable sense of excitement.

Goodman's down to his last twenty dollars, but tomorrow's a payday, so he splurges and orders a pizza. By adding the rest of the lettuce, Carmen manages to reproduce last evening's salad. They gather around the card table and play family. The usually appetiteless Kelly eats two slices of pizza and shares a third with Pop-Tart, and Goodman dares to believe for a moment that being reunited with him is what she's needed all along. His eyes suddenly fill, and he quickly brings his paper napkin to them, drying them and blowing his nose in one motion to hide his reaction. But as he lowers his napkin back to his lap, thinking he's pulled the maneuver off quite nicely, he catches Carmen looking at him. She misses nothing, he sees.

They watch an old episode of *Taxi* on TV. When it's bedtime, Carmen begs for a turn on the floor, but Kelly points out that there are more girls than boys, so the girls get the bed.

"Looks like you and me on the floor for sure," Goodman tells Pop-Tart, but he's wrong again. An hour later, he's still trying to cushion his hipbone, while the kitten sleeps peacefully on the sofa bed with Carmen, Kelly, and Larus.

"Looks like they're out for the count," Daniel Riley says to Ray Abbruzzo. The two of them have been shivering in a doorway on East Ninety-second Street, peering up at a fifth-floor window for the last two and a half hours. They had to get special authorization from a lieutenant to skip the evening's buy-and-bust operation and do this surveillance instead, and now all they have to show for it are a lot of frozen toes and a couple of stiff necks. They step out of the doorway and begin walking east.

"I can't figure this fucker out," Abbruzzo says. "He's definitely the guy that the Bradford kid met with. We know Bradford was walking around with a pocketful of pure shit. He even *told* us that the guy he was meeting was his connection. Yet the guy never looks behind him when he walks, and when we turn the place upside down, it's clean as a whistle."

"And now he's playing Mr. Family Togetherness." Riley rubs the back of his neck as he walks.

"We could stand out here playin' with our dicks for two weeks and not see a fuckin' thing," Abbruzzo says. "Maybe it's time to bring in OCCB, see if they'll spring for a wiretap."

Shortly after midnight, Big Red walks into the Uptown Lounge on 125th Street. He's recognized by the regulars, with whom he exchanges greetings and high fives.

"Hey Red. Howsitgoing?"

"Whassup, man?"

"Heard you spent a night at the Centre Street Hilton."

"Yeah, yeah." Red smiles. "How about that?" He spots the man he's looking for sitting at a table in the corner, and he heads that way. The man starts to stand, but Big Red motions him to stay put, lowering himself into the empty chair.

"Lookin' good, Red. They treat you awright?"

"Red carpet for the Red Man."

"Solid. Good to see you."

"So," Big Red says, leaning forward over the table, "how'd it go?"

"Like eatin' pussy," the other man smiles.

Big Red leans back and laughs. "You always did have a way with words, Hammer."

"So when do you wanna whack that shit up, Red?"

"I got the girls lined up for ten o'clock tomorrow night. I think we'll use that apartment up on Gun Hill Road."

"That's cool," Hammer says. "Want me there?"

"Yeah, you be there," Big Red says. "You an' ol' Buster Brown."

Hammer smiles. "Buster Brown" is street talk for a sawed-off shotgun.

{ 17 }

Thursday morning, Goodman explains to Kelly that he has to go to work later on, so he'll be dropping her back at her grandmother's.

"I want to stay with Carmen," she says.

"No," he tells her.

"Why not?" she pouts.

"Because I said so." Then, remembering his promise to himself never to justify things on such an arbitrary basis, he adds, "You don't have any other clothes here." And throws in, "And I'm sure Grandma misses you." What he's not ready to tell her is that sleeping in the same bed as Carmen is one thing—after all, he was right there, only six feet away—but he's not about to leave her in the hands of a virtual stranger for day care.

Kelly's pout shows considerable staying power. "Can I come back tonight, to sleep?"

He softens immediately. "You bet you can."

All smiles. Oh, to be six, Goodman thinks, when the whole world's so very simple. And the thought reminds him of her headaches and the MRI and tomorrow's spinal tap, and a sudden shudder runs through his body.

Shortly after eleven, Ray Abbruzzo and Daniel Riley have another meeting with Maggie Kennedy, the assistant district attorney who drew up the search-warrant papers with them.

"What can I do for you guys?" she asks.

Abbruzzo answers her question with one of his own. "Remember that guy you got us the search warrant for Saturday night?"

"The Mole? How could I forget?"

Abbruzzo nods.

"How'd it turn out?"

"Not so hot," he admits. "But there've been a few significant developments since then."

"Like what?"

"Like for one thing, the kid who gave us the information about him turned up dead. Stopped a coupla bullets with his back."

Kennedy narrows her eyes a bit. "I thought your tip was from an anonymous caller," she says.

"Yeah, it was," Abbruzzo says. "But through diligent investigation, we found out who the caller was."

"Hey, we do our homework," Riley assures her.

"Can you connect . . . the Mole—what's his name again?"

"Goodman."

"Goodman," she repeats. "Can you connect Goodman to the killing?"

"Not yet," Abbruzzo admits, remembering he's forgotten to call Homicide. "But the word on the street is that he right away suspected it was the kid who dropped a dime on him, and he swore he'd fix him for it."

"Meanwhile," she asks, "where's Goodman's stash, if it isn't in his apartment?"

Abbruzzo winks and points a finger at her, as if to say she's onto something there. "Could be anywhere," he says.

"They don't call this guy the Mole for nothing," Riley reminds her. "He could have this stuff underground, for all we know."

"Seems we're at a dead end," Abbruzzo says sadly. "Unless—"

"Unless I can get you a wiretap order," Kennedy says.

Abbruzzo smiles broadly. "Now *there's* an idea," he says, as though the thought had never occurred to him.

At work, Goodman finds the new bookkeeping systems he's installed greatly simplify things. Manny's back from whatever kept him away on Monday, and Goodman makes the suggestion that they open a second bank account in order to facilitate segregating deductible expenses from nondeductible ones.

"You think it's a good idea?" Manny asks him.

"Yes, I think so. You see—"

"Then do it," Manny says. "Don't tell me about it; don't explain it to me. Just *do* it. *You* think it's a good idea, then *I* think it's a good idea."

Goodman takes it as a vote of confidence, and goes back to the books. He'll continue to work until quarter of five, when Manny will pop in, peel off five twenties from his roll, and tell him to have a good weekend.

Obtaining a wiretap order—officially designated "an electronic-eavesdropping warrant, pursuant to Article 700 of the Criminal Procedure Law"—is somewhat more difficult than getting a search warrant. Maggie Kennedy works through her lunch hour with Detectives Abbruzzo and Riley, gathering the necessary information she'll need to prepare three affidavits: one for Abbruzzo, one for herself, and one for her boss, Robert Silbering, the citywide Special Narcotics Prosecutor. The affidavits must contain facts sufficient to establish probable cause that Michael Goodman is the subscriber of a particular telephone number at his residence; that he is engaged in illegal narcotics trafficking; that he uses his phone to call and receive calls from his suppliers, customers, and confederates; and that conventional means of investigation have been tried and proved unlikely to be successful in identifying those suppliers, customers, and confederates, or in learning the whereabouts of Michael Goodman's narcotics.

It is this last requirement—sometimes termed the *exhaustion requirement*—that the legislature has inserted into the law in an attempt to safeguard citizens from the unique intrusiveness of a wiretap, when less invasive law enforcement techniques (such as undercover buys or good-old-fashioned surveillance) might succeed in obtaining the objectives sought. But while the legislature may have acted in good faith in placing what would seem on its face to be a formidable hurdle in the path of overzealous law enforcement personnel, it turns out that police and prosecutors have been quick to learn just what magic words are sufficient to satisfy the requirement, and judges—seeing those magic words in place—are equally quick to rubber-stamp their assertions.

So, once she's accepted the assurances of Detectives Abbruzzo and Riley that Michael Goodman, aka the Mole, is indeed using his East Ninety-second Street apartment in furtherance of his heroin trafficking (in spite of the fact that an earlier search of the premises proved negative), and that he's using his telephone to converse with suppliers, customers, and confederates, Maggie Kennedy turns to the exhaustion requirement.

"How do we show that conventional investigative techniques are unlikely to succeed?" she asks them, pen in hand.

"Well," Abbruzzo sighs, "we've tried just about everything. Surveillance is virtually impossible because so many people go in and out of the building, it's impossible to tell which apartment they're going to." This one's a win-win category: If the suspect happened to live in a single-family dwelling, then surveillance would be virtually impossible because the officers' presence would be too obvious.

"What else?"

"The guy's just too suspicious," Abbruzzo confesses. "Whenever we put a tail on him, he's all the time looking around for it. You know—doubling back, circling the block, ducking into buildings. He's good."

"He's good all right," Riley chimes in.

"And the search warrant thing," Abbruzzo says. "We hear he got tipped off about that, moved his stash just before we hit the place."

"How about a buy?" Kennedy suggests.

"Too dangerous," says Abbruzzo, lifting the phrase verbatim from the statute. "He's already killed—or had killed—the person he thinks informed on him. We can't risk the life of a police officer."

"This is one dangerous guy," Riley agrees.

"I wish there was some other way," Abbruzzo says, turning his empty palms upward. "I really do."

Kennedy looks over her notes. "Well," she says after a moment, "I think we've got enough here. We can use the dangerousness thing in here, too. Let me get started with the paperwork. Want to come back tomorrow morning, say nine o'clock?"

"Sure thing."

"And fellas," she says.

"Yeah?"

"Give surveillance one more try tonight."

They're out of her office and alone in the elevator before Abbruzzo grabs his crotch and says, "Surveillance *this!*" They both burst out laughing in one of those rare moments of camaraderie that makes you feel good all over to be a cop.

Before leaving work, Goodman calls his mother-in-law to tell her he'll be stopping by to pick up Kelly.

"I'm not sure she's up to it," she tells him. "It's all she's talked about all afternoon—the kitten and this new friend of yours, Carmine."

"Carmen."

"Carmen. Don't you think it's a little soon for that? What with Shirley dead only three months?"

"It's not like *that,*" he assures her.

"I'm not telling you how to run your life, Michael. But it's all very confusing for Kelly. What kind of a name is Carmine, anyway? Not Jewish, certainly."

"Tell me about Kelly," he says.

"She tries so hard to be brave, but I can see she's in pain again. And her eyes—she keeps squinting, like the lights are too bright. I've got it so dark in here, I can barely see. You want to talk to her?"

"Yes."

"Hold on."

He does, and in a minute he hears his daughter's "Hi, Daddy." She sounds weak and far away.

"Hi, angel. How are you doing?"

"Okay," she says, but he has to press the phone hard against his ear to hear her.

"Do you want me to come over and get you, or would you rather wait till tomorrow, when you're feeling better?"

There's a short silence, then her voice again. "Would it be okay to wait until tomorrow?"

"Of course it is."

"You're not mad at me?"

His nose suddenly feels as it's been punched, and he's glad she's not there to see his eyes fill up. "Angel," he says, "I am never, never, never, *never* mad at you. Do you understand that?"

"Yes."

"I love you."

"I love you, too, Daddy."

Even before he reaches the door of his apartment, Goodman detects the aroma of home cooking. He can't quite identify the dish—it seems to be somewhere between brisket and vegetable soup—but its effect on him is nothing short of invigorating.

He lets himself in, and the aroma hits him full blast. He is all but drawn to the kitchen end of the room, where Carmen turns her head to smile at him over her shoulder. She's wearing a tiny pair of shorts, the kind that kids make by cutting off the legs from faded jeans—he can't remember what they're called—and a white T-shirt, and she's barefoot. He wants to say something about how terrific she looks, but he doesn't trust himself to make it come out sounding right.

"Something sure smells good," he says instead.

She lifts the lid off a pot and shows him a bubbly brown creation. "I hope you like veal stew," she says.

The truth is, he's stayed away from veal, not only because it's terribly expensive, but because once, driving south through Connecticut, he saw calves chained to what looked like doghouses, and he learned later that they do that so the animals don't get a chance to develop their muscles before they're taken to be slaughtered. The thought of a creature living its entire short life like that was too much for him to bear. But now, since Carmen's gone to all this expense and trouble, he knows he can't bring that up.

He settles on "It smells absolutely delicious."

He goes into the bathroom to wash his hands and face. He looks in the mirror, sees the same face he's been looking at for all of his adult life. A little more drawn now perhaps, a bit thinner in the hair department, where the first hints of gray are beginning to show at the sideburns.

He takes off his glasses and places them on the edge of the sink. He lowers his face, splashes water onto it, rubs it, and reaches behind him for a towel. He pats his skin dry and lowers the towel to dry his hands. The face in the mirror looks a bit younger suddenly, not so bookish—less the stereotypical accountant, perhaps. He leaves his glasses resting on the sink and turns off the light.

"You look better without your glasses," she smiles as soon as he rejoins her at the stove, where he notices a bottle of red wine. "Can you see without them?"

"Almost as well," he says. "I started wearing them years ago because I thought they made me look older, more serious."

"And why on earth would you want to look old and serious?"

"Job interviews," he explains, breaking off the end of a loaf of sourdough bread she's bought. "People expect accountants to look like accountants." The bread is soft and chewy.

"Do you want rice or noodles?" she asks him.

"Whatever," he says. "Rice, noodles. You decide."

He walks to the sofa, extracts his copy of the *Times* from his brief-case, and sits, happy to leave her in charge. But there's one thing that bothers him.

"Carmen?"

"Yes?"

"Where did all this food come from? I mean, two days ago, you told me you had no money. All of a sudden, you're showing up with veal."

She leaves the stove and comes over to the sofa, where she stands directly in front of him. "What did you do this afternoon, Michael?"

He shrugs before answering, "I went to work."

"Me, too," she smiles.

"What kind of work?"

"Work," she says. "And if that calls for a cross-examination, can it at least wait until after dinner?"

"I'm sorry," he says. "I'm glad you've got a job. I was just curious, that's all."

"I know," she smiles. "I didn't mean to jump." And she leans forward and kisses his forehead lightly before returning to her cooking.

He tries to immerse himself in the sports section, but can think only of her lips touching his forehead. He vows not to be the one to bring up her job.

The veal tastes every bit as good as it smelled, cruelty to animals notwithstanding. She's cooked it with these sweet baby onions, carrots, and other vegetables he can't name, and ladled it over rice. The sourdough bread is even better warmed up, and the wine is smooth and wonderful.

"Bravo," he tells her, giddy on his second glass. "Where did you learn to cook like that?"

"My mother, my grandmother," she says. "Cooking was very important in my family." He sees her reach for the wine bottle, but the gentleman in him tries to get there first so that he can pour for her. But his aim is slightly off the mark, and he ends up knocking the bottle sideways, spilling the last of its contents onto the tablecloth that was once a towel.

"*Marron'!*" she laughs, jumping up and out of the way.

"No damage," he assures her. Together they clear the dishes, and Goodman relegates the tablecloth to the hamper in the bathroom.

She washes while he dries, and they settle on the sofa while coffee brews in an improvised coffeemaker, complete with a single layer of paper towel Carmen's separated to serve as a filter.

"So how come a Carmen uses an expression like *marron'?*" he asks her. He's assumed all along she was Hispanic.

"Oh, don't be fooled by the Carmen," she smiles. "My father was a music lover, and he named me after his favorite opera character. How about the last name Pacelli? Is that Italian enough for you?"

"I think so."

"Or the middle name Ormento?"

"Pretty Italian," he agrees.

"Rumor has it that my grandfather John Ormento was a big shot in the Mafia. I've got an older brother who's trying to live up to the name, thinks he's in some kind of gangster-in-training program. Hangs out on Pleasant Avenue, bets numbers, sells drugs—a real success story."

Goodman pretends he didn't hear what she just said about having a brother who sells drugs, and he makes a promise to himself never to bring up the subject. For the last day or two, he's all but forgotten about the black duffel bag lying downstairs in his storage locker, but his financial picture certainly hasn't improved any, and his debts are approaching a critical mass. Still, he knows the last thing in the world he needs is to involve Carmen in that business of his.

The coffee is surprisingly good, and they sip it sitting on the sofa, along with rich fruit tarts that Carmen produces from a bakery box she'd hidden in the corner. Pop-Tart, already stuffed with veal stew, collapses between them.

"So," she says, tucking her bare feet underneath her. "Do you still want to hear about my job?"

"Only if you want to tell me," he says. He's a pretty quick learner.

"Is that a yes or a no?"

"It's an 'it's up to you.' "

"No fair," she says. "I decided on rice versus noodles."

"Oh, *that* world issue," he says. "Sure, I want to hear about your job."

She hesitates for a moment, as though she's trying to come up with the best way to describe exactly what it is she does. Then she says, "I'm a working girl."

"I know that," he says. "I thought you were going to be just a wee bit more specific."

She laughs again, that full-bodied, all-featured laugh of hers that he's come to like so much. "That's actually pretty specific," she says. "I'm a call girl."

Goodman can only stare at her, dumbstruck.

"A hooker?" she tries. "A prostitute?"

He lifts a hand to stop her. "I get it," he says.

"Sorry."

Neither of them says anything. The only sound comes from Pop-Tart's purring each time Carmen strokes the length of his back. Goodman finds himself overcome with an enormous blanket of sadness and hurt for this young woman who sits beside him.

"So that's what you did this afternoon?" he finally asks.

"No," she says, staring off into some world he's not a part of. "What I did this afternoon was I collected the last of some money I had coming to me."

He has no response, no questions. Just the sadness and the hurt.

"Is this a story you want to hear?" she asks.

Again he says nothing, afraid that the very sound of his voice will betray the depth of his reaction to all of this. But then she turns toward him without warning and—before he's had a chance to turn away—sees the look of anguish on his face and the tears welled up in his eyes. In what seems like a single motion, she moves the kitten to the other side of her, closes the distance between the two of them, and takes him in her arms. That gesture—that she should at this moment be somehow moved to comfort *him*—is more than Michael Goodman can bear, and he loses it all: The tears burst forth and stream hotly down his cheeks, and he sobs uncontrollably—for Carmen, for his daughter, for his dead wife, for himself, for all the terrible sadness in the universe.

Shortly after ten o'clock that night, a van pulls up in front of a building on Gun Hill Road in the Bronx. The driver, a thin black man they call Fox, gets out, walks around to the passenger side, and slides open the door. One by one, six black women file out of the van. Fox leads them inside the building to an elevator, where they're met by another black man. Fox returns to the van and drives off, his job over. For his hour's worth of work and the use of his van, he'll be paid a thousand dollars.

The black man and the six black women ride the self-service elevator to the eighth floor. There, the man leads them to the door of an apartment. He knocks once, then three times, then once again. The sounds of locks opening can be heard; then the door swings open. A tall black man holding a double-barreled shotgun, sawed off at both ends so it can be concealed inside the sleeve of a jacket, ushers the women inside. The man who brought them upstairs leaves. For his hour's worth of work, he'll be paid $750.

Inside, the apartment resembles any other apartment in the Bronx. The living room is pleasantly, if inexpensively, furnished. The curtains and blinds are drawn shut. The kitchen has formica counters and a vinyl tile floor. A sound system plays an old Smokey Robinson tape.

But the women are not here to lounge in the living room or work in the kitchen. The man with the shotgun leads them to the master bedroom. A few of them have been here before and know the way. There, yet another black man waits for them.

The master bedroom is actually not a bedroom at all. It is large room—nearly as large as the living room. It has no windows: The only window disappeared when the far wall was covered with imitation wood paneling. The only furniture in the room is a table—the type of table one would expect to find in a dining room, except that instead of being covered with a tablecloth, it is topped with a single piece of butcher paper—and six straight-backed chairs are arranged around it. There is an overhead light. Two electric heaters supplement the building's heating supply.

Without invitation, the women begin to remove their clothing. They remove all of it, until they are absolutely naked. There is nothing suggestive or sexy about the way they do this. Each woman in turn hands her pile of clothes to the black man who was in the room when they got there; he takes each pile out to the living room and places them neatly on the floor.

If the man with the shotgun is aroused by the sight of so much naked flesh around him, he shows no sign of it. Instead, as the women take their places in the chairs around the table, he opens a suitcase and begins removing objects from it and placing them on the table. These objects include three high-quality postal scales; a number of kitchen strainers, spoons, and knives; several rubber stamps and ink pads; half a dozen rolls of Scotch tape; a large box of rubber bands; six dust masks of the type commonly worn by painters or contractors; two large jars of powdered lactose, which is known on the street as milk sugar; and five large boxes full of small glassine envelopes. Then, from his jacket pocket, the man produces one more object, a blue plastic bag roughly the size and shape of a small brick. This he tosses onto the very center of the table. Taking a knife from another pocket, he snaps open the blade with the push of a button. With no less flair than a matador's aiming for the vulnerable nape of a bull's neck, he brings the knife down swiftly, almost invisibly, piercing the bag dead center. A puff of white smoke appears, and when he withdraws the knife, the blade is coated white. Then he carefully cuts away the plastic wrapping until nothing remains but a pile of white powder.

While the man completes the performance of that ritual, the women have been putting on the dust masks, covering their mouths and noses. This they do in order to inhale as little of the powder as possible, so as to avoid becoming sleepy or sick, or even overdosing, so potent is the powder they'll be working with. They've been required to remove their clothing so that they won't be tempted to try to steal, so precious is the powder. Their job is to mix the pile of pure heroin and six equal parts of milk sugar into a uniform consistency; to place single-dosage amounts of the mixture into the glassine envelopes, each of which they will have stamped with a brand name or other identifying logo; to fold and tape shut each glassine they've filled; and to count, stack, and rubber-band together bundles containing twenty-five envelopes each. For their evening's work, which will take about three hours, each of them will be paid five hundred dollars. The man with the shotgun, who goes by the name Hammer, will receive $2,500; the one who took their clothes, $1,000.

This operation is called a "mill." It is one of Big Red's mills. Three hours from now, as the result of this evening's work, Big Red will have about twelve hundred more bundles, or thirty thousand more bags of heroin, to sell on the street for five dollars apiece. Even after he's finished paying off Hammer and the six mill workers and his three other helpers, paying the rent for the apartment, and covering certain other expenses, Big Red will be looking at nearly $140,000 worth of profit from the kilogram of heroin he and Hammer took from Michael Goodman.

"I left home when I was sixteen," Carmen tells Goodman. "Not that there was much to leave, really: an out-of-work father who got drunk every other night and took turns beating his wife and his kids. I took a bus to New York. I had a little money saved up; I used it to put down two months' rent on an apartment on the Lower East Side. Landlord told me I was pretty enough to find work modeling."

"You are," Goodman says.

"I thought so, too," she laughs. "So I started going to agencies. You want to see *pretty?* Every one of them's blond, five ten, a hundred and two pounds, and nothing but lips and cheekbones. I felt like somebody's ugly kid sister. So much for the modeling career.

"So I got a job waiting tables, like everybody else who calls herself an actress or a model or whatever. Five bucks an hour, plus tips if you're willing to smile and flirt enough. Ever try paying rent in this town on five bucks an hour?"

Goodman regards it as a rhetorical question. He could say that he's having his own troubles at twenty-five an hour, but thinks better of it.

"Then I go to a party in midtown with one of the other waitresses, and I meet this guy, Paulie Mancuso. Real good-looking, nice clothes, wonderful way of looking into a girl's eyes while he's talking to her. By now, I know he does it with every girl he meets. But at the time, I was the girl whose eyes he happened to be looking into, and I was stupid enough to think it was about *me*.

"I gave up my apartment and moved in with Paulie a week later. Didn't know where he was from or what he did. All I knew about him was that he was making phone calls all the time and going out in the middle of the night.

"Then one day he tells me he's in terrible trouble, that he owes a bunch of money to some bad people who want to break his knees and stuff. If I love him, I'll help him out, he says. I love him. 'What do I have to do?' I ask him.

" 'You have to spend an hour with this guy,' he tells me. 'He won't hurt you or anything. Just do as he says, and he'll give you five hundred bucks.'

"I tell him *no way!* I cry for two days. I threaten to leave, though of course I've got no place to go. The next night, he comes home with his face cut. Tells me they caught him, but he managed to get away. He told me they were going to kill him next time, and I believed him. So I said okay.

"I went to this guy's hotel room. He had me take off all my clothes and bend over a big pile of pillows in the middle of his living room floor, facedown, while he stood behind me rubbing himself. I kept waiting for the pain. But he never touched me. He did his thing, zipped up, and handed me five one-hundred-dollar bills.

"It seemed like a joke: all that money just for letting some weirdo get his rocks off. So I did it again the next night, only the second guy was a little more hands-on. After that, there were other hotel rooms, other guys. Before I knew it, I was nothing but a high-priced whore. Paulie took every cent I brought in. Me, I was glad to give it to him. I thought I was saving his life, and I sure didn't want to keep the money.

"Then, to make a long story short, I found out that I wasn't the only one who was out there saving Paulie's life. We had a pretty good fight. He laughed at me, told me he'd cut his own face, that there weren't any debts or guys looking to kill him or break his knees, and that I was one of six girls he had working for him, and that he could do anything he liked with me. To prove his point, he tied me up, stuffed a washcloth in my mouth, and raped me. Afterward, he guaranteed me that if I ever went to the police, he'd have me killed. When he fell asleep, I untied myself, crawled out the window, and climbed down the fire escape. It was raining, so I found a place to get out of the rain. That's when you found me."

They sit in silence. Goodman wants to say something, wants to tell her it's all right, but he can't think of any words that seem to fit. "I'm sorry" is what he settles for, and it seems to be as good as anything, because it draws a smile from Carmen, though certainly not one of her *smiles*.

They have more coffee and they sit, mostly in silence. At one point, Carmen takes his right hand in her own, and they continue to sit.

That night, Goodman gives up his spot on the floor and lies on the sofa bed with Carmen. They are in their underwear: he in his wrinkled boxer shorts and sleeveless undershirt, she in matching pink bra and panties. They lie a good two feet apart, and—just to make certain that no funny business goes on—Pop-Tart plants himself squarely between them.

Nonetheless, Goodman doesn't have a prayer of falling asleep. He lies in the dark, feeling his pulse pound in his chest, his wrists, his temples, and even his penis. He tells himself it's the caffeine, but he knows better than to believe everything he hears.

Sometime around three, just when he's almost asleep, he feels a hand brush against his own. It will cost him another hour of restlessness.

[18]

Goodman awakes Friday morning to the smell of coffee brewing. He looks at the clock. 7:33. He figures he's gotten maybe four hours of sleep, tops.

Yet when Carmen brings him a cup of steaming coffee, she looks rested and gorgeous. She's put a denim shirt on. He catches a glimpse of her pink panties, then quickly looks away. He accepts the coffee gratefully.

"I've got to take Kelly to the hospital this morning," he tells her. "I'll probably be gone most of the day."

"Do you want me to look for a place to stay?" she asks. "I mean, I've got friends—"

In the firmest voice he can muster at this hour of the morning on four hours of sleep, he says, "I want nothing of the sort."

She leans forward and kisses his forehead. The thought that comes to him is that his nose has missed its turn.

At 0915 hours, Ray Abbruzzo and Daniel Riley are back at Maggie Kennedy's room on the sixth floor of the Special Narcotics Prosecutor's office. She has the papers for the eavesdropping order all drawn up, waiting for Abbruzzo's signature.

By 9:45, they're across the street in part 70 of the Supreme Court. Even though court's supposed to begin at 9:30, there's no judge in sight.

A few minutes after ten, a small woman with glasses perched on the end of her nose comes in from a side door and mounts the step to where the judge is supposed to sit. In a voice that can charitably be described as somewhere between a rasp and a whine, she asks if there are any ready cases.

"Not yet," says Tommy, the clerk.

"There's a wiretap order, if you want to take that," says Dennis, the sergeant.

"Okay," says Justice Arlene Silverman. "Come on up."

Maggie Kennedy, papers in hand, approaches with Detective Abbruzzo. She hands the papers to the judge, who, while she looks through them, asks Abbruzzo if he swears to the truth of his affidavit.

"Yes, I do," Abbruzzo says, right hand in the air.

"Very well," Justice Silverman says after a minute. She signs her name three times and tosses the papers to Tommy, who stamps them up.

After a quick trip to the clerk's office on the tenth floor to get a seal imprinted through the judge's signatures, Ray Abbruzzo and Dennis Riley have their wiretap order.

Goodman picks Kelly up at nine, and they walk over to Madison Avenue and then uptown toward the Mount Sinai Medical Center, Larus in tow. Kelly seems upbeat, doing her best to be brave in the face of whatever this day will bring. Only once does she ask if what they're going to do to her will hurt.

"I'm afraid it will," he says. "But the doctor said I could be right there with you, holding your hand, so I will be."

"Promise?"

"Promise."

His only wish at this moment is that he could change places with her, that her headaches could be his headaches, that whatever tumor lurks deep inside her tiny head could only be in his, and that the terrible needle they're readying for her spine could instead be aimed at him.

Almost as if she can read his thoughts, his daughter gives his hand a tiny squeeze and looks up at him. "I'll be okay," she announces.

They enter through continuously revolving doors—Kelly decides they're "magic portals," and Goodman is not for the first time astounded with her vocabulary—and follow color-coded signs down long corridors. It seems they have to walk underneath the hospital for almost as long as they walked *to* it. Finally, they reach an elevator that promises to take them to the Same-Day Procedure Unit.

They fill out papers together, Kelly contributing her full name, date of birth, and home address. When it comes to allergies, she says, "I really *hate* sardines. I almost barfed once when I tasted one. Does that count?"

"Why not?" Goodman agrees, and he lists sardines under allergies.

He has a bit more difficulty with the section entitled "Medical Coverage." He's tempted to list the insurance company from his old job, but he worries that he could be accused of fraud or misrepresentation or something, so long has it been now since he was fired. Instead, he simply writes, "None."

"None" doesn't quite seem to do the trick at the reception desk, however, and Goodman is directed to see the cashier. There, he's informed that the charge for the procedure is $825, of which $500 must be paid in advance when there's no proof of insurance.

"Does that include the doctor's bill?" he asks.

"Oh, no. That's extra."

"How much extra?"

"They generally charge somewhere between a thousand and fifteen hundred."

He takes out his credit card case. He's been using it ever since he lost his wallet—along with his pants, his shoes, and the first kilo of heroin—in his first attempt to become a drug seller. Behind the five twenties, behind the worthless credit cards, behind the expired library card, he finds what he's looking for: a single check bearing the imprint of the Bronx Tire Exchange. His hand shakes slightly as he fills it out and signs it. Walking back to rejoin his daughter, Goodman promises that no matter what happens, whatever it takes, he'll pay this money back to Manny, who's never done anything to him but hire him and trust him.

Shortly after noon, a white NYNEX truck with blue-and-yellow trim pulls into a block and double-parks. Two uniformed technicians climb down from the cab, assemble some equipment from the back, and head for the building listed on their work order. They ring the bell, wait a few minutes, and are met by the superintendent. He leads them downstairs and shows them the telephone wire panel that links each of the building's apartments with the incoming lines.

"You need anything else, just let me know," he tells them. "My name's Tony."

But they don't need anything else. One of them punches a seven-digit number on a red handheld phone strapped to his belt. The other one fastens a wire to a terminal on the panel by means of an alligator clip. Then he begins touching another alligator clip, connected to another wire, to other terminals, one by one. As soon as he touches the fourth terminal, there's an audible dial tone.

"That's a pair," he says, fastening the wires.

That easily, and that quickly, has Michael Goodman's phone been tapped.

As they pack up their equipment and prepare to leave, the first technician looks around. "Nice setup," he says. "I sure wish my building had storage lockers like this."

Goodman and Kelly are led by a nurse to a small room. There is an examining table, two chairs, a rolling cart with drawers in it, and two wastebaskets—one marked BIOHAZARDOUS. There is no window. Goodman seats Larus on one of the chairs.

The nurse hands Goodman two white gowns. "She needs to take off all her clothes and put this on," she says. "And if you're going to stay, you need to put this over your clothes, and wear one of these." She hands him a surgical mask, not unlike the masks Hammer distributed at Big Red's heroin mill.

Goodman unfolds the gowns, which turn out to be the same size. He helps Kelly on with hers; it's so big on her that her hands disappear, and he has to roll up the sleeves to find them. The strings in the back go all the way around her waist and can be fastened with big bows in the front.

"Is my butt covered?" she worries.

"I can't even tell you've got one," he assures her. He puts the second gown over his own clothes. Kelly ties the strings for him.

A second nurse comes in and tells Kelly to lie on the table, facedown. She unties the strings of the gown, completely revealing Kelly's tiny rear end.

"Hey!"

"Sorry," the nurse says, arranging the gown more discreetly. Then she proceeds to wash Kelly's lower back, first with soap and water, then with alcohol, and finally with some chemical that leaves the area a bright yellow color. "Stay like that," she says, and leaves the room.

What seems like a half an hour goes by. Kelly complains she's cold. Goodman suspects she's frightened or embarrassed, or both. He rubs her upper back, being careful not to touch the yellow area.

Finally, Dr. Gendel comes in, accompanied by yet another nurse. "How are we doing here?" he asks.

"We're cold," Kelly says.

"Well, we can't have that, can we?" the doctor says, leaving the room as quickly as he'd entered. He returns in a moment and says, "That should be better." Within seconds, the temperature has already begun to rise. If he can do that, Goodman tells himself, surely he can make my little girl better again.

While the doctor and nurse lay out instruments on a towel, Goodman puts on his surgical mask and takes a position at his daughter's head. He strokes her hair, tells her how much he loves her.

The doctor spreads Kelly's gown, exposing the tiny butt she's so protective of, but this time she doesn't complain. He swabs the center part of the yellow area with more alcohol. He probes the base of her spine with his fingers until he finds the spot he's looking for, then draws a circle with what looks like a Magic Marker.

The nurse hands him a small syringe with a tiny needle, and Goodman feels reassured, knows this is something Kelly can handle.

"This is going to sting," the doctor tells her. Goodman watches as the needle goes into the marked area, feels his daughter tense.

"Ow," she says softly. "That burns." But after a moment, he can feel her begin to relax. He's about to tell her that wasn't so bad when he sees the nurse hand Dr. Gendel a second syringe. This one is huge, and the needle attached to it looks like it could pierce an engine block. Goodman suddenly feels so light-headed that he has to place one hand on the examining table for support. The other hand continues to stroke Kelly's hair.

He cannot watch as the second needle pierces his daughter's skin, though he knows the exact moment from her tensing and beginning to whimper again. He grits his teeth and holds his breath as the needle knifes into flesh, through muscle, and finds the spinal column itself. He leans his weight against the table with one hand as the other continues to stroke his daughter's hair over and over and over again, until it seems as though his hand is no longer a part of him.

                              *   *   *

Ray Abbruzzo, Daniel Riley, and a third detective sit around a basement apartment across the street and two doors down from where Michael Goodman lives. The name of the third detective is Harry Weems; he and a fourth detective have been assigned by the Organized Crime Control Bureau of the New York Police Department to assist Abbruzzo and Riley on their investigation.

Until yesterday, this basement apartment was unoccupied: a single damp room with a sink, a hot plate, a motel-size refrigerator, and a bathroom down the hallway. The landlady had long ago given up on it as one of those rarest of all things—an unrentable Manhattan apartment.

That was before two men in business suits showed up inquiring about its availability. The landlady had looked them up and down slowly before shaking her head and saying, "You're not gonna be happy there. *No way.*"

Both men reached for their pockets, and for a second the landlady thought she was about to be murdered. But one had reached for a gold badge, and the other for a checkbook.

Before she knew it, she was looking down at a check in her hands in the amount of three thousand dollars, a sum representing two months' rent on the apartment.

She'd chuckled to herself later on. "Damn thing's worth no more'n a thousand!"

Overnight, the room has become a "plant." A collapsible aluminum table is covered with electronic equipment. There is a large tape recorder, capable of recording from as many as six phone lines simultaneously. There are headsets plugged into the recorder. There is a device called an automatic electronic impulse starter, which activates the equipment a thousand times faster than the human ear can pick up the ring of an incoming call or the hum of a dial tone. And there is a pen register, a machine that deciphers the electronic codes and spits out a continuous list of every call made and received, complete with area code, extension (if any), time of connection, and time of completion.

There are also telephones, log sheets, boxes of tape cassettes, pens, pencils, a space heater, and—because detectives work here—newspapers, guns, coffee containers, handcuffs, jelly doughnuts, spiral notepads, and antacid tablets. Come back in two days, there'll also be burger wrappers, pizza boxes, Chinese-food cartons, soda cans, ketchup packets, chicken bones, and an awful lot more coffee containers.

"Any activity?" asks Weems, who has been in the apartment less than ten minutes.

"Nothing yet," Abbruzzo says. "He must be out."

"Probably setting up a deal," Riley adds.

Weems nods thoughtfully. He's already been warned at a briefing session that this Mole guy is a major player, who's already had a CI killed and who must be considered very cautious and extremely dangerous.

"Who's going out for coffee?" Abbruzzo wants to know.

Goodman carries his daughter and her stuffed animal up the five flights to his apartment. The sound of his key in the lock is enough to bring Carmen, who swings the door open for him and, without saying a word, takes Kelly in her own arms. For somebody so slender, she is surprisingly strong.

Goodman opens the sofa bed, and Carmen lowers Kelly onto it and places Larus alongside her. Kelly is awake, but she's been told to keep her head from moving as much as possible. It's the fluid inside the skull that cushions the brain when the head moves. The spinal tap has drained much of that fluid and, until the body has time to replenish the supply, any sudden motion can cause the brain to collide with the inside of the skull, causing pain or even bruising of the brain, which can be serious.

Goodman is exhausted, physically spent from carrying his daughter and emotionally drained from worrying about her, and he collapses onto a chair. Carmen attends to Kelly, removing her shoes, loosening her clothing, asking her if there's anything she needs.

"Can I have a drink of water?" is all Kelly asks.

Carmen looks at Goodman, who nods. Fluids are good, he's been told: They hasten the replenishment process. He watches as Carmen pours Kelly a glass of water and finds a straw—something that Goodman didn't even know he had—so that Kelly can drink from the glass without having to lift her head. Watching this, Goodman is overwhelmed by the sheer tenderness of the act, and he's forced to look away, so that his tears won't give him away again.

Later that evening, the three of them sit on the bed and eat leftover veal stew, this time over noodles. Kelly eats very little, but Goodman tells himself not to worry, that that's probably to be expected. Pop-Tart is delighted.

After dinner, Goodman tells Kelly he's going to lower the lights and let her go to sleep. She looks paler than ever, but she still manages to smile.

"Not yet, Daddy?"

"Why not?"

"I need some more of our story."

The Ballerina Princess
(Continued)

So it came to pass that the Ballerina Princess had the Great Unfair Test, the one that really hurt. But with the brave and loyal Prince Larus at her side, and the Keeper of the Numbers at her head, the Ballerina Princess was wonderful. She said "Ouch!" and cried the tiniest bit, which was good, because otherwise the doctor might not have known she was still awake.

And when the test was over, the Ballerina Princess allowed the Keeper of the Numbers to carry her to the top floor of his castle and place her on the royal bed,

"You didn't put me on the bed," Kelly reminds him. "Carmen did."

with the help of his friend Lady Carmen

"The beauteous Lady Carmen," Kelly corrects him again.

the beauteous Lady Carmen, that is.

And all that evening, the Ballerina Princess was required to keep her head very still, lest her crystal crown fall off and shatter, causing seven hours of bad luck. And she decided that the best way to do that was to go to sleep right after dinner, so that she wouldn't forget and suddenly move her head. And that's exactly what she did.

After Kelly closes her eyes, Goodman wedges Larus against one side of her head and a pillow against the other. He kisses her softly on the cheek.

"Good night, Daddy," she says.

"Good night, angel."

He phones his mother-in-law to tell her that the test is over and that they're back at his place.

"How's our little girl?" she asks him.

"She seems okay," he says. "I just put her to bed."

"You think she's safe there?"

"Absolutely," he says.

"Okay," his mother-in-law says. "But keep an eye on her, all right? You can never be too careful, you know."

"I will," he assures her.

In a basement apartment across the street and two doors down, Daniel Riley sits up straight. "Did you hear that?" he asks.

"What?" Ray Abbruzzo asks.

"I just put 'our little girl' to bed, where she'll be 'safe.' Now if they're not talking about a load of drugs, my mother's not Irish."

"Could be," Abbruzzo agrees. "Could be."

"You *bet* it could be," Riley says. "I'm telling you, Ray—the fucking Mole is back in action."

The word in the South Bronx that evening is that a new load of shit has hit the street and that Big Red's people have got it. It's being sold in nickles and full loads—street talk for bundles. It's called "Red Menace" on 141st Street; on 125th, it's packaged as "Red Devil." And the talk is that downtown they're moving the same stuff as "Red Dawn," and up by the bridge they're calling it "Spanish Red."

By nine o'clock, more than twenty thousand bags have been sold. By midnight, except for a few leftovers here and there, it will all be gone, out onto the streets of the South Bronx and Harlem and Washington Heights, into the veins and up the nostrils of the city's walking dead.

{19}

Goodman spends Sunday afternoon as he always does, with Krulewich, the Whale, and Lehigh Valley. The Giants are playing the Cowboys at Dallas, so the game doesn't start until four o'clock New York time. In deference to Krulewich's poor eyesight, they turn the TV volume down and listen to the play-by-play on the radio. The Whale's not happy about the arrangement, because he really likes John Madden, who's one of the TV announcers. But the radio guys describe the action in a lot more detail, and are Giants fans themselves, so they let you know whenever the refs give the Cowboys a favorable call.

On this day, the Giants are no match for either the Cowboys or the refs, and the game's been pretty much decided by halftime.

GIANTS	6
COWBOYS	20

Nevertheless, the Whale wants to keep watching, to see if the total final score is more or less than the forty-one-point "over/under" line that the bookies have predicted. But he's outvoted three to one in favor of hearts, the game Lehigh taught them last Sunday.

Goodman plays cautiously again, all but forgetting to look for an opportunity to shoot the moon. But nobody else goes for it, either, and the final score after five hands is much closer than last time.

KRULEWICH   41
WHALE   39
GOODMAN   31
LEHIGH   19

"You guys are gettin' the hang of it awright," Lehigh tells them. "But you're still no match for the champ!"

They turn the ball game on in time for Goodman to see that at least he did better than the Giants.

GIANTS   9
COWBOYS   34

"I *knew* they'd be over!" moans the Whale. "I coulda cleaned up! I coulda won a *fortune!*"

"The spinal fluid shows a few abnormal cells," Dr. Gendel tells Goodman over the phone Monday morning.

"What does that mean?" Goodman asks.

"It's hard to say, really. She could have some kind of low-grade infection in the meninges, the lining of the brain. We'll put her on an antibiotic and see what that does. But what I'd really like to do is another MRI, this time with contrast."

A chill runs through Goodman's body. "That's where you inject dye into her?"

"That's right. It gives us much more definitive pictures."

Goodman's afraid to ask where they inject the dye. He remembers the huge syringe, tipped with its terrible needle; only this time, he pictures it filled with a dark purple liquid, aimed again at the base of his daughter's spine, or perhaps the back of her neck, or her temple, or the spot between her eyes.

"You really think this is necessary?" he asks.

"I wouldn't be suggesting it if I didn't," the doctor tells him. Goodman thinks he detects a note of defensiveness there. "But there is a little problem before we can go ahead."

"What's that?" Goodman asks, dreading more bad news.

"My office manager tells me that you've made no payments on your bill. And when she checked with the MRI facility, they told her it's the same story with the first test they did. Apparently, there's no insurance? Anyway, they say they won't do another one unless they're paid in full for the first one and up front for the second one."

"I've had some trouble . . ." Goodman starts to say, but his voice trails off.

"Well," Dr. Gendel says, "I'd hate to have to make a diagnosis without the proper tools. What is it you do for a living again?"

"I'm an accountant, a bookkeeper."

"Right. Well now, you wouldn't want to attack a complicated accounting problem without your . . . your calculator, would you?"

"No," Goodman says, feeling patronized. The truth is, he often does figures by hand, trusting himself more than machines, and also because he likes numbers—working with them pleases him. But he knows the point would be lost on the doctor, so he keeps it to himself. "I'll see what I can do," he says instead.

He says nothing to Kelly about the conversation. She's spent the weekend recuperating. She had a headache most of Saturday, but then again, it might not have been as a result of the spinal tap. Her back is still sore from the needle.

"Get dressed, angel," he tells her. "I'll drop you off at Grandma's on my way to work."

"Can I stay with Carmen instead?" she asks.

"I'm sure Carmen has things she has to do."

"Nothing that Kelly can't do with me," Carmen says.

"Please, Daddy?"

"I don't know—"

"Pleeeeeze?"

"Go to work, Daddy," Carmen says. "The women in your life will be just fine."

That seems to settle it.

At work, Goodman uses a double-entry system to hide the check he wrote to Mount Sinai. To anyone looking at the books, the entry will show up as a legitimate operating expense. It'll be a good three weeks before the canceled check itself comes back with next month's bank statement.

Manny's there but, as usual, pays no attention to Goodman and his work. He's upset about the price of the new Goodyears and preoccupied with a tire bath that's suddenly sprung a leak and flooded the back of the shop.

Around 3:30, Goodman calls home to find out how "the women in his life" are doing.

"We baked *bread!*" Kelly tells him. "I never knew you could do that, did you?"

"No, I never did."

"And we're going to make *curtains.* Carmen's going to teach me how to *sew.*"

"That's terrific," he says, wondering whatever happened to the feminist movement. "Let me talk to Carmen, okay?"

Carmen says, "Hello," just as there's a clicking noise on the line.

"What's that?" Goodman asks.

"I don't know," she says. "Sounds like somebody's tapping your phone. You into something I don't know about?"

"Right," he says. "That's why I've got all that money you see sitting around the apartment."

"So *that* explains it," she laughs.

"How you guys doing?" he asks.

"Great," she says. "But hurry home. We miss you."

After he hangs up, he tries to remember if he's ever been told that before.

"Stop playing with those buttons!" Ray Abbruzzo yells at Daniel Riley.

Riley takes his hand away from the equipment. "You hear that?" he asks.

"Yeah," Abbruzzo says. "The part about them hearing noises and figuring their phone's tapped."

"That's nothing," Riley assures him. "Only somebody who's doing something wrong thinks his phone's tapped. Ever hear of an innocent guy thinks that way? And did you hear the bit about there being money in the apartment?"

"I think he was being sarcastic, like."

"No way. This guy made a move over the weekend. I bet you anything he unloaded a package, and we fuckin' missed it."

Abbruzzo yawns. "You hungry?" he asks.

*   *   *

That night, with Kelly asleep on the sofa bed, Goodman and Carmen sit across the card table from each other, sipping the last of their coffee. The last crumbs of homemade bread dot the tabletop.

He's told her about his conversation with the doctor, told her about his inability to pay for his daughter's tests, told her about his pile of over-due bills. She's placed one hand over his, and now she strokes it softly, the same way he watched her stroke the kitten not long ago.

"I could go back to work," she says softly.

"To the *street?*" He pulls his hand away.

"It's not the street," she says. "I was a call girl, not a streetwalker."

"No way," he says. "I'll rob a bank before I let you do that."

"I could go back to waiting tables," she suggests.

"Your five dollars an hour, and my two afternoons a week," he laughs.

She takes his hand back in hers, this woman who's just offered to sell her body to strangers in order to help him pay his bills. He sits there, lis-tening to the hum of the refrigerator motor, until it abruptly shuts off, leaving the rise and fall of Kelly's breathing from the sofa bed as the only sound in the room. He looks over at her, and for some reason he re-members how upset she'd been at the hospital over the prospect of her naked butt being exposed. He's struck by just how vulnerable she is, how very fragile. He knows he has to do whatever it takes to protect her.

And right then and there, Michael Goodman does the unthinkable. Turning slowly back to Carmen, looking her straight in the eye, he does precisely that which he's promised himself he will never do.

"Tell me about your brother," he says.

Tuesday morning, Goodman makes Kelly bundle up, and they walk to Central Park. They enter at Ninetieth Street and circle the reservoir. It looks full from all the rain they've had lately. There's ice at the very edges.

"Do people really drink this water?" Kelly asks him.

"I think so," he says, though he's not really sure. He remembers hearing that the city gets its water from upstate somewhere.

"It looks so yucky," she says. "All those leaves and allergy."

"Algae."

"I like to call it allergy," she says. "How come Carmen couldn't come with us?"

"She's got something she has to do."

The thing Carmen has to do is to call her brother. Last night, after Goodman had broken his promise to himself and asked her about him, she'd naturally wanted to know why. So he'd started at the beginning: He'd told her about his discovery of the blue plastic bags in the spare tire down in Fort Lauderdale. He'd described his efforts to turn the drugs in, his decision to bring them to New York, his encounter with Russell, and the disaster in Carl Schurz Park. He'd also included the burglary of his apartment, and the search of it by the police later on. But he'd stopped short of telling her precisely how much heroin there is or just where he'd hidden it, and she hadn't pressed him for details there. He was grateful for that—he figured the less she knew about those things, the better for her.

Yes, she'd said, her brother Vincent—Vinnie to everybody but her—had boasted to her more than once that he'd been involved in big drug deals involving both cocaine and heroin. She had no idea if he was being truthful or not, but she'd learned over time not to put anything past him.

"But Michael," she'd said, "do you have any idea how dangerous this is? Do you know what could happen to us if we get caught?"

"Not *we*, paleface," he'd said. "I just want you to introduce me to your brother. Then I'll take care of the rest. I want you to stay completely out of it."

"Right. You'll take care of it like you did when they left you in your undershorts."

"I'll be more careful," he'd told her. "And if I screw up again, so be it. That way, if I go down, I go down alone. I don't have to destroy your life, too."

She'd looked at him hard at that point and said, "You *saved* my life, Michael. If this is what you decide you're going to do, I want to help you."

"No," he'd said. "Besides, all I did was bring you in out of the rain."

"No," she'd insisted, before repeating her words slowly and emphatically. "You saved my life."

They'd gone to bed shortly after, she on the bed with Kelly and Larus and Pop-Tart, he on the floor, fortified by her promise to call her brother in the morning. But, explaining that she was now more concerned than ever that his phone might be tapped, she'd told him that she'd do it from a pay phone. Just to be on the safe side.

"Are there fish in reservoirs?" Kelly asks him now.

"I suppose so," he says.

"How come they don't freeze?"

"They're New York City fish," he explains. "They're tough."

"How come they don't get sucked into the pipes that take the water to our faucets?"

"They're too big."

"How about baby ones?"

"I imagine there are screens to keep them out," he says.

"How about their poops? Can't *they* get through the screens?"

"Maybe," he has to admit. "But then they treat the water with chlorine and stuff before it goes into our faucets."

"It still sounds yucky to me," she says.

That evening, after Kelly's asleep, Carmen informs Goodman that she's succeeded in reaching her brother. As he waits for whatever she's going to tell him next, Goodman finds himself half-hoping that it'll be that Vinnie's interested in the idea, and half-hoping to hear that he wants nothing whatsoever to do with it.

In fact, the news turns out to be a combination of the two.

"He's interested all right," she says, "but he's afraid to meet you. Thinks you might be a narc. Are you a narc, Michael?"

"I think I can safely say that I am not a narc," he says.

"I actually took the liberty of telling him that. But you've got to understand Vincent's pretty paranoid. When he heard what I was talking about, he made me give him the number of the pay phone I was at, so that *he* could go to a pay phone and call me back at *my* pay phone. I swear, I felt like I was in the CIA or something. Next he started asking me if I was angry at him for anything. He finally admitted he's afraid *I* might be trying to set him up."

"So—"

"So, after all that, he said he wants in, but only if he can send someone else to deal with you."

Goodman digests the news for a moment. "So what do you think?" he asks her.

"I don't know, Michael. You asked me to call him, I called him. He said he's interested. It's up to you now."

"Who's this guy he wants to send me?"

"They call him T.M.," she says. "I met him once or twice years ago. He went to school with Vincent, taught him how to steal cars."

"Hey," Goodman says. "What are friends for, anyway?"

She laughs, but it's not one of her best. It's clear to him that she has reservations about this business. He wishes he had a choice, wishes he could come up with some other way to raise the money.

"So," he says. "Let's say I want to get together with Vincent's guy, T—"

"T.M."

"T.M. How do I arrange that?"

"Vincent's pay phone is going to call my pay phone at exactly noon tomorrow," she says. "If you want to do it, you go there with me. If not, you pass. Only, one thing?"

"What's that?"

"Call him Vinnie, okay? Anybody but me calls him Vincent, he's liable to freak out. Somebody once told him it's a fag name."

"Fair enough," Goodman says. "Vinnie it is."

Abbruzzo and Riley are off duty that evening, and the plant is being manned by the two OCCB detectives, Weems and Sheridan. They've been on for almost seven hours, with hardly a single phone call to log in.

"I'm telling you, it's too quiet in there," Sheridan says. "Something's going down."

"Nah, they're probably in the sack, playing Hide the Salami."

"That little fucker?" Sheridan laughs. "He don't look like he can even get it up."

"Don't be so sure," Weems says. "Those little guys can surprise you sometimes."

But at that moment, the only person Michael Goodman is surprising is himself. He lies on his now-familiar spot of the floor, wondering how it is that he's so quickly yielded to temptation all over again, barely a week after getting so badly burned the first time.

For already he knows that he'll be with Carmen when she goes to the pay phone at noon tomorrow. He doesn't even allow himself the luxury of pretending that he may yet decide to pass. No, he'll go, and he'll take his chances again, even if that means taking his lumps again.

His hope, as he lies there in the dark of his apartment, staring up at the ceiling, is that this time he'll manage to be just a little bit smarter about it.

It's already ten minutes past noon on Wednesday when Goodman turns to Carmen and asks, "This guy T.M., he's not black by any chance, is he?"

They've been waiting in the cold at a pay phone at the corner of Eighty-sixth and Third—the same phone from which Carmen called her brother Vincent ("Vinnie to you") yesterday. Kelly is with them, working on a pretzel they bought from a chestnut seller. The chestnuts looked yucky, she said.

"Pay phones don't call *you*," she now tries to explain patiently to the two adults. "They're there for you to call someone *else*."

While Carmen suppresses a laugh, Goodman does his best to justify what they're doing here. "The someone else knows this number, and he wanted to call us right around this time, when we knew we'd be here."

"What about?"

"About work," Goodman says. "A new job, maybe."

"Sounds weird to me," Kelly says.

"Can I have a bite?" Goodman asks. He's reaching for the pretzel when they're all startled by a loud ringing noise.

"There," he says. "You see?"

Carmen picks up the receiver and speaks into it. After a minute, she hands it to Goodman, mouthing the initials T.M. Goodman pulls a scrap of paper and a pen out of his pocket. He waits until Carmen's walked Kelly out of earshot before he says "Hello" into the phone.

"Hello," says a raspy voice. "You her friend?"

"Yes."

"I hear you got sompin speshul."

"That's right," Goodman says.

"My people are interested in checkin' it out," the voice says. "Whaddaya need for a quadda oh-zee?"

Goodman doesn't know what to say. He has no idea what T.M. has just asked him. He scribbles down what it sounded like, but he's afraid to try to answer whatever the question was.

"Too large be okay?" the voice asks.

Goodman is stumped again, but he figures he's got to say something. "Sure," he says, "that'll be okay."

"You know the big bookstore over on Lexington?" the voice wants to know. "The Barney Noble?"

"Yes."

"We'll meet there same time tomorrow—in the travel book section. You be carrying some flowers wrapped up in white paper. Put the thing inside the paper. But make sure it don't get wet. That's very important. Okay?"

"Okay," Goodman says. "How will I recognize you?"

"You won't," the voice says. "I'll recanize *you*. Remember, I'm the one's stickin' my neck out here."

"What do I call the girl in my report?" Riley asks Abbruzzo as they sit shivering in the wiretap plant, trying their best to keep warm from the space heater. The phone they're listening in on has been quiet all morning. Riley is bent over a three-page document, about halfway through filling in blanks. Fortunately, most police reports tend to be multiple choice in format, or, at worst, short-answer. Essays are rarely called for.

"I don't know," Abbruzzo says. "We don't have her name yet."

"No," Riley says. "I don't mean her *name*. I mean like 'girlfriend' or 'companion'—that kinda thing."

"I think 'companion' is when they're gay," Abbruzzo says. "How about 'lady friend'?"

"Too English."

" 'Lover'?"

"Too romantic," Riley says. "We're supposed to be making this guy sound like a major drug violator, remember? Not a fucking movie star."

"I've got it," Abbruzzo says. "She's his *paramour.*"

"Ooooh, that's good—pure Mafia." It's a few seconds before he looks up from his writing. "P-A-R-A?"

"M-O-R-E," Abbruzzo says.

"Right," says Riley.

T̲hat evening, after Kelly's fallen asleep, Goodman fishes out the scrap of paper from his pocket and flattens it out on the table for Carmen to help him decipher. They stare at the writing on it.

Quadda ohzee?

Too Large

Barnes & Noble Lex
same time tomorrow

Travel books

Flowers—white paper

Keep dry!

"What was he talking about when he said these things?" Carmen asks.

"The Barnes & Noble part I understood," Goodman says. "That's where we're supposed to meet tomorrow. I guess at quarter after twelve. I'm supposed to be in the travel section, with the stuff in a bunch of flowers. It's the first part I'm confused about. I think he was telling me how much I'm supposed to bring."

"And that's when he said, 'Quadda—' "

" 'Quadda ohzee.' "

"Sounds like a Quarter Pounder with cheese," Carmen says.

"That's it!"

"What's it?"

" 'Quaddah' is *quarter,*" he announces with all the pride of a spy who's just cracked the enemy's master code, "and 'ohzee' is *oz.,* as in *ounce.*"

"They want a quarter of an ounce," Carmen agrees. "Like a sample. Did you discuss price?"

"I think so," Goodman says. "I think that's where the 'too large' came in."

"That's the price," she says.

"What's the price?"

"Two large."

"What's too large?" Goodman asks, beginning to feel like he's caught up in an Abbott and Costello routine.

"Two large means two thousand dollars," she explains. "Paulie was all the time talking like that. 'Two C's' or 'two yards' would mean two hundred. 'Two G's' or 'two big ones' or 'two large' is two thousand. You know—God forbid he should've spoken English."

But Goodman's no longer paying attention. His accountant's brain has taken over once again. If a quarter of an ounce goes for two thousand dollars, then an ounce is worth eight thousand. Multiply that by sixteen, and a pound will bring close to $130,000. A kilo, or 2.2 pounds, should be $286,000. And twenty kilos brings you slightly over $5.7 million.

"These guys pay a lot more than the black guys," he says softly.

"As I remember the story, the black guys weren't into paying anything. Weren't they the ones who took your pants?"

"Yup," Goodman says. "What do you think these guys'll try to take?"

"Oh, not much. Your liver, your heart."

"Nothing important."

"That's why you're going to let me help you," Carmen says, putting her hand on his.

"Right," he laughs. " 'Cause you're so good about holding on to *your* pants."

She pulls her hand away as though from an open flame. "That was cruel," she tells him.

"I'm sorry," he says. "I didn't mean it that way." And when he reaches for her hand, she reluctantly lets him take it back. But in that brief exchange, Michael Goodman knows this: There's a tiny part of him that *did* mean to hurt her just now, a part of him that blames her, that's angry at her for having given in to Paulie, for having surrendered—what, her body, her love? Not quite trusting himself to put these feelings into words just yet, he says nothing. Instead, he gives her hand a gentle squeeze.

Hours later, Goodman lies on the floor and listens in the dark to the sounds that come from the sofa bed. After awhile, he's able to recognize the tiny exhalations of his daughter. Ever since she first came home from the hospital as a newborn, she's been a mouth-breather. He remembers how, in the first days and weeks of her life, he would stand beside her crib and listen to the rhythm of her breathing, marveling at this tiny creature with a life of her own. In later months, he would find himself in the doorway to her room, checking to make sure she was safe, hearing again the little puffs of air coming from her lips. Now he hears them again, identifies them as hers as surely as a mother seal can pick out her own pup by its smell from thousands on the beach.

Next, he hears the occasional purr of Pop-Tart, a miniature motor idling so gently that he knows he'd miss it altogether if he didn't know to listen for it.

Finally, he makes out the sound he's been searching for: yet a third noise, this one so soft that he's dependent not on its volume but upon its frequency. Twenty years ago, Michael Goodman was an ensign in the navy on a training ship hugging the coast from New London, Connecticut, to Norfolk, Virginia. Too sick to sleep one night, he'd come up on deck and clung to the rail, afraid he might die, and afraid he might not. He remembers now picking out the beacon of a distant lighthouse not by its brightness—there were hundreds of stars and other lights on shore that were brighter—but by the constant, regular intervals that punctuated its flashes.

He does his best now to filter out the sounds of his daughter's exhalations and the purring of the kitten, so that he can isolate this third sound and concentrate on it. He times the intervals at six seconds, thinks how that might appear on a nautical chart as "BS 6sec"—breathing sound, every six seconds. Only when he's completely certain that the rhythm is too regular to mean anything but deep sleep does he rise as quietly as he possibly can, tiptoe in his socks to the door, and slip out silently, wedging a sock in the door frame to avoid making a clicking noise.

Down in the basement, he aims his flashlight and works the combination of his lock. He unzips the black duffel bag and retrieves the same blue plastic package as before. Carefully, he taps some of its powder into a small baggie, stopping when he guesses he has a quarter of an ounce. Then he replaces things as they were, makes his way back upstairs, and returns to his spot on the floor. When his own heartbeat finally quiets, he's able to pick out his daughter's tiny exhalations, the kitten's occasional purring, and the six-second breathing sounds that he knows can only belong to Carmen.

At the plant, Abbruzzo and Riley share a pizza and a six-pack of warm Pepsi. They're working twelve-hour rotations now, beginning with the graveyard shift, midnight to 0800. They'll be on until noon Thursday.

"Looks like Mr. and Mrs. Excitement are down for the night," Abbruzzo says.

"No question about it," Riley agrees. He enters a notation on the log sheet:

> 2315 Subject & paramore asleep. No further calls or
> suspicious activity.

Michael Goodman stands in the travel section of Barnes & Noble and does his best to pretend he's browsing. This is not easy to do, because his right hand holds a large bunch of daisies wrapped in plain white paper.

But while Goodman has pretty much followed the instructions given him over the phone yesterday by an individual known to him only as T.M., he's also departed from those same instructions with respect to one detail. Specifically, the plastic baggie containing the white powder is not inside the paper that holds the flowers.

This departure is partly the product of Carmen's concern and partly the product of Goodman's willingness to listen to her suggestion, limited only by his continuing reluctance to allow her to get involved in this business of his.

After calling the Bronx Tire Exchange and asking Manny if he could come in tomorrow instead of this afternoon, Goodman and Carmen had dropped off Kelly at her grandmother's. Then they'd made a stop at a florist.

"I want some flowers," Goodman had told the clerk, "but I need them wrapped in white paper."

The clerk had checked his inventory. "I got blue and I got lavender," he'd reported. "I got a white background with a pink-and-green pattern. I got red, white, and blue stripes left over from Independence Day. I got silver and gold foil—"

"I need plain white," Goodman had said.

"Then I'm afraid I can't help you."

And all had seemed lost until Carmen had come to the rescue, pointing out that all one had to do was to reverse the white background with the pink-and-green pattern, and—voilà!—one suddenly had plain white paper.

Then, on their way to Barnes & Noble, she'd spoken up again. "You're asking to get robbed again if you put the package in there," she'd told him. "All they have to do is see some guy standing around holding a bunch of flowers in white paper. They grab it from you and run out the door. End of scene."

Goodman had been forced to admit that she had a point there. "So what do we do?" he'd asked her.

"We'll both be in the store," she'd suggested. "Only we won't stand together. We'll act like we don't know each other. You'll hold the flowers," she'd said. "Let me hold the package. If T.M. shows up with the money, have him give it to you. Then I'll be the one to hand him the package."

"No good. I told you, I don't want you messed up in this, and I mean it. There's got to be some other way of doing it, without getting you involved."

"All right," she'd said then. "How about this? Once he shows you the money, you tell him to wait a minute. You come over to me, and I'll give *you* the package. That way, you're the one who gives it to him, and I stay out of it."

And they'd agreed to do it that way.

Now he studies *Fodor's Paris, London on $50 a Day, Trekking in the Himalayas,* and *Street's Cruising Guide to the East Carribean.* He had no idea there could be so many travel books, and he's astonished to find that they've all ended up in a single store. He crouches down, zeroing in on a whole shelf of books on the West Indies. He has to squint just a bit to read the titles, because he's not wearing his glasses. Carmen's convinced him to leave them home. Not only that—she's actually *dressed* him. She's made him give up his jeans for a pair of black cotton slacks. She said they looked more "hip," whatever she meant by that. And she found in his drawer a black imitation Lacoste shirt, from which she'd painstakingly removed the alligator logo with a razor blade. An almost-black suit jacket and a pair of black shoes and socks had finished off the outfit.

"You look like Batman, Daddy" had been Kelly's only comment.

Finally, Carmen had insisted on wetting his hair and had tried to slick it back, but she'd succeeded only in making it look something like wet Brillo.

"Pickin' out a nice place to go to with all that money you'll be gettin'?"

Goodman recognizes the gravelly voice before he even sees who's addressing him. He straightens up but finds he still has to look slightly upward into a heavy-featured face dominated by bushy dark eyebrows that barely break in the middle. Everything about the man suggests power, perhaps even violence—everything, that is, except the bunch of flowers wrapped in white paper he holds tucked under one arm like a football.

"Lookathat, we musta both bought flowers at the same place," the man says, nodding at Goodman's.

"I guess so," Goodman acknowledges, realizing that the man hasn't made a grab for Goodman's flowers after all, though certainly Goodman would be totally powerless to stop him. He wonders for the first time if this might actually turn out to be the deal it's supposed to be, and not another rip-off, as they'd feared.

"This one looks good," the man says, pointing to a book on the bottom shelf. As he lowers himself to one knee, he removes his flowers from under his arm and places them on the carpeted floor.

Goodman has to squat to read the title of the book that's drawn the man's attention. He's lip-reading *Pacific Northwest* when the man makes a suggestion to him: "Put your flowers down."

And suddenly, Goodman gets it. He's supposed to lay his flowers right next to the other bunch. Then, when it's time to get up, they'll do a switch—Goodman will end up with the money flowers and the man will end up with the drug flowers. Just like he's seen it done in the movies.

Only thing is, Goodman knows the drugs aren't *in* his flowers.

"Put your flowers down," the man repeats. This time, it sounds more like a command than a suggestion. Goodman does as he's told.

Sure enough, after a second or two, the man places a meaty hand on Goodman's flowers and straightens up into a standing position. With no choice, Goodman follows his cue. He's struck immediately by the fact that his new flowers are much heavier than his old ones.

"You got a phone where I can get back in touch with you?" the man asks, and before Goodman can think of a reason not to, he's given him his home number.

"Listen," he tells the man, knowing he somehow has to break the news that the drugs aren't in with the flowers as they're supposed to be. But before he can explain that he has to get them, Carmen is there between the two of them.

"Excuse me," she says as she reaches with one hand for a copy of *Frommer's New England*, her other hand finding its way into the flowers in the man's hand. There's nothing stealthy about the way she does it—she just *does* it, gives them each a wink, and continues down the aisle, nose in her book, boning up on Cape Cod, or maybe Martha's Vineyard.

The startled look on the man's face gives way to one of confusion. Goodman decides he'd better say something. "You know how it is. In this business, you can never be too careful" is what he says. Then he follows Carmen toward the front of the store and out onto Lexington Avenue.

Across the avenue, Abbruzzo and Riley huddle with Weems and Sheridan. All four detectives are there because, just before 1020 hours, Abbruzzo picked up a call from Goodman to an unidentified female that he'd be dropping his daughter off in a while so he could attend to "some business."

"Sounds like a deal all right," Riley had agreed.

Then, around 1100, they'd spotted the three of them headed out—the Mole, his daughter, and his "paramore."

"They're makin' a move," Abbruzzo had announced.

They'd followed them on foot, contacting Weems and Sheridan to let them know what was happening. They'd seen Goodman take his daughter into a building on Seventy-second Street, then waited for him to emerge. Their log entries chronicle each activity that followed:

> 1129   Subject exits premises without daughter. Rejoins
>   paramore. Walks N on Lexington.

> 1136   Subject & paramore enter florist at 83rd St.

> 1142   Subject & paramore exit florist. Subject in
>   possession of 1 boukay of flowers.

> 1153   Subject & paramore enter bookstore at 86th St.

> 1209   Subject & paramore exit bookstore. Subject still in
>   possession of boukay.

Now the four of them—Abbruzzo and Riley, who should be off duty by now, and Weems and Sheridan, who've just begun their tour—fall in behind the two people and resume following them. In the process, they fail to note a large man with dark eyebrows and a thick neck, who comes out of the store moments later, carrying a very similar bunch of flowers. By the time he crosses Eighty-fifth Street and joins another man, the four detectives are heading north, trailing the first man and the woman he's with. Riley enters one final log entry before handing the book over to Sheridan:

> 1227   Subject & paramore return on foot to subject's
>   residence & enter premises. Still with boukay.

"I guess it was nothin' after all," Riley shrugs.

"Yeah," Abbruzzo agrees. "The lovebirds must just be into flowers, is all."

But if the lovebirds are into flowers, they show their interest in a somewhat peculiar fashion. As soon as they're back inside the apartment, they lock the door behind them and attack their new possession. They don't bother to notice that the paper is white on both sides; evidently, T.M. *didn't* shop at the same florist they did. Nor do they pause to admire the flowers themselves, which are actually a tasteful mixture of red roses and white baby's breath. Instead, they pull them apart and go directly for a white envelope that's been wedged between the stems. Goodman retrieves it gingerly from the thorns that guard it and begins to tear it open. He's ready for anything—play money from a Monopoly set, cut-up pieces of newspaper, even a note that when unfolded will tell them they've been duped.

What he finds instead are twenty-five one-hundred-dollar bills.

That evening, in Michael Goodman's apartment, the two of them sit facing each other across the card table. Between them are two cups of coffee, two paper napkins, a single spoon, and a stack of one-hundred-dollar bills.

"I'm a drug dealer now," is Goodman's first spoken thought.

"Depends on how you look at it," Carmen says.

"It's how I look at it," he says soberly. "Why'd you change the plan all of a sudden? You were supposed to give the package to *me*, not to T.M."

"You looked a little lost," she tells him, putting a hand on his forearm that tells him not to take it as a criticism. "And besides, like I said, if you're in this, I'm in this, too. You know that old saying, When someone saves your life, you owe them forever. You have to be willing to follow them into hell."

"I never heard that."

"Well, it's something like that," she says.

He lets it go. "What do we do with the money?" he asks her, as though he's not quite sure he's ready to do *anything* with it.

"Well," Carmen says, "I think the first thing you should do is take it to some bank you have nothing to do with, where nobody knows you. Have it changed into smaller bills. People tend to notice hundreds—no use arousing suspicion if you don't have to. Then you can spend it."

"How?"

"Money orders. You take Kelly's most urgent medical bills, and you start there."

Goodman tries his best to visualize doing what she suggests. As always, he reduces it to a matter of numbers. "I guess I could start by paying off the first MRI test and part of the neurologist's bill," he says, "and still have something left over to give them toward the new MRI." He realizes that his getting engrossed with the numbers is his way of ducking more difficult issues, in this case the little matter of spending money he's earned by selling drugs. But then he pictures his daughter's tiny pale face and imagines it contorted in pain, ravaged by a brain tumor that could have been treated, if only he'd had the money for the doctors and the tests she'd needed. And he knows without any further thought that first thing tomorrow, God help him, he'll spend this money.

Money is on Big Red's mind, too, as he drives his Bentley home well after midnight. He's got over sixteen thousand dollars in cash in his pocket, and—although he's accustomed to dealing with amounts far larger than that—he doesn't like to be driving around with it on him. Never can tell when some hotshot cop might take offense at the idea of a black man sitting behind the wheel of a fine car, decide to pull him over and go through his pockets. So, just to be on the safe side, at the next red light, he takes the money from his pocket and goes to stuff it up into the special compartment in the springs underneath the passenger seat.

Only as he does so, he feels something in his way, something flat and smooth. Then he remembers—it's the wallet that was in the pants he and Hammer took off that Caucasian guy they relieved of the kilo. He removes it and places the money in the spot where it had been.

The light turns green. He slips the wallet into his pocket and continues on his way home.

24

Goodman is up early Friday morning, and by nine o'clock he's at the Chemical Bank on Eighty-sixth Street. It's a branch he hasn't been inside for thirty years, and he figures it ought to be as safe as any.

The teller gives him a look when he says he wants to buy $2,500 worth of money orders, but he decides it's only because it's work for her. At one point, he thinks he sees her whispering to someone he imagines is her supervisor, but when she comes back, she has the money orders—four for five hundred dollars, three for one hundred dollars, and three for fifty dollars. He has to use the last fifty dollars to cover the commission the bank charges.

He leaves the bank and heads back to his apartment, where he'll match the various denominations with the stack of bills and envelopes he has, then begin filling in the payees' names.

He doesn't notice the two men who fall into step behind him as he crosses Lexington.

"He must be laundering his money," Sheridan says to Weems. "Maybe one of us oughta go back to the bank and talk to the teller he dealt with."

"I wouldn't chance it," Weems says. "From what Abbruzzo says, this guy's a real piece of work. I guarantee you he does business at this bank all the time. That woman he dealt with inside, she's gotta be his regular contact. He pays her off to wash his cash without making any record of it. We approach her, next thing you know, she'll be tippin' him off. Could blow the whole thing."

"Good thinking, Harry," Sheridan agrees. "When you're right, you're right."

Weems smiles. "Hey, I've learned a thing or two after twelve years on the job."

"So this Mole is some slick operator, huh?"

"You got *that* right."

On his way to the subway to the Bronx, Goodman stops at a mailbox and deposits three envelopes. Each contains money orders in various denominations. He checks to make sure that the envelopes have dropped down into the box. Despite the fact that he's been doing that for as long as he can remember, he's yet to find one piece of mail that's defied gravity and hung there in midair. But he continues to check anyway.

He checks coin returns after using pay phones, too, though he's almost never found any money that way. But habits are funny things, and Michael Goodman seems to derive some sense of pleasure from the ritual itself, separate and apart from any more tangible reward that might be at stake.

At work, nothing is mentioned about Goodman's having come in Friday rather than Thursday. Manny continues to take the position that he doesn't much care how or when the work gets done, so long as it gets done. Goodman suspects that back when Marlene was keeping the books, Manny had to pay much more attention to details. Now he seems happy to have someone who can take over for him.

By four o'clock, he's pretty much finished whatever work he has to do. He dials his mother-in-law's number, hears her pick up on the second ring.

"Hello?"

"Hi, it's Michael."

"Hello, Michael."

"How's everything?"

"So-so," she tells him. "She's still getting the headaches. But she did say the spot in her eye doesn't bother her as much as it did before."

"Well, I guess that's something. Can I talk to her?"

"Sure. Hold on."

After a moment, he hears his daughter's voice. "Hi, Daddy."

"Hi, angel. How you doing?"

"I'm fine. When are you coming to get me?"

"I'll come straight from work, okay?"

"Good," she says. "And Daddy?"

"Yes?"

"You owe me *two chapters!*"

"*Two chapters?*" he laughs. "Then two chapters it'll be! See ya later, alligator."

"After awhile, crocodile."

"In a shake, snake."

"Watch out for your gizzard, lizard."

Long after he hangs up the phone, he marvels at how she never seems to forget a single thing he teaches her.

Manny comes back into the office a little before five and peels off his customary five twenties. For some reason, it doesn't seem like so much cash this time.

"Thanks," Goodman says.

"My pleasure," Manny says. "Have a good weekend."

On his way to catch the train at 161st Street, Goodman makes another stop at a mailbox. The envelope he drops in this one contains a Bronx Tire Exchange deposit slip and the last of the five-hundred-dollar money orders, covering the check Goodman had written to Mount Sinai Hospital a week ago for his daughter's MRI.

As always, he opens the mailbox lid a second time and looks inside. Just to be sure.

"So what's the story on Michael Goodman?"

The person asking the question is Assistant District Attorney Maggie Kennedy. She's asking it of Detectives Ray Abbruzzo and Daniel Riley, whom she's summoned to her office this Friday afternoon.

"He's a slick one," Riley tells her.

"Well, slick or not, I owe my boss an interim report on the results of the eavesdropping investigation. So you better give me something I can tell him."

"We know he's in action," Abbruzzo says. "We've got him discussing deals, making meets, talking about moves."

"We seen him launder his money, too," Riley offers. "Weems and Sheridan spotted him in the bank he uses. He's got a special teller, pays her off in cash. Won't deal with anyone else."

"Have you learned who his co-conspirators are?" she asks.

"To a certain extent," Abbruzzo says. "There's a mystery woman involved. He sometimes calls her "Grandma," never refers to her by name. And there's a guy up in the Bronx, looks like a muscle man, prob'ly uses him as a slugger, for protection."

"And don't forget his paramour," Riley reminds him.

"Yeah," Abbruzzo says. "He's shackin' up with this broad—"

"Excuse me?" Kennedy interrupts him.

"He's cohabitizing with a female individual," Abbruzzo says. "And we're pretty sure she's in on the thing, too."

"The Molestress," Riley explains.

"Well," says Maggie Kennedy, "you guys better come up with something pretty soon if you want to stay in business on this one."

"I got a feeling he's gonna make a move this weekend," Abbruzzo says.

"I hope so," Kennedy tells him. "Otherwise, they'll be pulling the plug on us the minute our thirty days are up."

Goodman stops at his mother-in-law's to pick up his daughter. As soon as he sees Kelly, he knows she's having one of her headaches. She doesn't mention it, and she's even learned to be less obvious about shielding her eyes from the light. But he can tell anyway. Her skin looks pale and slightly translucent, and feels a bit clammy to the touch. And though she smiles as soon as she sees him and laughs when he hugs her and tickles her ribs, her smiles seem somehow forced and her laughter subdued.

"I'm all packed for the weekend," she tells him, pointing to a small red overnight bag that sits on the carpet, just inside the front door. The bag is dwarfed by Larus, who is also apparently ready to leave.

Before they go, Goodman thanks his mother-in-law for looking after Kelly. The worried look she gives him mirrors his own concerns.

They stop and buy a pizza on the way home, which means that for the last three blocks Goodman must balance the pizza, his briefcase, and Larus. Kelly carries her overnight bag. At each intersection, she dutifully takes her free hand and grasps his elbow before stepping off the curb. He knows this isn't so much because she's worried about crossing—at six, she's already proclaimed she's quite old enough to cross herself—but because she's wise enough to know *he* worries about such moments, and therefore she willingly defers to him.

Carmen greets them with hugs and kisses, and the thought occurs to Goodman that the three of them are settling into playing family pretty comfortably. He looks on as Kelly and Carmen reacquaint themselves, and he can't help wondering how long it'll be before Carmen decides to pick up and get on with her life, and what the damage will be to his daughter when she loses a mother figure all over again. From there, his thoughts move on to how Carmen's leaving will affect *him*. He goes to the sink, washes his hands, tries to busy himself with chores that need no attending to.

Kelly shares one slice of pizza with Pop-Tart, and only picks at the salad Carmen's put together, finally admitting that her head hurts.

"Grandma said the spot in your eye seemed to be getting a little smaller," Goodman says.

"I think so," Kelly agrees brightly, happy to have some good news to report. "I notice it mostly at the end of the day, or when I'm real tired."

"Like now?" Carmen asks.

"Yeah, a little."

"Too tired for a story?" Goodman asks her.

"No *way*, José."

While Kelly gets ready for bed and Carmen clears the table, Goodman opens the sofa bed. Again he's struck by the family roles they've fallen into, and the loss he and his daughter will soon be facing. He fluffs the pillows on the bed and concentrates on the next part of the story.

The Ballerina Princess
(Continued)

Now you may recall that when we last left the Ballerina Princess, she had just fallen asleep after going through the Great Unfair Test, the one that really hurt.

"It didn't really hurt that much, Daddy," Kelly tells him.

"You're just trying to be brave," he says. "It's okay to say something hurts when it does."

"It wasn't that bad. Honest."

Be that as it may, the Great Unfair Test was partially helpful to the royal doctors. And it seemed to help the Ballerina Princess a little, too. The spot she'd been seeing in one of her eyes seemed to get a little smaller afterward, and sometimes she couldn't see it at all.

So the Ballerina Princess asked the Keeper of the Numbers a very natural question. She wanted to know if that could be the last of the tests. Which meant that the Keeper of the Numbers had to go to the Lord High Royal Doctor and ask him. And what do you think the Lord High Royal Doctor told him?

"More tests," is Kelly's answer.

"One more test," proclaimed the Lord High Royal Doctor.

"What kind of a test will it be?" asked the Ballerina Princess and the Keeper of the Numbers. "A test like the one where they put you inside the big machine and scare you, or a test when they stick a needle in your back?"

"Well," said the Lord High Royal Doctor, "since this might be the very last test, we're going to scare *and* hurt the Ballerina Princess at the same time! First, we're going to stick the needle in her back, and then we're going to put her in the big machine."

"Why in kingdom do you have to do *both* of those terrible things?" they asked.

"Because," explained the Lord High Royal Doctor, "the combination of doing both of those things will show us exactly where these headaches are coming from. And then maybe—just maybe—we'll be able to make them disappear for once and for all."

"Like magic?" Kelly asks. She's turned over onto her side, and her eyes are already closed.

"Just like magic."

"Do you believe in magic, Daddy?"

"I very much believe in magic," he tells her. "How else could such a funny-looking guy like me have ever have become the father of such a wonderful, beautiful, brave, smart girl like you, if not for magic?"

In place of a spoken answer, the familiar sound of his daughter's breathing tells him she's already asleep.

From Maggie Kennedy's office at 80 Centre Street, Ray Abbruzzo and Daniel Riley went to Dominick's Clam Bar in Little Italy, where Riley dutifully noted in his log that they "did have meal." For the lowly civilian, policespeak is a wondrous thing to behold. Why, for example, should one settle for "got out of the police car" when the far more graceful "did proceed to exit the departmental vehicle" is available? Thus "gun" becomes "officially authorized weapon," "cop" turns into "member of the force," and—as here—"ate" gives way to "did have meal."

"Meal" in this particular case consisted of two double orders of fried clams in Dominick's seventh and very hottest red sauce, referred to on the wall menu as "Armageddon." (Its six less lethal cousins begin with "Slow Death" and "Sudden Death," warm up to "After Death" and "Way After Death," before smoldering to "Meltdown" and "Purgatory.")

There were huge beds of linguine to soak up the sauce, and crusty bread to wipe up that which hadn't been soaked up. A bottle and a half of Barolo, compliments of the house, added a pleasant tingle to the experience, to say nothing of the .08 blood-alcohol percentages the two men had in common as they drove uptown to begin their evening shift at the wiretap plant. Not quite "intoxicated" under the Vehicle and Traffic Law, but legally "impaired"—nothing, of course, that a couple of experienced detectives couldn't easily compensate for.

They'd reached the plant by eight, bullshitted with Weems and Sheridan for half an hour. The main topic of conversation had been trying to figure out which team was better off—Weems and Sheridan, who got to go home now to their wives and kids on Long Island, or Abbruzzo and Riley, who didn't have to.

By 2200, they've settled in, popping Tums and chewing Rolaids in a futile attempt to quiet the belches and ease the heartburn that's all that remains from their having "had meal" at Dominick's.

The call comes in at 2216.

Goodman grabs the phone on the first ring, not wanting it to wake Kelly. Before even speaking into the receiver, he glances at the clock, wonders who can be calling him at 10:15 at night.

"Hello?" he says.

"Hello," says a man's voice he doesn't recognize. "This Mikey?"

Goodman can't remember the last time he's been called Mikey. Few people seem to think of him as Mike, let alone Mikey. Those are names that conjure up flannel shirts and work boots. Goodman, with his ledgers and briefcase and pocket protector, has always considered himself decidedly Michael. Nonetheless, he now hears himself saying, "Yes, this is Mikey," and as soon as the words are out of his mouth, he realizes he should have gone for "Yeah" instead of "Yes."

"This is Vinnie," the voice says. "Carmen's brother." Only he says it *Cah'men.*

"How do you do?"

"I do good," Vinnie says.

Goodman wonders why the previously paranoid Vinnie is all of a sudden not only using the phone but also identifying himself over it. He decides there must be some sort of trouble.

"Is there a problem?" he asks.

"No," Vinnie says. "No problem at all."

"Everything was okay?" Goodman's pleased with himself for being clever enough to speak vaguely. He figures no one listening in could possibly know what they're talking about.

"Everything was wonderful," Vinnie assures him. "That book was terrific. That's why I'm calling you."

It takes a moment, but it registers in Goodman's mind that "book" is Vinnie's code word for the sample. An inspiration from the exchange at Barnes & Noble, no doubt.

"I'm glad you liked it," Goodman says.

"Yeah," Vinnie says. "I'll be ready to do some more reading pretty soon. Maybe you can tell me how many more books are in that particular series."

Goodman hesitates. He wonders if Vinnie's not being too obvious here. But then he figures, Who am I to outparanoid the paranoid Vinnie?

"That particular book was one of four volumes, just as your friend requested. And there are thirty-five volumes to a . . . a series."

"And how many serieses are we talking about here?"

"Altogether," Goodman tells him, "I understand the publisher has nineteen left. Less that one book, of course."

Vinnie lets out a low-pitched whistle. "An' they're all as exciting as the one I read?" he asks.

"Every one's a classic," Goodman says.

"Whattaya say we get together and talk tomorrow afternoon, Mikey boy? Just you an' me."

"Sounds okay," Goodman says, though the truth is, he's not sure if it really sounds okay or not.

"How 'bout right in front of the library? You know, the main one, with the two big lions and all those steps?"

"Sure," Goodman says. He decides Vinnie's a bit too much into extended metaphors, but at the same time he figures the Forty-second Street library ought to be as safe and anonymous a place as there is.

"Three o'clock okay?"

"Two's better," Goodman says, for no particular reason other than wanting it to appear as if he's exercising a tiny bit of control in this thing.

"Holy motherfuckin' shit!" exclaims Daniel Riley as soon as the conversation is over. "Did you hear *that?*"

"I heard that," Ray Abbruzzo says, although the word *heard* is somewhat difficult to understand, since it comes out part word and part belch.

"This guy's sitting on *nineteen kilos* of pure!"

"And now he's got some wiseguy looking to buy the whole load off him."

"Unfuckingbelievable!" Riley can barely contain himself.

"We gotta get some backup," Abbruzzo says, "cover that meet tomorrow. What time did he say it was on for? Three o'clock?"

"Yeah," Riley agrees, still a notch off his game from the three-quarters of a bottle of Barolo in his system.

"What was that all about?" Carmen asks as soon as Goodman hangs up the phone.

"Our man Vinnie," he says. "Wanted to know how much more there is. Seems like the sample was a big hit."

"You two talked like that on the *phone?*"

"Not like that," he assures her. "It was all very top secret. By the book, you might say."

"Nothing's secret on the phone, Michael."

"All we did was arrange a meeting."

"For when?" she asks.

"Tomorrow. Two in the afternoon."

"Where are we meeting him?"

"*We* aren't," he tells her.

"Excuse me?"

"Vinnie was quite clear about that. 'Just you an' me, Mikey boy,' to be precise."

"Mikey boy?" she parrots.

Goodman feels himself begin to blush a bit.

"Good old Vincent." She shakes her head. "In my brother's world, everybody's gotta have a nickname. He was always hanging out with people like 'Jimmy Blue Eyes' and 'Frankie Tonsils' and 'Bobby the Geek.' Jesus, *Mikey boy!*"

"Sounds like I could have done worse," Goodman says. "I think it's actually got a nice ring to it."

"Besides which," she tells him, "you're not going alone."

"Listen—"

"Don't *listen* me," she cuts him off. "Vincent's my brother. He doesn't tell me what to do."

For Goodman, it's a side of Carmen he hasn't seen before, a fiery stubbornness that takes him by surprise. But he knows that part of him will be very happy to have her there tomorrow, with the two big lions and all those steps.

That night, he lies on the floor. After a bit, he hears his daughter's breathing and Pop-Tart's purring. But the third set of sounds is irregular.

"You awake?" he says softly into the darkness.

"Yes," Carmen says.

"Me, too."

There's a rustling noise, and then she's on the floor next to him. Emboldened by the dark, he reaches an arm around her and draws her to him. He feels the back of her T-shirt, tries to remember if he peeked at the color of her underpants before they turned the lights out. Has to settle for imagining them red. They lie like that for what seems like a long time. Goodman knows that Carmen has come to him to express her caring and her feelings of closeness to him. He understands on an intellectual level that her gesture isn't sexual in nature. Nonetheless, it's been months since Goodman has been next to a woman in any way remotely like this, and while the last thing he wants to do is to misread her gesture, he's only human, and he finds himself completely powerless to control either his galloping pulse or the growing stiffness at the front of his undershorts. As he lies there in an excruciating mixture of delight and dread, he wonders which of his twin embarrassments will be first to betray him—his heartbeat or his hard-on?

Morning comes, and Goodman realizes he's made it through the night. Evidently, his pulse must have finally returned to double digits; somehow, his penis must have managed to behave itself. He vaguely remembers Carmen kissing him sometime while it was still dark, then slipping away from him and retaking her place on the bed with Kelly and Pop-Tart. He does his best to convince himself that the kiss carried with it some unspoken promise of wonderful things to come. But the truth is that he remembers it being delivered not hotly upon his mouth, but softly against his cheek, in a fashion that bespoke far more of sisterly love than animal lust.

Morning begins with breakfast. Kelly announces that she wants "shapes." "Shapes" are pancakes, only Goodman pours the batter onto the skillet in such a way as to create animals, stars, snowflakes, and other creations. Each shape is awarded to the first person able to identify it. Carmen dutifully holds back, allowing Kelly to name almost all of the shapes. Somehow, though, it's Pop-Tart who ends up with the tallest stack of prizes.

Morning also brings laundry duty, and the three of them—Pop-Tart is excused as too full to join in—traipse down to the basement with arms full of clothes, detergent, bleach, and wire hangers. The washer and dryer happen to be next to the storage room, and their path takes them directly past its open door. But if Carmen notices the bins inside, she makes no mention of them.

Next comes a trip to the supermarket, where Goodman, in a rare display of extravagance, tells Kelly to pick out things she wants. But years of exposure to her father's frugal ways have left their imprint on her, and it takes considerable encouragement from both adults before she settles on Mallomars, raisins, orange sherbert, and Count Chocula cereal. She's much less resistant when she gets to PET NEEDS, in aisle 8, where only the most appetizing flavors of cat food will do, and two twenty-five-pound bags of environmentally friendly Kitty Litter become a must, because the store is featuring a "buy one, get one free" special. Together with items Goodman and Carmen pick out, the bill comes to $53.67. Goodman pays for it with three of Manny's twenties, leaving them a little over $40 to get by with until his next payday.

By the time they're back home and finished unloading their purchases, it's almost noon. Kelly has shown no sign of headaches so far, but her energy level has dropped a notch or two, and she looks pale to Goodman. He helps her curl up in front of the television with Pop-Tart and Larus, and the three of them soon seem absorbed in a program about grizzly bears.

"Don't forget we have a meeting with Vincent at two o'clock," Carmen reminds him as they put away the groceries.

"I haven't forgotten," he assures her. "But I'd like you to stay here with Kelly while I go. I just don't feel it's something she needs to be around."

But Carmen disagrees. "I don't trust my brother," she says. "I know he's less likely to try to take advantage of you with me in the picture. Besides, all you're going to be doing is talking," she says. "I'll keep her off to one side. She's not going to know what it's about."

"She's tired," he says.

"She's resting now."

"It's cold out."

"You know, Michael, it's just possible that in loving your daughter so much, you end up babying her. Treat somebody like they're really sick, soon enough you convince them they are. You may need to consider if you're not hurting her by being so overprotective."

It's something he *has* thought about, and he knows she may be right about this. But he finds himself totally unable to do things any differently. He remembers reading a book some years ago about a father so worried about his little boy that he was forever imagining disasters that might happen to him. Finally, there was a car accident, and the father, reaching his injured child, hugged him desperately as he imagined the life draining out of his tiny body. It turned out that the boy hadn't been mortally injured after all, but the father, in his panic and grief, proceeded to squeeze his son so tightly that he suffocated him, thereby accomplishing what the accident hadn't.

Is Carmen right? Is he that father now, suffocating the life out of his child in some misguided perception of the level of danger she's in?

He feels a hand on his arm and is brought back to the moment. "She'll be okay, Michael," Carmen tells him. He looks into her face for more, for some promise—some absolute, unconditional, money-back guarantee printed in indelible ink. Her eyes hold his for a moment, but then she averts them, searching over his shoulder for some space in his tiny cabinet that might be big enough for the box of Count Chocula she holds in her other hand. And in this instant, from that seemingly insignificant loss of eye contact, he knows that as much as she'd like to, she will not give him that promise; she cannot.

Michael Goodman isn't a child. He knows that in life there *are* no guarantees, that indelible ink is something from way back in penmanship classes. But over the days to follow, he'll remember this moment and be drawn back to it in an attempt to understand Carmen's hesitancy, revealing itself as it did at the very moment when he'd most needed her reassurance, and when she should most have wanted to give it to him.

What he doesn't notice—what he cannot see as Carmen reaches past him to wedge the cereal box into a space barely large enough to contain it—is that she's biting her lower lip hard enough to draw blood.

"We gotta cover a meet at fifteen hundred hours," Ray Abbruzzo barks into the phone to his lieutenant. "The Mole is settin' up what sounds like an nineteen-kilo deal. We need a surveillance van, video equipment, a parabolic mike—"

"Whoah, whoah," Lieutenant Spangler stops him. "Today's Saturday. You know you gotta requisition that stuff by noon Friday if you want it over the weekend."

"Since when is that?"

"Since Salvaggi and Wilcocki got caught using the stuff to drive down to Philly and tape the Giants-Eagles game, that's when."

"This is *nineteen kilos*, Lou!"

"I don't give a rat's ass if it's nineteen *hundred!* I'm not putting my shield on the line. Cover it on foot."

"It's cold out there."

"Wear your mittens," the lieutenant says. "You got binoculars?"

"Yeah."

"Use 'em. You wanna get high-tech, bring a camera. You know how to work one?"

"Yeah."

"Make sure you put film in it," Spangler adds. "That dickbrain Jensen once shot thirty-six exposures of a wiseguy funeral, forgot to load the fuckin' thing."

"I'll load it," Abbruzzo says. "Can I get a few extra men at least?"

"Whaddayou, fuckin' kidding me? I got two thousand cabbies converging on City Hall, protesting they gotta learn English. I got the President's wife in town all fuckin' weekend, promoting equal rights for retards. There's talk of a counterdemonstration on behalf of nonretards. The borough commander's been pulling guys offa their RDOs to work with the feds on security detail. And I'm supposed to find you extra men? Get fuckin' *real*, willya!"

"Just thought I'd ask."

"You asked. Now cover the fuckin' meet, and don't fuckin' blow it."

Abbruzzo hangs up the phone.

"How did it go?" Riley asks him.

"Not bad. He says we should cover the meet."

"You look funny, Daddy," Kelly tells Goodman as he tries his hardest to slick his hair back. He's wearing his all-black drug dealer–impersonation costume again, but they forgot to buy styling gel this morning, so once again his hair refuses to cooperate.

"No comments from the peanut gallery," he tells her, then ignores her confused look. If *he* can't remember where that saying comes from, how can he expect *her* to understand it?

"Where are we going?" she asks him.

"To the library," he says. "I've got to meet somebody there, so you may have to wait with Carmen for a few minutes."

"No problem," she says.

Goodman locks the door behind them and they head downstairs, Kelly leading the way, Carmen following her, and Goodman bringing up the rear. From the spring with which Kelly takes the steps, Goodman won-

ders if maybe Carmen was right after all. Stop treating your daughter like
an invalid, he tells himself.

They head west, toward Fifth Avenue.

In the plant, it's 1310 hours. Abbruzzo is the only one there. He sent Riley
out fifteen minutes ago to buy film. Neither of them knows what kind of
film the camera takes, so Riley took it with him.

The phone in Goodman's apartment has been quiet all morning. The
way Abbruzzo figures it, with the meet set for three o'clock, the Mole
won't show himself again for another hour or so. Weems and Sheridan
have been directed to proceed straight to the Forty-second Street library
and have the steps staked out by 1420. In other words, everything's covered. So Abbruzzo permits himself to lean back and close his eyes for a
few minutes. No harm in that.

At Fifth Avenue, they catch the number 3 bus. Kelly insists they ride in
the very back, where it's warmest from the motor and where there's
room enough for her to sit between Goodman and Carmen.

"What are you meeting this man about, Daddy?" she asks.

"Business," he tells her.

"What kind of business?"

"It's an investment opportunity," he says. "It's a bit too complicated
for me to explain it to you."

"Sounds like *monkey business* to me," she says.

Carmen laughs. "That's a pretty good guess," she says. Goodman shoots
her a look, but she either misses it or chooses to ignore it.

Lighten up, he tells himself. After all, he can only get about five hundred years in prison for what he's doing. If somebody doesn't kill him first,
that is.

Riley gets back to the plant with the film. "Did we want Kodacolor or
Kodachrome?" he asks Abbruzzo.

"How the fuck am I supposed to know? Why didn't you ask them at
the store?"

"I did," Riley says. "But you know these Koreans—they can barely speak English. Wanted to know what *speed* I needed. Did I want prints or slides or contack sheets?"

"What are contack sheets?"

"Beats the shit outa me."

It takes the two of them twenty minutes to load the camera, and when they're finished, they're still not sure they've done it right.

"Anything new in Moleland?" Riley asks.

"Nah," Abbruzzo says. "Watch—he won't leave the burrow for another half hour. It's got to the point where I know this guy real good. Right now, he's sittin' on his butt in front of his TV set."

In fact, Goodman's butt is at that very moment lifting itself up from the backseat of the number 3 bus and following the rest of him toward the exit.

At street level, he puts on his imitation Ray•Ban sunglasses to complete his outfit. He gets a look from his daughter that he interprets as "I used to know you." It's Carmen's hand she reaches for as they head for the library steps, he notices.

"What does Vincent look like?" he asks Carmen.

"Vinnie."

"Vinnie," he repeats.

"Like a wanna-be gangster," she says before smiling and looking him up and down. "Same as you."

"Hey," he reminds her, "this was your idea, remember?"

"I do remember. If you'd have shown up wearing your pocket protector, my brother would've flipped out. At least this way, he'll think you're both members of the same species."

"Can I have a hot dog, Daddy?" Kelly wants to know, pointing at a dark little foreigner behind a Sabrett wagon.

"No—"

"Of course you can," Carmen says, overruling him and heading that way with Kelly.

"You have no idea what they put in those things," he calls after them.

"They sell a million of them every day, all over the city," Carmen calls back. "They're probably safer than the air she's breathing."

Goodman relents. After six years of parenting, he's getting a crash course in lightening up. It doesn't come easy for him, but he's trying his best to go with it. He runs after them. "I'll take mine with mustard and onions," he says, trying to catch up with them in more ways than one.

They eat their hot dogs sitting on the steps, in the warmth of the sun, leaning against the base of one of the lions. "Not bad," Goodman is forced to admit, though when he burps a moment later, it tastes of onions, mustard, and something that only approximates any meat he's familiar with.

"There's Vincent now," Carmen says.

"Vinnie," he corrects her, turning to where she's looking. Making their way up the steps are two men. Goodman recognizes one of them as T.M., the guy he exchanged flowers with at Barnes & Noble. The other one is smaller, dark-haired, and a bit dangerous-looking. He wears mirrored aviator sunglasses, the kind that make it impossible to see his eyes. He gets within a few feet of where they're sitting before Goodman notices a long, thin scar on the side of his face. Completely ignoring Goodman, he addresses Carmen.

"What are *you* doing here?" he asks.

"What's *he* doing here?" She gestures at T.M. Then, without waiting for an answer, she introduces them. "Michael, this is my brother Vinnie."

"Pleased to meet you," Goodman says.

Vinnie grunts something unintelligible. There is no offer of a handshake.

Carmen stands up and reaches for Kelly's hand. "Why don't you and I take a walk, young lady?" she suggests.

"No problem," Kelly says. He watches the two of them head down the steps, wondering if "No problem" is going to be his daughter's latest in a long line of favorite expressions.

Vinnie looks at Goodman, who in turn stares at T.M. until Vinnie seems to catch on. "Give us a minute," he says to T.M., and the bigger man shrugs before walking across the steps to the other lion. There he takes up a position facing in their direction, arms crossed and legs spread like some sort of sergeant at arms, out of earshot but still very much in sight.

Vinnie pulls out his cigarettes, mentholated ones in a green-and-white pack. He offers one to Goodman, who shakes his head no. Vinnie finds a lighter in the pocket of his sport jacket. The jacket is beige, and it looks Italian and expensive; the lighter is slim and gold-colored. He lights his cigarette and blows long streams of smoke out his nostrils. Goodman wonders if he'll try for rings next.

"That was a nice thing, the other day," Vincent tells him.

"So they tell me," Goodman says. He assumes Vinnie's referring to the sample, but he has no way of being certain, so he keeps his answer as non-committal as he can.

"If I understand you correctly, you've got nineteen keys of the same stuff."

"Sounds like you understand," Goodman says, deciding this gangster talk is kind of fun.

"I got some people who are interested in the whole load."

"I hope they're wealthy people," Goodman says, trying to do his best Al Pacino imitation.

"They're way beyond wealthy," Vinnie says. "But they're also very cautious. They want to make sure that what they're getting is every bit as good as the first thing was."

"That's understandable."

"That your kid?" Vinnie asks, looking over toward Carmen and Kelly. Goodman nods.

"Nice-lookin' girl," Vinnie says. "Sure would hate to see anything bad happen to her."

Goodman feels a chill run up his spine. He hasn't counted on threats against his daughter. "If anything bad should happen to her," he says slowly, "I better already be dead."

"Oh, don't worry," Vinnie says easily. "You would be. But then I don't expect any problems. Do you?"

"Not me."

"Good." He lets his half-smoked cigarette drop, then grinds it out with the pointed toe of a boot that's made out of snake or lizard or some other endangered species. "My people are willing to go to two million."

Goodman's figured things out in his head so many times and so many different ways that his laugh comes easily to him. The quarter-ounce sample was two thousand. An ounce should be eight thousand. At thirty-five ounces to a kilo, that's $280,000. Multiply that by nineteen, and you're up to $5.32 million. "Go tell your people they don't have a prayer," he says.

"Hey," Vinnie smiles. "The negotiations gotta begin *somewhere,* right?"

"Not if you're here to waste my time," Goodman says, realizing he's shifted over to Robert De Niro.

"Why don't you tell me what you're lookin' for," Vinnie says.

"Me? I'm looking for five million." He rounds it off. No use in being greedy.

"Get serious," Vinnie laughs. "I'm authorized to go to two point five."

"You're not even close," Goodman says, amazed that he's able to keep a straight face while turning down two and a half million dollars. But it's become a game to him, and he finds he's surprisingly good at it. Maybe that has something to do with the fact that none of this seems even remotely real to him. This could just as easily be Monopoly.

"Two point seven five," Vinnie says. "That's my absolutely final offer."

"Too bad," Goodman says, starting down the steps. "And to think you probably could have had it for four—"

"Three," says Vinnie, falling in behind him, matching him step for step.

"Why don't you tell your people you tried your best? I'm sure they'll understand."

"Three two," Vinnie pleads. "I gotta make something on this for myself."

"Not a chance."

"Three three?"

Goodman waits a second just for effect. He decides he's played the game long enough, and is about to agree.

But Vinnie speaks first. "Three *five?*"

"Deal," says Michael Goodman.

Vinnie lets out a deep breath. "You drive a hard bargain," he says.

"This isn't exactly my first deal," Goodman explains.

"It's gonna take my people a few days to put their bread together," Vinnie tells him. "I'll call my sister when we're ready to go. Is that all right?"

"No problem." First Al Pacino, then Robert De Niro. Now all of a sudden, it's Kelly Goodman he finds himself imitating.

Vinnie extends his hand and they shake.

"Good-bye," Goodman says.

Vinnie winks and says something that sounds like "Chow." Goodman's heard people say that before, though he can't for the life of him figure out why they say it. As he heads down the steps to rejoin Kelly and Carmen, he succumbs to his nervous habit of checking his watch. It's exactly 2:15. One thing about dealing with white guys is they show up on time.

Detectives Weems and Sheridan show up at the library steps on time, too; and Weems, at least, is anything but white. But *their* on time is 1420 hours, which is 2:20 in civilian time and a full five minutes after Goodman and

Vinnie conclude their business. Because Goodman, Carmen, and Kelly dawdle a bit at the bottom of the steps before crossing Fifth Avenue and walking east toward Madison, Weems and Sheridan actually miss them by less than half a minute. But miss them they do, and—in surveillance—almost doesn't count; a miss is a miss.

Nonetheless, Weems and Sheridan now take up separate observation positions on the steps, trying their best to blend in with the crowd. This isn't all that easy for them to do. For one thing, they're both over two hundred pounds. That and their bellies, the direct and prodigious results of too many jelly doughnuts, buttered rolls, and slices of pizza. Finally, the fact that one of them's black and one of them's white would be a sure tip-off to any interested party that they're some sort of law enforcement.

But there *is* no interested party to be tipped off. Weems and Sheridan will do their observing for the next hour and a half, or until it occurs to Sheridan to call the plant and find out what's going on. Or, more precisely, why *nothing* is going on.

Abbruzzo stands by the window of the plant, watching the door of Goodman's building through binoculars. He takes another look at his watch. It's almost 3:45.

"I don't get it," he says. "Guy's supposed to make a three o'clock meet a half hour away. Shoulda left his crib two-fifteen, two-thirty, two-forty at the lastest. Here it is, quarter of *four*, for Chrissakes, and he hasn't budged."

"And he didn't call to say he's running late or he's not going to show," Riley says, playing with the strap of the camera. "And nobody's called *him* to say, 'Where the fuck are you?' "

"I don't get it," Abbruzzo says again, lowering his binoculars but continuing to watch the door across the way.

But then, all at once, he does get it. He gets it not because he figures out some subtle point he's been overlooking, nor because he decides to approach it from a different direction, nor even because of some brilliant insight that suddenly comes to him. He gets it because, as he watches, into his vision come Michael Goodman, his daughter, and his "paramour." But instead of coming *out* of the building like they're supposed to be doing, they're going *into* it.

"Cock*suck*er!" he roars just as the phone rings.

He picks it up and barks, *"What?"* into it.

"Ray?"

"Yeah?"

"Ray, it's me, Sheridan. You okay?"

"No, I'm not okay."

Sheridan seems to take that in stride. "Harry and I have been out here freezing our asses off for an hour and a half," he says. "This guy gonna show or what?"

"No," Abbruzzo says. "He's not going to show. Come on back." He puts the phone down before turning to Riley. "This guy is one clever piece of work," he says.

"I been trying to tell you that all along," Riley reminds him.

As soon as he gets upstairs, the clever piece of work collapses onto his sofa with Kelly and Carmen. Pop-Tart jumps up to join them, ready to eat or play, whatever their order of preference may be. But the three of them are exhausted from their long walk back uptown. Climbing the five flights of stairs was the final cruncher.

"Boy, we're going to sleep tonight!" Carmen observes.

"Not me," Kelly moans. "I'm going to *die* tonight!"

Michael Goodman feels his heart stop beating for an instant. He says nothing, but he catches Carmen looking at him, and he knows without her saying a word that the color has drained completely from his face.

"I'm going to get this guy," Abbruzzo announces. He and Riley have been joined in the plant by Weems and Sheridan. "First thing Monday morning, we're gonna pay another visit to Maggie-O." "Maggie-O" is their nickname for Maggie Kennedy. Cops, like wiseguys and athletes, are among the top 2 percent of the world when it comes to creating nicknames.

"What for?" Sheridan asks. "Another search warrant?"

"Nope," Abbruzzo says. "We're going to get us another eavesdropping order. Only this time, we're going to pull off a little black-bag job, plant us a *bug* in there."

Because Kelly gets to pick the menu, they dine on grilled cheese sandwiches and tomato soup, a combination that particularly pleases Pop-Tart, who eats himself into semiconsciousness and then collapses for the night with Kelly. For Goodman and Carmen, it means their first opportunity to speak about the meeting with Vinnie.

"So how did it go?" she asks, drying dishes.

"Okay, I guess. First, he threatened my daughter, then we *hondled.*"

"*Hondled?*"

"Bargained," he translates. "He offered a million, I asked for five."

"And?"

"We more or less split the difference. I figured that's how these things are supposed to work."

"*Three million dollars?*"

"Three and a half, actually." He tries to sound nonchalant about it, but the truth is that he's delighted with her disbelief, and accepts it as a testament to his negotiating prowess.

"When is this supposed to happen?" she asks. "And *how?*"

"He's going to call us. Says his people are going to need a few days to get ready."

"And *you,* Michael?" She looks at him hard. "Are you sure *you're* ready to do this?"

"I'm ready," he says. "As long as I don't think about it too much."

"You understand," she says, "I really could go back to work for a while. She doesn't define "work," but it's clear to him she's not talking about waiting tables.

"No way," he says.

"Look at it this way," she says. "I get busted, it's a night in jail. *You* get busted, it's a *lifetime.*"

"My daughter's not going to die because I can't pay her medical bills, and you're not going to go back to—*to work.* I'm not sure of much in this world, but I'm sure of those two things."

He glances in her direction, hoping for some show of appreciation at this manifesto of gallantry he's just served up. What he sees instead is a look that falls somewhere between serious concern and total panic. Though neither of them says another word, it's clear to both of them that Michael Goodman is hopelessly overmatched in a game so far out of his league that it might be laughable if only it weren't so deadly serious.

Sunday afternoon finds Goodman with his navy buddies again, Krulewich, Lehigh Valley, and the Whale. Again there's a Giants game on, but it's a home game that started at one o'clock, and by the time Goodman arrives, it's almost over. One look at the score tells him it's going to be another long season for his team:

EAGLES   28
GIANTS   10

They try to play a card game called Oh, Hell, which they used to play on shipboard, but nobody can quite remember the rules. The Whale wants to play poker ("not for money or nothin'—maybe just quarters"), but there are no takers. In the end, they fall back on hearts again.

As always, Goodman plays cautiously. But he's modified his game plan just a bit. In addition to stripping his own hand of hearts, he keeps a wary eye out to make sure no one else—particularly Lehigh—is going to shoot the moon. He decides it's a good policy to win at least one heart trick, or at least save a high heart or two, as insurance against such a possibility. The strategy seems to pay off, and after four hands, he's in second place, just four points behind Lehigh.

KRULEWICH   30

WHALE   34

GOODMAN   22

LEHIGH   18

Lehigh deals the final hand, and Goodman sorts his cards.

A, K, J, 7, 5, 2	hearts
A, 10, 9	spades
A, Q, 8	diamonds
2	clubs

He recognizes instantly that it's a hand with which he could shoot the moon if everything were to fall right. But he's never tried it—in fact, he's only seen Lehigh do it once, and it worked for him purely because everyone else got caught napping.

He leads his two of clubs. Everyone else follows suit, meaning that no hearts get played on the trick. The Whale, who's won the trick with the queen, continues clubs, leading the five. Krulewich follows with the seven, Lehigh with the ten. Goodman sees he's reached the moment of truth: With no clubs left, he's free to play any card in his hand. He can dump the queen of spades right now and stick Lehigh (whose ten of clubs is going to win the trick) with thirteen points. Or he can throw a low spade or diamond, immediately tipping his hand that he's going to shoot the moon.

He studies his hand, knowing that even his hesitation is likely to give him away.

"What did he play?" Krulewich asks, unable to see if Goodman's thrown a card onto the table.

"Nothin', you bat," says the Whale.

"Man's thinkin' about a moon shot," Lehigh says. It hasn't taken him long to catch on.

Goodman chickens out and decides to play it safe. He throws the queen of spades. Lehigh picks it up and shifts to diamonds, leading the three.

It turns out that Goodman is able to dump only two of the six hearts in his hand. He ends up with ten points—his remaining four hearts, as well as six others that his opponents play on tricks that Goodman is forced to win.

KRULEWICH	32
WHALE	35
GOODMAN	32
LEHIGH	31

He replays the hand in his head over and over again on the way home, kicking himself for not having gone for it. He'd been dealt a hand with real and obvious possibilities. The cards had been staring him in the face, daring him to take a chance. All it would have taken was the nerve. And yet, when the opportunity had presented itself, Goodman had shied away from it and had chosen instead to play it safe, as always. And playing it safe had cost him the game, had kept him in the losing column.

Michael Goodman is resigned to the fact that in this life there are those who take risks and there are those who play it safe. He understands that he'll always be a card-carrying charter member of the Safe Group. He guesses it's a good thing to know himself, to understand his limitations, to appreciate that he simply doesn't have whatever it takes—that sense of abandon, that *recklessness* that's required to risk everything on the all-or-nothing long shot: to take a chance, to shoot the moon.

First thing Monday morning—which in lawyer terms means anytime after nine—Assistant District Maggie Kennedy gets a surprise visit from Detectives Ray Abbruzzo and Daniel Riley. They've even brought her a container of coffee.

"And what brings you gentlemen here so early?" she asks them. "Did Michael Goodman announce on his phone that he's the Unabomber?"

"No," Abbruzzo says. "But he's getting ready to unload his entire stash."

"And what might that consist of? An ounce of sinsemilla?"

"How about nineteen kilos of heroin?" Riley asks her.

"And remember," Abbruzzo adds, "our information is that it's *pure.*"

"Right," Kennedy says. "And that was the anonymous identified dead kid who told you that, if I remember correctly."

Abbruzzo reaches into his jacket pocket and comes out with an audiocassette. "Listen for yourself," he says, tossing it onto Kennedy's desk.

Kennedy pries off the lid of her coffee container and sits down. Out of habit, she blows on the coffee to cool it before taking the first sip. It turns out to be an unnecessary precaution. "Set it up," she says, pointing to a tape player by the window.

Soon all three of them are seated with their coffee containers, listening to the voice of Michael Goodman, aka the Mole, as he speaks with an outside caller who identifies himself as Vinnie.

GOODMAN: Hello?

VINNIE: Hello. This Mikey?

GOODMAN: Yes, this is Mikey.

VINNIE: This is Vinnie. Carmen's brother.

GOODMAN: How do you do?

VINNIE: I do good.

GOODMAN: Is there a problem?

VINNIE: No. No problem at all.

GOODMAN: Everything was okay?

VINNIE: Everything was wonderful. That book was terrific. That's why I'm calling you.

GOODMAN: I'm glad you liked it.

VINNIE: Yeah. I'll be ready to do some more reading pretty soon. Maybe you can tell me how many more books are in that particular series.

GOODMAN: That particular book was one of four volumes, just as your friend requested. There are thirty-five volumes to a . . . a series.

VINNIE: And how many serieses are we talking about here?

GOODMAN: Altogether, I understand the publisher has nineteen left. Less that one book, of course.

VINNIE: [Whistles] An' they're all as exciting as the one I read?

GOODMAN: Every one's a classic.

VINNIE: Whattaya say we get together and talk tomorrow afternoon, Mikey boy? Just you and me.

GOODMAN: Sounds okay.

VINNIE: How 'bout right in front of the library? You know, the main one, with the two big lions and all those steps?

GOODMAN: Sure.

VINNIE: Three o'clock okay?

GOODMAN: Two's better.

"What was that last thing he said?" Riley asks.

"Nothing," Abbruzzo says. He's just realized for the first time why they missed the meeting Saturday, but now isn't the time he wants to talk about it.

But Riley doesn't get the message. "Did he say 'together'?" he asks. "Fuckin' guy's always *mumbling*. Was that 'together' or 'two's better'? Play that last part again, will ya, Ray?"

"Later," Abbruzzo says.

If Riley's a bit slow to comprehend things this morning, Kennedy isn't. "You missed the meet," she says. It's spoken somewhere between a question and a statement.

"Yup." Abbruzzo nods.

"The guy's so fuckin' *sneaky*," Riley explains. "You just heard how he changed the time at the last second, just to throw us off?"

Kennedy and Abbruzzo exchange glances.

"Now what?" she asks him.

"I was hoping we could get an order to bug his place."

"So *that* explains the coffee." Kennedy smiles.

Michael Goodman figures the money orders he mailed out Friday morning should've arrived at their destinations by now, so while Kelly reads *Stuart Little* to Carmen, he calls the MRI place and schedules the new test, the one with contrast.

"How about tomorrow at three?" they ask him.

"Tomorrow at three will be good." *Good* being a relative term, he tells himself. He decides he won't tell Kelly until tomorrow. No reason for her to have to think about it all day and spend half the night worrying herself sick.

He looks over at her. She's sitting in Carmen's lap now, listening as Carmen takes her turn reading Kelly's favorite part.

"In the loveliest town of all," Carmen reads, "where the houses were white and high and the elm trees were green and higher than the houses, where the front yards were wide and pleasant and the back yards were busy and worth finding out about, where the streets sloped down to the stream and the stream flowed quietly under the bridge, where the lawns ended in orchards and the orchards ended in fields and the fields ended in pastures and the pastures climbed the hill and disappeared over the top toward the wonderful wide sky, in this loveliest of all towns Stuart stopped to get a drink of sarsaparilla."

"What's sarsaparilla?" Kelly asks, though Goodman's told her each time they've come to the word.

"It's what people used to drink long ago," Carmen explains. "Way back, before there was Juicy Juice."

Composing the affidavit for the bug turns out to be harder than any of them anticipated. Like the wiretap order, the bug order is an eavesdropping warrant. The first application had to establish, among other things, that conventional investigative techniques had failed and were likely to continue to fail. Now this second application must demonstrate that convential techniques still aren't enough, *even when coupled with the wiretap.*

"How do we get over *that* hurdle?" Kennedy wonders. "Especially when you bring me a tape that proves he *talks* on the phone?"

"He's stopped talking?" Abbruzzo tries.

"Yeah," Riley agrees. "The Mole muted up."

Kennedy ignores him. "How can you be so sure?" she asks Abbruzzo.

"He said so. We heard him say it on the phone. 'No more talkin' on the phone,' he said."

"Do you have that conversation on tape?"

"No," Abbruzzo says, looking her squarely in the eye. "We were right in the middle of changing tapes when he said that. Missed it." Ray Abbruzzo takes special pride in his ability to maintain eye contact at all times. Once he convinced a murder suspect that in addition to being a detective, he was also an ordained Catholic priest. Got the guy's confession, too. Then, at the suppression hearing in court, he denied that he'd ever said that. Under oath. All the time looking the defense lawyer right in the eye.

The papers are drawn up by noon, then approved and signed off on by 12:30.

"Any chance we can get some judge to do this before the one o'clock break?" Abbruzzo asks.

"If we hurry," Kennedy says.

"Some judge" turns out to be the Honorable Leslie Crocker Snyder, who sits in part 88 and presides over some of the most serious narcotics cases—and the murders, assaults, and gun possessions that seem to accompany them—in the court system.

Judge Snyder is an attractive woman with long blond hair that may or may not get occasional help from a colorist, now that she's reached fifty. She is smart and hard-working. A former prosecutor—some of her critics would argue that the *former* could be dispensed with—she's made no secret of her aspirations to become police commissioner or district attorney, and she will appear on just about any panel show where there's a camera and a spare microphone. Off the bench, she is warm and friendly, displaying a ready sense of humor that includes the ability to laugh at herself. But as soon as she puts on her black robe, the warmth dissipates, the friendliness disappears, and the humor develops a decidedly caustic aspect to it: She becomes a defendant's worst nightmare. Accordingly, she is a prosecutor's best friend, and the judge to see when you need an eavesdropping order signed. Even at quarter to one.

Maggie Kennedy, being an experienced assistant district attorney in the Special Narcotics Prosecutor's office, knows all this, so it's no accident that she's brought Ray Abbruzzo to part 88.

Judge Snyder reads the papers carefully. She wants to make sure that the allegations in them add up to probable cause and also demonstrate an exhaustion of conventional investigative techniques. She reads them carefully because, should the bug eventually lead to a major seizure of drugs, she doesn't want to see some clever defense lawyer get those drugs suppressed because the allegations weren't sufficient.

What she *doesn't* pause to worry about is whether or not the allegations themselves happen to be *true*. Now, in Judge Snyder's defense, her particular New York City is some light-years removed from the underbelly inhabited by those who use, sell, or seize illegal drugs; and the possibility that police officers occasionally bend the truth may be truly too difficult for her to fathom. In any event, in Leslie Snyder's rather narrow interpretation of the law, such an inquiry simply isn't required of her. The statute permits her to assume the truth of the police officers' allegations, and she's delighted to cloak herself with that permission.

Now she signs the order and smiles at Abbruzzo. "Good luck, Detective," she says.

"I can drop her off at her grandmother's," Goodman tells Carmen as he gets ready to leave for work.

"You just *try* it," Carmen says.

"You just *try* it," Kelly chimes in.

"On second thought, I don't think I'll try it," Goodman decides.

"I *love* Carmen," Kelly announces, throwing her arms around Carmen.

"I love you, too, sweetie," Carmen says, returning the hug so hard that Kelly squeals. They both look over at Goodman.

"I just wish you two would learn to express your feelings a little," he says. "What do you want for dinner?"

"Pizza!" Kelly shouts.

"Pizza!" Carmen echoes, laughing.

"I guess that'll teach me to let a couple of kids be in charge," Goodman says. Then he's out the door and off to the Bronx.

At the plant, Weems and Sheridan have been joined by two members of the OCCB technical team, DeSimone and Kwon. They've been assigned at the request of Detective Abbruzzo, who called in this morning from Maggie Kennedy's office, the moment she'd agreed to apply for permission to bug the Goodman apartment.

"There goes the Mole," Sheridan says, lowering his binoculars.

Weems checks his watch. "It's twelve-twenty-five," he says. "He's going to work, won't be back till seventeen-forty-five. Now if only we could get the girls to leave."

"How much time do you guys need?" Sheridan asks.

"Studio apartment?" DeSimone asks. "We can be in an' out in thirty minutes."

"As long as we don't have trouble with the locks," Kwon adds.

"I remember one time we wanted to bug some wiseguy's home out on Staten Island," DeSimone says. "Only his old lady would never leave the place. Seems their marriage was falling apart, and she was afraid to go out, thought he might change the locks on her and never let her back in. So finally we had to sneak into the basement, light some newspapers on fire to smoke 'em out. Then we waited for the firemen to show up, and went in with them. Lucky thing they got there when they did, too, cause the goddamn *paneling* caught on fire. We almost burned the whole fuckin' *house* down!"

They all have a good laugh over that.

It's business as usual at the Bronx Tire Exchange. Having just worked Friday, Goodman has less to do than he ordinarily would. He brings things up-to-date, then uses the latitude given him by Manny to set up yet another checking account. This one he calls Larus International and opens it with twenty-five dollars, which he draws against Bronx Tire Exchange, Special Account. Not much of a balance, but you've got to start somewhere. He phones the bank, and because Bronx Tire is a good customer, they promise to have checks and deposit slips printed up the next day and delivered by priority mail.

"So what'll it be, kiddo?" Carmen asks Kelly. "The park, the zoo, the museum?"

"It's cold out," Kelly says. "Have you ever been to the *Planetarium?*"

"Never," Carmen admits. "You?"

"Me, too. Never."

"Well, put on your space shoes, girl—we're going where no woman has gone before!"

Kelly finds her sneakers and begins lacing them up. "Is it scary?" she asks.

"I don't know," Carmen says. "But if it is, we'll start screaming, they'll have to give us the heave-ho, and then we'll be outa there. Deal?"

"Deal," Kelly agrees.

"Lookathis," says Sheridan, holding the binoculars, so of course no one else can see.

"What?"

"The kid and the chick are outa the crib."

"Okay," Weems says. "You take 'em. And if they get more than a half an hour away, call us and let us know, and we'll go in."

"How come I never get the fun jobs?" Sheridan whines.

" 'Cause I got six years and fifty IQ points on you, that's why."

"Great. You guys get to sneak into the Molehill, while I gotta spend the afternoon freezing my balls off, following the broads."

The "broads" take the Lexington Avenue bus down to Seventy-ninth Street, then the crosstown to Central Park West. Kelly spots the dome of the Planetarium from the bus.

"There it is!" she shouts.

The good news is that there appears to be no line at the doors. The bad news becomes apparent once they get close enough to read a small sign on the center door.

CLOSED FOR REPAIRS

"The nerve!" Carmen says.

"They could at least say, '*Sorry,* Closed For Repairs,' " Kelly observes.

"So much for outer space, kiddo. What's your second choice?"

"How about the museum?" Kelly suggests. "It's right around the corner."

"The museum it is," Carmen says.

As they head back up the walkway, a man in a tan coat is walking toward them. Evidently, they're not the only ones to be disappointed this day.

"Don't bother," Kelly tells him. "It's *closed.*"

"Oh," says the man. "Thank you."

The museum is open, and Kelly—who knows every square inch of it—leads Carmen around by the hand, showing her all of her favorite places.

"I wonder what the movie is?" Kelly asks.

"Movie?"

"Yup. They have this giant movie screen, and if you sit up real close, you think you're part of the movie. Like being in a plane, or underwater. It's so cool."

"Then let's check it out," Carmen says.

"We're at the fuckin' *museum.*" Sheridan is talking into a pay phone outside the IMAX Theater. "They're watching a goddamn *movie.* You guys got all the time you need."

"Which museum?" Weems asks him.

"The whatchamacallit—the National History."

"On the West Side? The Museum of Natural History?"

"Yeah," Sheridan says. "Cost me four-fifty for a cab, too. You shoulda seen the look on the Arab's face when I jumped in and told him, 'Follow that bus!' "

"Okay," Weems says. "We're going in. You stay with the girls. They decide to rush back home all of a sudden, you do whatever you gotta do to slow them down."

"Sure thing. I can always throw myself in front of their bus."

"Not a bad idea," Weems says.

"Fuck you," Sheridan says. "I hope the guy's got a five-hundred-pound pit bull and it bites your black ass off."

The giant movie screen is featuring a film about Antarctica, and Kelly and Carmen enter a full twenty-five minutes before the three o'clock showing, just so they can race down the aisle and grab seats in the middle of the very front row.

"We'll go blind," Carmen complains. "That is, if we don't die of stiff necks first."

"This is the only place to sit," Kelly insists. "Trust me."

Carmen laughs. "Remind me never to go on a roller-coaster ride with you," she says.

Gradually, the theater fills up. Almost all of the seats are taken by families or by children accompanied by adults. The one exception seems to be a man in a tan coat, who takes his place in the very last row. Quite clearly, he lacks the benefit of a child to assist him in finding the best vantage point.

At three o'clock, the sound track starts and the lights begin to dim. On the giant screen, the image of an emperor penguin appears. It looks startlingly human in its tuxedo feathering, and there are "Ooohs" from the audience.

"Look at the cute penguin!" Kelly whispers.

Thirty rows back, the man in the tan coat can be heard to grumble, "Fuckin' penguin," before he's shushed by those sitting to either side of him.

Harry Weems checks his watch nervously outside the door to Michael Goodman's apartment, sees it's 1452. They were able to get into the building by slipping the downstairs lock with a credit card, but the deadbolt lock is too sophisticated for such a primitive technique. Nonetheless, it yields easily enough to David Kwon's expertise with a set of picks.

Once inside, the three detectives remove their shoes. Though their entry is pursuant to court order and therefore perfectly legal, the last thing they want is to arouse the suspicion of some downstairs neighbor, who might hear intruders and tip off the target of their investigation.

Kwon snaps open a briefcase and begins removing small items.

"No use bugging the phone," Weems points out. "We've already got a tap on it."

Kwon carries a chair to the center of the room and places it directly underneath the ceiling light fixture. "How about a parasite right here for starters?" he asks.

"Go for it," Weems agrees. As Kwon stands on the chair, DeSimone hands him a tiny parasite microphone, so called because it draws its power from the electricity that feeds the light. Then he replaces the lightbulb in the fixture with a brand-new long-lasting one of identical wattage. This is a precaution to make it less likely that the bulb will burn out and require changing—and result in the possible detection of the microphone—at any time in the near future.

"Where do you think they talk?" Kwon wonders out loud, taking in the sofa bed, the kitchen wall, and the card table.

"The sofa's no good," DeSimone says. "Looks like the kind you open up and make a bed out of."

They settle on the table. Kwon takes a fully integrated transmitter—a unit the size of a sugar cube, containing both a microphone and a battery—and attaches its adhesive side to the underside of the card table.

"Bathroom?" DeSimone asks.

"Why not?" Kwon says. He finds a magnetic Kel minimike and places it on the back side of the pipe leading to the toilet tank.

"This guy farts, you're going to know it," DeSimone tells Weems.

Back in the main room, they check to make certain that all three devices are transmitting on the same frequency and that there's a minimum of static and no chance of feedback.

"We're outa here," Kwon says, packing up the briefcase. They slip their shoes back on and relock the door on the way out. Weems checks his watch: 1511. Counting the four minutes it took them to get inside, the entire operation has taken less than twenty minutes.

It's some time after noon when Big Red wakes up. The hours of a drug dealer tend toward the nocturnal, and Big Red often sleeps until three or four in the afternoon. But something has him up earlier than usual today.

It's nothing he's terribly worried about. Things have been going well enough for him lately. No one's bothered him about the unfortunate accident that took Russell Bradford's life. His own day in "the system" following his arrest was a small price to pay for an alibi. Hammer and Tito and the rest of his people are behaving themselves. As far as he can tell, nobody's stealing from him too blatantly.

The something that's woken Big Red up earlier than usual this Monday comes under the heading of "business opportunity." He's found out over the years—and in this business, even a couple of years operating at his level is generally considered a pretty fair run—that in order to stay on top of things, you have to be constantly alert for new opportunities to develop and expand your business.

The kilo of pure he and Hammer took off the little Caucasian guy was a good example of just such an opportunity. From an investment of absolutely nothing, Big Red was able to turn a profit of nearly $140,000, virtually overnight. He now realizes—from the fact that the bags and bundles sold so quickly, and from the number of customers who've come back asking for more of the same product—that he probably could've whacked the stuff even harder. He'd had his mill workers cut it six times; now he knows it could've easily taken a seven, maybe even an *eight*. He tries to remember the last time he's had his hands on something so pure. He'd have to go all the way back to the early eighties, when he was buying direct from the Italians on Pleasant Avenue. And even then, the stuff they were calling "pure," some greaser had already stepped on it.

What bothers Big Red is that he realizes he may have been a little quick to kill off the goose that laid the golden egg. Sure, he's got no way of knowing if the guy had any more after the kilo. And yes, he did hedge his bet by giving his DEA buddies Zelb and Farrelli the guy's name and address from the wallet in his pants. That way, if they hit the place and came up with anything else, they'd turn in part of it and throw the rest of it his way to put out on the street for their mutual benefit.

But the thing is, it's over two weeks now, and he hasn't heard squat from Zelb. What Big Red's thinking now is that maybe it's time for him to do a little investigating of his own. He gets out of bed, walks to his closet, and starts going through the pockets of his jackets. What he's looking for is a wallet, the same wallet he found in the pair of pants he and Hammer took off the guy who had the kilo of pure.

He finds the wallet in the inside pocket of a red suede jacket. He carries it to his bed, where he turns it upside down and spills its contents onto his satin sheets. He smiles when he spots the driver's license with the inked-in new address. It's landed heads-up, a good omen for sure.

He sits down on the bed and lights his first cigarette of the day, inhaling deeply. Then he reaches for the phone beside the bed and slowly punches in the number code for Hammer's beeper.

Goodman finishes up at work and heads to the subway. He's grateful for the job, which has at least given him a place to go two afternoons a week and supplied him with a bit of spending money. But he knows that's all it is—spending money. Even if he saved every penny of it, he could never hope to begin to pay for Kelly's medical expenses, let alone the pile of other bills he has.

He wonders when he'll hear from Vinnie about their deal. Can it really be that Vinnie's people will be able to come up with three and a half million dollars? The number is so staggering that it seems totally unreal to him. So he tries to blot it out of his mind, concentrates instead on the five twenties in his back pocket. Now *that's* real, he tells himself.

The Antarctica film is a big hit with Kelly, and she's still talking about it as she and Carmen climb the steps back up to the apartment.

"Didn't those bears look like they were about to jump right off the *screen?*"

Carmen laughs. She finds that in spite of herself, she's become terribly attached to this little girl. "They reminded me a little of Larus," she says.

"After my mommy died, I carried Larus around wherever I went," Kelly says. "He was my security blanket, if you know what I mean."

"I know what you mean," Carmen says, doing her best to match Kelly's suddenly serious tone.

Carmen unlocks the door. Inside, Kelly's first stop is the refrigerator. After a quick inventory, she reports on her findings. "We need more *kid food* in this place," she announces.

"I'll be sure to pass that suggestion on to the management," Carmen says.

With the first sound of a key in the lock of Goodman's door, the plant springs to life. Abbruzzo and Riley have joined Weems, who's waiting for Sheridan to "bring home" Michael Goodman's kid and girlfriend. The two technicians, DeSimone and Kwon, are hanging around to make sure the bugs are operating properly. As they listen, they hear, "Didn't those bears look like they were about to jump right off the *screen?*" The voice comes through loud and clear, almost as if the speaker is in the same room.

"Beautiful." Abbruzzo smiles.

"Hey," Kwon says, "we do good work."

The next thing they hear is, "They reminded me a little of Larus."

"That's the broad," Weems said.

"No shit."

They continue to sit around the receiver and listen to the conversation. This they do despite the fact that they've all been given precise type-written instructions on what the wiretap statute calls the "minimization requirement." By that, the law specifies which conversations they're permitted to listen in on: those to which the person who's the target of the investigation—or someone else reasonably believed to be involved with him in his criminal activity—is a party, and—even then—only those portions that relate to the criminal activity. At all other times, the detectives are supposed to "spot-monitor" the apartment by turning the equipment on at occasional intervals, just long enough to see if criminal conversations are taking place. If the conversation is about anything else, they must turn the equipment off immediately.

Or so the theory goes.

In actuality, the detectives pretty much leave the equipment running all the time. They justify doing so on several rationales. They start by assuming that the girlfriend must be in on this business. So whenever she and Goodman are talking, they could lapse into "relevant conversation" at any moment, without notice. And even when Goodman's not around, and it's just the girlfriend and the kid, one of them could drop a remark about what Daddy's doing, which could, in turn, tip the detectives off to a deal about to go down. So everything becomes relevant.

Besides which, listening in on an eavesdropping device is pretty dreary stuff. People watch television, they read, they talk about drivel. When they're not talking, they sing off-key, they hum, they belch, they fart. The bugs pick it all up. So you end up listening for two things: conversations about the criminal activity (because that's your job) and about sex (because that's the only other thing you're ever going to hear that could be of any possible interest to you).

And while no one says anything about it now, every detective in the room could tell you that tonight, when Goodman's back in the apartment with his girlfriend and the kid's been put to bed, whichever team's in the plant will somehow get a second wind—they'll find themselves hunching over the receiver and turning the volume up a notch, desperately hoping to catch the telltale sounds of the Mole and the Molestress going at it, *doing it.* Grown, married men, somehow transformed back to the mentality of their high school teens, or the barracks behavior of their early twenties. Listening Toms.

It may sound silly, but police work tends to do that kind of thing to you.

Goodman arrives home around six, bearing the requested pizza and a six-pack of soda.

"Yea, Daddy!" Kelly cheers.

"Our hero!" Carmen joins in. Goodman can't tell if she genuinely shares Kelly's taste for pizza or if she's simply being an awfully good sport about it. But then again, he reminds himself, she *is* Italian.

"I got an invitation to a party Friday night," Kelly announces. "Can I go?"

"Where is it?"

"Far away," she says solemnly. "Two hundred West Tenth Street."

"Of course you can go." He thinks—but doesn't say—If you're feeling up to it. Be optimistic, he tells himself.

The good thing about pizza is that there's not much in the way of dishes to wash afterward. Kelly is permitted a half hour of television before getting ready for bed.

"Aren't you forgetting something?" she asks her father.

But the truth is, he hasn't. All afternoon and evening he's been thinking about her MRI test tomorrow afternoon, wondering if there's any way he can use his story to help her deal with the anxiety she must be feeling over it. But nothing's come to him, and now he's forced to improvise.

The Ballerina Princess
(Continued)

It was the night before the very last test, the one where they were to give the Ballerina Princess the injection *and* put her into the scary machine. The Ballerina Princess was sitting around talking with her father, the Keeper of the Numbers, and with the beauteous Lady Carmen. They had just finished devouring the royal pizza.

"I don't want any more tests after this one," said the Ballerina Princess. "Can this *really* be the last one?"

"Yes," replied the Keeper of the Numbers. "This shall be the last one."

"Do you promise?" asked the Ballerina Princess.

"I promise," he said.

"Suppose they say I have to have *more* tests?" the Ballerina Princess asked. "What if they *make* me?"

"Then," said the Keeper of the Numbers, "we shall flee the kingdom. We shall go into hiding, and the Lord High Royal Doctor will never be able to find us."

"But what of the brave and loyal Prince Larus?" the Ballerina Princess asked. "We can't abandon him, can we?"

"Of course not," the Keeper of the Numbers agreed. "He shall flee with us."

"And what of our cat?"

"Ah, yes," said the Keeper of the Numbers. "The strange and peculiar Kat Mandu. We could never abandon him, could we? He shall come, too."

"And what of the beauteous Lady Carmen?" Kelly asks. "We can't abandon *her*, either." She reaches out for Carmen's hand.

"No, I guess that wouldn't be fair, would it?" Goodman is forced to admit.

"No way."

"Well," Goodman says, "if it ever comes to that, we'll have to give Lady Carmen the choice, won't we?"

"Yes," Kelly says. Then, turning to Carmen, she pleads, "Will you come with us, Carmen?"

"I don't know, sweetie" is the best Carmen can offer her. "We'll have to see."

"Listen to that!" Riley exclaims. "They're planning their fucking *getaway!*"

"Could be," Abbruzzo says. They're the only two detectives left at the plant. Weems and Sheridan had gone off duty 1800; DeSimone and Kwon split as soon as it was evident that the bugs were working well. "Or it could just be a story," Abbruzzo offers as an afterthought.

"Bull*shit* it's just a story," Riley says. "I'm telling you, Ray. The Mole's going to do his deal and then he's going to cut and run. Only thing is, we're going to be standing smack on top of his tail."

"Take it easy," Abbruzzo tells him. "I don't even know if moles *have* tails."

L

ater, Goodman and Carmen sit across the card table and finish the last of the wine.

"No word from Vinnie yet?" Goodman asks.

"No," she says. "Michael?"

"Yes."

"Would you really leave if it happens?"

He thinks for a minute. "I guess we might have to," he says. "I can't imagine sitting around here, waiting for someone to come and get us."

"And me?"

"You heard the story," he tells her.

"That's just a fairy tale."

"Fairy tales can come true." He tries to sing it, but he's never had much of a voice, and they both end up laughing.

Getting up from his seat, Goodman—who holds his wine about as well as he carries a tune—trips over his own feet and bangs noisily into the card table.

In the plant, Abbruzzo and Riley cover their ears in pain.

B

ig Red picks Hammer up just after midnight. The temperature has fallen to the low thirties and steam rises from manhole covers, joining smoke from tailpipes. But inside the Bentley, it's warm and quiet. They head south, across the Madison Avenue Bridge into Manhattan, then head down Second Avenue. At Ninety-sixth, they cut over to Lexington and continue to Ninety-second, where they make a left turn.

"That's the building, right there," Big Red says as they pull to the curb a hundred feet east of Michael Goodman's building. See if his name's on the buzzer.

Hammer's out of the car for less than a minute. When he returns, he's shivering, but there's a smile on his face. "M. Goodman," he says. "Apartment 5F. We gonna pay him a visit?"

"Not just yet," Big Red says, putting the car in gear and pulling away from the curb. "But soon."

[28]

The phone rings shortly after nine Tuesday morning, while Goodman, Carmen, and Kelly are cleaning the apartment. Goodman dries his hands on his shirt and picks up.

"Hello."

"Hey, Mikey boy."

"Hello, Vinnie."

"Wanna take a little walk, Mikey?"

"If it's important."

"It's important," Vinnie assures him.

"Okay."

"Write this number down," Vinnie tells him. He reads off a number—555-3318—which Goodman jots down. "Go to a pay phone and call it."

"When?"

"*Now* when. I'm waiting at a pay phone, and it's *cold* out here."

As soon as he hangs up, Goodman tells Carmen and Kelly he's got to go out to get some Clorox. Kelly takes him at his word; Carmen knows better, and catches his eye.

"Be smart, Michael," is what she says.

"Shit!" is what Harry Weems says. He and Sheridan have been manning the plant since 0800. They heard the call come in, heard Goodman identify the caller as Vinnie, heard Vinnie assure Goodman that it's important they speak. But next thing, they're arranging a secure conversation—pay phone to pay phone—which means the detectives can cover it visually, but they'll have no way of knowing what's being said.

"Follow him," Weems tells Sheridan. "See what phone he uses."

"Me again?" Sheridan whines.

But Weems ignores him. He's already on the phone, trying to reach Telephone Security. It takes him two minutes to get through to the unit he needs.

"This is Detective Weems of OCCB," he says. "I need an address on a local number, ASAP."

"Go ahead," says a voice.

"It's five-five-five–three-three-one-eight," Weems says.

"Area code two-one-two?"

"Yeah."

"Please hold."

Weems drums his fingers on the phone receiver as he waits. He knows he's got only a matter of minutes to get the address of the phone, call Communications, and have the nearest precinct send an unmarked car to respond. If he's lucky, they'll get there in time to get a look at this Vinnie guy. If he's *real* lucky, they'll be able to get a plate number, take him home, maybe even get a full ID on him.

"That's an unlisted number," the voice tells him. "It'll take me a few minutes."

"I'll hold," Weems says. *Shit!* is his first thought. His second is a bit more cerebral: Why should a pay phone have an unlisted number? But then he answers his own question—it must be someplace where they don't want you calling back and bothering them, or tying up the phone without putting money in it.

"Sir, I'm unable to locate a record for that number," the voice tells him.

"Shit!" says Harry Weems again. "Shit, shit, shit!"

"Have a nice day," says the voice.

It's colder than he figured outside, and Goodman uses the first pay phone he finds, one of a pair at the corner of Ninety-third and Lexington. He drops a quarter in and dials the number Vinnie gave him.

The phone is answered almost before it has time to ring.

"Mikey boy?"

"Yeah."

"What took you so long?"

"I thought I'd put shoes on—"

"Okay, okay."

"What's up?" Goodman asks. It's so cold he can see his breath.

"What's up is, my people got their thing together. They're ready to go."

Goodman waits for his heart to restart itself.

"We can do it tonight if you can," Vinnie says. "Otherwise, we gotta put it off till Friday night."

Goodman remembers the MRI. "Tonight's no good," he says. "I've got to take care of my daughter."

"Your *daughter?*" Vinnie sounds incredulous. "You remember how much we're talkin' about here, Mikey?"

"Sorry," Goodman says. "First things first." The truth is, all this has happened much too fast. He feels almost grateful to have the MRI as an excuse to put things off.

"Awright," Vinnie says, disappointment in his voice. "I'll call you again in a day or two. We'll talk the same way, okay?"

"Okay."

Goodman hangs up. He stops into the store on the corner of Ninety-second Street to pick up a copy of the *Times*. Coming out, he almost bumps into a man in a tan coat. The man looks familiar, but Goodman's unable to place him.

"I think he made me," Sheridan tells Weems as soon as he gets back to the plant. "He ducked into a newsstand to see if he was being followed, and he almost got me. From now on, you better take him."

"Where did he go?" Weems asks.

"Corner of Ninety-third."

"What happened?"

"Whaddaya mean, 'what happened'? He talked on the fucking phone and I froze my fucking ass. That's what happened."

"We gotta get that phone," Weems says.

When Kelly's out of earshot for a moment, Carmen asks Goodman how it went.

"He says they're ready," he says. "I put him off till Friday night. He'll call again."

"Are you sure about all this, Michael?" she asks him.

"Of course not," he says.

The conversation ends there. It's been brief, and they've kept their voices low. But it's taken place at the very center of the studio apartment, directly under the ceiling fixture.

"Bingo!" shouts Harry Weems. "Friday night it is. We gotta get that phone," he says again.

By "get that phone," Harry Weems means tapping the corner pay phone Goodman used to call Vinnie back. Weems calls Ray Abbruzzo at home and brings him up-to-date on the morning's events.

"We gotta get that phone, Ray" is how he sums things up. "You think Maggie-O will go for it?"

"I doubt it," Abbruzzo says. "We've been to the well too many times already. We got the search warrant, we got the tap, and we got the bug. And we still got diddly-squat to show for it."

"We're getting close."

"This ain't horeshoes, Harry."

"So what do we do?" Weems asks.

"We call in the Fu Man."

Fu Man Feldman is the closest thing the NYPD has to a black-bag-job specialist. A former detective himself, Feldman was forced into early retirement when an investigation revealed that, in addition to his official duties, Feldman had a one-third interest in a hazardous-waste-removal company. That interest probably never would have been discovered, except for the fact that two company employees accidentally started a fire while dumping flammable chemicals underneath an overpass of the New Jersey Turnpike.

Physically, Feldman has been likened to a fireplug, a bowling ball, a toad, a stump, and no doubt many other objects—most of them physically squat, more than a few of them decidedly loathsome. Squat, because at an even five feet tall, Feldman weighs in at close to 230 pounds. Loathsome, because he is rude, foulmouthed, and generally unpleasant to be around.

That being said, Fu Man Feldman (his first name, Isadore, having been replaced long ago by the nickname that derives from his droopy mustache and goatee) has always been in great demand, both when he was on the job and since his retirement. The reason is simple: Fu Man Feldman can tap a phone, bug a room, hot-wire a car, crack a safe, or do any number of similar chores. He can do these things quickly. He can do them with his own equipment. And, best of all—unlike Detectives DeSimone and Kwon from the technical team—he's willing to do them without a court order.

Feldman works for cash, something many detectives are happy to pay out of their own pockets in order to avoid the paperwork, legalities, and headaches that come when you go through proper channels. His rates are actually quite modest—a hundred here, a fifty there. The truth is, Feldman rather likes doing the occasional job, even aside from the pocket money it brings him. He enjoys being around cops, even though you'd never know it from the way he treats them. He likes to keep his skills sharp. And he loves to show off.

Feldman arrives at Ninety-third and Lexington at one o'clock in the afternoon. For the occasion, he's wearing a NYNEX hard hat and a telephone repairman's belt, complete with an assortment of tools, wire loops, and a handset. He carries an official-looking metal box.

He spots two pay phones on the northeast corner. He has the equipment to tap both, but he knows that won't be necessary.

To the casual observer, the two and a half minutes Feldman spends at the phone are devoted to servicing the equipment, making sure all the connections are tight, and checking to see that the wire-jacketed cord is intact.

In fact, Feldman does none of these things. What he does is to loosen the cover of the phone box, reach behind it, isolate the two wires that form the pair unique to the phone's seven-digit number, and clip a tiny remote transmitter to those wires.

Then he sets the frequency of the transmitter to match that of a "middleman," a relay unit capable of receiving the signal and forwarding it to a third unit located anywhere within a quarter-mile radius.

The only drawback to the middleman is that it needs an AC power source. This problem Feldman solves at the corner lamppost, where he unscrews the plate at the base and connects the unit to the live wires inside. A green light on the unit flashes three times, informing him that the system is in business.

Next, he goes to the second pay phone. Fishing a self-adhering sticker out of his toolbox, he pastes it onto the phone, covering the coin slot. Experience has taught Feldman that that little sticker is all it takes to ensure that any caller will now use the first phone, the one he's tapped. The message on the sticker is short and to the point: "Sorry. Out of Order."

By two o'clock, it's time for Goodman and Kelly to leave for the MRI place. Kelly asks Carmen if she can come, too. When Carmen hesitates just a second before responding, Goodman answers for her.

"I'm sure Carmen's got things she has to do."

"No," Carmen says. "I'd like to come."

Kelly is so pleased, she decides to leave Larus home. "He can keep Pop-Tart company," she explains.

Walking along, holding one of his daughter's hands as Carmen holds the other, Goodman tries to remember the last time Kelly's complained of a headache. He's tempted to ask her but fears the power of suggestion. He settles for daring to hope that she might be getting better, that there may be no tumor after all.

The MRI place is busy. They repeat the registration process, and the questioning regarding Goodman's lack of medical insurance. They take his Bronx Tire Exchange, Special Account, check in the amount of $550.00. They are led to the same procedure room as last time, where Kelly trades her clothes for a gown.

"I'm afraid only one parent may remain during the actual test," says an attendant.

Carmen makes a move toward the door, but Kelly asks her to stay. Goodman bends down to kiss his daughter good-bye. "I don't want to hurt her feelings," she whispers into his ear. "Okay, Daddy?"

This from a six-year-old.

He walks back to the waiting room, takes the only empty seat, across from an old Hispanic man wearing a patch over one eye. They smile at each other. He wonders what misfortune has brought the man here. Has he already lost an eye to the ravages of a malignant brain tumor?

Goodman finds an issue of *Time* magazine from last December; there doesn't seem to be a more recent one. He skims an article about the fragile peace accord in Bosnia, ignores an analysis of what seems to be shaping up as a Clinton-Dole campaign, and glances through an editorial about Princess Diana's bulimia. The story that begins on the next page stops him.

THE RESURGENCE OF HEROIN

The article discusses how emergency-room admissions, police statistics, and prisoner interviews over the last year all point to a "disturbing trend." The use of heroin—which had declined steadily for almost a decade—is on the rise again. Users who had been scared off by fears of getting AIDs from shared needles, or drawn to less expensive and more plentiful crack cocaine, have been returning to heroin, lured by higher quality and greater availability. A public health official is quoted as saying that the good news is that heroin users tend to be less violent than crack users. Police Commissioner Bratton warns of turf wars already beginning to break out among rival drug sellers. And Representative Guy Molinari blames needle-exchange programs, calling for their immediate curtailment and demanding the death penalty for all drug dealers.

Goodman closes the magazine. Is he about to do his part in contributing to this "disturbing trend"? How many new addicts will be created as a result of the heroin he sells to Vinnie and his people? How many overdoses will there be? How many *deaths?* In his battle to save his daughter's life, how many other lives will be destroyed?

He shuts his eyes, pinches the bridge of his nose. Wonders if it's too late to stop this whole business, if there isn't some other way. . . .

"Mr. Goodman?"

He opens his eyes, realizes he's been asleep. For a moment, he has no idea where he is or whose face it is that peers down at him.

"You're Kelly's father?" the face asks him. It belongs to a black woman with a pleasant smile.

"Yes," Goodman says, embarrassed at having dozed off.

"We're all done," she tells him. "Your doctor will have the results tomorrow morning."

"Thank you," Goodman says, pulling himself to a standing position.

"Why don't you come with me; we'll go back and join your wife and daughter."

Goodman's about to correct her, but as he begins to move, he finds his foot has fallen asleep. He half-walks, half-hops down the hallway, causing the woman to turn around at one point.

"We don't give group rates, you know," she cautions him.

The side effects of an MRI with contrast fall somewhere in between those associated with a spinal tap and those with a simple MRI. So while Kelly's head doesn't have to be held rigid afterward, her head hurts, her back is sore, and she's somewhat wobbly from the procedure.

Carmen takes one look at Goodman hopping into the room and says, "I guess I'll have to carry *both* of you home!"

But they get a cab to carry all three of them, and by six o'clock, Kelly's asleep on the couch, joined by Larus and Pop-Tart. She's so exhausted, she doesn't even think to ask for another chapter of the story.

"Thank you," Goodman says to Carmen.

"Thank you for letting me be part of your family for a while," she says.

He says nothing further, but the phrase "for a while" burns into his memory. Is she gone, then, this person who came into his life so suddenly, so unexpectedly? Is she history as soon as this business with her brother Vincent is finished? He can't bring himself to ask her, so afraid is he that she will say yes.

Ray Abbruzzo sits in the plant alone. With things under control, he's let Daniel Riley have the night off to go watch his kid play in a fourth-grade basketball game, though Abbruzzo has his doubts about the ability of fourth graders to reach the basket. What's the final score going to be, anyway—four to two?

They know now that the Mole and Vinnie are going to do their deal Friday night. Abbruzzo and his team have got the building entrance under surveillance, the apartment bugged, the phone tapped, and the corner phone covered, as well. You just can't do much more than that.

The way Ray Abbruzzo sees it, the good guys are sitting pretty.

The way Big Red sees it, he's given No Neck too much time already.

"Remember that apartment we checked out last night?" he asks Hammer over a drink at the Homeboy Lounge on 127th Street?

"Yeah," Hammer nods.

"Well, I think it's about time we paid our respects to our little friend."

"Tonight?" Hammer's always ready. It's one of the reasons Big Red knows he can rely on him.

Big Red thinks for a moment. "No," he says. "We'll wait till the Man's gone home to the suburbs for the weekend. We'll do it Friday night."

First thing Wednesday morning, Goodman calls Dr. Gendel's office to get the results of the MRI.

"Doctor isn't *in* right now," a receptionist tells him, as though she's speaking to a small child. "But he left a message asking that you come in and see him this morning at eleven, if that's convenient with you."

"Does he want me to bring my daughter?" he asks.

"Well, she *is* the patient, isn't she?"

He thanks her and hangs up the phone, his palms already slippery with sweat. What can this mean but bad news? he asks himself. Had the pictures shown nothing, surely they could have told him so on the phone. Leaving a message for him to come in is a truly ominous sign, a sure indication that things are so bad that whatever the news is, it has to be delivered *in person*, the way you tell someone that a loved one has *died*. "We've scheduled her for immediate brain surgery this afternoon," he can hear Dr. Gendel saying.

He tries to avoid Carmen's eyes, but there's no hiding from them.

"The doctor wants to see us at eleven," he tells them, trying to make it sound as matter-of-fact as he can. But he fools no one. Nothing else is said, but Carmen bites her lower lip and breaks off eye contact. Kelly walks to the corner of the room and picks up Larus. Even Pop-Tart sulks away.

It's cold and gray outside, and they take a cab to Dr. Gendel's office. No one questions Carmen's coming along this time. Once or twice during the ride, Goodman tries for small talk, but he soon gives up. They stare out of the cab windows, as though the streets of the city have suddenly become so interesting as to demand their full attention. Goodman is reminded that he's all but promised Kelly that there'll be no more tests. How does he now tell her that he was wrong, that he *lied?* He's afraid there's only so much mileage you can get out of "Life isn't always fair" with a six-year-old.

"Doctor still isn't in," they are told when they arrive, and they take seats in the waiting room. They are the only ones there. Goodman sits Kelly in his lap, and together they leaf through a copy of *National Geographic.* He's determined to do his best to keep her occupied, fearful that she might otherwise ask him to fill the time with another chapter of their story. He doesn't know precisely what lies ahead for the Ballerina Princess, but he's so certain it isn't good that he's afraid even to think about it.

Carmen sits without so much as a magazine as pretext, her stare more or less aimed at the pattern of the wallpaper.

Goodman is explaining to Kelly what makes certain animals marsupials when the receptionist pokes her head into the room. "Doctor will see you now," she says.

The three of them follow her. Goodman wonders when the doctor arrived, and through what side door. Or has he been there all along, stalling, trying to compose the words he'll use to break the news to them?

They're ushered into Dr. Gendel's empty office and take seats. Goodman says one of his silent little prayers, asking for his own death if that will spare his daughter's life.

"Good morning, folks," Dr. Gendel says, walking into the room in a white lab coat. Goodman tries to read meaning into his casual air but finds it difficult to do so. Is it really casual, or is an act, put on to disguise his anguish? Goodman wonders if they train doctors in medical school how to hide their emotions. Poker Face 101, three credits, pass/fail.

"I'm Dr. Gendel," the doctor tells Carmen, and Goodman is forced to mumble an apology for having forgotten to introduce them.

"How are we feeling today, young lady?" Gendel asks Kelly, motioning her to join him behind his desk.

"Okay," she replies in a small voice, circling the desk and ending up in front of him. He takes her hands in his.

"Okay, but *freezing!*" he says. "Cold hands, blue lips. Doesn't your daddy bundle you up enough?"

"I dress myself," Kelly tells him. "And my daddy takes very good care of me."

So serious is her tone, so protective her words, that Goodman actually feels his chest inflate with such intense, aching love for his daughter that he has to concentrate on his breathing. He's aware of Carmen's hand on his arm, is happy to have it there.

Dr. Gendel opens a drawer and fishes out a device similar to the one he used last time to examine Kelly's eyes. He fits the contraption around his head and flicks on a light that's part of it. Then, spreading his knees apart, he draws Kelly closer to him, pinning her little body with his knees.

"See this funny-looking nose of mine?" Dr. Gendel asks Kelly.

"Yes."

"Well, I want you to watch it as hard as you can, okay?"

"Okay."

He examines one eye, then the other, pausing to make notes on a pad of paper. Then he snaps off the light and removes the contraption.

"Do you still see the spot?" he asks her.

"Only sometimes."

"Which eye?"

She raises her hand to her right eye.

"Is it the same size as before?"

"No," she says. "When I see it, it's smaller."

"What color is it when you see it?"

"Yucky color," she says.

"What's yucky color?"

"Yellowish brown."

"Sounds yucky to me all right," Dr. Gendel agrees. "Was it always that color?"

"I don't remember."

He looks through some notes in his file. "Last time, you told me it was brown. Is it different now?"

"I guess so."

He opens his knees and releases Kelly from their grip. She seems happy to escape, and retraces her route around the desk to join Goodman and Carmen.

Dr. Gendel swivels his chair to face them. Goodman braces for the worst. Isn't it good that the spot's fading? Isn't yellowish brown better than all brown? Doesn't that count for *something?*

"I'm going to confess, I'm just a little bit baffled here," Gendel says. "The MRI pictures are clear—there's no tumor I can see. The spot on the eye *has* faded some—Kelly's absolutely right about that.

"My best guess is that we're looking at a case of atypical pseudotumor cerebri here. That's when we have an overabundance of spinal fluid, and we see symptoms mimicking those associated with a tumor: headaches, visual spots, and so forth. Though the truth is, we usually find that condition in teenagers, and, more often than not, where obesity plays a contributing part.

"The diagnosis—or lack of diagnosis, really—could explain why we're seeing some improvement following the spinal tap. We draw fluid out and that relieves some of the pressure."

"So she's getting better?" Goodman's voice sounds far away to him, unlike his own.

"Well, she's certainly holding her own," Gendel says. "And the pictures are negative, even with contrast. We've got to be very happy about that."

"We are," Goodman agrees.

"What next?" It's Carmen's voice.

"Next is continued close monitoring," Gendel says. "Someone's got to keep watching that spot. It provides us with a convenient barometer of the pressure inside. The spot grows bigger and darker, the pressure's building up. That means it's time to do another tap, draw off some fluid. Should it get real bad, she might need to have a drain inserted. On the other hand, the spot continues to get smaller and lighter—*yuckier,* I believe the technical term is—the less we have to worry about. The important thing is that somebody's got to keep an eye on the spot."

"Somebody?" Goodman asks. He's aware that twice now, Dr. Gendel has distanced himself from Kelly's case.

Dr. Gendel rises from his chair. "We can talk about that if you like," he says, looking at Kelly and Carmen as if to tell them that they're dismissed now, this is man-to-man talk. Something else they must teach in medical school, Goodman decides.

Carmen takes the cue, and she and Kelly say their good-byes and head back toward the waiting room. Dr. Gendel closes the door.

"Is this about money?" Goodman asks.

"Partly," Dr. Gendel admits. "My office manager tells me you have no insurance of any sort."

"I'm going to be able to pay your bill," Goodman says.

"This is a very expensive proposition," Dr. Gendel says. "We've made accommodations, but you're already several thousand dollars behind. Your daughter needs to be watched. There may have to be more procedures, possibly many of them." He shrugs. "You know, there *are* city hospitals. I don't want to see your daughter go untreated. But it's just not fair to the rest of my patients."

The phrase "city hospitals" stings Goodman's ears. He's not about to turn his daughter's care over to some medical student or first-year intern. "I'm going to be able to pay your bill," he repeats dumbly. "Whatever it comes to."

"Don't get me wrong—I know you have the best of intentions—"

"You said 'partly,' " Goodman reminds him. "Is there some other problem?"

"Problem? No. Suggestion? Yes."

"What's that?"

"Your daughter's *cold,* Mr. Goodman. She damn near has chronic hypothermia."

"She's nervous about all of this."

"She's *freezing!*"

"So?"

"So," Dr. Gendel says, "take her on vacation. Take her someplace where it's *warm.* Give the kid a chance to *thaw out,* for God's sake!"

Thawing out is very much on Daniel Riley's mind, too. He shivers in a doorway opposite the entrance to Dr. Gendel's office, waiting for the reappearance of Michael Goodman, his daughter, and his girlfriend. They've been inside for forty minutes now. Outside, where Riley is, it's thirty-three degrees and windy.

Riley's back on duty after a rare night with his family. He watched his son's fourth-grade basketball team lose to a team of what seemed to Riley to be a bunch of *high school kids.* At least one of them looked like he was *shaving* already. *They* certainly had no trouble reaching the basket. The final score had been twenty-three to nine. Riley's kid went scoreless, missing two free throws in the last minute from a foul line that couldn't have been more than five feet from the basket.

Riley takes his orders from Ray Abbruzzo on this assignment, and Abbruzzo's convinced the deal is going down Friday night. Still, he's decided to cover the Mole full-time between now and then, just in case he makes a side trip from one of these family outings to meet with his customers.

To Abbruzzo, full-time coverage means sitting by the heater in the plant. To Riley, it means standing out in the cold, getting pneumonia.

Seniority is a big deal in the NYPD, even among detectives. Especially in winter.

Preoccupied with his futile attempts to keep warm, Riley almost misses Goodman hailing a cab across the street. He flags down one of his own and jumps in. It feels almost as cold inside the cab as outside. Riley's forced to show the driver his gold shield in order to convince him to make an illegal U-turn. The driver mumbles something in a strange language. Riley takes his eyes off the other cab just long enough to glance at the driver's name on the ID card: Viktor Gromechki. That probably goes a long way toward explaining why there's no heat on in the cab.

Back home, Goodman, Kelly, and Carmen celebrate the good news—or at least the absence of *bad* news—by toasting marshmallows over the burner of the stove. Kelly, standing on a chair and using a long serving fork, under Carmen's close supervision, holds her marshmallow high over the flame, rotating it patiently until it gradually turns a golden brown, just the way Carmen says she likes hers.

Goodman is less careful, allowing his marshmallow to get too close to the burner, until it catches fire. By the time he succeeds in blowing out the flame, he's left with a charred crust and an oozing interior that burns his fingers when he goes to pull it off the fork.

As they sit around the card table, eating their snack, Goodman asks Kelly if she's warm enough.

"Yup," she says absently, busy trying to coax Pop-Tart into tasting the inside of a marshmallow.

But to Goodman, her lips look thin and just slightly purple. He will watch her for the rest of the afternoon and well into the evening, looking for signs of shivering, of cold—of chronic hypothermia.

[30]

It's even colder Thursday, with temperatures down around thirty. The news is filled with stories about record-breaking temperatures for October. Goodman bundles up for the ride to work, tells Carmen and Kelly to promise him they'll stay indoors.

"No *way*," Carmen says. "We've got to go out to find a costume for Kelly's party."

"We're not *babies*," Kelly tells him. "And you're not the boss of us."

"You're *my* babies," he says.

"Excuse me?" Carmen chimes in.

"Just a figure of speech," Goodman says, blushing.

"What's a figure of speech?" Kelly wants to know. "Is it like a figure eight?"

"Not exactly," he smiles. "It's when you say something that's not exactly true."

"So why do you say it?"

"To make a point," he explains. "You know, like, 'I'm so hungry, I could eat a horse.' "

"Yuck."

Goodman's been at work a little over an hour when Manny comes into the office, closes the door behind him, and sits down across the desk from him.

"You doing anything wrong, Michael?"

Goodman thinks immediately of the accounts he's opened and the checks he's written against them. Did he slip up somewhere? Has the bank notified Manny?

"Like what?" he asks, trying to sound surprised at the question but knowing that if he was hooked up to a lie detector, the needle would be jumping off the page.

"I dunno," Manny says. "But two minutes after you walked in, two guys in a blue Ford parked across the way. They been sittin' in their car since, drinkin' coffee the whole time."

"Who do you think they are?" Goodman asks.

"Well, one's black and one's white. To me, they gotta be cops. So I was just wonderin' if it's you they're interested in."

"I can't imagine why they would be," Goodman says.

"Me neither," Manny agrees. "Don't worry about it." While he's there, he pulls his usual roll of bills from his back pocket and peels off five twenties for Goodman.

But not worrying about it proves to be more easily said than done, and worry about it is about all Goodman can do for the rest of the afternoon.

At quitting time, he bundles up for the trip home. On an impulse, he purposefully leaves his briefcase in the office. As he steps out onto Jerome Avenue, he sees a blue Ford across the way. It's easy to spot: The windshield's fogged up, and there's visible exhaust coming from the tailpipe.

He walks a block uptown in the cold before stopping in his tracks. He smacks his forehead like the guy used to do in the "I coulda had a V-8" commercial. Then he turns around suddenly and heads back downtown. As he does so, the blue Ford passes right by him, and he gets a good look at the occupants. The driver is a heavyset black man he doesn't recognize. But the passenger, a white man, looks very much like the guy he saw at the store the other day when he was buying a newspaper.

"Shit!" says Harry Weems as soon as they've driven past Goodman. "Shit! Shit! Shit!" It's become a staple of his vocabulary since he's been assigned to this investigation.

"Did you see that?" Sheridan can't get over it. "Motherfucker doubled back on us like a *pro!* I *told* you he was good."

Knowing they've been burned, they continue on to the plant. No use making things worse than they already are. Besides which, they already know the Mole's pattern: walk to 161st Street, take the subway home. Maybe stop off for a pizza, if he's feeling really rich.

When Goodman comes back out of the Bronx Tire Exchange again, this time with his briefcase, the blue Ford is nowhere in sight.

As always, it's dark as he walks to the train station, and he pays attention to his surroundings, something he's been careful to do since his first encounter with Russell.

He wonders what Russell's up to. He hasn't seen him since the ill-fated attempt to sell the first kilo of drugs. He tries to figure out how long ago that was, but has trouble remembering. As good as he is with numbers, that's how bad he is with time.

He has occasion to think of Russell again just before he gets to 161st Street. There's a tall, skinny black kid leaning against the building, and for just a moment, Goodman thinks maybe it *is* Russell. But then he sees that the kid isn't really a kid after all, but a man in his thirties or forties. As Goodman passes him, the man comes away from the wall, hunched over, eyes closed—sleepwalking. But for some reason totally unfathomable to Goodman, he doesn't fall over, just staggers around in a circle, oblivious to everything around him. "Drunk as a skunk" is the expression Goodman is reminded of.

If Goodman knew a little about pharmacology, he'd understand that the man isn't drunk at all. Drunks fall down, because alcohol adversely affects the drinker's sense of balance. Opiates have no such effect: The heroin user can be quite literally "out on his feet" without ever losing command of his internal gyroscope, his unconscious ability to maintain his balance.

Of course, Michael Goodman may find it easier to assume that the man is drunk. It is Thursday after all. Tomorrow is Friday, the day he and Vinnie are to conduct their little business. How appropriate that they should have picked Halloween, the scariest day of the year to begin with.

Which reminds him—he's promised Kelly he'd pick up a pumpkin on the way home. So, at the corner of Ninety-sixth and Lexington, he stops at a hybrid Spanish-Korean store called the Bodega Palace and picks out what seems to him a reasonably sized pumpkin. He fishes out a few dollars to pay for it, wondering how much they can charge for what is essentially an overgrown orange squash. The Korean woman behind the counter puts it on the scale and rings it up.

"Nine dolla," she says.

Jesus, he thinks. But comes up with it.

"Whaddaya mean, he *burned* you?" Abbruzzo asks Weems and Sheridan as soon as they rejoin him at the plant. At Abbruzzo's request, Lieutenant Spangler has assigned five more men to the investigation, meaning they're back to eight-hour shifts, three men to a shift.

"He doubled back on us," Sheridan explains. "Made us for sure."

"Sonofabitch," Abbruzzo says. "I hope this doesn't spook him."

"How are we ever gonna cover the deal?" Weems wonders. "With this guy so hinky. He'll make any car we use."

Abbruzzo thinks for a moment. "We'll get the MOUSE," he says. The MOUSE is the Mobile Operations Unit for Surveillance Enhancement. From the outside, it appears to be a delivery van, one of countless thousands New Yorkers are accustomed to seeing making a variety of deliveries, pickups, installations, or repairs. Inside, it's equipped with one-way viewing glass, video and still camera ports, and parabolic microphones capable of picking up whispered conversation a block away. For extended periods of surveillance, there's a small refrigerator, a microwave oven, and even a chemical toilet.

"Good thinking," Weems says.

"This is shaping up as some battle," Sheridan decides. "The Mole versus the MOUSE. It's like *Wild* fucking *Kingdom.* You gotta wonder who's gonna survive."

"Do yourself a favor," says Ray Abbruzzo. "Put your money on the MOUSE."

Goodman, Carmen, and Kelly are in the middle of dinner when the phone rings. Goodman's in the process of swallowing a mouthful of tuna casserole as he reaches for it.

"Hello?" he says.

"Hello. Who's this?"

Goodman recognizes Vinnie's voice. "Michael," he says.

"You sure? You sound funny."

"I'm eating."

"Go outside," Vinnie tells him. "Gimme a call at this number—"

"Wait, wait," Goodman says, looking around for something to write with. He finds a pen, says, "Go ahead."

"Five-five-five–five-nine-six-two."

Goodman writes the number on the palm of his hand. "Give me fifteen minutes," he says.

"Fuck fifteen minutes!" Vinnie shouts. "I'm at a pay phone. You got any idea how *cold* it is out here?"

"Don't tell me," Goodman says. "I'll call you in five minutes." He hangs up the phone.

"I have to run out," he tells Carmen and Kelly. "I'll be back real soon."

"Dress warmly," Kelly tells him.

He exchanges a look with Carmen. She knows what the call was about.

Ray Abbruzzo knows what the call was about, too, and he loses no time in calling Telephone Security's night line.

"Get me an address on two-one-two–five-five-five–five-nine-six-two as fast as you can. I think it may be a coin box." Then he hands the phone to Weems. "You guys are hot," he says. "I'll take the Mole. See if you can get a unit to respond to wherever Vinnie's phone is. But no RMPs."

Abbruzzo puts on his coat. As soon as he spots Goodman coming out of his building, he's out the door, following him at a safe distance, from across the street.

"That's a coin-operated phone located inside the premises of One thirty Tenth Avenue," a woman's voice tells Weems.

"What the hell's at One thirty Tenth Avenue?" Weems asks.

"It's a restaurant," she tells him, "called La Luncheonette."

"What's the cross street?"

"How am I supposed to know?" she asks. *"You're* the detective."

He hangs up, calls Communications, and requests a PDU—a Precinct Detective Unit operating out of the local station house—to respond to the location. He tells the operator he'll hold on to give the unit instructions.

"No units are answering," the operator tells him. "It's cold out there."

"Bullshit!" he roars. "Make it a ten-thirteen!" A 10-13 is the highest priority job there is—"Officer needs assistance." If Martians were landing a flying saucer in Central Park and a 10-13 came over the air, every cop would be out of there in seconds.

"You know I can't do that," the operator says.

"Fuck!"

"Wait a minute—I've got a unit that'll take it," the operator says. "Twelve minutes ETA."

"*Twelve minutes?* I don't *have* twelve minutes!"

"Sorry, sir."

Goodman is shivering by the time he reaches the corner. The phone he used last time has an "Out of Order" sticker on it, but the one next to it is working. He drops in a quarter and calls the number he's written on his palm.

While Weems continues to hold on, waiting for the Communications operator to come back, Sheridan turns the volume all the way up on the receiver Fu Man Feldman added to the growing list of electronic equipment in the plant. The voices come through loud and clear.

VOICE:	Hello?
GOODMAN:	Hello, Vinnie.
VINNIE:	Hey, Mikey boy. You sound better now. Don't be eating anything my sister cooks for you, man. You could be taking your life in your hands.
GOODMAN:	What's up?
VINNIE:	We're set. Tomorrow night, eight o'clock.
GOODMAN:	Eight?
VINNIE:	Yeah. Whassamatta?
GOODMAN:	Well, it's just that my kid's got to be at a party tomorrow night.
VINNIE:	Jesus, I don't know if I can change it.
GOODMAN:	Well, leave it at eight, then. I'll see what I can do. But you know how kids are. Where's this supposed to be?
VINNIE:	Someplace quiet.

Goodman remembers the last time he did a deal at "someplace quiet." He ended up losing his drugs, his shoes, and his pants. He wants no part of that this time around.

GOODMAN: You sure it's got to be at eight?

VINNIE: Jesus, I awready told 'em—

GOODMAN: Okay, okay. Then it's going to have to be near where the party is.

VINNIE: Where's that?

GOODMAN: Downtown somewhere. I don't remember.

VINNIE: Fuck.

GOODMAN: I can call you back tomorrow with the address.

VINNIE: No, no, that's awright, I'll call *you*. You be home around noon?

GOODMAN: I'll make it a point to be.

VINNIE: Good, you do that. And Mikey boy?

GOODMAN: Yes?

VINNIE: No funny stuff, okay?

The phone goes dead.

"Shit!" Harry Weems slams down the phone. He'd hoped the conversation would last for eight or ten minutes. That might have given the responding unit a chance to get to the restaurant in time to see who was on the phone, or at least who was coming out of the place looking as if he'd just used the phone. One time, Weems had been able to find out who had used a pay phone last by yelling out that the quarter had ended up in the coin return slot, then waiting to see who claimed it. Guy who claimed it ended up doing five years, too—either because he was really the one who'd made the call or because he was greedy and tried to steal the twenty-five cents. Whatever.

But Goodman stayed on the phone less than a minute, making it impossible for anyone to get there in time to get a look at this Vinnie guy.

On the other hand, they *have* learned that the exchange is scheduled to go down at eight o'clock tomorrow night. And while they don't know the location yet—other than "downtown somewhere"—they should have that by noon tomorrow.

The door opens and Ray Abbruzzo comes in and joins them. "How'd you do?" he asks them, still shivering from the cold.

"No luck on IDing Vinnie," Weems says.

"But we did get the details of how the deal's going to go down," Riley says.

"Good work." Abbruzzo seems genuinely pleased. "When's it set for?"

"Eight o'clock tomorrow night."

"Where?"

Riley checks the notes he made of the conversation. "Uh . . . someplace downtown."

"Great," Abbruzzo says. This time, there's not the slightest suggestion of pleasure in his voice.

Goodman is back home in time to finish his tuna casserole.

"Where's that party you're supposed to be going to tomorrow night?" he asks Kelly.

"I already *told* you," she says.

"I know," he admits. "But tell me again."

She shoots him a look that says, *Grown-ups,* but she gets up and finds the invitation. " 'Two hundred West Tenth Street,' " she reads. " 'Corner of Sixth Avenue. Apartment Six B. Six to nine P.M.' Janie says there's a *parade* that goes by, and we'll be able to see it from her living room. *Neat,* huh?"

"Very neat," Goodman says. A Halloween *parade?* Must be something new. Probably a dozen weirdos running around in silly costumes.

"Me and Carmen bought *material* to make me a costume," she says.

"Carmen and I," he corrects her.

"No, *you've* got to carve the pumpkin. Remember?"

"I remember," he assures her.

"And give it a scary face."

He nods.

"Not *too* scary."

With no developments expected for another eighteen hours, Abbruzzo all but shuts the plant down. He figures they can all use a good night's sleep before getting ready to cover the deal tomorrow evening. He leaves one of the newly assigned men on duty, with instructions to beep him right away if anything out of the ordinary happens. Then he calls Lieutenant Spangler at home to get permission to requisition the MOUSE for tomorrow evening.

"Okay," Spangler says. "But don't forget to put in the paperwork for it."

"Right," is what Abbruzzo says. What he *thinks* is, This job really sucks—you want to use a stupid van to make a legitimate collar, you gotta *ask permission to request it.* And God forbid you don't submit the proper fucking forms in triplicate or quadruplicate or whatever, some stiff from IAD is going to have your ass on the carpet first thing Monday morning, accusing you of using police property for personal business.

"Anybody need a drink?" he asks.

There is a chorus of "Yeahs."

Goodman sits at the card table, trying to carve a not-too-scary jack-o'-lantern. He's never seen so many pits in his life. They're all over the place—on the table, under the table, in his lap, down his shirt. Pop-Tart seems amused by them at first, but soon becomes overwhelmed by the sheer number of them.

"Save those," Carmen says from the bed, which she and Kelly have opened up to use as a work surface for their costume making.

"Save what?" he asks. "The *pits?*"

"They're not *pits,*" she laughs. "They're *seeds.* And I want to season them and bake them. They're delicious."

Pop-Tart hops up onto the bed and begins attacking the material Carmen and Kelly have stretched out there.

"I *knew* the guy at Woolworth's was making a mistake," Carmen says. "We brought him this roll of black satin marked five-ninety-five, and he just rang it up. It was supposed to be five-ninety-five a *yard.* That'll teach them to let *men* work in responsible positions."

"We've got *miles* of it," Kelly shouts, rolling it onto the floor, where Pop-Tart pounces on it.

"Wouldn't it have been the honorable thing to point out the poor fellow's mistake to him?" Goodman asks.

"Honorable shmonorable!" Carmen says. "It's not *his* money."

"Honorable shmonorable," Kelly giggles.

And it occurs to Goodman: Who am I to talk?

It's after ten by the time they're finished. Goodman has created a respectable jack-o'-lantern, complete with a Chanukah candle. Kelly is a very convincing witch, all in black satin: a tall peaked hat, a floor-length cloak, and black tape to produce the illusion of thigh-high boots. A broom completes the outfit. Almost.

"Can I bring Pop-Tart?" she begs. *"Pleeeease?"*

"It'll be much too cold out," Goodman tells her.

"Maybe we could take a cab?" Carmen suggests.

"Who's side are *you* on?"

"My side!" Kelly squeals, hugging Carmen. "My side! My side! My side!"

"And who wound *you* up?" Goodman asks. "We'll see about it."

"That means yes," Kelly whispers to Carmen.

"It means *we'll see,*" Goodman tells her. "When did I lose control around here?" he wonders aloud.

Cleanup is next. Carmen and Kelly gather up bits and pieces of material, while Pop-Tart makes an occasional charge. That leaves Goodman to crawl around on his hands and knees in search of pumpkin seeds. They're covered with stringy yellow stuff, which makes them slimy and hard to pick up. There are so many underneath the table that his hands fill up.

"Hand me that bowl over there, would you?" he asks whoever's in earshot.

"Here."

He feels the bowl against his left shoulder. With both hands occupied, he has to lower himself to the floor before turning to reach behind him. It's a strange position he finds himself in—underneath the table, looking upward. But it's the only position from which he can see the bowl.

And something stuck to the underside of the tabletop.

But to Goodman, given the distance, the awkward position he's in, and the poor lighting under the table, it looks like a piece of used chewing gum. He's about to say something about it to Kelly, but then it occurs to him that it might have been Carmen who stuck it there.

"Are you going to take the bowl, or what?" Carmen's asking him.

He takes it from her hand, empties the seeds into it, and crawls out from under the table.

"It's story time," Kelly announces, already under the covers with Larus and Pop-Tart. He forgets about the gum.

The Ballerina Princess

(Continued)

Now it came to pass that the Ballerina Princess received an invitation to a ball—

"A ball?"

—which happens to be another word for a fancy party where the guests all get dressed up in strange and beautiful outfits, which are sometimes called costumes.

Because the Ballerina Princess was so beautiful, she decided that for once it would be fun to go dressed up all in black—a black hat, a black cape, even long black boots. And on her face, she wore green and yellow makeup. By the time she was ready to go, she was so ugly that she was scared to look in the mirror, for fear that she might cause it to crack.

"Did her cat go with her?"
"Quiet, you," he says. "I told you we'd *see* about that."
"It's only a *story,* Daddy," she reminds him.

At the ball, nobody had any idea who the girl dressed all in black was, but everyone agreed that she was the ugliest, scariest, most evil-looking creature they'd ever seen. In order to figure out who she was, they decided to wait until the end of the ball—to see who came to pick her up.

At the stroke of nine, the doorbell rang, and all the other children ran to see who the two people were who'd come to pick up the little girl. But, to their surprise, the man and the woman at the door were dressed up in their *own* costumes, and even as they reclaimed the little girl and fled off into the night with her, not a soul knew who they were. Or who the little girl was.

"Ever?"
"Ever."

Spike Schwartz is the lone police officer on duty at the plant. Spike's full name is Adalberto Schwartz. He's a Puerto Rican Jew, and he's been called "Spike" ever since seventh grade, when somebody figured out you could compress two ethnic slurs into a single syllable. The nickname stuck. Spike and his wife—her name is Norma, though she's referred to by her husband's friends as "the Spikestress"—are the proud parents of six-week-old twin boys. People keep assuring Spike that, with a little time, the babies will adjust to each other and get themselves onto the same feeding schedule, more or less. So far, it's been less. Spike arrived for work this evening on less than three hours of sleep over the last thirty-six.

Spike's a good cop, and he tries his best to stay alert and monitor the electronic equipment properly. But no phone calls come in at all, and the only thing the bug seems to pick up are dishes being washed and some goofy guy telling a story about a ballerina who dresses up like a witch.

By 2100 hours, Spike's starting to yawn.

Goodman lies awake in his spot on the floor that night, watching the shadows cast by the candle burning down in the jack-o'-lantern.

Tomorrow, he thinks. Tomorrow he becomes a certified, blue-ribbon, wholesale narcotics dealer. He wonders if there's still time to pull out of it, to tell Vinnie that he's changed his mind, or chickened out, or whatever. He thinks about the guy he saw staggering around on 161st Street this afternoon, thinks about Russell. He thinks about the Resurgence of Heroin.

The same old dilemma comes back to him. He knows it's wrong to be putting the drugs out onto the street. But he also knows now that Kelly, even if she's to continue getting better, is going to require expensive medical attention for the foreseeable future—medical attention he means to provide for her, no matter what.

"Are you awake?" Carmen's voice.

"Yes."

"I kinda figured you might be," she says. "Want company down there?"

"I'd love some."

Then she's next to him, all warm in an old flannel shirt of his.

"I need to ask you something," he says.

"Ask."

"If anything happens to me, will you—would you look after Kelly? You know, see that she gets to her grandmother's?"

"That's it? Just like that?" There's a sharp edge to her voice.

"What do you mean?"

"I mean, *think what you're saying.*" She's up on one elbow, face-to-face with him. "The kid's *six years old.* Her mother died. She's sick, maybe real sick. *What do you think happens to her if she loses her father now?*"

"I—"

" 'Look after Kelley'? 'See that she gets to her grandmother's'? This isn't some rag doll you're talking about, Michael. This is a *child,* a little girl, and she's not going to survive losing you."

He puts a hand on her arm. "I don't intend on losing me, either," he says, trying his best to sound self-assured. "I'm just saying those things *in case.*"

She lies back down and says nothing more. He watches the orange light flickering across her face. It plays tricks with her features, making her nose look long one moment, short the next. For a while, it hides the tears that well up in her eyes. But only for a while.

He says nothing. He's never known what to say when a woman cries— not to his mother, when his father finally lost his long battle to cancer; not to his wife, when their occasional arguments would bring her to tears; not now to this woman who lies next to him.

"You can't do this, Michael," she says softly.

"I've got to."

"You can't." The urgency of a moment ago is gone from her voice, re-placed by a flatness. She says the words not so much as though she seeks to persuade him, but more to let him know that she's in a better position to understand how things really are—as if she knows something that he doesn't.

So he asks her. "Why not?"

"You just can't."

"Why?"

"Because Vinnie's a federal narcotics agent."

"No way," he says. Part of him is sure she's joking. The other part of him involuntarily pulls his hand back from her arm. "What makes you think so?"

"I don't *think* so," she says. "I *know* so."

"How can you know that?"

The tears well up again, only this time there's no stopping them. They overflow, producing long streams that run down her cheeks. It's awhile before she answers him, but finally she does.

"Because I'm one, too," is what she says.

Several minutes pass before Goodman's able to speak. He wonders if this is what it feels like to get hit with a sledgehammer.

"You're a DEA agent?" he asks dumbly.

"Yes," she says. "Or at least I was until this moment."

"I don't believe you," he says. "You're just saying this so you can talk me out of going through with the deal." But even as he says the words, he knows he's grasping.

Carmen doesn't say anything right away, and for just a moment, Goodman dares to take her silence as confirmation that he's right, that none of this is true, that he's seen through her little ploy.

When finally she begins to speak again, it's in an emotionally exhausted monotone. It's the same voice he heard moments ago, when she told him he couldn't go through with the deal. It tells him she's way past arguing.

"My name is Cruz," she tells him, "Carmen Cruz. I've been with DEA eleven months. I do undercover work. A couple of weeks ago, we got a tip that you had some pure heroin, possibly a lot of it. We checked you out, found out from the super that you were the kind of person who couldn't bear not to let a stray kitten in. We figured you'd have the same reaction with a stray *person.*"

"The beating, the rape—"

"That was all an act," she says, "a performance. Makeup, stage blood."

Goodman fights to understand, but he can't even begin to. "The stuff about Paulie—"

"Stuff," she says, "lies. There's no Paulie. I've never been a prostitute. Before I was a DEA agent, I was an investigator with the state police."

"*Cruz?* You told me you were *Italian,*" he says dumbly.

"I *lied,*" she says, and the tears start again. "I'm half Puerto Rican, half Cherokee. They concocted the Italian bit so I could mention that I had a brother with Mafia connections. Remember my full name—Carmen Ormento Pacelli? The initials spell out *cop.* My partners thought that'd be a cute touch—they knew you'd never notice."

"I never noticed," Goodman says. He still isn't sure she's telling him the truth. But it's slowly beginning to dawn on him that she *must* be. "And Vinnie?" he asks.

"Vinnie is Frank Farrelli. Nine years in DEA."

"And the other guy—T.M.?"

"T.M. is Jimmy Zelb," she says. "Six years in DEA. They call him 'No Neck.' And T.M. stands for 'The Man.' Another little joke of theirs."

" 'The Man' ? "

She laughs softly. "You don't even know, do you? 'The Man' means the law, the police. We've been playing games with you, Michael. And you're so, so—"

"—dumb—"

"—that you don't even get it when I explain it to you."

But, in spite of himself, he's beginning to. "Why are you suddenly telling me all of this?" he asks.

"It's not all that sudden, actually. I've been having trouble ever since the day you took me in. You were *supposed* to be *nice*—they warned me not to be fooled, said that you would be—but you weren't supposed to be *that* nice. You thought I was a whore. Yet you treated me like a lady. My God, you treated me like a *lover.* And your *daughter*—I wasn't ready for *that.* By the time of your meeting with T.M. at the bookstore, I had serious doubts that I could go through with it. That's why I had to work it so that *I* was the one to hand him the package, not *you.* Otherwise, they'd have you for a sale already."

"My God," Goodman says, letting it all sink in. "I feel so stupid."

"Stupid?" She's up on her elbow again; it's he who lies flat on his back now. "You're *wonderful,* Michael. You're caring and loving and trusting and gentle and all the things a person could ever want. We took advantage of that. I got you to bring me into your home and take care of me so that I could betray you. *We're* the ogres here, not you. Can't you see that?"

And, at last, he can. "Everything was lies," he says. It's not a question so much as an acknowledgment.

"Not everything," she says in a voice barely above a whisper. "Thinking you're wonderful wasn't a lie. Learning what it feels like to be cared about wasn't a lie. Falling in love with your daughter wasn't a lie. Falling in love with *you* hasn't been a lie." She lies back down. The light from the candle continues to play on the contours of her face.

For Michael Goodman, there is a cruel, terrible irony in this last remark. Short of Kelly's recovery, nothing in the world could have made Goodman happier than to hear this woman lying next to him profess her love for him. It's something that he hasn't even dared to *think* about, much less bring up in conversation. But now that he hears her utter the words, the circumstances in which they're spoken rob him of any pleasure he might otherwise have taken from them. He lies on his back, feeling totally exhausted—*deflated,* as though everything's been sucked out of him.

"What happens now?" he asks.

"I don't know."

"Do you arrest me?"

"I can't *do* that, Michael. That's why I'm telling you all this."

"What about you? What about your job?"

"I'll figure something out," she says. "I'll tell them you found me out somehow, or that you got cold feet. They won't like it, but without proof that I told you, there won't be anything they can do about it. They'll give me a reprimand, maybe transfer me to another city. At DEA, when they want to get rid of you, they don't fire you—that requires hearings, good cause, lots of messy stuff. Instead, they just transfer you. Then, as soon as you get settled in some new city and buy a home—boom!—they transfer you again. Pretty soon, you get the message and put in your papers. Maybe they'll do that to me; I don't know."

"Suppose I decide to go through with the deal anyway?"

She laughs. "You can't do that."

"Why not?"

"Because it's a trap."

"Like *entrapment?*"

"Oh," she laughs again, but bitterly. "We went *way* past entrapment. I took advantage of your goodness to come into your *home,* into your *life.* I've shared your daughter's *bed.* I was the one who told you about some brother I don't even have, just to give you the idea of selling the drugs in the first place. You never would have done it otherwise."

"I'm not so sure about *that,*" he confesses.

She says nothing.

"So there's no three and half million dollars?" he asks.

"Oh, there is," she says. "They'll put it together, just in case you insist on seeing that it's all there. But they won't let you walk *away* with it. Not *that* kind of money."

"What happens after they show it to me?"

"They'll ask to see the drugs."

"And?"

"And as soon as they're satisfied you've got the drugs, they give a signal of some sort. Usually, it's opening the trunk of their car. You know, in order to put the drugs inside it. As soon as that happens, twenty guys with shotguns and DEA jackets swoop down on you like you're the Sundance Kid. Next time you see daylight over your head, you'll be eighty years old. Why are you asking me all of this?" she says. "Don't you *get* it, Michael? It's *over.*"

He knows she's probably right, but he says nothing.

"Do you have any idea how *many* of them there are?" she asks him, making it clear that if *he* doesn't know, *she* does.

"I've seen some of them already," he says. "They've been following me."

"Who?"

"A black guy and a white guy, in a blue Ford."

"There's no black guy on our team," she says. "And DEA has no reason to follow you. We'll know exactly when and where the deal's going down, because Vinnie *is* the DEA. And so am *I*. Part of my job is to slip out and call them every once in awhile, fill them in on your innermost thoughts."

"Have you been doing that?"

"I did at first," she says. "I'm dangerously overdue."

"Maybe you should call in."

She looks at him. "Why are you saying that?" she asks.

"No matter what, it makes sense."

She seems to ponder that for a moment, then nods in agreement. "And what do I tell them?"

It's his turn to ponder. "Tell them everything's right on course."

"Is that navy talk?" she smiles.

"I guess. I used to be—"

"I know," she says. "U.S. Navy, enlisted in 1976—Six September. Stationed Norwalk, Connecticut; Norfolk, Virginia; Vieques, Puerto Rico. Six months on the USS *Charleston*—"

"The first four in sick bay—"

"—before being discharged Fifteen August 1979— And we knew about the sick bay, too. Just one more reason the investigation got code-named 'Pushover.' "

"Pushover," he repeats. "That's me, huh?"

"Yes," she says. "But you're *my* pushover." They both try to laugh at that; the combined result can best be described as a snort. "I even have DEA's permission to—how did they put it?—'to have consensual relations' with you if it becomes necessary 'to protect the integrity of the investigation.' Which is the only reason I *haven't.*"

"Haven't what?"

"Made love with you, silly."

In spite of everything, Goodman instantly feels his twin libido sensors react—pulse and penis. "I understand the DEA's thinking of withdrawing their permission at any moment," he says.

She laughs—a real laugh, an honest-to-goodness Carmen laugh. He has to shush her, for fear she'll wake Kelly.

"I don't get it, Michael. After what I've told you, you're supposed to *hate* me. You're supposed to want to *kill* me."

But Michael Goodman's learning center has traveled far south by this time and is presently operating out of Testosterone Command. Now it adopts his voice and utters its first pronouncement.

"Hate can wait."

"How can you forgive me for this?" she asks, but at the same time, she comes to him. The sensation of flannel against his bare upper body is electric. Pulse and penis seize full command of the operation.

"If what you say is true," Goodman reasons, "this could be my last night of freedom until the year 2036. I figure we better make the most of it."

"I like the way you figure," Carmen says, and with that, she is over him, pulling his pajama bottoms off him in what might have been a single motion, had it not been for one of his commanding officers standing at attention and getting slightly in the way.

Goodman reaches for the top button of her shirt. But as he does so, the jack-o'-lantern gives off a final burst of orange light, then dies, leaving them in blackness.

She rolls to one side of him, and he hears her voice against his ear. "Put another log on the fire, would you?"

He rises to his hands and knees and gropes towards the kitchen end of the room, drawn by the smell of burned wax, smoke, and pumpkin. Eventually, his eyes adjust to the point where he can see outlines and shapes. He locates the matches, the Chanukah candles, succeeds in lighting one and putting it in place.

The distraction might well have managed to soften the resolve of another man's will. But Michael Goodman has not made love to a woman for months, and it's going to take more than a brief time-out to soften any part of him. Carmen notices this phenomenon now, not because she's watching Goodman at this moment—she isn't—but because a critical portion of his anatomy is suddenly backlit by the new flame in the jack-o'-lantern, causing a *huge* shadow to be cast against the far wall, where her gaze happens to be directed.

"My God," she mutters.

"Is something the matter?" he asks as soon as he gets back to her.

"No," she says. "Nothing's the matter—just be gentle."

He tries. He tries as he reaches again for the top button of her shirt. Tries as he fights to stop the trembling in his fingers, exaggerated by the flickering of the candlelight. Tries as he works his way down the row of buttons, until at last he frees an impossibly perfect pair of breasts, tipped with rigid dark nipples. He tries as he slips the shirt off her back, spreading it out beneath them on their makeshift floor bed. But when she presses her body against him and kisses his open mouth with hers, he completely forgets what it was he was supposed to be trying. And when she takes him with both hands, he hears himself make a sound somewhere between a groan and a roar, less befitting a human than some jungle beast that's gone a year without a kill.

"Maybe we should open a window or something," Carmen suggests, "before you explode." But instead of letting go of him, she holds him tighter, squeezes him—

—and explode he does. Too suddenly, too violently. And far too quickly.

It takes him awhile before he can catch his breath and speak. "Sometimes I can actually make it last a little longer than that," he tells her, and she breaks into laughter again, forcing him to smother her into silence.

And then, somehow, his body frees him to make love with her—silently, gently, lastingly. It goes on for what seems like hours, days, weeks. More precisely, it goes on a full two Chanukah candles. They light a third one, neither wanting it to end.

"Once you burn one candle, you've got to buy a whole 'nother box anyway," he explains. "They do it like that on purpose."

"What's that?" Carmen asks.

"Chanukah candles. They put—"

"No, *that*," she says, pointing to the underside of the card table, underneath which their heads have ended up.

He looks. "Oh, *that*. A piece of gum."

"No it isn't," she says. And, putting a finger to her lips to silence him, she raises her body to examine it.

Her change of position presents her bare bottom to him. Impossibly, he feels his commanding officer begin to come to attention once again. Merely following orders, he reaches out and touches her, but she pushes his hand away, as though to tell him that this is serious. He lifts himself up to see what he still thinks is gum but what her superior vision has apparently revealed is something else altogether. And as he looks closer, he realizes she's right. The shape of the thing is simply too geometrical. It's a perfect rectangle, perhaps the size of sugar cube. It appears to be some sort of miniature electronic device, complete with a tiny wire antenna.

And then it hits him: It's a bug.

He looks at Carmen. Her expression tells him that she figured it out before he did. She stands up now and heads for the bathroom, motioning him to follow her.

Goodman closes the bathroom door behind them. "What do you—" he starts to say, but she hushes him. She bends over to turn on the water in the tub. He locks his hands behind his back to fight temptation.

"Come on in," she beckons him, lowering herself into the tub. He follows her dumbly, until they sit in the water, facing each other. "No bug in the world can pick us up over this noise," she explains.

"Who put it there?" he asks her. "Your DEA friends?"

"I don't think so," she says. "It doesn't look like one of ours. I think it's more likely some other agency, like the NYPD. Probably the same guys who've been following you."

"What does *that* mean?"

"Well," she says, "for one thing, it means they know about tomorrow night's deal. For another, they've heard me tell you who I am, and who Vincent and T.M. are."

"What'll happen to you?"

"Meet your codefendant," she says. "Maybe they'll be kind enough to arrange adjoining cells for us."

"What do you mean?"

"Obstructing justice, interfering with governmental administration, hindering prosecution, conspiring to distribute a Schedule One controlled substance. The beat goes on."

"You're sure they've heard everything?" He finds it hard to believe.

"Oh, they've heard everything," she says. *"Everything."*

In fact, they've heard nothing.

Spike Schwartz has been dreaming. He's been dreaming about his bachelor days, before there were twins and midnight feedings, 2:00 A.M. feedings, 2:30 A.M. feedings, 3:15 A.M. feedings, 4:00 A.M. feedings, and bottles to warm, and diapers to change.

He's awakened suddenly by a noise that sounds like a water main has burst somewhere nearby. He grabs for the volume button on the wiretap recorder and turns it down. Nothing happens. He does the same with the room bugs. Number one, nothing. Number two, nothing. Number three, the noise disappears. He turns it back up, and the noise returns.

"Fucking static," Spike says out loud. Well, he figures, two outa three ain't bad. He kills the power on bug number three. Then he remembers he's supposed to make entries in the logbook. He finds the book, studies his last entry.

> 2100   Subject tells a story about someone beautiful who dresses up like a witch.

He checks his watch, is surprised to see it's almost four in the morning. He decides he must've dozed off for a few minutes. He picks up a pen, enters a notation recording the next important development.

> 0355   Bug #3 malfunctions, delivering only static, and is shut off. Subject asleep.

"What do we do now?" Goodman asks.

"I don't know," she admits. "The problem is, we've already committed enough crimes to put us each away for twenty years."

"How can that be?"

"Take conspiracy," she says. "All that's required is an agreement to break some law, and that one of us does some overt act in furtherance of it."

"What's an overt act?"

"*Any*thing," she says. "It doesn't even have to be an *illegal* act by itself. My handing the sample to T.M. Your returning one of Vincent's calls. Our having the conversation we just had. I wouldn't be surprised if *Washington*'s heard about that by now."

"So we're kind of in this thing together, huh?"

"Looks that way. Any ideas?"

"Yeah," he says. "Pass the soap."

[31]

In his dream, Goodman is flying above the earth, peering down through the clouds at the city's skyline. He's not alone—it's as though he's the leader of a V-shaped flock of geese. Fanning out behind him are Carmen and Kelly and Pop-Tart and Larus. He wants to see if they all have wings, but for some reason, he's unable to turn his head to the side to look back at them.

All of a sudden, there are noises, the zinging of bullets whizzing by them. He knows they'll all be shot, all be killed.

"Daddy! Daddy!"

He recognizes the voice of his daughter, but still he can't see her; still he can't move his head.

"Daddy! Daddy! It's for *you!*"

His heart almost bursts at the thought of whatever it is she's doing for him.

"The telephone, Daddy! It's for you."

He opens his eyes and finds he's on the floor of his apartment, his head wedged against the wall. Above him is Kelly, extending a telephone receiver in his direction. He takes it from her, puts it to his ear.

"Hey, Mikey boy. Sleeping late this morning?"

It's Vinnie, of course.

"Take a look outside your door, Mikey," Vinnie says. And then the phone goes dead. After a moment, there's a dial tone.

"What time is it?" Goodman asks.

"Eight-thirty," Kelly tells him.

He rubs his eyes and looks around. For a moment, he wonders if *all* of last night was a dream. Then he notices his pajama bottoms are on backward. At least they got back onto him somehow. He spots Carmen on the bed, totally dead to the world. He goes to get up, but finds he has to do it in stages—his balance is slightly off, and his knees are decidedly wobbly.

"Are you *sick*, Daddy?"

"No," he assures her, "just tired."

"Maybe you should sleep on the bed tonight," she suggests. "I can take a turn on the floor."

"We can talk about it later," he says. He stands there, trying to remember what it was he was about to do. Then he recalls the phone conversation. What was it Vinnie wanted him to do? Look outside the door—that was it.

He walks to the door, unlocks it, and cracks it open, half-expecting to find Vinnie standing there. But there's no one in sight. He's about to close the door when his eyes are drawn downward. There's something there, right on top of his doormat. He pulls the door open farther, sees it's a suitcase, a large one—the awkward, heavy type people used to lug on trips before soft lightweight luggage became popular. It's particularly ugly, too—a yellow-and-green floral print. There's a big tag on it that reads IN-NOVATION LUGGAGE.

He grasps the handle and braces himself for its weight—he has no interest in throwing his back out again. But when he lifts it, he finds it's only moderately heavy, a sure sign that it's empty. He carries it into the apartment and closes the door.

Kelly has exhibited the good sense to make her own breakfast, and the even better sense to make something that doesn't required the application of heat. She resumes her seat at the card table, over a bowl of cereal of some sort. He remembers the bug, wonders if right now there are ten guys at CIA headquarters listening to his daughter chewing.

"Are we going somewhere?" she asks between mouthfuls.

He looks at her. She looks at the suitcase. He looks at the suitcase.

"Oh, that."

"We can talk about it later," she says.

Carmen's still asleep. Goodman notices that somehow she managed to get back into her flannel shirt before passing out. He wonders which one of them had the presence of mind to put some clothes on their bodies. A thought suddenly occurs to him, and he looks over at Kelly, but she seems to be thoroughly occupied with her cereal.

He heads for the bathroom.

"Someone called at oh-eight-thirty," Spike Schwartz briefs Abbruzzo and Riley, who arrive at the plant at nine. "Told the Mole to look outside the door."

"And?"

"And nothing," Schwartz shrugs. "Whatever was there, it didn't make noise."

"Mighta been a note," is Abbruzzo's guess.

"Sonofa*bitch!*" Riley mutters. "Fuckers are communicating in *writing* now—to beat the tap and the bugs. Maybe we need to get a *video camera* in there, Ray."

Abbruzzo ignores him. It's too late for that. Though he must admit he likes the idea—can you imagine catching a couple *doing it* on video?"

"Did they do it last night?" Abbruzzo asks Schwartz.

"Do what, sir?"

"It."

"It?"

"Did they become acquainted in the biblical sense?"

Morning is apparently not Schwartz's best time of the day. He stares blankly at Abbruzzo, waiting for the next clue.

"*Did they fuck?*"

"*Them?*" Schwartz catches right on. "No way. They were down for the count by twenty-two hundred."

"It's the big day," Riley says. "They wanted to be well rested."

Looking in the bathroom mirror as he wipes the last traces of shaving cream from his face, Michael Goodman feels anything but well rested. What he does feels is a growing sense of dread, which he recognizes as the prelude to eventual panic. He feels outnumbered, outwitted, and absurdly out of his league. He feels a little bit like he's just woken up on the morning he's scheduled to be executed.

But then again, he feels totally, helplessly in love.

There's a knock on the bathroom door. Goodman pushes it open, and

Carmen slips in, flannel shirt and all. Her smile reassures him that not all of last night was a dream.

"Good morning," she says, running the back of one hand down the side of his face. He's never been so glad he's shaved in his life.

"Morning," he smiles, heading out the bathroom door.

"Your pajamas are on backward," she tells him.

Jimmy Zelb wakes up around 9:15. Remembers he's been looking forward to this day for some time. Today, after all, is the day they're going to take Michael Goodman down.

Zelb has directed Operation Pushover since the beginning, since Big Red told him about the guy living on East Ninety-second Street who was dealing pure heroin. It was Zelb who convinced Lenny Siegel, his group leader, to let him put Carmen Cruz in with Goodman. It was Zelb who concocted the rape scenario, knowing that Goodman would be sucker enough to take her in. And it was Zelb who created Vinnie and T.M. In fact, the cute initials—T.M. and C.O.P.—were Zelb's idea, too.

And it's all worked like a charm.

Goodman went for the bait like a bear goes for honey. Bought the whole line about Cruz's fight with her pimp boyfriend, her threat to go back to the street, her connected brother. And before you knew it, Zelb—playing the role of T.M.—had a sample. True, it was actually Cruz who handed him the sample. (But when it came time to do the paperwork, they'd taken care of that little detail by writing Cruz out of the transfer altogether. No big deal.)

And what a sample it turned out to be!

Zelb had taken it to the police chemist himself, bypassing the lab messenger they usually called for. He'd watched as Dr. Krishna or something like that—the "Dr." no doubt being some sort of an honorary degree, seeing as no Ph.D. chemist would ever stoop to work for what the city pays—had opened up the baggie and examined the contents.

"Notice the gray cast to it," he'd told Zelb. "And the graininess. I hear South Florida is starting to see this kind of stuff."

"Where's it come from originally?" Zelb had asked.

"Colombia, most likely. Though we're seeing more and more high-quality heroin coming out of Peru lately, too."

For the next fifteen minutes, Zelb had watched as Krishna had weighed the powder, taken small samples from various parts of it, and added drops of different solutions to the samples, comparing the colors that resulted against standard color samples on index cards. Then he'd turned to Zelb.

"We won't know the exact numbers until we run it through a neutron activation analysis," he'd said. "But I'll stake my reputation on this stuff's being better than ninety-eight percent pure."

It turned out that his reputation was safe. The analysis showed the sample to be heroin hydrochloride, 99.8 percent pure. Though Zelb doesn't know it, heroin in its soluble form is anhydrous—it craves water, tending to combine even with the moisture in the atmosphere, meaning it will almost never test out at 100 percent purity under normal conditions.

Then there'd been the negotiations between Goodman and Vinnie, who was of course none other than Zelb's partner, Frank Farrelli. Goodman had driven an unexpectedly hard bargain, insisting on $3.5 million for the nineteen kilos he has left. But the truth is, Farrelli had been prepared to offer as much as five million if he'd had to. Money is no object when you're not going to spend it. But Farrelli had nevertheless been compelled to *seem* reluctant to meet Goodman's price: As any drug dealer knows, if a buyer agrees to pay too much, he's either intending to rip you off or he's the Man. But then again, Goodman wasn't just any drug dealer. An exhaustive search of the files of DEA, FBI, and even Interpol revealed no mention of him, except for a three-year stint in the navy in the seventies. To this day, nobody's been able to explain how he suddenly appeared on the drug scene. There's been some speculation that he may even have stolen someone else's stash. That notion's recently been fueled by an unconfirmed report from an informer that in the past day or two a handful of Latino heavyweights have flown up from the Miami area to reclaim something they consider to be rightfully theirs.

But that's all idle speculation and rumour, what the Justice Department classifies as "soft" information. Jimmy Zelb likes to deal in *facts*. And the *fact* is that today's the day Michael Goodman's going to bring them nineteen kilos of the purest heroin law enforcement has seen in three decades. And he's going to put it right in their hands.

"Going somewhere?" Carmen asks, eyeing the suitcase as she comes out of the bathroom, drying her hair with a towel.

"We can talk about it later," Kelly says, cutting between them to take her turn in the bathroom.

"It seems your 'brother' had it dropped off on our doorstep," Goodman explains.

Carmen examines the tag on the suitcase. "It's brand-new," she says. "They've no doubt bought another one just like it. That means they want to do another switch."

"Boy, they think of everything."

"Oh, they're three moves ahead of you, Michael. First, this forces you to get the drugs out of hiding so you can transfer them to the suitcase. Next, it's nice and visible, so you'll be easy for them to spot when you show up. Finally, it's big and unwieldy, so you can't disappear with the money that'll be in the other suitcase."

"They really *do* think of everything."

She takes his face in both hands and makes him look her in the eyes. "Promise me you'll tell Vinnie you can't go through with it, Michael."

"Promise me my daughter's not going to keep needing tests," he says.

She releases his face but not his eyes. "Your daughter needs *you*," she says.

By midmorning, the plant is packed with cops. Abbruzzo and Weems, by virtue of their seniority, will run the operation from there. Lieutenant Spangler is the supervisor, and he'll act as field commander from his car. Riley and Sheridan will cover the buy location, aided by a dozen plain-clothes police officers. DeSimone and Kwon will be nearby if technical assistance is required. They've even thought to have a female officer assigned, in case they arrest Goodman's girlfriend. And someone from the Bureau of Child Welfare is on standby, since it's possible they may end up with a *kid* on their hands. All told, there are twenty-one people assigned to the operation at this point, not counting Maggie Kennedy, who'll be at her desk in the DA's office should legal advice be needed.

In addition to cellular telephones, each unit has a handheld radio to keep in touch with all other units. Finally, the deputy commissioner in charge of Public Affairs has been briefed; he, in turn, has notified certain trusted contacts in the media. If all goes according to schedule, the seizure should make both the eleven o'clock news and the morning papers.

At 1145 hours, a call comes in from the Special Equipment Unit telling them the MOUSE is ready for their use. Abbruzzo tells Sheridan and Riley to go pick it up. "And don't be playing with any of the gadgets, for Chrissakes."

"You want us to bring it back here?"

"Fuck no," Abbruzzo says, looking around for his Maalox tablets. "I don't want the Mole to see it anywhere around here. I want you to call me when you got it, then just hang loose until we find out where this thing is going to go down." He finds the Maalox, pops one.

"Then we head for the set?"

"You don't do *any*thing," Abbruzzo says, "until I tell you to." He downs another Maalox.

Gustavo Fuentes wakes up Friday morning in a suite he's rented for the weekend at the Waldorf-Astoria Hotel. It's a large suite, which the Waldorf categorizes as one of its "premiere" accommodations. It consists of a large sitting room, a bedroom, a dressing room, a full bathroom, and a half bathroom off the sitting room, for guests. It has a service area complete with refrigerator, cooking facilities, dining table, and a full wet bar. It rents for $1,850 per night. Yet it somehow fails to please Mister Fuentes.

"It's so, so *old,*" he said when he first saw it.

Mister Fuentes wakes up this Friday morning with the same headache he's been waking up with for several weeks now. It has proved to be a very stubborn headache, the kind that doesn't seem to go away with even extra-strength Tylenol.

Over time, Mister Fuentes has learned that his headache has a name. Its name is Michael Goodman. Mister Fuentes has had enough of his headache. He's come all the way to the East Side of Manhattan, in New York City, to get rid of it. And as he wakes up this Friday morning, his very first thought is that today is the day he's going to do precisely that.

Carmen and Kelly are curled up on the sofa, watching something on Channel 13 about why people sneeze. Goodman sits at the card table, staring off into space. When the phone rings, it startles him. He looks at his watch. 12:18. Even as he reaches for the phone, he knows who's calling him.

* * *

At the sound of an incoming phone call, the plant springs to life. Abbruzzo turns down the volume on the three bugs—whatever the static problem was with bug number three has been fixed—so they can listen to the conversation directly from the wiretap.

GOODMAN: Hello?

VINNIE: Hey, Mikey boy. How ya doin'?

GOODMAN: Okay.

VINNIE: Today's the big day.

GOODMAN: Yup.

VINNIE: Everything cool?

GOODMAN: I don't know. I've been thinking. I'm not sure this is something I really want to do. I mean—

VINNIE: What the fuck are you saying?

Abbruzzo has to turn the volume down, Vinnie's voice is so loud.

GOODMAN: It's just that I've never done anything like this. It's *wrong,* for one thing—

VINNIE: *Don't you get cold feet on me now, man!* I know where you live. I know you got a little kid. You can't back out now—not after my people've put everything together. We're goin' through with this thing—that's all there is to it. *You hear?*

There's a pause.

GOODMAN: I hear.

VINNIE: Good. I picked out a place. It's downtown, like you said.

GOODMAN: Yeah?

VINNIE: Yeah. Tenth Avenue, cornera Nineteenth Street. It's real quiet over there at night. Nobody'll bother us.

GOODMAN: No, that's no good. I told you, I have to take my daughter to a party. We'll have to make it near where she's going to be.

VINNIE: Where's that at?

GOODMAN: Sixth Avenue and Tenth Street.

VINNIE: No good. I'll never find a parking place over there.

GOODMAN: You'll have to double-park, I guess.

VINNIE: Shit. Hold on a minute, will ya?

There's a pause, and Vinnie can be heard in muffled conversation with somebody in the background at his end. Abbruzzo turns the wiretap volume switch all the way up, but they can't make out the words. Then Vinnie's back on the phone.

VINNIE: You there?

GOODMAN: I'm here.

VINNIE: Okay. If it's gotta be, it's gotta be.

GOODMAN: It's gotta be.

VINNIE: Which corner?

GOODMAN: Make it the southwest.

VINNIE: Okay. Hey, you get the present we dropped off?

GOODMAN: Yup.

VINNIE: Use it.

GOODMAN: I will.

VINNIE: Okay. Southwest corner a Sixth Avenue and Tenth Street, eight o'clock sharp. And Mikey?

GOODMAN: Yeah?

VINNIE: Stop worrying so much. It's natural to worry about these things, but it's gonna be okay. Trust me.

A cheer goes up in the plant as soon as they hear Goodman and Vinnie hang up.

"Quiet down!" Abbruzzo yells, but even he can't help smiling. "Okay," he says. "We've got a location."

Goodman's first thought after hanging up the phone is to wonder why Vinnie has suddenly been willing to take the chance of talking on Goodman's home phone. Then he remembers: *Vinnie's* not taking any chances—Vinnie's a federal agent. All that stuff about needing to have one pay phone call another pay phone was just part of the act, part of the charade to help convince him that Vinnie was a typical drug dealer—cautious to the point of being paranoid. Evidently, they're now satisfied that Goodman has bought the performance and they no longer feel the need to keep playing the pay-phone game.

His second thought is that, for a federal agent, Vinnie sure got upset when he learned that Goodman was having second thoughts about going through with the deal. Shouldn't he have been *happy* to hear that a would-be heroin dealer was considering the wrongness of what he was about to do? And didn't he step way over the line when he told Goodman it was too late to back out, that he'd *do something to Kelly* if that happened?

He wants to ask Carmen these questions. But when he looks over at her on the sofa with Kelly, he knows this isn't the time to do it.

He looks at his watch. It's 12:25. Less than eight hours left.

Big Red wakes up a little after one o'clock. He remembers right away there's something he wants to do today, but he can't recall just what it is. He reaches for his cigarettes and lights one, inhaling deeply, holding the smoke in his lungs as long as he can.

There's a stirring in the bed, and Big Red recalls he's not alone. A body alongside him groans, lifts her brown head an inch or two, opens one eye, and groans again. Then she turns away, covering her head with a pillow.

Big Red tries his best to remember. First, he tries to figure out who it is that's in his bed. He recalls a party at an after-hours spot, a fair number of vodka and cranberry juices, and a sweet young thing sitting next to him in the Bentley awhile later. He has a vague memory of arriving home, putting on a couple of CDs, downing another vodka and cranberry juice or two, and doing some slow dancing. After that, nothing. He wonders how good this little girl was. He wonders what her *name* is, for that matter. Something with a *G*, he thinks. Georgia? Gina? Georgina?

And right about then, he remembers Goodman. Goodman, the little Caucasian guy they relieved of his pants. *That's* what he wants to do today—go visit the guy and see if he's got any of that pure shit of his left. 'Cause that fuckin' lazy sonofabitch No Neck Zelb never followed up on it, that's for *damn* sure.

Big Red reaches for the phone and punches in the number of Hammer's beeper. Then he lifts the covers off the lower half of the body alongside him, revealing as fine an ass as he's seen in a *long* time. He'd like to remember more about last night but cannot. He rolls to his side, places a hand on the ass. It's a beautiful milk-chocolate color, warm to the touch and wonderfully firm. He begins tracing a finger slowly down the line where the cheeks meet, from top to bottom. He's about halfway when the phone rings.

He gives the ass a good slap. The head bobs up again, this time both eyes open, staring at him with some mixture of indignation, confusion, and expectation.

"Get packin', sugar," he says. "Big Red's got some business to take care of today."

"Daddy, is it time for me to get into my costume?" Kelly wants to know.

"It's only two o'clock," he tells her. "The party isn't until six."

"We'll all start getting ready around three-thirty," Carmen says. "That'll give us more than enough time."

"We can't all go," Kelly says.

"Why not?"

" 'Cause if Daddy drops me off, all the kids at the party will recognize him and know who I am."

"You've got a point there," Carmen admits. "Michael, I've got good news and bad news for you. The good news is, you don't have to drop Kelly off at her party. The bad news is, you have to make dinner while I'm gone."

"Deal," he says, though he's barely heard what she's been telling him. He walks over to the suitcase with the yellow-and-green floral print. "Will you two excuse me for a few minutes?" he asks, lifting the suitcase. He unlocks the front door, opens it, and steps out of the apartment. Closing the door behind him, he heads down the stairs.

"Fuckin' guy," Abbruzzo marvels. "Excuses himself when he goes to the fuckin' *bathroom.*"

"Whitey gonna have hisself a little *adjustment* problem when he gets to Rikers Island," Weems observes.

"Oh, they'll *adjust* him pretty good out there," Abbruzzo says. "Specially the brothas."

"Sheeet." Weems laughs. "Give him two days of good black lovin', he'll be beggin' for more. Kinda like the white dude who gets tossed into a cell with this big brother been locked up for ten years, been doin' nothin' but weight training? The brother introduces himself. 'You gots two choices,' he tells Whitey. 'You can be the husband, or you can be the wife.' Whitey thinks a minute, finally says, 'I'll be the husband.' 'Okay,' says the brother, 'come on over here now and suck your wife's dick!' "

The room dissolves into laughter.

In the basement, Goodman sets the suitcase down and sits on it in front of his storage locker, facing the black duffel bag. Inside the bag, he knows, is either eternal wealth or eternal prison. He thinks of a "Peanuts" comic strip he once saw: Snoopy's composing a love letter. "And I shall be yours forever," he writes. "*Forever* being a relative term, that is."

Eternal wealth or *eternal prison* being relative terms, Goodman thinks now. But not too far from being completely accurate.

Goodman realizes that there *is* one component of his dilemma that's been eliminated. Before, he had to contend with the fact that, by selling the heroin, he was going to be responsible for its getting out onto the street and into the hands of addicts—kids, some of them. Now, he knows that's not going to happen. Since Vinnie turns out to be a DEA agent, once Goodman sells him the drugs, they're kept *off* the street. Then again, so is Goodman.

He only wishes he could think of some way to have it both ways. But he knows that's asking the impossible. He reaches for the lock and starts dialing the combination.

By 2:20, he's back upstairs. With the suitcase.

Sheridan calls in to the plant a little after 2:30.

"This is MOUSE," he says over the radio. "Standing by for instructions."

"Where are you, MOUSE?" Abbruzzo asks.

"I'm at the garage, on Delancey Street. I been checking out the equipment on board. This thing is *great!*"

"You break anything and I'll have you back in uniform by morning," Abbruzzo warns him.

"What?"

"*Don't break anything!*"

"Say again? Hello? Testing, testing—"

Just what I need, Abbruzzo thinks, a fuckin' *comedian*. He looks around for his Maalox.

By three o'clock, Kelly's insistent that it's time for her to put on her costume. "And you've got to put one on, too," she tells Carmen. "Otherwise, they might see you someday with my Daddy and figure out who I am."

Carmen has a little trouble with the likelihood of that particular scenario, but she's a good sport about it. While Kelly starts changing, Carmen makes a quick run to a stationery store on Eighty-ninth Street, where they're selling inexpensive masks. She narrows it down to two but can't decide which she likes better. Seeing they're each $3.95, she ends up buying them both—that way, Kelly can decide for her.

Heading back to the apartment, Carmen remembers Goodman's suggestion that she call in. She stops at a pay phone, punches in the number for her office.

"Group Two." It's the secretary's voice.

"Hi, Emilia, it's Cruz. Is No Neck around?"

"No, but they're on the air. Want me to raise them?"

"How about the boss?"

"Lenny? He's here."

"Let me speak to him."

"Hold on."

After a moment, she hears Lenny Siegel's voice. "Cruz?"

"Hi, boss."

"Where are you?"

"At a pay phone, Ninetieth and Lexington."

"What's going on?" he asks her. "You don't write. You don't call."

"Everything's fine," she tells him. "I just don't get out much, that's all."

"He doesn't suspect anything?"

"This guy doesn't suspect he's *alive*," she assures Siegel. "He's truly dumber than a stick."

"He's got the goods?"

"Sure seems that way."

"Is he armed?" Siegel asks.

"You kidding or what? This guy's a pussycat."

"You been stroking his fur, huh?"

"What's *that* supposed to mean?"

"You know—did you 'consensual-relation' him, like we said you could?"

Carmen controls herself, knowing this is no time to lose her cool. "You'll have to read my report," she says.

"Don't be putting stuff like that in your report," he tells her. "We've cut a few corners in this one already, you know."

Tell me about it, she wants to say. Instead, she settles for, "Gotta run."

Sheridan radios the plant back a little while later.

"Had you worried, huh, Ray?"

"Had me *pissed,*" Abbruzzo snaps, forgetting for a moment he's on the air.

"Sorry about that, chief."

"The deal's going to go down at the corner of Sixth Avenue and Tenth Street," Abbruzzo says. "It's not supposed to happen till eight, but I want you set up there ahead a time. So stay by your radio, okay?"

"Ten-four."

Two of the plainclothes cops come back into the plant.

"Whad she do?" Abbruzzo asks them.

"She went into a card store," one of the officers says. "Bought somethin' smallish. Stopped at a phone on the way back, made a call."

"You get any overheards?"

"I walked by her one time," the other officer says. "I think she was saying, 'I got the runs.' Then she hung up."

"That's it? You do a *walk-by,* and all you hear her say is she's got the *runs?*"

"Sorry. She looked like she was sorta checking for a tail," the officer says. "I didn't wanna spook her."

"Watch your language there, boy," says Harry Weems.

By the time Carmen gets back to the apartment, Kelly's all witched up in her black hat, cape, and boots. Carmen finds the leftover black satin and cuts herself a piece long enough for a cape. She stands in front of the bathroom mirror, trying to drape it different ways. She couldn't believe it when she first discovered that Goodman had no full-length mirror anywhere in his apartment. A *guy* thing, evidently; certainly no *woman* could ever live like that.

"Come in here, Kelly," she calls.

Kelly pops her head in, witch hat and all.

In her best crone voice, Carmen says, "Take off that hat, me pretty, and come here. It's time for a little makeup!"

The rest of Kelly follows her head into the bathroom. The giggling begins almost immediately.

Back in the living area, Michael Goodman has begun to pace. Every so often, he stops to take a look at his watch. Last time he looked, it was 3:53.

"Stop that giggling in there!" he shouts now.

"Sorry," Carmen calls. "We'll be leaving you in peace in ten minutes."

"I need to talk to you first," he says, walking toward the bathroom. The door swings open, but it's Kelly who slithers out, looking positively scary in black-and-green makeup.

"My God!" he shrieks, not entirely in pretense.

Her answering giggles sound very familiar.

"Could you help me in here a moment, Michael?" Carmen calls from the bathroom. As soon as he joins her, she takes his hand, pulls him over to the bathtub, and turns the water on full force. "Talk," she says.

"That's the same static as last night," Spike Schwartz says.

"That's not static," Abbruzzo says. "That's *water*. Guy's taking a fuckin' *shower.*"

"Gonna pretty his ass up for jail," Weems says.

"One time I locked this broad up in her apartment," Abbruzzo remembers. "I had her for a rob one, and on topa that, she owed parole five years and change. So she was *going*. And all she cared about was, could she shave her legs? I said no. So she hiked up her skirt, made me feel the stubble, even started *crying*. So I said okay, okay, she could shave her legs. Now, I wasn't going to be a *pervert* and stand there while she did it, so I waited right outside the bathroom door. Next thing I knew, I heard this *crash*. I rushed in; she'd fallen down, slit her fuckin' *wrists.*"

"Jesus. She die on you?"

"Nah, it was one a them little disposable razors. She was lucky to break the skin. But I tell you—ever since then, a prisoner of mine needs to do something, *no way*. You gotta take a piss? That's good, 'cause we're going to the station house *right now*, find you a nice little rest room, you can piss all night. Fuck 'em, I say."

Weems says something that sounds to Abbruzzo like "Amen." Then again, it might have been "Fuck 'em."

"Daddy, they just said on TV that it's forty-eight degrees out. Isn't that warm enough for me to take Pop-Tart?"

Goodman takes time out from his pacing long enough to look at his daughter. He knows she's just asked him a question, but he has no idea what it is. He remembers Carmen once telling him he needs to lighten up, become less protective of Kelly.

"Sure," he says.

She runs off, singing, "Yaaaaaay!" as only a six-year-old can. Pop-Tart, apparently sensing that something's up, heads for the corner of the room and hides behind Larus.

Goodman resumes his pacing.

"Daddy, can I take Larus, too? Pop-Tart wants me to."

"Isn't it time for you guys to leave?" he asks.

"*Can* I?"

"What?"

"*Take* him."

"No, honey," Carmen interjects. "We'll have our hands full as it is."

Next thing he knows, they're standing in front of him, waiting for good-bye kisses. He hugs them each in turn, longer and harder than usual, he realizes. "Here," he says to Carmen, reaching into his pocket and pulling out one of Manny's twenties. "You better take a cab."

She thanks him, and they're out the door, stuff and all. As he watches them head for the stairs, Goodman suddenly notices they've got Pop-Tart with them. He can't believe it. He opens his mouth to object, but the door closes and they're gone.

The apartment suddenly seems eerily quiet. Goodman looks at his watch. 4:20.

"There go the kid and the girlfriend," Weems says, watching them through binoculars. "Think we oughta put somebody on them?"

"Nah," says Ray Abbruzzo, "let 'em go. We wanna concentrate our manpower on the Mole."

* * *

At 1702, Sheridan pulls the MOUSE over to the curb at Tenth Street, just west of Sixth Avenue and right past a row of orange cones that someone's put down. Sheridan's found the perfect parking spot: the first car from the corner, with the back of the van closer to the intersection. That way, the observation ports—which from outside the vehicle appear to be nothing more than side and rear reflectors—have an unobstructed view of the corner.

Sheridan's about to slide open the partition separating the cab from the rear of the van—so that he can join Riley and the other two men already back there—when there's a knock on the driver's side window.

"No standin' here, pal," a uniformed officer tells him.

"I'm on the job," Sheridan tells him before reaching for the pocket his shield is in. He remembers the first time he did that, some years back. He'd reached for his pocket without first saying the magic words. The cop—turned out to be a rookie, a probationary officer just two weeks out of the Academy—had pulled his weapon and dropped into a combat position, ready to blow Sheridan's head off.

"How long you gonna be?" the officer asks him.

"Not long," Sheridan tells him. Fuck him, he thinks. You want to write me a ticket? Write me a ticket. The lieutenant'll take care of you. He climbs into the back, sliding the partition closed behind him and leaving the van looking empty and unremarkable to anyone passing by.

From the back, Riley radios the plant. "MOUSE to Geranium," he says into the microphone. Someone's decided you shouldn't say the word *plant* over the air. Everything's gotta have a code word.

"Go ahead, MOUSE."

Riley recognizes Abbruzzo's voice. "We're on the set," he announces.

"Can you see good?"

"Ray, if Barbie walks by, we're gonna be able to see the hairs on her little—"

"Never mind. You got a legal spot there, where nobody's gonna bother you?"

"The best."

"Okay," Abbruzzo says. "Stand by. We'll keep you guys posted."

"Ten-four."

If there's anything cops know how to do, it's stand by. "Hey, you guys got any food in here?" Sheridan asks.

It turns out there's not that much: a dozen doughnuts, four packs of Twinkies, a bag of potato chips, a box of pretzels, some Slim Jims, and a pint of something that's either potato salad or cottage cheese—no one seems too sure. In the process of taking inventory, however, everybody's too busy to notice the woman, the short witch, and the cat getting out of a cab right next to them and heading for the entrance of the corner building.

It's 7:15 and dark by the time Goodman leaves his apartment. The suitcase is heavy and difficult to maneuver going down the stairs, and by the time he reaches the ground floor, he's sweating. He realizes he should have worn his windbreaker instead of his old navy survival jacket. Its bright orange color makes it a good thing to have on if you're knocked overboard, but its quilted lining makes it much too heavy for the weather. He didn't realize how much it had warmed up. He wishes someone had told him.

He walks to the corner, shifting the suitcase from one hand to the other every twenty feet or so. He squints his eyes against the headlights coming down Lexington, searching for an empty taxi.

"He's moving! He's moving!" Weems reports, binoculars following every step Goodman takes. "And he's got a big suitcase. Looks like it's a *load.*"

"Waters! Gleason!" Abbruzzo shouts. "You guys take him on foot. But don't let him make you—we already know where he's going." The two plainclothes officers are out the door.

"We could take him right now, Ray," Weems says. "That suitcase has got the shit in it, or my name isn't Harry."

"No, no," Abbruzzo says. "We wanna take him down at the set, soon as he hands it over to this Vinnie guy. That way, we got 'em both."

"Well, don't let's lose him."

"Don't worry," Abbruzzo says. Then he hits the Send button on the radio. "Geranium to all field units," he says. "The Mole has left the burrow. He's headed toward Lexington. And he's dirty as can be. Repeat, the Mole has left the burrow."

"This is Charlie car," a voice comes back. "He looks like he's trying to flag down a cab on the corner of Ninety-second and Lex. We're on him."

"Baker car here," comes another voice. "We got him in our sights from the west. We'll fall in behind you, Charlie."

"Ten-four, Baker."

* * *

Cab after cab go by, but all of them are occupied. Goodman can't imagine why, until some kids in costumes walk by him. It's Halloween, he remembers. People are going trick-or-treating, heading to parties.

Finally, he gives up. Picking up the suitcase, he takes a deep breath and begins the six-block walk to Eighty-sixth Street.

"He's heading downtown," a voice crackles over the radio. "On foot."

"Whozat? Whozat?" Abbruzzo shouts into the microphone.

"Charlie car, sir," comes the reply.

"You got him, Charlie?"

"Affirmative. My partner's behind him on foot. I'm hanging back, just in case he grows wheels."

"How 'bout you, Baker?" Abbruzzo asks.

"Same thing. And I can see Waters and Gleason across the street. They're on him, too."

"Good," Abbruzzo says. "Don't lose him, but don't get burned, either."

Despite changing hands frequently, Goodman has to stop walking altogether three times to catch his breath. The twin green globes that mark the entrance to the subway are a welcome sight when he finally spots them.

"This is Baker car. He's going down into the *subway.*"

Abbruzzo can hear the surprise in the voice. Drug dealers drive cars; they hire limos; they take cabs. They never take the *subway.* "That's okay; that's okay," he says. "He's a tricky one. Probably trying to shake you."

"Not gonna happen," Baker reports. "We got four guys on foot, heading down after him."

"Good," says Abbruzzo. "You and Charlie car head for the set, Sixth Avenue and Tenth Street. Repeat, Sixth Avenue and Tenth Street. You copy?"

A "Ten-four" comes back over the air in duplicate.

"You know what, Harry?"

"What, Ray?"

"We're gonna get this fucker."

"I hope so," Weems says. "I got kids, you know."

Goodman takes the first downtown train that arrives on the platform, a number 5. It's crowded, and he has to stand. He straddles the suitcase, looking around for a seat that's likely to open up. There are people in costume on the train, young people mostly. There are clowns and ghouls and devils. Some are fully costumed; others wear masks and street clothes. Goodman has a vague sensation of being in a scene from a Fellini movie.

No seats open up at Fifty-ninth Street, but one toward the middle of the car does at Forty-second. He lifts his suitcase and heads that way, even as he sees a man coming from the opposite direction who's got a good two steps on him and no luggage to weigh him down. Goodman slows down, determined to be a good loser about it. But at the last moment, the guy surprises him by pulling up and graciously gesturing to Goodman that he should take the seat.

Goodman does take it, offering warm thanks.

It's only after the man tips his hat, turns away, and heads for the next car that it occurs to Goodman that there was something very familiar-looking about him.

"Boy, that was *close*," Lee Waters tells his partner, George Gleason. They both look through the glass doors, toward where Michael Goodman sits in the next car.

"He make you?" Gleason asks.

"Not a chance," Waters assures him. "This hat a mine fooled him."

"You sure?"

"Sure I'm sure."

Goodman's pretty sure the man is one of those he's noticed following him over the course of the last couple of days. He wonders if the guy's DEA, or NYPD, or what. If he's one of the good guys or one of the bad guys. He ends up deciding he must be a city cop. He's too clean-cut-looking to be a bad guy, he figures, and the feds should be better at following someone than that. Then again, he realizes he's just making a guess.

It occurs to him that it would be nice if the rest of the decisions he makes this evening are based on something just a bit more substantial than guesswork.

He gets off at Fourteenth Street, lugging the suitcase onto the platform and looking around for signs. Before leaving home, Goodman carefully studied the subway map in the front of his Manhattan Yellow Pages. The most direct course seemed to be the L to Sixth Avenue, but he sees no sign of it. He notices that the man with the hat has gotten off also, and that he and a friend of his seem to be having some difficulty getting their bearings, too.

The L turns out to be down the end of a long corridor, and Goodman suddenly feels alone and vulnerable. Without even turning around, he's begun to be able to sense that he's being followed, and he knows that's the case now. If they were to decide to jump him right here—and arrest him, steal his drugs, slit his throat, or whatever—there's absolutely nothing he could do about it. So he just keeps walking.

He sees some kids in costumes coming toward him. There's a Spider Man, a ghost, and a scary-looking hockey goalie. As they pass him, Goodman sneaks a glance over his shoulder, as though he's still watching them. His peripheral vision picks up two men following him at a distance. But they don't look like the same two men as before. My God, thinks Michael Goodman. I'm being followed by an *army*.

The L is crowded, too, with an even greater concentration of costume wearers, and Goodman's forced to stand. He tries to look around casually for the men who've been following him, but he doesn't spot them in his car.

But when he gets off at Sixth Avenue and sets his suitcase down at the bottom of the steps, there they are—four, possibly five of them. One, he notices, appears to be wearing a hearing aid, except that it's got a wire running down from it into his jacket. Goodman starts up the stairs, wondering if it would be presumptuous to ask one of them to carry the suitcase for a while.

Even before he hits street level, Goodman is absorbed by a crowd of bodies more dense than any rush hour he's ever been in. He finds that individual progress is impossible—the crowd moves as one, at a single pace, like some giant slug pushing steadily ahead, all the while wiggling tiny nodules that make up its body. Goodman is simply one of those nodules.

Fortunately, the creature seems intent on heading downtown, and one by one, the street markers overhead inform Goodman that he's crossing Fourteenth Street, then Thirteenth, then Twelfth.

"What's going *on?*" he asks a young couple crushed against each other to his right.

"It's the *parade,*" they tell him in unison.

And then he remembers: Kelly's party is all about watching the Halloween *parade,* that thing where anyone who feels like it puts on a costume and marches through Greenwich Village. Funny, he's always thought of the Village as more on the East Side; now he realizes this must be what they mean when they say the *West* Village.

By the time it nears Eleventh Street, the slug seems to have lost some of its mass as people begin breaking away from it to find vantage points five and six rows deep behind blue wooden barriers that have been set up parallel to the curb.

Before crossing Eleventh, Goodman stops and finds a spot where he can put the suitcase down for a minute. He leans against the building while he fights to catch his breath, wishing he was in better shape. Then again, he realizes, lugging forty pounds around—in a suitcase that's plenty heavy to begin with—would probably tire out just about anybody.

He looks at his watch, sees it's 7:44. He's got one block left to walk, and sixteen minutes to do it in. Early as always. He moves the suitcase right up against the building wall and sits on it, using the wall as a backrest. If he's going to kill time, he might as well make himself comfortable.

"He just sat down on the goddamn suitcase!" comes a voice on the radio.

Abbruzzo grabs the microphone. "Where?"

"Corner of Eleventh. He's just looked at his watch."

"He's gonna let the clock run down," Abbruzzo says. "How many of you guys are on him?"

Four units respond.

"MOUSE?" Abbruzzo calls.

"MOUSE here. Go ahead."

"You hearing all this?"

"Affirmative."

"Can you see him yet in the scope?" One of the more sophisticated pieces of equipment on board is a tiny periscope that peers out of a vent in the top of the van. It has infrared capability for night vision. Sheridan has been practicing on it by following a pickpocket who's been working the crowd. By zooming in on the guy, Sheridan has actually seen him dip into two handbags. On one of the dips, he scored a wallet or a change purse. No question about it.

"You should see this thing!" Sheridan exclaims. "It's fuckin' unbelievable!"

"Gotta tell you something, Ray." It's Riley's voice. "There's gotta be a million people on this corner. I'll let you know when we spot him. He's ahead of schedule, remember."

If Goodman is ahead of schedule, Zelb and Farrelli are decidedly late. The two agents are in the lead car of a procession of four DEA vehicles, the other three being a Jeep, a cable TV truck, and a yellow cab. Caught in traffic at Fourteenth Street and Seventh Avenue, they've got the siren of their unmarked car on, but are still doing no better than a block every two minutes or so. There's simply no place for the cars ahead of them to pull over in order to let them by.

"Shit!" Zelb mutters. "We'll never make it at this rate."

"Maybe we oughta fuck the car and do the rest of it on foot," Farrelli suggests. He's already in character, talking like Vinnie.

"What?" Zelb asks. "And leave three and a half million dollars sittin' here double-parked on Fourteenth Street?"

"We can carry it, man."

"Fuck that," Zelb says. "Besides, we need the car. How else are we gonna give the signal for the backup guys to move in? Am I gonna open the trunk of my dick, or what?"

Farrelli has to think about that one for a moment. He takes a look at his watch. "Shit, Jimmy. It's five minutes to eight."

Zelb unseats the microphone from the car radio. "Two-oh-three to two-oh-one," he says into it. He's calling group leader Siegel's car, a champagne-colored Cadillac seized from a drug dealer just last month. The supervisors get the best cars.

"Two-oh-one," comes back.

"Hey, Lenny, we're down to a crawl here—"

"Is that your siren?"

"Yeah."

"Turn it off," Siegel says. "I can't hear you."

Zelb releases the siren button. "How's that?"

"Better. Where are you?"

"Stuck in gridlock at Fourteenth," Zelb says. "We're never going to make it."

"What's your ETA?" Siegel asks.

"Next Tuesday, at this rate."

"Are the other vehicles with you?"

"Yeah."

"Pull it over, then," Siegel tells them. "Take a couple of men out of the other units, grab the suitcase, and hoof it."

"*Hoof it?*"

"Walk! Run!" Siegel shouts. "I don't care how you do it. Just don't blow this meet. We need this case."

It takes Zelb a full minute and a half just to pull over from the middle lane to the curb. He slams the car into park. He pulls the trunk latch, opens the door, climbs out, and meets Farrelli at the back of the car. They're joined by three other agents, one of whom takes Zelb's keys from him and climbs behind the wheel of the car.

"I'll take the first shift," Zelb says, yanking the suitcase out of the trunk. "Jesus!" he groans. "This must weigh a ton!"

He's exaggerating, of course. Empty, the suitcase weighs six pounds. With its contents of 35,000 hundred-dollar bills, it comes to 39.7 pounds. But as the old army saying used to go: After a couple hundred yards, you think the decimal point's dropped out.

Zelb and Farrelli head for Sixth Avenue. The other two agents fall in right behind them, their instructions abundantly clear: At all costs, protect their fellow agents and the money. Though not necessarily in that order.

Goodman, sitting on his suitcase, looks at his watch, sees it's 7:59. Taking a deep breath, he stands, yanks the suitcase up from the sidewalk, and begins the last block of his walk.

"He's moving! He's moving!"

As soon as they hear the transmission, every man in the MOUSE springs into readiness. All are armed; each has checked his weapon within the last fifteen minutes. Sheridan works the infrared periscope while Riley mans the radio. One of the officers peers out an observation port disguised as a taillight while the other waits for the signal to fling open the back door and lead the charge to arrest the Mole and Vinnie and anyone else foolish enough to get in their way.

Which means, of course, that none of them is in a position to see what's going on up at the front of the van.

Street security for the Halloween parade is the joint responsibility of the NYPD and the DOT, the Department of Transportation. It is an understatement to say that these two agencies have never had an overabundance of love for each other. The antagonism dates back to the very inception of the DOT, a well-intended measure to free police officers from the rather mundane business of directing traffic and issuing parking summonses. The first salvo was fired by the "Brownies." (The nickname dates back to the original color of their uniforms, but it is equally descriptive of the skin tone of most of their ranks, and has managed to survive a recent switch to blue-gray outfits.) They began ticketing the illegally parked personal cars of police officers, in direct violation of an unwritten but longstanding policy that exempted cops from all parking laws. The officers quickly retaliated by arresting scores of Brownies for interfering with governmental administration, defacing city property, disorderly conduct, loitering, and a variety of other charges. Although an uneasy truce was ultimately worked out, occasional sniping still occurs, and relations between the Brown and the Blue continue to be strained.

So, about twenty minutes ago, when an NYPD sergeant pointed out to a DOT captain that a van parked at the corner of Sixth Avenue and Tenth Street was involved in official activity, the captain had nodded absently, not overly impressed. Now, some twenty minutes later, when he gets a call on his walkie-talkie from a DOT truck, telling him there's a vehicle illegally parked on one of the side streets, he forgets all about the earlier advisory. In his most professional-sounding voice, he issues what in his business amounts to an official directive.

"Hook the fucker up," he says.

Now, saying "Hook the fucker up" to a Brownie behind the wheel of a tow truck is kind of like saying "Run" to a gazelle or "Eat" to a great white shark—you don't have to stand around too long to see what's going to happen next.

*   *   *

"I think I see him!" Sheridan whispers, his eyes pressed against the view box of the periscope.

Riley hunches forward in his seat at the radio controls, and for a moment, he assumes that the shifting of his weight is what's caused the van to lurch slightly. Riley catches himself, knowing that any sudden activity inside the van can be detected outside and can therefore give them away. But he has the distinct sensation that his movement—even though it's ended—continues to rock the van in a sort of ripple effect. But without a window to look out of, he has no way of knowing for sure, and he decides it may be only his imagination at work.

Sheridan experiences the phenomenon slightly differently. Just as he's spotted the Mole—or thinks he has, at least—the periscope starts playing tricks on him. Instead of responding to his fingertip commands, it now suddenly seems to have taken on a mind of its own, intent on viewing first the Mole's legs, then his feet, and finally the pavement in front of him. Within a matter of seconds, Sheridan's lost sight of him altogether and is focused instead on other pedestrians and parade watchers.

As for the two officers at the very rear of the van, they find themselves inexplicably pressed up against the inside of the back door. They're able to sense that the van is in some kind of motion, but—just as is the case with Riley—without a view of the outside world as a point of reference, they're disoriented as to just what the motion is. They look at each other, hoping for some clue.

"We're moving," one of them says.

"No," says the other. "We're *lifting off!*"

The truth is, of course, that they're *both* right: The van is simultaneously rising (at least at the front end, that is) and moving forward, a phenomenon made possible by the DOT's latest piece of equipment, a hydraulic speed-lifter, affectionately nicknamed the "bump and run," after a popular defensive technique on the football field.

And by the time any of them realizes what's happening, the MOUSE is pulling away from the intersection.

"Open the door!" Riley shouts, and the officer pressed up against it yanks desperately at the handle. Success would all but guarantee him serious injury, since the moment the door opens, the combined effect of the van's speed and the forces of gravity would land him on the asphalt of West Tenth Street. But here some clever engineer at General Motors has come to the rescue: An automatic locking mechanism—designed to prevent children, pets, and cargo (and, in this instance, cops) from tumbling out of the moving vehicle—kicked in ten seconds ago, as soon as the van attained a speed of five miles per hour.

The officers, being resourceful young men, will ultimately figure out how to override the device, and they'll eventually manage to open the door and tumble out of it, just as the van reaches its destination. But by that time, they'll be at the DOT pier on Thirty-ninth Street and the Hudson River, along with several thousand other illegally parked vehicles. Just an average day's catch for the dedicated men in brown.

Goodman arrives at the intersection of Sixth Avenue and Tenth Street at precisely eight o'clock. He crosses Sixth first, then Tenth, all the while looking for Vinnie or T.M., or a suitcase identical to his own.

He sees no sign of any of them.

Jimmy Zelb is taking his second turn carrying the suitcase as he and Frank Farrelli finally near the corner of Sixth Avenue and Tenth Street from the west, closely followed by the only two backup agents in sight (all of the others being hopelessly stuck in traffic back up near Fourteenth Street).

Zelb, despite his football background, is sweating and out of breath. He was a lineman, after all, and the only running he was ever called upon to do was in short spurts, with frequent rests between plays. And never while carrying a loaded suitcase.

If Zelb and Farrelli are late in arriving for their meet with Michael Goodman, they're just in time for the parade. For a moment, Zelb is clueless enough to think that the cheering he hears is for his own arrival. But soon it dawns on him that all eyes—which at first seemed riveted on him—are looking past him, down Sixth. He turns his head slowly in that direction in order to see just what it is that has suddenly created such pandemonium.

Jimmy Zelb is a Presbyterian, raised on a family farm outside Dusty Gulch, Nebraska; educated in Wooster, Ohio. He spent a year and a half as a cop in Toledo, and another five as a DEA agent in Detroit. He's been in New York City eight months, and he thinks he's seen it all. But nothing, *nothing* in his background has prepared him for this moment. Coming toward him is a majorette, tall and blond, decked out in a sparkling silver hat, the miniest miniskirt of all time, and shiny high boots, and flinging a gold baton high into the air every fourth step. She is completely topless, and her breasts are everything Zelb has ever dreamed of since the age of twelve, when a dog-eared copy of *National Geographic* had taken him down the Amazon River and into the storm cellar of his parents' house for the next two hours. They are *gigantic.* The are *humongous.* They bounce with every step she takes. They are tipped with awesome brown nipples. And, best of all, *they are heading right at him!*

How on earth is Jimmy Zelb—with no real sense of New York history—to know that the event he is watching originated some years back as the gay parade? Or that to this day almost half of its marchers put on their wildest drag-queen outfits, created just for the annual occasion? Or that the particular majorette of Zelb's dreams goes by the name of Rick Verchinsky, shaves twice a day, played his own football as an outside line-backer for the Citadel, and works five nights a week as a bouncer at the Palladium?

Zelb knows none of these things, of course. All he knows, as he puts his suitcase down on the sidewalk and out of his mind (so that he can stare openmouthed and undistracted at the Breasts), is that he's *in love.*

Frank Farrelli, who by this time should be well into the role of Vinnie the drug buyer, can't help noticing Zelb's sudden change in focus. He swivels his body and follows his partner's gaze in an attempt to see just what it is that's suddenly captured Zelb's attention.

And Farrelli sees what Zelb sees: the Breasts. And, more or less, he does what Zelb is doing: He stares. (Though to be fair to Farrelli, it should be pointed out that in the days and weeks to follow, he would steadfastly in-sist that he knew all along that the majorette was in fact a major, that the breasts were only real in the virtual sense, and that he was staring at them purely out of a sense of detached curiosity. As for the momentary lapse in concentration on the job at hand, however, neither agent would have much to offer in defense of his performance.)

Goodman, too, hears the crowd break into a roar, and the sudden turn-ing of heads en masse tells him that the first paraders have come into view as they work their way up Sixth Avenue. He strains forward to see, but there are so many bodies in front of him that his view is completely blocked: All he can see are the backs of other watchers.

And a suitcase identical to his.

There can be no doubt about it—the same size, the same shape, the same yellow-and-green floral print.

Then, just as quickly as the suitcase had come into view, it's suddenly obscured, and he can see only the backs of the two men standing closest to the spot where he saw it. But even from behind them, he can tell that one of them is slender, while the other is broad-shouldered and thick-necked.

Vinnie and T.M.

Michael Goodman has always been a careful person, slow to react, cautious in the extreme. He's an old-fashioned accountant, wary of calculators—one who trusts his own ability to add a column of numbers better than that of some Japanese- or Mexican-made gadget whose battery might or might not be dependable. He likes to start at the top and add up the numbers, see what he gets. Then he adds them up again, this time starting from the bottom. (That way, he can't make the same careless mistake twice, such as 29 + 6 = 33.) If he ends up with the same answer, he still might want to do it a third time, particularly if it's essential that he get it right. And after that, if there's a calculator that happens to be handy, it never hurts to double-check the answer, just to be on the safe side.

But something in Goodman tells him that there's no time for all of that now, that spotting the suitcase at the very moment that the beginning of the parade is coming up the avenue is a good omen of sorts, and that it might be a mistake to hesitate. So before he can analyze the situation too closely, he forces himself to start off again, making a straight line for the two men, suitcase approaching suitcase.

As the leader of Group Two, Lenny Siegel is supposed to be directing the DEA agents from the radio in his Cadillac, close to where the deal's supposed to go down. But Siegel finds himself stuck in the same gridlock traffic that's earlier forced Zelb, Farrelli, and the rest of the field agents to abandon their cars on Fourteenth Street.

"This is fucked up," Siegel now tells his driver. "What street is this?"

"Twenty-third, sir," replies Luis Sandoval. At twenty-two, Sandoval is the youngest agent in the group, and the newest, with less than two months on the job. Fresh out of John Jay College, he's yet to make an undercover buy, be present at an arrest, or take part in a seizure. He doesn't drink, smoke, curse, or seem to understand the occasional need to testify creatively in court. As a result, there are still serious doubts about Sandoval's potential to fit into the law-enforcement community. Siegel has appointed him his personal driver for the time being, since none of the other agents wants to be burdened with such an untested agent as a partner.

"This is really fucked up," Siegel says, looking at the wall of traffic ahead of them. "Make a U-ey, Louie, and we'll head uptown, get ourselves out of this fuckin' mess."

"Yessir," says Sandoval.

Goodman comes up on Vinnie and T.M. from the rear, and can tell that they're totally absorbed in the parade. He sets his suitcase down a few feet behind theirs. For a moment, he wonders if he might actually be able to slide theirs out from between them. It's a maneuver he's seen his daughter make when playing Pickup Sticks—gently pulling one stick free without disturbing those on either side of it. But he sees that T.M. has his leg pressed against the suitcase, and decides he better look around for another move.

The noise is overwhelming. The first marchers are passing right by them, led by some guy dressed up like a majorette, wearing these huge rubber tits. Behind him are a couple of people wearing Newt Gingrich and Bob Dole masks, waving to the crowd. Two others are dressed up as huge ears, suspending a tiny likeness of Ross Perot between them. Next comes a huge smoke-breathing dragon, held aloft by a dozen people in black costumes. A full calypso band can be seen—and heard—coming up the avenue.

There's so much noise—music, shouting, cheering, laughing, and applauding—that Goodman finally has to tap Vinnie and T.M. on their shoulders to get their attention. They spin around in tandem. For a fleeting instant, Goodman imagines he reads disappointment on their faces, or even sexual rejection. But he's sure he must be mistaken—it's only a *parade* they've been watching, after all.

"Hi, fellas," he says.

"Hi," they respond in unison, looking a bit out of their element. The greeting "Hi" is apparently not real big in either drug parlance or DEA agent machismo.

"How's the parade?" Goodman asks them.

"Good," Vinnie answers, his eyes now darting back and forth between Goodman's suitcase and their own. "How do you want to do this?"

Goodman starts to answer, but his voice is completely drowned out by a giant roar of laughter from the crowd. Passing them is a huge float, featuring an outrageously attired couple engaged in mock fornication on a purple velvet four-poster. The breasts of the "woman" are every bit as bare as those of the majorette before her, and every bit as awesome. Above the display is a giant reproduction of the Nike logo—apparently corporate sponsorship has extended yet another tentacle into American life—and the slogan JUST DO IT.

"Let's just do it," Goodman says. And with that, he reaches for their suitcase with his left hand, yanks it off the sidewalk, and gives them a crisp salute with his right.

Dumbly, Vinnie and T.M. return the salute. T.M. takes a step toward Goodman's suitcase, grasps the handle, and picks it up. He smiles slightly, apparently reassured by the discovery that it's even heavier than the one he's been lugging.

"Let's do this again sometime," Goodman says. As he backs away, he stumbles over something. Looking down, he sees it's a big orange cone, one of those high-visibility rubber markers they use. He picks it up and looks for a place to toss it, but every inch of the sidewalk seems to be already occupied by a body. He shrugs and turns into the crowd.

To Zelb and Farrelli, the switch has happened faster than their wildest dreams. They'd counted on the fact that Goodman, as an accountant, would surely want to crack open their suitcase to assure himself that the money looked right. That would've given them time to do the same with his, to make certain the drugs are there, before signaling the backup team to move in. But Goodman's sudden departure has thrown them off.

On top of that, not having been able to bring their car to the set has forced Zelb and Farrelli to abandon their original signal, which had, of course, been the traditional opening-of-the-trunk move. They'd hastily switched to an exchange of high fives, a gesture considered obvious enough to be easily spotted by the backup team.

Finally, with the gridlock caused by the parade, the backup team—once close to twenty strong, complete with vehicles and radios—has been reduced to two men on foot. And at this very moment, those two men are doing their best to follow Michael Goodman and the suitcase full of the government's money, while at the same time watching Zelb and Farrelli for signs of anything approaching a high five.

Desperately, Zelb drops to his knees right there in the middle of the sidewalk as Farrelli does his best to keep the crowd from trampling them.

Zelb needs to check to make sure that the drugs are there before they can give the signal for the backup team to move in. Otherwise, it may turn out that the seller has engaged in what's termed a "dry run"—a delivery of something other than narcotics, just to see if the police are going to swoop down at the moment of the transfer. (Zelb knows of one case in which a wary seller delivered ten pounds of sanitary napkins to test whether things were safe for the actual sale.)

Zelb opens one latch, then the other. Then, holding his breath, he snaps the lid open and peers inside. What he sees is nineteen large plastic bags, each packed full with a grayish white powder.

He breathes. He slams the lid shut, fastens the latches, and jumps to his feet. "Bingo!" he shouts to Farrelli, who has to lip-read his answer, because the crowd has broken into a roar once again. Then the two give each other a series of high fives that are, at least by white male standards, more or less identifiable.

The only problem is that at that moment a marcher dressed up as a giant Barney the Dinosaur has begun to throw candy into the crowd. Not anything wonderful—chocolate Kisses, M&M's, Neco Wafers, and the like—but more than enough to cause people who've been standing around in the cold for an hour and a half to react. And the way they react, naturally, is to raise their hands high as they attempt to catch the treats in midair.

This activity by the crowd lasts just long enough (and is just similar enough to the high fives of Zelb and Farrelli) to confuse the two backup agents, who are forced to hesitate a moment longer before closing in on Goodman and his suitcase. The last they see of him is his suitcase and his bright orange jacket, framed against the entrance of a large apartment building on the corner.

"That's it!" one of them shouts. "That's the high five, the signal!"

Joined by Zelb and Farrelli moments later, they will still be arguing over whether Goodman went into the building or somehow disappeared into the crowd.

"Calm down," Zelb tells them. "We've got a backup system." He reaches into his pocket and produces an object that looks like an electronic garage-door opener but is actually the locator unit of a powerful state-of-the-art homing device. He presses the On button. Immediately, a red light begins to flash every two seconds or so, accompanied by a beeping sound.

"He's still nearby," Zelb announces, "probably inside the building. This little gadget'll tell us as soon as he makes a move."

"You mean as soon as the *money* makes a move," Farrelli corrects him.

"Same difference."

"It's a switch! It's a switch!"

The voice is that of Lee Waters, coming over the radio to Ray Abbruzzo at the plant.

"Who's with you?" Abbruzzo asks.

"Just me and Gleason."

"Can you see the MOUSE?"

"No," Waters says. "They drove off."

"Drove off?" Abbruzzo can't believe his ears. "MOUSE! Come in, MOUSE!" he shouts over and over again.

Finally, he hears Daniel Riley's voice, and a timid "MOUSE here."

"Are you still there?" Abbruzzo asks.

"Not exactly," comes the reply.

"Can you tell me where the fuck you are, then?" Abbruzzo screams into the microphone.

"Uh, not exactly."

"What is this, some Hertz commercial? *What's going on out there?"*

The answer that finally comes sounds small and far away, and almost like a question of its own. "We're being towed away?"

Abbruzzo grabs the neck of the microphone as if to throttle it. Twice, he starts to say something; twice, he stops. Finally, he releases the microphone, reaches for his Maalox tablets, and downs whatever's left of them, wrapper and all.

"What should we do, Ray?"

Abbruzzo suddenly remembers he's got Waters and Gleason standing by, waiting for orders.

"How many of them are there?" he asks.

"Hard to tell," Waters says. "Looks like three or four of them, and the suitcase."

"Think you two can take them?" Abbruzzo asks.

"Shit, yeah."

"Go for it."

Zelb, Farrelli, and one of the other DEA agents are still in front of the apartment building, playing with the locator device. The fourth agent is stationed at the service entrance of the building, a couple of doors down.

"From the way it's giving out a constant signal," Zelb explains, "he's gotta be inside. Otherwise, we'd be losing him."

"I don't know," Farrelli says. "It feels like we've already lost him."

"Have a little faith in technology," Zelb tells him, his eyes on the flashing red light.

"Freeze, motherfuckers!"

Zelb looks up and sees two crazy guys pointing toy handguns at them from combat positions. "Go march in the fuckin' parade," he tells them. "Cancha see we're busy here?"

"I said, *freeze!"*

Zelb takes a closer look. Maybe the guns don't look so much like toys after all.

Lee Waters keeps his gun trained on the guy with the big neck, the one closest to the suitcase. On Waters's left, George Gleason has both hands on his own gun, pointed in pretty much the same direction.

What Waters is thinking is that this is a career-defining moment for him. With the rest of the troops nowhere to be found, he and his partner have saved the day. They've brought down three perps with a suitcase full of pure heroin. This will mean a commendation at the very least, perhaps a *promotion*. Possibly even an appearance on the eleven o'clock news. He can't wait to see his face on TV as he stands flanked by the mayor and the police commissioner, drugs displayed in front of them, answering Gabe Pressman's questions in a steady, self-assured voice.

Instead, the voice he hears comes from the guy with the big neck. "We're on the job, here, assholes! Who the fuck are *you?"*

Now if the one with the big neck had said, "We're cops," or "We're police officers," or even "We're federal agents," Waters might be having his doubts right about now, might even be cocking the hammer of his weapon to show just how much he means business. But "on the job" is a magic phrase, and as soon as he hears it, Lee Waters experiences a sinking feeling. He's not sure yet, but he senses already that the whole Gabe Pressman interview is down the tube, so to speak.

The standoff continues for a few minutes, each side demanding to see the credentials of the other but afraid of any move toward a pocket. There's some swearing and name-calling, as well as an accusation or two that one agency has interfered with another's investigation. But in the end, nobody gets shot, punched, or even arrested. Which is a pretty fortunate thing, considering how these jurisdictional disputes usually seem to wind up.

Zelb continues to monitor the locator device, which blinks and beeps a steady indication that their target is still nearby. Farrelli uses a portable radio to call the group leader, Lenny Siegel.

"Stay on the building," Siegel tells them. "We couldn't get any closer with all the traffic, so we're heading uptown. We'll swing by his house. If he slips past you guys, we'll be waiting for him at his house."

"Don't worry, boss," Farrelli says. "No way he's gonna slip past this team."

"Why am I not convinced?" Siegel asks. He clicks off before Farrelli can answer.

But by this time, the team consists of six men, including Waters and Gleason. They represent the United States Justice Department's Drug Enforcement Administration and the New York Police Department's Organized Crime Control Bureau. All told, they have eight guns, two hundred rounds of ammunition, five pairs of handcuffs, and the locator device. They're waiting for a little unarmed guy with a big suitcase to walk out of the building and into their arms.

Now those are the kind of odds you've got to like.

Shortly before 8:30, Big Red pulls his Bentley into Ninety-second Street, finds a parking place that's more or less legal, and kills the engine. He taps a pack of Marlboros and extracts one of them. Before it reaches his mouth, Hammer has lighted a match and holds it ready.

"What's the plan, Red?" Hammer asks.

"We gonna jus chill here a few minutes," Big Red explains. "Then, if everything looks cool, we gonna pay Mr. Pure a little call."

Not thirty feet away, Harry Weems studies the Bentley in his binoculars.

"Two wrong-looking characters sittin' in a red Rolls-Royce right in front of us, Ray." By "wrong-looking characters," Weems, of course, means blacks. But being African-American himself, he chooses to state it somewhat differently.

"What are they up to?" Abbruzzo asks.

"Hard to say," Weems says. "But nothing legal, that's for damn sure."

"Keep an eye on them."

"Oh, I will," says Harry Weems. "I will."

The black Mercedes 500S cruises slowly down Lexington Avenue. Johnnie Delgado is behind the wheel. Mister Fuentes sits alongside him. Two guys known as Papo and Julio ride in the back.

"What street we looking for?" Mister Fuentes asks, turning up the heat. He wishes he were back in Miami.

"Ninety-second," Johnnie Delgado says. He knows the block well. He's known it ever since a couple of their men followed the gringo there—the same gringo who stole the heroin Raul Cuervas was supposed to pick up at the airport in Fort Lauderdale. That little mistake had cost Cuervas his life.

"Raul Cuervas was my cousin, you know," Mister Fuentes says. He's always had this uncanny ability to know what's on the other person's mind.

"I didn't know that," Johnnie Delgado says, not sure if it's really true or not.

"Yes, it's true," Mister Fuentes says. "That's why it's so important for me to avenge his death."

Which strikes Johnnie Delgado as a bit strange, given the fact that it was Mister Fuentes himself who ordered the death of Raul Cuervas.

"That was business," says Mister Fuentes.

"And now?"

"Now we find our little gringo and avenge Raul's death."

Johnnie Delgado has the feeling that there's more involved here. Mister Fuentes hasn't flown up from Miami just to kill some Anglo. He could have done that with a phone call.

"And while we're at it," Mister Fuentes continues, "we'll see if there are any black duffel bags lying around his apartment. Heh, heh, heh." As usual, he's his own best audience.

"Good thinking," says Johnnie Delgado.

The two guys in the back of the car say nothing. Johnnie Delgado can't remember if they speak English or not. In any event, they're along for a reason, but it's not to express their opinions.

Big Red stubs out his cigarette. "Let's take us a little walk," he tells Hammer.

They step out of the Bentley, slam the doors, and cross the street.

"You packin'?" Big Red asks Hammer. "Packin' " in this case means "strapped"—carrying a gun. Big Red doesn't like to pack. Possession of a loaded weapon is a class D felony, get you seven years upstate. That's one of the reasons he has Hammer.

"I do believe I am," Hammer replies, patting an area just to the right of his belt buckle.

"Is it clean?"

"Clean as a whistle."

Here, Big Red's jargon leaves just a bit to be desired. *Clean,* when it comes to a gun, is a word that can be used to mean that the gun's been cleaned since the last time it was fired, not only so that it will operate properly but so that if it's seized by the police there will be no evidence of discharge visible upon examination. And indeed, it's precisely that meaning of the term that Hammer has in mind when he assures Big Red that he's recently cleaned the gun.

But a clean gun has a second connotation altogether, and it's actually that second connotation that Big Red was concerned about when he posed the question in the first place. A clean gun also refers to one without a criminal history, a gun with no "bodies" on it. Since guns and bullets can be matched by microscopic comparison, a seized gun can occasionally link its possessor to an unsolved homicide.

But when you come right down to it, Hammer has a rather childlike mind. He tends to take things literally. So it's really no surprise that he attaches the more literal meaning to Big Red's use of the word *clean*. The gun is clean, he knows, because he cleaned it himself—just the other day, in fact.

"Our two wrong guys are out of the Rolls," Weems tells Abbruzzo.

"What're they doing?"

"Crossing the street . . . looking around . . . Shit, Ray! They're going into Goodman's building!"

"*Are you sure?*"

"How sure do I gotta be?" Weems asks. "They're already inside, if that helps any."

"What's going on in the apartment?" Abbruzzo asks.

Weems aims the binoculars at the fifth-floor window. "Nothing," he says. "It's still dark."

"Keep an eye on it."

Hammer uses a thin piece of steel to slip the ground-floor lock of Michael Goodman's building. It's the same implement he uses when he wants to borrow someone's car and can't seem to locate the door key.

Big Red checks the names on the mailboxes in the lobby. He finds what he's looking for: M. GOODMAN, 5F

With no elevator in sight, they begin climbing the stairs. They're both smokers, and though they both work (after a manner of speaking), physical labor appears on neither of their job descriptions. By the time they reach the fifth floor, they're both seriously out of breath.

Big Red knocks on the door of apartment 5F and waits for an answer. There is none. The nice thing about the way the building's laid out, he decides, is that there are only two apartments on each floor. (Though why they're lettered *F* and *R* he can't imagine. White people too good for *A* and *B*?) He knows that a little noise won't alarm anybody, particularly on Halloween. He steps aside and motions to Hammer.

The trick to kicking in a door is understanding what's keeping it shut in the first place. Hammer understands this, and he now spends a moment studying the lock pattern on Michael Goodman's door. First, he notices that there's no Fox police lock, a contraption that consists of a long steel bar with one end set into the floor and the other wedged against the center of the inside of the door. Then he assures himself that there's no crossbar, a heavy metal plate running horizontally across the width of the door. Either device could spell disaster for someone foolish enough to make a run at the door—the first because it could impale him, the second because it could sever his body at its midsection.

Next, he inspects the frame—which in this case seems to be fairly substantial—and the composition of the door itself. It appears to be constructed out of several pieces of wood, a thick border surrounding a recessed center panel. Hammer taps softly on the border, listening to the solid sound of the wood. Then he taps on the center panel. A hollow sound answers him, causing a smile to spread across his face.

As Big Red stands off to one side, Hammer takes one step back, plants his left foot, and drives the sole of his right foot clear through the panel, which splinters like the plywood it is. Then he extracts his foot, reaches his hand inside the hole he's made, unlocks the door, and opens it wide for Big Red.

It's dark inside, and Big Red flicks on the light switch.

"They're inside!" Weems shouts. But he needn't have, since Abbruzzo has already heard the crash of the door panel giving way and is now picking up sounds from inside the apartment.

FIRST MALE: What's all this white stuff all over the place?

SECOND MALE: Beats me.

Abbruzzo distinctly feels his heart skip a beat. He leans forward, not wanting to miss a word.

FIRST MALE: Careful you don't get it on your clothes there.

SECOND MALE: Shit, man, it's all over the place. There must be *tons* of it here.

That's more than Ray Abbruzzo can stand. Grabbing his gun and his handcuffs, he's on his feet. "Come on, Harry!" he shouts. "We're going to save this day yet!" Then he's out the door and running across the street, with Weems struggling to keep up, the binoculars looped around his neck and banging painfully against his chest.

They slip the downstairs lock with a credit card and are in the building seconds before the black Mercedes makes the turn into the block from Lexington Avenue.

Lenny Siegel and Luis Sandoval find the traffic much lighter uptown, well away from the Greenwich Village area. By 8:30, Sandoval has the Cadillac in the Eighties, heading up Park Avenue.

"Hang a right at Ninety-second," Siegel says.

"Yes, sir."

"And don't *sir* me."

"Sorry, sir."

*   *   *

Abbruzzo and Weems huff and puff their way up the stairs to the fifth-floor landing. They're both overweight—Weems by eighty pounds—and a steady diet of pizza, doughnuts, coffee, soda, and cigarettes has somewhat underprepared them for this particular event. Abbruzzo fishes around in his pockets for his Maalox before remembering he finished the roll awhile back.

Johnnie Delgado leads the way from the Mercedes into the building, followed by Mister Fuentes, Papo, and Julio. They find the stairs and begin the climb to the fifth floor. They proceed slowly. For one thing, they feel no particular urge to hurry. Beyond that, by the fourth floor, they're all beginning to feel the effects of a lunch of rice and beans, habanero peppers, tequila, and *pulpo y olio*. *Pulpo y olio* is a delightful concoction of baby octopus and fried garlic cloves swimming in olive oil, but it begins to repeat on you just a bit during strenuous stair climbing.

"What's that?" Johnnie Delgado says, trying to quiet the rest of the climbers. It takes a moment, but eventually their burping and belching subside and they're able to hear the sound of heavy breathing other than their own. It's coming from the stairs directly overhead. They press their bodies against the wall to stay out of sight, and listen. They strain to make out the conversation coming from above them.

"Nice job they did on the door," the first man is whispering. His voice is that of a gringo.

"If nothing else, we got a felony burglary here," the second one says. He sounds black. "These fuckers give us any trouble, we blow 'em away, get their stories later," they hear him say.

The next sound they hear is that of an automatic pistol being jacked as the first round is lifted from the magazine and chambered into firing position. It is a sound that Johnnie Delgado, Mister Fuentes, Papo, and Julio all happen to be familiar with. Without so much as a word or a glance among them, they begin backing slowly down the stairs, looking something like a caterpillar in retreat.

It's turned out to be a very productive evening for Fingers Nelson. "Fingers"—a nickname that replaced the somewhat more formal Francis around the time of Nelson's third arrest for picking the pockets of unsuspecting New Yorkers—has been working the crowd of parade watchers up and down Sixth Avenue, between Christopher and Eleventh streets. Next to New Year's Eve, which Fingers likes to celebrate at Times Square, Halloween is his favorite night of the year. He's done so well, in fact, that he's had to remove his jacket and use it as a satchel to conceal the four wallets, three change purses, two credit card cases, and assorted other treasure that he's accumulated over the past two hours.

The problem with success, of course, is that it has its price. And the particular price that Fingers is paying right now is that he's cold without his jacket. As a result, he's been forced to seek temporary shelter between the outer and inner doors of a large apartment building on the corner of Sixth and Tenth Street. He knows he can't stay there long without being asked to move by a doorman or a tenant, but there are so many people milling about that he decides he's safe for a little while. But, just to be sure, he occasionally glances over his shoulder into the lobby to see what's going on.

Luis Sandoval makes a right turn off Park Avenue at Ninety-second Street and heads down the hill in the champagne-colored Cadillac.

"Take it slow when you get into the next block," Lenny Siegel tells him. "We'll see what's going on."

What's going on is that there's a light on in Michael Goodman's fifth-floor window, and two guys can be seen walking around inside.

"That's strange," says Lenny Siegel.

The retreating caterpillar of Johnnie Delgado, Mister Fuentes, Papo, and Julio inches its way down the five flights of stairs to ground level. Johnnie Delgado is about to lead them out of the building when he sees a champagne-colored Cadillac pull up in front and double-park. Something about it—perhaps the dual antennas, perhaps the unlikely combination of the two men inside, the young Hispanic driver and the older white passenger—causes him to hesitate.

"*El Hombre,*" he whispers to Mister Fuentes.

Mister Fuentes nods. They look around for some sign of a rear exit from the building but see none. What they do see is another stairway, this one leading down. With no other avenue of escape, they take it.

*   *   *

"He's coming!" Jimmy Zelb hisses. The red light on the locator device is suddenly blinking faster and faster, and the intervals between the beeps have almost disappeared, leaving a shrill pulsating tone. The only short-coming of the device is that it has no directional capability: It tells them how close they are to the sending unit (in this case, the suitcase full of money), but not the heading they need to follow in order to reach it. But there can be no doubt that their target's heading their way and must be almost on top of them—the red light is constant now, and the beep has turned into a steady, piercing whine. They look around frantically, ex-pecting to spot their quarry any second among the mass of people on the corner.

A roar goes up from the crowd once again, and all eyes are suddenly turned to a group of marchers dressed up as O. J. Simpson and his de-fense team. There's a strutting Johnnie Cochran, a chart-carrying Barry Scheck, an F. Lee Bailey wrapped in a marine flag, and a Robert Shapiro distancing himself off to one side. O.J. himself is smiling broadly and blowing kisses to the crowd, who respond with a tumultuous mixture of cheers and boos: No one seems undecided about this particular entry in the parade.

And then Zelb spots him.

Not twenty yards away, a small man wearing a bright orange jacket and carrying a large yellow-and-green floral-print suitcase is disappear-ing into the crowd. By the time Zelb reacts, the man has turned the cor-ner and is heading west on Tenth Street.

Jimmy Zelb, an offensive lineman in his football days—very offensive, according to some of his opponents—was never known as fast; never-theless, he was what professional scouts termed "quick off the ball," mean-ing he had an explosive quality about him, an ability to catapult himself from a set position into the opposing team's secondary and toward a line-backer, cornerback, or anyone else foolish enough to get in his path. Only a serious knee injury his senior year kept him out of the pro draft and de-prived him of a promising career in the National Football League.

It is that same quickness, that same explosive quality, that Zelb exhibits now as he bolts forward toward the receding orange jacket. Much as he used to knock opposing linemen aside as though they were tenpins, Zelb now clears a broad path through the crowd that his fellow DEA and NYPD teammates quickly fill as all six of them—a half a ton of hurtling human beef—zero in on their target.

So intense is Zelb's concentration that not once does he take his eyes off the combination of the orange jacket and the suitcase in front of him. He shortens the distance to fifteen yards, to ten, to five. Away from the avenue, the crowd is thinner and finally parts altogether, giving Zelb an unobstructed path to his prey. Gauging the speed at which the orange jacket is moving away from him, Zelb now instinctively adjusts his stride to that of his quarry, closing the gap between them to three yards, to two . . .

Offensive linemen are trained to block, not to tackle. They're schooled in the art of using their shoulders, their bodies, even their *heads* to fend off opponents and open holes for teammates. They're drilled for hours on end on how to avoid costly penalties for holding, or illegal use of the hands, or face-mask grabbing. They must endure bitter envy and endless frustration, as the same rules that hamstring them freely encourage their defensive counterparts to grab and tug and hold to their hearts' content. So—just as every receiver has always longed to turn the tables and throw a touchdown pass, just as every nose tackle has always imagined scoring a touchdown off a tipped pass or a bouncing fumble—every blocking lineman who ever played the game has at one time or another found himself dreaming of making the perfect open-field tackle: of being allowed, *just once,* to use his hands, his God-given *arms,* to grasp the enemy and bring him crashing down to earth.

Not that any of the specifics of this rationale go through Jimmy Zelb's conscious thought process as he closes in on his target, to be sure. But years of frustration are at play here nonetheless: frustration from his hand-tied football days, frustration from his career-ending knee injury, frustration from a life in law enforcement, in which he's paid a meager salary to uphold inadequate laws against millionaire drug dealers, frustration from the traffic jam earlier in the evening, frustration from losing sight of the Mole once already tonight.

Jimmy Zelb's frustration is about to end.

A yard from his target, he takes a deep breath and launches himself into the air, head down, arms spread wide, every ounce of his body prepared for impact: a perp-seeking missile locked onto his target with an intensity that is awesome to behold.

It takes Johnnie Delgado, Mister Fuentes, and the two others a few minutes to get acclimated to the darkness of the basement. One of them finds a book of matches, and halfway through it, they discover an overhead lightbulb that responds to the pull of a cord.

They look around and are able to see that it's a storage area of some sort that they've taken refuge in. There are individual bins, each full of household items, each secured with a padlock.

While Johnnie Delgado listens for noises upstairs, Papo and Julio, still panting from their exercise on the stairs, find a small bench and sit down on it. Mister Fuentes spends his time walking down the row of storage bins, looking at the contents. He sees a dusty TV set, a broken green chair, two pairs of skis, a child's bicycle, a black duffel bag, an old vacuum cleaner—

And he stops right there.

Taking two steps back, he stares at the bin in front of him. He doesn't even notice the tiny "5F" scratched into the gray paint above it. He doesn't have to. Mister Fuentes has found the gringo's storage locker, and in it the black duffel bag.

He looks at the lock, the only thing in the world that at this moment separates him from the bag. It is a small combination lock, the kind they sell in Kmart or Target for a dollar or two. He allows himself a broad grin.

"*Compadres,*" he says, "I think we may have avenged the tragic death of Raul Cuervas."

Jimmy Zelb's tackle turns out to be a wonder to behold, a perfect ten, a one-play human highlight film. He hits his target around the waist, just below the bottom of the orange jacket. Zelb's shoulder drives into the small of the man's back, simultaneously lifting him into the air and knocking him prone. For a long moment, both tackler and tacklee are airborne, as though the beefy Zelb is stretched out atop a sled that's suddenly lifted off and taken flight.

Then, gravity doing what it generally tends to do, they begin descending for what can only be described as a *series* of landings. Witnesses (and there were quite a number) will later disagree whether the pair bounced two times or three before finally coming to rest against a trash can. According to measurements taken for a civil suit filed sometime later, the trash can was a full forty-seven feet seven inches from the original point of impact, that point being assumed from the position of a pair of shoes from which the man had apparently been ejected at the instant of the big bang. As for the suitcase, it took a slightly different flight path, somewhat to the north, traveling thirteen feet two inches before hitting the pavement, springing open, and spilling its contents onto the roadway.

It is the nature of these contents that first alerts the agents and officers to the possibility that something has gone slightly wrong with their game plan. Instead of $3.5 million of the government's money being strewn about, all that can be seen are four wallets, three change purses, two credit card cases, a pocket watch, a badly wrinkled jacket, and (upon closer inspection) a miniature device called a sending unit, said to be capable of transmitting a variable-range electronic signal to a second device.

And instead of it being Michael Goodman who lies facedown on the sidewalk, struggling to regain consciousness, it is, of course, Francis Teller Nelson. Or, as all his friends at Rikers Island call him, Fingers.

It takes Papo and Julio all of thirty seconds to break the combination lock on the storage bin. As Mister Fuentes watches, Johnnie Delgado reaches forward, grabs the black duffel bag by its handles, and pulls it out onto the basement floor. He crouches over it, unzips it about four inches. He sees blue plastic packages.

"Let's go," he tells the others.

Mister Fuentes nods in agreement and leads the way to the stairs. In their greed and their haste, both Mister Fuentes and Johnnie Delgado have completely forgotten about the Cadillac outside and the two men who looked like *el Hombre*. Papo and Julio, if *they* remember, understand that it's not their place to say anything.

Ray Abbruzzo and Harry Weems are inside Apartment 5F before the two burglars know it. They have the handcuffs on them without a struggle. Both are charged with first-degree burglary, a class B felony punishable by up to twenty-five years imprisonment. A search of one of the two—the one who answers to the name Hammer—reveals a fully loaded 9-mm semiautomatic pistol.

"There's something going on up there," Lenny Siegel tells Luis Sandoval. "Let's go take a look."

They climb out of the Cadillac and head for the entrance of Michael Goodman's building. They find the front door locked.

"You got a credit card?" Siegel asks Sandoval. Siegel hates the things himself, refuses to carry them.

"Let me see, sir," Sandoval says. He pulls out his wallet, finds one, and hands it over to Siegel.

Siegel works at the lock. He was a good field agent in his day, but as a group leader, he spends most of his time at his desk or somebody else's, and his street skills have grown rusty. He's still working at the lock when the door suddenly swings outward, knocking him onto his butt.

A short middle-aged Hispanic man stands on the other side, backed by three younger Hispanic men. One of them is carrying a large black duffel bag. They look startled.

Startled is hardly the word for Luis Sandoval. Ever since Siegel said, "Let's go take a look," Sandoval's adrenaline has been pumping. In his seven weeks with the DEA, he's yet to make an arrest, or even be *present* at one. After graduating from his training class "Most Eager to Succeed," he's succeeded at nothing, in fact, but chauffeuring senior agents around. Now, the sight of his superior being knocked to the ground, coupled with the sudden appearance of what to Luis Sandoval looks like a band of Cuban thugs, causes the tightly wound Sandoval to spring into action.

"Freeze!" he shouts, pulling his service revolver and pointing it at the forehead of the Hispanic man nearest him.

The man's jaw drops open, joined by the jaws of his three companions. There is a loud *thud* as the duffel bag drops from the hands of the second man and lands heavily. All four men raise their arms as though they're part of some mass surrender of string puppets.

"Jesus, Luis!" Siegel shouts, still sitting where he landed. "You can't *do that!* They're just four guys coming out of the *building.* They didn't mean to knock me over. It was an *accident,* for Chrissakes."

Accident or fate, Luis Sandoval is far too pumped to back down now. He uses his handcuffs and Siegel's to secure all four men to the handrail of the outside steps.

Lenny Siegel continues to sit. "We're going to be sued; we're going to be sued," he mumbles. "My mother was right; my mother was right. I'll never work again."

Farrelli, the two other DEA agents, and the two NYPD officers are far too preoccupied with the injuries to Fingers Nelson and Jimmy Zelb (who also had been knocked unconscious by his landing on top of Nelson), and the contents of the suitcase, to pay attention to anything else. The cold seems not so cold anymore. The crowd noise fades into the background. The parade continues to march by, only a half a block away.

There are Bill and Hillary Clinton, the reincarnation of Richard Nixon, and all manner of ghouls, goblins, and ghosts. There are dancing bears and bare dancers. There are creatures from other galaxies. There is even a strange family of five: a man, woman, and child all draped in black satin material and wearing witches' hats (the man's looking suspiciously like the material's been wrapped around an orange traffic cone). The man and the woman wear inexpensive masks, the kind they sell at stationery stores for $3.95 apiece, that make you look like the Lone Ranger, or Zorro, or the Cat Woman. The woman carries a slightly spooked black cat in her arms, while the man lugs a huge stuffed animal that looks as though it must weigh close to forty pounds.

But all the agents and cops are too busy to notice any of these things.

Lenny Siegel finally gets up off the sidewalk. It's not his own job he's worried about, he decides. All he did was land on his rear end while trying to sneak into a building, a relatively minor transgression, certainly nothing more serious than a criminal trespass. It's what Luis Sandoval has done. Sandoval, still a probationary agent, has just arrested four men and chained them to a building, all because they happened to have opened a door at the wrong moment.

Siegel walks over to the first man, the one who appears to be the leader. "My apologies, señor," he says. He starts checking his pockets, trying to remember where he keeps his handcuff keys, so he can release the man.

Luis Sandoval walks back over to the door. It's propped halfway open at the moment by the black duffel bag the second man dropped. Sandoval gives it a tug and is surprised to find out how heavy it is. He peers inside where the zipper has worked its way open an inch or two. Sees a bunch of blue plastic packages. They seem to have a grayish white substance inside them.

"Excuse me, sir," he says to Lenny Siegel. "I think you might want to have a look at this."

"No, we're not checking any luggage," the man says. "We've just got these carry-on items." He points to a large stuffed animal he's carrying, as well as an oversized shoulder bag that the woman's wearing and a trick-or-treat bag the little girl's got.

"Must be nice to travel light," says the ticket agent.

"It's the only way," the man agrees with a smile.

"Your flight will be ready for boarding in ten minutes. Gate twenty-two is right down that corridor. And have a nice time in the islands."

"Thanks," the man says. "We'll do our best."

And they head down the corridor—the man, the woman, the little girl, and the stuffed animal. Every once in a while, the woman's shoulder bag appears to shift just a little bit, all on its own. But nobody seems to notice.

EPILOGUE

The days following Halloween prove to be busy ones at the laboratory of the United States Chemist in lower Manhattan. First, the suitcase delivered by Michael Goodman to Agents Jimmy Zelb and Frank Farrelli is brought in. It's found to contain nineteen packages of a grayish white powdery substance. Each package weighs approximately 2.2 pounds, or one kilogram, although the weights turn out to vary considerably, as though someone has used a bathroom scale to weigh them instead of the precision equipment generally favored by wholesale drug dealers. Extensive laboratory testing reveals that the grayish white powdery substance is a compound consisting of 97 percent highly absorbent nontoxic clay, 2 percent coloring, and 1 percent deodorant. It is known commercially as Kitty Litter.

The large black duffel bag, seized by Agent Luis Sandoval from Johnnie Delgado, Mister Fuentes, Papo, and Julio, is brought in next. It, too, contains nineteen one-kilogram packages of a grayish white powdery substance. These packages are wrapped in blue plastic, and considerably more attention seems to have been paid to their weighing. Testing reveals them to be uniformly 99.8 percent pure heroin hydrochloride.

That leaves only a large quantity of "white stuff" recovered by Detectives Ray Abbruzzo and Harry Weems during the arrests of Dwayne ("Big Red") Reddington and Leroy ("Hammer") Pendergrass for the burglary of Michael Goodman's apartment. Microscopic analysis reveals the substance

338

to be a synthetic material in the polystyrene family, patented by Du Pont under the trade name DuoFill, and commonly used as stuffing in the manufacture of pillows and toy animals.

The Ballistics Unit of the NYPD is busy, too. There, the 9-mm semiautomatic pistol found by Detectives Abbruzzo and Weems in Hammer's waistband is test-fired into a large water tank. The weapon is found to be operable with the ammunition found in it. Microscopic examination of the test-fired slugs establishes that they contain the identical land-and-groove markings as the bullets removed several weeks earlier from the body of one Russell Bradford, up on 129th Street, over by the Hudson River.

In a word, the gun is "dirty."

Charged with Bradford's murder, Hammer quickly "turns" and agrees to testify against Big Red as the one who ordered him to kill Bradford. Both men ultimately plead guilty in exchange for sentences of twenty-two years to life.

Papo and Julio agree to cooperate with the United States Attorney's Office against their bosses, Gustavo ("Mister") Fuentes and Joaquin ("Johnnie") Delgado, who are as a result convicted of possessing heroin in excess of ten kilograms and sentenced under the federal guidelines to seventeen and fifteen years in prison, respectively. In exchange for their testimony, Papo and Julio themselves receive eighteen-month sentences.

In time, investigators locate all of the rightful owners of the various items that spilled from the suitcase being carried by Francis ("Fingers") Nelson at the moment of his tackle by Jimmy Zelb. Three of them even come downtown to view lineups.

The lineups are somewhat unusual, to be sure, in that all of the look-alikes are required to wear huge bandages across their noses, so as not to be readily distinguishable from Fingers, with his own bandaged and painfully broken nose. In addition to the broken nose, Fingers turns out to have severely bruised elbows and knees, as well as several cracked ribs. Nonetheless, Fingers is identified not only as the man who was carrying the suitcase but also as the one seen picking it up and walking off with it (along with a shiny orange jacket that had been folded over it) only moments earlier, just inside the lobby of an apartment building on the corner of Sixth Avenue.

In addition to his injuries, Fingers turns out to have a lengthy record for larceny arrests, mostly as a pickpocket. He eventually pleads guilty to criminal possession of stolen property as a felony, and receives a sentence of two to four years. He also receives a settlement of $75,000 under the Federal Tort Claims Act, as compensation for the pain and suffering he underwent as a direct result of the "unreasonable and excessive force" inflicted upon him by Agent Zelb.

In the days following Halloween, several physicians and medical institutions receive checks in the mail for the full amounts of balances they've been owed for some time by one Michael Goodman for services provided his daughter. Checks are also received by Marvin Krulewich (permitting him to go to a private hospital to get his cataracts operated on and his diabetes brought under control), by Lehigh Valley (enabling him to buy a modest home for the foster parents who raised him), and by Wilbur ("the Whale") Bishop (who donates half of the money to Gamblers Anonymous and is last seen heading to Atlantic City with the remainder).

All of the checks are drawn against an account entitled Larus International. It turns out that a recent deposit of cash more than covers the total amount of the checks.

A hastily called press conference is announced to celebrate the success of Operation Clean Sweep, the first in what is promised to be a continuing series of joint ventures between the DEA and the NYPD. With the well-executed seizure of forty pounds of pure heroin (estimated to be worth upward of fifty million dollars on the street) and the arrests of major interstate traffickers all the way from the Bronx to South Florida, the authorities hail the breakup of a ring that they say they've been investigating for many months. "This will put a serious dent in the narcotics business on the East Coast for years to come," announces the mayor. All of the agents and police officers involved in the operation receive promotions. All but one, that is.

That particular agent, one Carmen Cruz, vanishes, as does Michael Goodman and his daughter. For a time, there is a discreet search for them, as well as a certain 3.5 million dollars of missing United States currency. But a number of hints are received from Agent Cruz that she's been offered almost as much to sell the networks her version of the events leading up to the success of Operation Clean Sweep. There is considerable disagreement and debate, but over time, top officials at DEA decide to permit Cruz to retire quietly, and they write off the loss of the money as a "miscellaneous operating expense—no further information available."

To this day, Michael Goodman, Carmen Goodman-Cruz, and Kelly Goodman live in a two-bedroom apartment in Manhattan with their cat, their memories, and a slightly lumpy stuffed animal, exact species unknown. Mr. Goodman is employed several days a week as an accountant in the Bronx, and also manages the family trust. Mrs. Goodman-Cruz works as a paralegal and a homemaker.

The Ballerina Princess
(Concluded)

And so it came to pass that the Ballerina Princess took the last test of all, the one in which the royal doctors tried to scare her and hurt her at the same time, first by sticking the needle in her back, and then by putting her in the big machine.

But they hadn't counted on just how brave and strong the Ballerina Princess was, and she came through the last test with flying colors. The spot in her eye gradually grew smaller and smaller, until it disappeared altogether.

As for the Ballerina Princess, she flew off and disappeared for a while, too, along with her four faithful companions, the Keeper of the Numbers, the beauteous Lady Carmen, the brave and loyal Prince Larus, and the strange and peculiar Kat Mandu. They all played in the sand by the ocean, drank juice straight from coconuts and pineapples, and lay in the sun, smiling a lot.

After a while, when they were all nice and warm and tan and rested, they returned to Yew Nork, which was still their favorite city in the whole kingdom, so that the Ballerina Princess could be near her grandmother and her friends from school, whom she had begun to miss.

Needless to say, she never had another headache, and she lived happily ever after.